Advance Praise for Things to Do in Denver When You're Un-Dead

"If you like quick wit, sadistic charm, and bad-ass gadgets, then you will enjoy the hell out of this book … no pun intended."

—Shay Fabbro, award-winning author of the *Portal of Destiny* series

Five stars: "This book was an absolute pleasure to read. It is witty, funny, dramatic and a well thought out paranormal with very fine storytelling. I couldn't put it down! That's a first for me in a long time …. I plan to be a loyal fan. Well done, Mark, and please, write me more?!"

—Clarrissa Lee Moon, author of the series, *The Nightwolves* and *Celeste Nites*

"I have really enjoyed reading this book…. The story could just be one of guns, blood and guts and magic, but … Mark Everett Stone has made these characters seem real."

—Michele Herbert, Fantasy Book Review

"This is not a story for the faint of heart or stomach, nor for those wanting a plot with any connection to reality. Personally, I'm really looking forward to the promised sequel."

—Gordon Long, TCM Reviews

"A fantastic read and very easy to follow. The way Mark combines magicians, zombies and super ghouls with a Bogart-style ultra sarcastic officer of the 'Bureau' makes you want to keep on reading. I highly recommend this for everyone—not just those into stories of the un-dead."

—G.R. Holton, author of Soleri, Guardian's Alliance and Deep Screams

"Five stars, two thumbs, fantastic! From the moment I began the first page to the final flip of the last, I was hooked .... The writing is sharp, fast and engaging. The characters are fun and/or not so fun in all the right places. Mark has captured the soul of his lead character so well that it's like the reader is sitting having a $300 bottle of vodka, chased with an aromatic and equally expensive cigar, while Kal spins tales of his heyday, punctuated by live action reenactments so real you wish you hadn't eaten dinner."

—Patti Larsen, author of *Fresco, Wasteland* (10/2011), *The Diamond City* (2012), and *The Ghost Boy of MacKenzie House* (2012)

"The blending of dark twisted humor in this chilling tale is utterly perfect, written with a sure hand. Comedic timing is everything, and author Stone has perfected the classic one-liner.... Make no mistake folks, this isn't for the faint hearted ... the sarcasm is used as a brief respite in the fastest paced action horror that I have read in a very long time."

—Suzannah Burke, aka Stacey Danson, Author of *Empty Chairs*

"In a first and quite brilliant novel, Stone proves himself equally adept at feverishly fast-paced action, edgy wit and banter, and the weaving of a richly satisfying and fresh world of mystery and intrigue. Write on, my friend."

—Michelle Izmaylov, author of *The Galacteran Legacy: Galaxy Watch*

Things to do in Denver When You're Un-Dead

From the Files of the BSI

Things to Do in Denver When You're Un-Dead

From the Files of the BSI

Mark Everett Stone

CAVEL
PRESS
Seattle, WA

CAMEL
PRESS

Published by Camel Press
PO Box 70515
Seattle, WA 98127

For more information, contact www.camelpress.com
www.markeverettstone.camelpress.com

Cover design by Sabrina Sun

THINGS TO DO IN DENVER WHEN YOU'RE UN-DEAD
Copyright © 2011 by Mark Everett Stone

ISBN (Paper): 978-1-60381-859-9
ISBN (eBook): 978-1-60381-860-5

Printed in the United States of America

To Professor Steven W. Stone, who helped make
this book possible. I miss you, Dad.

Contents

Chapter One

Monday Bloody Monday

Mondays suck. Always. Standard rule in life. In fact, it might just be rule #3, right after Feces Occurs and Anything That Can Go Wrong Will. Monday is the day when your boss will hit you with the Next Big Thing that the corporate office reckons will change the paradigm of whatever business you find yourself in. It's also the day that you have to play catch-up for whatever might have occurred on the two previous days you were off.

For me it wasn't the Next Big Thing as much as it was the Next Big Bad Thing That Wants To Rip Your Damn Fool Head Off, so it was with my usual sense of dread that I parked my blue Honda Accord in my assigned spot and staggered toward the brown brick building that housed the Denver offices of the BSI.

Spyeyes surrounding the building tracked my arrival and the Shape of a ward spell tingled against my feet as I stepped over gray-painted gold wire draped hither and yon over the asphalt walkway.

Working for the Bureau was always interesting, and I mean that in the Chinese curse sort of way. Don't get me wrong, the pay is great and I get to wear a gun, which is always fun, but the life expectancy at the Bureau of Supernatural Investigations (BSI) is usually one to two years. If you're good, maybe three. If you're great, maybe between four and six.

I've been at the job for ten and the odds were that I'd get my ticket punched any day. I knew the current Dead Pool was at Thursday before noon. I'd been beating the Pool for years now and figured I would for many years to come.

Jingling through my head, as it did every morning, were the words Robert Frost etched on my mind years and years ago, ones that echoed my own fatigue and bone-weary sense of resignation:

> But I have promises to keep,
> And miles to go before I sleep,
> And miles to go before I sleep.

The promises I'd made and the burden of responsibility I shouldered would keep me going and going like the Energizer Bunny until I figured it was time for me to shuffle off my mortal coil. And then, maybe, I could relax, finally ease into that eternal sleep that wasn't haunted by what I do, what I'd become, and things I'd left undone. Shaking my head, I stuffed these dark, tired thoughts into the back closet of my mind. I hurt too much and my teeth were far too fuzzy for me to be in such a mood on a Monday morning after a weekend bender. The Bureau had billions of dollars at their disposal and still hadn't come up with the cure for a hangover.

The front door threw a pale reflection at me. I drew near and noted that my favorite tie sported a suspicious reddish-brown stain. I hoped it was only blood; the piano keyboard tie was a gift from Mom on my thirtieth. My mind quickly juked toward the business of surviving the next few moments as I passed through the bulletproofed glass and steel door marked 'McClennan Statistical Analysis.' Nobody ever wants to go to a place marked Statistical Analysis. For the Bureau, it's blessed anonymity.

Time flowed back to the seventies as I stepped onto thick avocado-green shag carpeting surrounded by walls covered in tacky lilac wallpaper that looked like it was five minutes from peeling off in strips. Cramped and dingy, the foyer was made more so by a solid chunk of desk made of faux dark wood with a really creepy looking brown Formica top. Sitting behind that monstrosity was our Receptionist, Patricia, a woman most would call handsome rather than pretty. Long brown hair with the back pulled up in a mini bouffant, full-figured with enough hard-edged muscle showing underneath her sea-green silk blouse to give a linebacker pause. A buff, killer Peg Bundy sitting in front of a three-year-old Mac, all stainless steel and sex appeal.

At that moment, Patricia had her right hand under her desk. Cold blue eyes bored into mine as I slowly walked toward her.

"Howya doing, Pat?" I asked, slowly lowering my hands onto the cool Formica top with its silver and gold glitter pattern.

Her glance never wavered. "Looks like better than you, Kal." She pronounced it correctly: 'Kahl.' Taking in my slightly disheveled appearance and keyboard tie, her lips quirked a fraction. "What's her name?" While her face lacked warmth, her voice carried enough heat to thaw the polar ice caps—soft, sweet and luscious. It made you think of waking up next to her on a sleepy Sunday morning. The only thing that spoiled it was the fact that she had a swivel-mounted shotgun loaded with silver-tipped deer slugs aimed right at the family jewels.

"Who remembers names anymore?" I replied. "It probably ends in 'y' or 'i.' " Underneath my palms the silver spell Shapes warmed the Formica as they analyzed my handprints, aura, heat and electrochemical signatures and compared it to those in my file. If any didn't match, Pat would pull the trigger and several people would appear out from the back rooms and, very efficiently, disappear my remains to some lab where they would be examined down to the last cell for any trace of Supernatural influence.

There came a cheery *ping* from Pat's Mac and I breathed a sigh of relief, having survived another morning at the game. Fortunately, my ridiculous government salary is worth the stress. Most of the time.

The ice melted in Pat's eyes and she gave me a small smile that invited warm and squishy thoughts. "Go on in. You have a meeting with BB at noon in Comms."

I tipped her a halfhearted wink and headed toward a section of wall to the right and behind the desk, the hidden door *clicking* open to reveal the hallway leading to the heart of the Denver BSI.

The offices weren't big or fancy. I had only a team of four other field agents and a magician, but thanks to our budget, it was decorated in warm, rich tones and sported the finest in advanced hardware we managed to swipe from the NSA and a few they hadn't heard of yet. That all sounds great, I know, but the best perk was fresh Jamaican Blue Mountain coffee brewed every day. Starbucks had nothing on us.

K. Hakala, Senior Agent read the silvery plaque on the dark oak door to my office. I went in and sat at my massive mahogany desk that my pet Brownies had shined to a mirror finish and waited a few seconds for Alex to arrive.

Alex Dumont, the BSI techie/quartermaster/magician, entered a few seconds later, on time and impeccably dressed. Mondays were his Sweater Vest Day, with a blue striped Oxford button down shirt (heavily starched) and beige Dockers with creases so sharp you could shave with them. At a little over five feet tall, he looked like the quintessential geek with black hair and birth-control glasses. He was whistling a jaunty tune (the *Curly Shuffle,* I think) as he handed me the weekend crime report. It was my job to scan them for Supernatural activity.

Every office, every corporation, has an Alex—that one person the company can't do without. Meticulous, efficient as hell, and smarter than a bushel full of Einsteins, if he was in the private sector he'd be the CEO of a multinational corporation inside a week. But we pay much better than a mere CEO's salary and what the Bureau offers in tech would make Bill Gates faint.

Too tired to read, I tossed the report on the desk and turned on my Mac. "Just tell me," I grumbled. "Anything extraordinary happen over the weekend?"

His smile didn't slip an iota. "Nope, Kal, all's quiet on the Western Front." That smile faded at the edges a bit when I slipped him a gimlet stare.

"Bad mood today, sir?"

I grunted. "No 'sirs' here, Alex. Kal will do just fine." The Mac chimed its readiness and I swiveled the chair so I could face the *Dawn of the Dead* wallpaper. It always made me smile. If George A. Romero only knew …

"Pardon me, Kal, but is that *blood*?" he asked, pointing at my piano tie.

"God, I hope so," I moaned as I leaned back in my chair, scrubbing my face with my hands. Not even the zombie on the computer screen could lift my spirits out of the mire of my hangover.

"What did you do last weekend? Or should I say, *who* did you do?"

A nasty smile pasted itself on my face. "Do you really want to know?"

He shook his head quickly.

"Good." Nice kid, but a little sensitive. "Now clear off, I have to pretend to do some work around here."

"Okay." Alex cleared his throat. "I'm to remind you that you have a meeting with BB at noon. I think it might be about the Brownies." Before I could say something scathing, he left in a whisper of hyper-efficient motion.

A few months ago I rescued a Catholic church that was infested with the little guys. Smaller than mice and quicker than a wink, they terrorized the place with pranks and minor vandalism because the priest didn't adhere to the old ways. All they wanted was to exchange cleaning and repair services for a bowl of milk set out every night. I had lured them out with Oreos and milk, right into a toy Winnebago the size of a shoebox. I kept them under my desk, our arrangement a congenial one. For the price of cold whole milk and a few cookies, my office was neat and my dry cleaning done overnight. I took them everywhere I went, to whatever city the Bureau sent me because 'cleaning' and 'laundry' are four-letter words.

At that moment, soft music wafted from the toy RV. I recognized Samuel Barber's *Adagio for strings*—better known as the soundtrack from *Platoon*.

It was only a little after nine. Nearly three hours to kill before my meeting with BB, so I spent my time alternating between zoning out and fine tuning my final report on the zombie problem that brought us to Denver in the first place. Fortunately for the good citizens of the Mile High City, we came, we saw, and we kicked undead ass, ridding the place of a smelly, rotting menace. The only tarnish on the silverware was our inability to locate the witch who created them.

When you were a kid, did you ever look at the clock right before school let out? Those final few minutes took forever and a day to tick by. You felt so anxious, like time was standing still and you'd never see your parents again. You'd be stuck in school forever watching the clock tick away to nothing.

That's how time in that office on a Monday felt to me. The report only took a couple of minutes to complete, the rest of the time, mine to burn. Frustration fizzled at the hindbrain, sizzling its way to the back of my eyeballs and caused my head to pound with the beginning of a headache. Being hung over didn't help, either.

I looked at the Mac and the zombie wallpaper just stared back with a hint of menace. Tick-tock. With a snort, I reached into my secure drawer and pulled out my Lahti L35, a Finnish-made semi-automatic pistol that closely resembles the German Walther P38. It fires a 123-grain FMJ bullet with a muzzle velocity of 320 m/sec. I had custom clips made to house 13 rounds, giving the handle an elongated look, but those extra rounds had proven quite useful in the past. After stripping and re-assembling the heavy pistol about a dozen times (almost impossible to do a Lahti without LOTS of practice) I donned a shoulder holster and tucked the pistol away. There went ten minutes.

Before my frustration level could rise to overload, I locked the door to the office and set the alarm on my smart phone. Sighing, I lay on the floor and commenced to saw some logs. I prayed no one would call on me in the next couple of hours.

At noon I sluggishly strode into Comms (a 15x10 room dominated by a large, blond-wood table) and flopped into an expensive brown leather chair that made me want to catch some more Zs right then and there, but I knew that BB (known as Benjamin Bauer to the higher-ups) would be back any second. Instead I looked around the plain grayish/black space with its shiny, glossy, walls and twiddled my thumbs.

"Hello, Kal," came a voice seemingly out of mid-air.

"Hiya, BB," I replied, unable to stop the yawn that cracked my face wide open.

"Did you tie one on last night?" An 8x10 foot section of wall flickered to life, showing a slender middle-aged man with more forehead than gray hair. A pair of wire-rimmed glasses fronted two gray, slightly watery eyes. Looking at him you might think, 'Hey, who's the English Lit professor?' You'd never know that he once held the all-time record for active fieldwork until I came along.

"No, BB," I drawled. "I tied quite a few on the last two days."

He gave me a disapproving stare. "Two days? That's a little excessive considering you and your team are in play, monitoring the World Under in the Denver area."

"It's okay, boss. I never really got that drunk. Consider it a two-day buzz."

Butter wouldn't have melted in his mouth. "Be that as it may, Kal, please refrain from heroic bouts of debauchery until the job is complete. Can you do that?"

"Of course, sir," I soothed, feeling his disappointment through the giant screen.

Apparently my contrite reply proved to be enough. "Good. Now … is that blood on your rather hideous tie?"

"Sure is. And before you ask, I'm reasonably sure it's mine."

His look told me more than words ever could, but he didn't bother with a lecture. Instead he pulled out a smart phone and poked at it a few times with a slender, well-manicured finger. "Be that as it may, Kal, I want you on your best behavior. I'm sending you the data on a new recruit and I want your input."

I should have heard alarm bells, but my hangover drowned them out. "What? You hiring another Green Pea? Why? Don't we have enough agents?" The Bureau kept a steady fifty agents on the roster at all times. No more, no less.

"We lost an agent in the Appalachians. Karen Rinaldi."

I met her once. Tough lady, a two-year agent with shoulders like a weightlifter. "How did she go?"

"Her team was tasked to clean out a nest of harpies."

Oh … nasty. Those half-eagle, half-woman monstrosities not only had the attitude of a psychopathic pit bull, but their talons carried a poison that could rot the flesh from your bones in a half hour with one scratch. No antidote had yet to be discovered, so I had no doubt that Karen eased herself into the afterlife with the help of a bullet before she could see her flesh liquefy into something that resembled strawberry yogurt.

"Kal, keep a look out for more … activity around the Denver area. There's bound to be something popping up in the next few days," he said absently, staring at his phone. Supernatural happenings were like cockroaches: once you experienced one, you knew more were on the way. Last year in New York there were three troll sightings, a haunted house that ate passersby and a spider the size of a Buick living in Central Park. All cropped up within a week of the first sighting. When normal people (or Straights, as we call them) started noticing the extraordinary, you knew there was a supernatural critical mass building. The World Under was anything but subtle.

"I got my bloodshot eyes on the situation, boss." My phone buzzed. "Okay, got the data you sent. Anything else?"

"Yes, about those Brownies of yours …"

Both my hands came up in a warding gesture. "Uh-uh, boss. I need those little guys. If they go, I go."

He almost cracked a smile. "You feel that strongly about them?"

"I sure do. Who else am I going to trust with my dry cleaning?"

Gray eyes bored into my baby blues and I felt a slight chill. "Your sarcasm is noted."

"Really, boss, I'm quite fond of the little guys," I rumbled contritely.

"You're lazy."

I nodded. "That, too."

"Fine, but when you go on vacation to see your folks, take them with you." He sniffed. "I don't trust them out of your care."

My parents had a nice place in a remote area outside of Grand Rapids, Minnesota, near the Chippewa National Forest. Go figure that a couple of Finns would fly a gazillion miles to settle in a place that was just as cold and miserable as the country they had left. "You got it, boss." I reckoned Mom wouldn't mind a maid and handyman service happening overnight for the price of a bowl of milk.

"Fine. Review the file on the recruit." BB's thin lips twitched. "And get some sleep. You look like hell." With that, his image vanished and the wall once again became a gray/black window to nothing.

I might have looked like hell, but I felt like refried crap. I still felt that way an hour later when I decided to check the file BB had sent me. I aimed my smart phone at the printer, hit the proper app button and a few seconds later, with a whirr and a hum, nice white paper began to feed out of the top of the machine. Most agents like to read files on a RediPad, an 8x10 flat pc that Mac would release in a couple of years, but I like old fashioned hard copy.

Scanning the file, I felt my heart drop and acid boil in my stomach. Agent Ariel McMillan, DEA. DEA? God, I wanted to throw up day-glo. DEA, a bunch of cowboys who wound up getting killed faster than those red-shirted security guys on *Star Trek*. The Bureau was obligated to the DEA for much of its funding from seized assets, but the worst thing in the world was trying to train

DEA Green Peas, who thought the sun rose and set in their pants. They usually took that arrogance straight to the grave, did not pass GO, and did not collect two hundred dollars. And there were worse things than being dead.

My eyes continued to scan the pages of her life. Recently completed SEAL training in Coronado. Good, very impressive for a woman, considering how hard the men there treat the opposite sex. A former marine, so she didn't have to go for a refresher at Parris Island first. The lady read like a who's who for tough women.

Somewhere in that file was the one thing that had led her to the BSI and I kept reading until it popped through my eyes and into my achy brain. Assets taken from DEA evidence lockup (Assets=Money/Drugs), no witnesses, evidence clerk on duty unconscious with no idea how he got that way and the digital copies from surveillance cameras wiped clean. A partial thumbprint on the shelf from where the assets were taken matched our Ms. Ariel McMillan. Of course. Then my eye caught the last sentence in the file: 'Kal, show Ms. McMillan all due respect as she will be your Green Pea for the foreseeable future.—BB'

"BB, you son-of-a-," I whispered hoarsely. Another Green Pea to train, another gaping grave to fill. Angrily, I threw the file across the room in a childish display of pique that, oddly enough, made me feel better. Just as the last paper floated to the floor, there came a rap-tap-tapping at my office door.

"Nevermore!" I shouted.

Alex poked his head in. "Raven joke, good one, Kal."

My head hurt so much. "What can I do for you, Alex?"

From the small smile of satisfaction on his face I knew the news wasn't good. "You have a visitor."

I made a shooing motion with my hands as dread seeped through the pores of my skin. "Tell them I'm dead. Thank you and goodbye."

His head disappeared for a second. "He wants me to tell you he's dead." The smugness in his voice made my hands itch to draw my Lahti and fire a few rounds through the door. "Let her in, dammit," I hollered instead.

And in she walked.

Wow.

Maybe five inches shorter than my own six-four, she halted a few feet away and let me take a generous eyeful, which I did without hesitation. The testosterone levels in my bloodstream rose with such force that they burned away the last vestiges of my hangover. Skin like coffee with just the barest hint of cream, thick pouty lips and dark, dark eyes that threatened to suck you in and never let you go. Dark skirt to the knees, showing enough finely muscled and shapely leg to let the imagination run wild. Her hair was cut in the usual business bob, but worn in such a way as to render it as sexy as the rest of her.

Double wow.

"You seen enough?" snarled Ms. DEA.

"Shut up," I snapped with enough heat to rock her back on her three-inch black stilettos.

"What did you say to me?" she growled, fury lighting her deep eyes.

Standing to my full height, I squared my shoulders and rounded the desk, coming nose to nose with her, surprised to see that she didn't take a step back. A show of guts that raised her a notch in my estimation. "I. Said. Shut. Up." The smell of her tickled my nose. Musk and the faint trill of deodorant. That raised her another half-notch, but she was still in the basement. "I don't care what they call the new recruits in the other agencies: cherry, fish, probie, rookie, fresh meat or whatever. Here you are a Green Pea until I say otherwise or until you die. When I say 'jump,' you don't say 'how high,' you just better be airborne. I am the leader of Team Epsilon and your trainer, so if you don't do what I say when I say it, I'll send your behind back to the DEA so fast your *descendants* will get whiplash." *That hit her*, I noted as her eyes widened slightly in alarm. Not fear, but alarm. She sure as hell didn't want to go back.

She knew there were rodents in the DEA's woodpile.

"I know what you did, Pea," I continued, remorseless. "Evidence goes missing in lockup and the trail points to you, even though a rookie can tell it's a frame job. Someone wanted your butt on a plate with a side of fries, so the Director of the DEA sent you the Bureau via Coronado because he thought you were too good an agent to cut loose." I leaned in and realized her breath smelled of peppermint. "Here you are a waste of protoplasm. You hear me? A waste." Cracking my knuckles, I walked around her slowly, measuring, feeling the anger roiling off her in waves. Was I cruel? Maybe, but in the Bureau, it's sink or swim. "It's my job to mold you into something useful, something that won't die, because right now, out here in the world no one sees, the World Under the World, dying is all you're really good for."

I planted my fundament back behind my desk. "Now, Pea, you're lucky you got me; I'm a total sweetheart. If you had pulled any one of the other trainers you might have had a real hard time of it. As it is, I'm just going to make your life a living hell. Got me, Pea?"

"Got you, sir." I could tell the worlds almost cut her throat like glass.

My smile was pure greased nasty. "What do we do here, Pea?"

She blinked a couple of times in surprise. "We investigate—"

"*Ehhhnnk!*" My derisive honk forced her back a step. "Wrong! I'm so sorry; you do not win our Grand Prize of Happily Ever After." I held my hand to my ear. "Judges, what does she win? Why, a beautiful case of being dead. That's right, folks, she gets to die a horrible, gruesome death! And that's not all!" I was in full Bob Barker mode now, enjoying myself immensely. "She gets a nice little plot in Arlington for her service to her country while she was in the Marines, no doubt preparing for a life that would end abruptly at the tender age of thirty-three."

My smile faded and my voice became barbed wire and razors. "We don't investigate diddly-squat here, McMillan. We find whatever Supernaturals are killing the Straights and we finish them. Period and End of Story. No trials, no prisons, because we have nothing and nowhere that a Supernatural can't escape from. So we punch their tickets before they punch ours."

"So what are we? Government hit men?" The indignation in her voice was thick enough to cut. I appreciate idealism, but even that can get you killed faster than a politician could steal your wallet.

"We're soldiers," I snapped back. "The last line of defense between the Straights and the Supernaturals. We are the best and we receive the best of everything. The downside is, the mortality rate for a two-year agent is fifty percent. For a three year agent it's forty, and a four year, about twenty-five. Besides me, there has been only one agent in Bureau history to sign up for multiple contracts and that's the Director." The chair creaked as I leaned back, steepling my fingers under my chin. "Of all the fifty agents in the Bureau, I'm the best. I've been alive at this game longer than anyone in its entire history. That makes me your best bet at living past next week. That makes me your best bet at enjoying many more birthdays to come. If you can't handle that, you head right back to that bunch of idiots in the DEA with a nice government-sanctioned Interdiction that will keep you from spilling the beans about the Bureau." What she didn't know is that the Interdiction had been laid upon her before the ink dried on the contract she signed. There was no way she could, in any fashion, divulge the existence of the BSI. Not until someone lifted that Interdiction and, to my understanding, the only way to dispel it was to get yourself an executive case of dead.

"So," I continued. "You copasetic with playing by my rules for the foreseeable future, or do you want to head back to your drug chasing pals?"

I had to give her another notch up; she held her composure a lot better than I would have. A grudging appreciation for her began to form in my belly. "I'm good, sir." I could tell that hurt her right down to her toes.

"No sirs around here," I rapped. "Call me Kal or Mr. H. Or Mr. Hakala. But I'm not a 'sir.' I work for a living."

"Yes, Kal." She sure didn't sound as meek as her words implied, in fact, she sounded like she wanted to see how I'd fit in a food processor. Good. In my business, the only way the meek inherit the earth is when they're buried in it.

"Groovy. Now pay close attention. Your shoes … wear flats. I see stiletto heels again I'll stab you with 'em. Next, wear pants. Skirts are nice for showing off the goods, but you can't wear an ankle holster. Before you leave, have Alex set you up with the basic weaponry needed for this job. Tomorrow I want you to have all of them secreted around your person in such a manner that no one will be able to tell that you're loaded for bear. Got it?"

Ariel looked me straight in the eye and muttered, "Got it." It was the same tone of voice you'd use to say, "Screw you, buttwipe."

"Great, now get thee out of my sight and be here at eight in the morning. Sharp."

After she left, back all straight and indignant, I went to the lounge and poured a bowl of milk for the Brownies. That stain on my tie had to go. God, I hoped it was *my* blood.

Mondays suck.

Chapter Two

Breakfast Serial

The great thing about work is that it eventually ends. My day had started with a hangover and unwanted responsibilities and ended with mild nausea and scummy teeth. Leaving the office was a heck of a lot less dangerous than entering and I felt a profound sense of relief when I climbed into my Honda and plugged in my iPod. The Ramones began to lull me into a nice state of mental oblivion. *I wanna be sedated* ... Yeah, you and me both, Johnny.

Home for me was a large apartment at 40th and Chambers, almost due north from the office. Fifteen hundred square feet of lavish space furnished by the Bureau for the team leader. In the past month I'd come to like the casual opulence of the place with its huge flat-screen TV, fully stocked kitchen and maid service, Monday through Friday.

The only thing I'm meticulous about (besides staying alive) is my espresso machine. It's the one thing besides my weapon I take to any new locale. Gleaming stainless steel and chrome, it looks like it belongs in a *Star Wars* movie. With a little finely ground coffee and some tenderness, it yields me a cup of liquid heaven. God knew what he was doing when he invented caffeine and I thanked him for it.

With a cup of liquid love in one hand and the TV remote in the other, I began an evening of channel flipping. I sank into my hideously overstuffed leather couch, letting my eyes glaze over as I skipped through the usual sludge of reality TV, prime time game shows, soap operas for those who didn't get enough of them during the day, and sports. Nothing caught my eye so I decided to zone out and watch what passes for BIG NEWS in Denver.

Crap, crap, crap. More crap. Human interest crap. Weather crap. Sports crap (I couldn't care less about the Broncos, Nuggets, Avalanche, or Rockies. If it's not from Minnesota, it doesn't matter).

Before my eyes could droop shut the news finally gave me something I was at least partly interested in.

The Organ Donor.

On the big screen, a talking head stared seriously out at me, his hair perfectly coiffed, not a strand out of place. He spoke in deep, sonorous tones about Denver's most notorious serial killer to date, the Organ Donor. This guy (or gal) had been terrorizing the city for the past month-and-a-half, kidnapping people, harvesting their organs and leaving their bodies posed in very public places. The police would get a call from a disposable phone telling them where to find the organs, the caller's voice electronically altered to confound identification. The organs from each victim were always stowed on ice in a Styrofoam chest, along with a note written in crayon that read, "Give them to someone worthwhile."

So far the victims had one thing in common: they all, at one time or another, had been on the wrong side of the law. All of them had records, all them were loners—people who wouldn't be missed. The talking head told me that a new victim had been found that morning near an alleyway in Lower Downtown, also called, creatively, LoDo. At 6:18 a.m. thirty-seven-year-old William Krouse had been found lying face down in a gutter, organs missing. A couple of hours later the police received another call from the Donor. The organs had been found behind a dumpster in an alley at 17th and Wynkoop, near a bus stop.

What made this news report different was a photo of the victim. Denver PD had run an effective media blackout, but this time someone had managed to snap a shot and the media had plastered it all over my big screen. Krouse used to be a large man, plenty of fat and plenty of solid muscle. The photo showed him on his stomach, naked, one arm on the sidewalk, another on the street. His legs were splayed unevenly on the concrete. It looked like he had fallen out of the sky and landed there. At least the media had had the decency to pixelate the area from lower back to mid-thigh. Lying face down hid the gaping wound in his torso, where his organs had been removed. Good thing, too; last thing I wanted to see was a big red slash against his bone-white skin.

Bone white?

I vaulted off the sofa and peered at the flat-screen, studying the grainy photo closely. No blood in the gutter, and what looked to be no moribund lividity from pooling blood inside the body. Yep, the big guy had lost most if not all of his blood during dissection. Or vivisection.

Curious, I unsheathed my cell and said, "Call Alex." Within a few seconds he came online.

"Hello?" He sounded tired.

"Alex, it's Kal. Got a minute?"

"Sure, Kal. What do you need?"

"I need you to send me everything you have on the Organ Donor."

"What?" He no longer sounded tired.

"The Organ Donor. Everything you can get. Background on the victims, where they were dumped, times of the calls to the police." A thought hit me. "Heck, Alex, get me everything. I even want the personal notes from the lead detective on this."

"Right," he said without missing a beat. "You want the FBI's notes? They're also in on this. I can have it on your desk first thing in the morning."

"How about now?"

"No can do. I'm not anywhere near a computer."

"Since when are you not near a computer?" I asked, surprised, figuring that he'd have his RediPad handy.

"Since I'm in a girl's bed and she doesn't own one," he replied with more than a trace of smugness.

Alex had never even talked about girls, let alone hinted he might actually sleep with one. "Great, Alex. I'm really happy for you. Honest." Small hesitation. "Is she a fembot?"

"Har-de-har-har. Listen Kal, if you need it now, I can always call Ghost for you."

The temperature of my stomach reached zero Kelvin in less than a second. We got along fine, but Ghost was just that … a ghost. He haunted cyberspace, unhampered by anything trivial like firewalls or top-level encryptions. Around six years ago he had come to the Bureau's attention and managed to resist exorcism; the Bureau had never discovered his true name, so no exorcism could work. Since then there existed a fragile truce: the Bureau wouldn't make an effort to erase him and the only naughty activities he would indulge in would be on the Bureau's behalf. Sometimes, if you asked nicely, he would do you a favor or three, but the damn thing still creeped me out sometimes. It had a power I couldn't fathom. He was a Supernatural, and in my business Supernaturals were always suspect.

"Kal, you still there??

"Yeah," I said, still contemplating the Bureau's very own *Deus Ex Machina*. "Go ahead and get hold of him. Tell him I'd like to have everything downloaded to my RediPad ASAP."

"Anything else?"

"No thanks, Alex."

"It should be there soon, Kal." The cell clicked as he hung up.

Sighing, I turned to the cupboard and started prepping my favorite evening meal—Lucky Charms. As the multi-colored marshmallow-filled cereal *tinked* into my Scooby-Doo bowl, I couldn't help a silent chuckle at Alex's expense. He'd joined the Bureau some six years ago as our resident techie/magician, a geeky mix of MacGuyver and Q from the James Bond movies. So dang smart and efficient, I often forgot that he was still basically a naïve kid with mad skills. So sensitive, so much like an adolescent with wide eyes believing in the basic goodness of humanity and the world in general. It was my job not only to take his advice when necessary, but also to treat him with kid gloves because the Bureau needed him a hell of a lot more than a tired old agent like me.

Hip deep into my second bowl, my cell buzzed. "Whatcha got, Alex?" I mumbled through a mouthful of whole grain yumminess.

What came through the phone was more an insect-like buzz than a human voice. "I have the files you requested, Kal." Asexual, horribly jangling, the buzz sent a shiver up my spine and down again all the way to my toes.

A couple of seconds passed as I forced a half-chewed lump of cereal down my suddenly too tight throat. "Uh, thanks, Ghost. Thanks a lot."

"Are you all right, Kal? You sound nervous."

How did I tell a cyberspirit that sometimes he really spooked me the hell out? "I'm fine, Ghost. Just a little tired, you know. Fighting the good fight."

'That's good, Kal. I hate to think I make you nervous."

It was frustrating, having the same conversation with a dead person every time your paths crossed, like talking to an Alzheimer's patient. I'm pretty sure Ghost did it to get under my skin. It worked, too. "Thanks, Ghost. I'd hate to be nervous."

"Are you still happy in the Bureau, Kal?"

The question took me by surprise. For a few seconds I did nothing but blink, my mouth doing a pretty good impression of a landed fish. "Doing okay, I guess," I answered finally, unsure where this was leading.

"Then why do you seem so tired and on edge lately?" That gender-neutral buzz sounded rather ... sad somehow, and I felt a tug in the silent places of my heart.

"It's a tough business, living life alone for so long. Sometimes it gets to me."

The cell vibrated on the counter, humming its way toward the edge, but I was too tired to pick it up. Finally it stopped just at the edge, millimeters from falling to the linoleum. "Has the loneliness gotten to you? You know, Alex and I can help you out."

I cudgeled my brain for a reply that wouldn't make the spook angry. "I think he's a great kid and the smartest person I know. I like him well enough, but you know the circumstances, Ghost." My voice was even, calm. "I can't call anyone a friend. The life of an agent is short, brutal and emotional attachments make us weak. That's why when and if we do attempt a long-term relationship, it's grounds for immediate resignation. No ifs, ands, or buts."

Bzzzz …"You should resign, then."

"It's the nature of the business, Ghost."

"Okay, Kal. Just don't let the job get to you."

I frowned. "Eventually it gets to all of us; then we quit or die."

"True."

For a moment I was irritated about having a debate with a cell phone, but I stowed the aggravation and broached a topic I hadn't raised in a while. "I appreciate that, Ghost, I really do, but can I ask you to do a favor for me?"

"You can ask."

Great, a flip phone. I crossed my arms. "Remember the package Alex asked you to deliver for me some time ago?"

"Of course. I do not forget anything. Why?"

"Do you think you can deliver another one for me?" I asked, crossing my fingers.

Once again the cell vibrated, but this time away from the edge of the counter. "That should be no problem," he said slowly.

"Okay, Ghost, maybe later."

His voice suddenly became crisp and brisk. "I've downloaded all the relevant files to your RediPad, Kal, and I've sent them to the printer in your office. There are forty-three pages for you to peruse, all the data I was able to sift from the FBI and the DPD. I trust that will be sufficient?"

"Uh, yeah, thanks." A chill crept on sneaky feet up and down my spine. If Ghost could access my printer from the phone, what was to stop him from accessing anything with a computer chip? Every time that thought crossed my mind my flesh got all goosepimply.

"Goodbye, Kal."

"'Bye, Ghost."

"Oh, and Kal? Have a good evening." The phone clicked.

"Ghost? Ghost." I picked up the cell, but it was cold and still in my hand. He was gone.

"Well, crap," I muttered while stalking toward my office, miffed that the cellular spirit had gotten the last word.

In my office, the printer was chugging its way toward the end of the file, that distinctive hot toner smell stinking the place up. A few seconds later the last page rolled out of the feeder into the hopper. I snagged the stack and began to thumb through it.

The more I flipped through the pages the more impressed with Ghost I became. Everything was neatly organized and laid out in a linear fashion from first to last victim with FBI's and DPD's notes also neatly arranged on the same timeline. I know cops, I've had to impersonate plenty, and most of them are never organized enough to produce what I held in my hands. The fact that it … no, *he* … had done it in such a short time freaked me out just a little.

Clearing away a section of my desk, I sat down and got busy doing the one part of my job that I really hate … research.

April 7th, a month and a half ago, the body of Sheree Brydendorf (a prostitute) had been found by a street sweeper on the 16th Street Mall at 6:05 a.m., a half hour before sunrise. The body had been splayed in a gutter much like Krouse's. In fact, its positioning had been virtually identical, right down to the arms and legs. Flipping through the police photographs, I saw that all the bodies had been arranged the same way. Creepy? For sure. A message? Maybe. If it was, it was one known only to the Organ Donor.

Whoever dumped the bodies, assuming it was the murderer and not an accomplice, had guts. Pardon the pun. He/she/it disposed of the remains in very public places, in full view of busy intersections and businesses. All in the wee hours of the morning, just before sunrise. Soon after the bodies were found, the calls to the

DPD came in, telling them where the organs could be found. I quickly scanned the pages, found the notes of Detective Lieutenant Wilkes of Denver Homicide and saw that he'd come to the same conclusion I had. Someone had been at the scene, watching, waiting for the body to be discovered then phoning it in when it was. The killer? An accomplice? Whoever it was called himself the Organ Donor, which surprised me because it was usually the cops or the media who liked slapping labels around. Strange and stranger.

Frowning, I read more of Lieutenant Wilkes notes and saw that he felt the DPD was being jerked around, that the organs, all placed in fairly easy-to-find locations, were a blind, a distraction from the rest of the case. From his notes, the crisp, concise writing and well-thought-out logic, I pictured him as a pretty sharp cookie. This was a good cop—one who could probably crack the case if no one stumbled into his way.

And then came the FBI. Someone pulled the emergency brake, most likely a politician, and screamed for the Feds to aid in the investigation after the third murder. After reading the lead agent's notes, I came to the conclusion that the guy was a total tool. That man turned out to be Special Agent Avery Briegan of the National Center for the Analysis of Violent Crime's (NCAVC) Behavioral Analysis Unit (BAU). From what I read, the man sure thought his feces contained no odor and, unfortunately, that particular malady is epidemic among law enforcement officers working at the federal level.

Agent Briegan, along with the rest of the BAU, thought the organs were the key to catching the killer. They had every forensic specialist they could find going over them and the containers they were packed in with a fine-toothed comb.

So the BAU and the local feds had come in, virtually taken over the case and, if my ability to read between the lines still worked, promptly ignored one Detective Lieutenant Wilkes entirely, probably raising his blood pressure several hundred points. Usually the BAU coordinated efforts with local law and the feds, but this time it seems they'd stepped on toes.

I made a mental note to get all the dirt on this Briegan when I made it to work in the morning. Something about this case bugged me and I was damned if I was going to let it go. It was an itch I had to scratch.

Shaking my head, I continued to flip through the file, reading every word, trying my best to bumble my way through some of the more dense passages. Sometime later, when the yawns were coming thicker than flies on cow flop, I finally had had enough. Even though my curiosity bump was itching up a storm, I was too damn tired to figure out why.

As I lay in bed I wondered what the rest of my week would look like. The way things were going, I really didn't want to find out.

Chapter Three

Ruby Tuesday

My style is di bomb digi bomb dideng dideng digidigi
Oo-oo Oo-oo OoOoOo Oo Oo
Car rude boy no play with di bomb dideng dideng digidigi
Oo-oo Oo-oo OoOoOo Oo Oo

The nonsensical lyrics of the Teddybear's *Cobrastyle* jerked me out of the kind of sleep where you're all warm and cozy with a light sheen of sweat on your brow. The deepest and most fulfilling sleep I'd had in weeks.

I reached over to the side table, grabbed my cell, and gave the screen a poke to turn the alarm app off. The song would reverb in my head for the rest of the morning, like it did every weekday, but it was catchy enough not to drive me completely crazy.

Before I could even think about getting out of bed, the cell chirped twice … an incoming call from Mom.

"Hei, Äiti (hello, Mother), how'ya doing?" My voice came out as a scratchy mess from a throat full of sand.

"Hei, Kalevi (Hello, Kalevi). I am well," she returned much more energy than I felt. "I woke you up?"

"Good guess, Äiti. It's morning."

"It's eight o'clock there. You should be awake already." She sounded disapproving, making me feel about an inch tall, an ability she always used with the practical ruthlessness of a person who believes she's right.

"I know, Äiti, I know. Late night, that's all." And I was going to be late for work. Oh, well … wouldn't be the first time.

A different voice came online. Pekka Hakala, my father.

"Kalevi, you hip deep?" Fifty-four years old, an ex-marine and still tougher than bad beef jerky, my dad had the body of an athlete half his age. He knew what I did for a living, and so did my mom. Both had Interdictions to keep them quiet. As far as I knew, they were the only outside people in the last hundred years who had knowledge of the Bureau.

"Not yet, Dad, just doing research on a sick bastard of a serial killer."

"That Organ Donor fella I heard about on the Nightly News?"

"That's the scumbag."

"But I thought you looked into ... other things?"

I sighed, which made a whooshing sound in the cell's speakers. "I still do, Dad. I have a feeling about this case. My gut tells me it may fall into my jurisdiction."

Then he said what I knew he'd say. The thing that a father worried to death for his only surviving child would utter. "Son, don't you think it's time you got out?"

I gave him the same answer I've given dozens of times. "Not yet. I still haven't found a way to kill it."

Exasperation roughed his voice. "It's been twenty years ..."

"And I've only been in the Bureau for ten. I'll stay in for as long as I need to."

"Lord knows I want you to, son. More than anything, but this is Iku-Turso we're talking about." Desperation crawled into his words.

"It's a monster, Dad, not a god. I kill monsters for a living."

"But *ten years*, Kalevi. I know the attrition rate at your job. The fact that you're alive still amazes me."

This conversation, repeated so many times, still twisted and pulled my guts like fishhooks. For some reason, maybe fatigue, this time it really pissed me off. However, I kept my tone respectful. Big and tough as I may be, Dad could kick my ass any day of the week and twice on Saturdays. "Enough, Dad. I won't quit. Not ever. Not until I find what's needed to kill Iku-Turso."

Long pause. "Okay, son. I love you." Another pause. "Please be careful."

Something stung my eyes and I wiped away a bit of moisture. "Always am, Dad."

There came muffled voices and Mom's worried tones caressed my ear. "You be careful and come to visit, okay?"

"Yes, Äiti, I will."

"Näkemiin, Kalevi." (Goodbye, Kalevi.)

"Näkemiin, Äiti." (Goodbye, Mom.)

Click and the line went dead. I love my folks, but so many feelings get stirred up when they call that it's hard to carry on with the rest of my day. Right then what I needed most was a nice, scalding hot shower that would bring me into sync with the rest of the day.

Fiery needles stung my skin and turned it bright red, the water rushing its way over my body in streams that both caressed and scalded. I stood there, getting hotter and hotter, breathing in the steam that cleared my head and chased away any vestige of lingering hangover.

One and a half bowls of Lucky Charms later, I dressed in a soft pair of khakis, a blue polo bearing the Izod alligator, and a cream-colored sport coat. I had to admit, I looked pretty snazzy. I drove slowly to work, the Honda purring along Chambers Road nicely, passing about a zillion other Hondas and quite a few Subarus— seemingly the State Car of Colorado. The late May sky shone bright blue with hardly a wisp of cloud. Everything looked so bright and cheerful in total contrast to my mood. Even the smog seemed less oppressive and brown. If a blue jay decided to land on my shoulder when I exited the car, I was going to draw my Lahti and blow its little birdy brains out. I wasn't feeling very *Zippity-Doo-Dah*.

"Hello, grumpy," Patricia snorted as I swung through the door. "Get up on the wrong side of the blonde?"

I hefted my briefcase that contained the files printed out the night before. "Woke up on the wrong side of studying," I said defensively, dropping the case and laying hands on the desktop. "You know me and research. I'm an action man."

Pat's Mac *pinged*. "Well, 'action man,' your Green Pea is chewing the walls in your office, waiting for your lazy butt." Her smile broke through like the sun through dark clouds. "Funniest damn thing I've seen all month."

My answering grin matched hers tooth for tooth. "The only good thing about training Green Peas is torturing them."

Mood much lightened, I trotted into my office, holding up a finger to forestall any explosions of feminine wrath.

"Pop quiz, hotshot," I rapped. "A serial killer is leading the FBI and the DPD around by their noses. After a body is found, he calls up to tell them where the organs are. He could leave them someplace public, or at a hospital, but doesn't. Why? Oh, by the way, I see three of the weapons Alex gave you. Deduct two points. Do better next time."

Ariel shut her mouth with a snap and I knew it cost her dearly not to spew molten anger all over the room. Instead, she considered the question for a few seconds before speaking. "It's about the Organ Donor?"

I nodded.

"Then it's not our jurisdiction," she said primly.

The look I tossed at her should have burned a hole through her skull but she remained unimpressed. "It's my jurisdiction if I decide it is. Now, answer the damn question."

"You want to know why he calls the cops?"

"Yeah."

She tapped a forefinger against her chin. "He just wants to jerk the PD around."

I shook my head. "Too simple. He goes to the effort of buying disposable phones to make the calls and leaving calling cards handwritten in crayon. Why? It doesn't jibe with me. A smart killer doesn't take that many risks."

Her eyes narrowed. "Maybe he's not that smart." Ariel

frowned. "But he is," she continued. "He's smart enough to dump the bodies in public and not get caught. Not by traffic cams or ATM cams. Nobody sees this guy."

"Exactly," I stated emphatically. "He's so damn smart he shouldn't take extra risks. So why do it?"

The gears in her noggin were churning full bore as she considered the problem and I took the opportunity to study her. Ivory blouse, black jacket and slacks (with ankle holster, I noted), hair pinned back, exposing a broad forehead and oval face. A damn fine looking woman, but I couldn't let myself be distracted like that. You get too close to someone, a partner, a friend, lover, whatever, and you'll find it's a one-way ticket to Deadsville ... population: you.

"I wish you wouldn't stare at me," she commented with surprisingly little heat.

"I'll stare, I'll curse. Hell, I'll sing the 'Star Spangled Banner' if I want, woman. If you can't work under pressure, then get thee gone. You're of no use to me."

"A distraction!" she blurted.

"So, I'm distracting you—"

She shook her head. "Not *you*, Mr. H, the Organ Donor."

"Go on," I urged, intrigued.

A bit of a smile curled the corners of her mouth and she dimpled prettily. "He wants the DPD and the Feebs to run around chasing their tails. When he calls in, I'll bet you dollars to donuts that it sends everyone scrambling." Her brow furrowed. "If he had them distracted, then he could focus on something else, some other sort of illegal activity; that might be the reason he takes the organs in the first place." She shook her head. "But it doesn't make sense. We can't apply logic to this nutjob."

Of course! I smacked myself on the forehead in sudden insight. "Actually we can," I uttered breathlessly. At her confused look, I smiled. " 'Nuts' doesn't mean dumb. There are plenty of variants of crazy." My smile must have resembled a shark's. "Think about it. Sure he/she/it is crazy, but it takes a lot of careful planning, intelligence, and research to carry off the murder of half a dozen people without getting caught. Plenty of smarts and enough control to plan something else. Something unexpected." Mentally I added to her tally of notches because, according to the reports Ghost had secured, Ariel had offered more insight in three minutes than the BAU had presented in weeks. She was rising pretty high on my Respect-O-Meter.

Excitement burning in my chest, I turned to my Mac and clicked on an icon in the dock. When the blank document appeared, I began to type furiously. "You," I told Ariel. "Get to go to the head of the class, hotshot. I like you. You might just live past Friday."

I could almost feel the heat of her appreciation and knew that if I turned around I'd see a face full of dimples. We all like to be appreciated. "Listen, Pea, while I do this, let's see how well you paid attention in class."

"Pardon me?"

"I will if you pass, Pea. Tell me … who founded the Bureau in America?"

Her answer was prompt. "George Washington, 1789." I guess she had paid attention to the briefings.

"What was it called?

"The Committee of Unnatural Affairs."

"Who's been read in on the Bureau and its mandate?"

"The President, Vice-President, Secretary of State, the Joint Chiefs, and the directors of all the major law enforcement alphabets."

"Okay, hotshot," I threw over my shoulder as I typed. "You obviously know the hierarchy. Goody for you. Let's move on to practical application. What is magic?"

A very long pause. So long that I nearly turned around. Finally, "Magic is a force or forces that have no explanation as to—"

"*Beeep!* Wrong!" I stopped typing and swiveled in my chair, crossing my arms. "Magic, my dear Green Pea, is science by other means. We have twenty magicians and a roomful of eggheads in R&D back in DC trying to figure it out."

I chuckled at her look of incomprehension. "Listen, Pea, magic follows the laws of physics, the Laws of Conservation of Energy, Cause and Effect and all the rest. In fact, it won't be too long before we understand it fully." I started counting on the fingers of my right hand. "One: magical energy is everywhere. You find it in people, animals. It can be found in special places, such as Easter Island, and you can even generate a large amount by such means as murder—what's known as Necromancy." My second finger went down. "Two: the use of magic comes from the will to use it and the ability to tap into it. Runes, jujus, candles and pentagrams are all tools to help the mind focus on what it wants. A magician Shapes the spell in his or her mind and releases it. Three: what you can do with it is directly proportional to the energy it is supplied with, i.e., ... use a little magic energy, do little things ... use a lot, do a lot. Four: it's genetic; not everyone can do it. If your mom could, chances are fifteen percent that you can. We know; our lab has isolated the gene. Really cool stuff, by the way." One finger left. I saved the middle one for last. "Five: if you don't try to understand it, learn to recognize it, it will kill you. Sooner rather than later. We take on a lot of magic users who think they should run things. They're our number one source of headaches around here."

Her face screwed up like she'd tasted something sour. "Magicians, really?"

"Really and truly. There've been magicians on this planet as long as there have been humans. Ben Franklin, Thomas Jefferson, Alexander Graham Bell, Henry Ford, JFK ..."

"JFK?"

"Hmph. For some reason, all the Kennedy boys were, except for JFK Junior. It passed him straight over; all he got were the looks." I paused for a second. "It seems that all magicians are highly intelligent, or that magic increases intelligence. Maybe ambition has something to do with it, but if you look at all the great men and women in history, and all the infamous ones, many were magicians. Spooky, eh?" She should have been briefed on magicians as part of her orientation, but that never happened. Someone wanted to throw her into the shark tank to see if she'd swim or become breakfast. I had a strong suspicion that she'd take the sharks on, bite for bite.

The soles of her shoes made a soft *whish whish whish* as she began to pace. "This is strange, but looking at it cockeyed, it makes a bizarre sort of sense. If you accept magic, you have to accept magicians."

"It gets weirder, trust me." With a flourish I finished my typing and sent the interdepartmental email winging its way through cyberspace.

"How? How does this get weirder?" she muttered.

If she had looked up, my smile might have scared her out of her wits. "Hitler was a magician."

Instantly she stopped. "Okay, now I know your razzing me, I just know it. No way!" Her voice carried equal amounts of resentment and wrath.

Time to hit her hard. If you can't take the heat ... "What do you think the death camps were all about? One of the greatest sources of magical energy is death, the more sudden, the greater the output of energy. Kill a lot of people, generate a lot of energy. Auschwitz, Bergen Belson, Sobibor, Treblinka ... they were some largest magical batteries known to mankind. All used by Hitler to fuel the continuation of the Third Reich."

Ariel took a deep breath, and I could see the wheels spinning in her head as she crossed her arms defensively. "So he killed all those poor Jews for his own agenda?"

"You think that's bad? *Six million* people were exterminated, sacrificed so that madman could prosecute his war. But look at Josef Stalin ... *eighteen million* people killed in his pogroms. It's the main reason Russia held Stalingrad, the deaths of millions of people."

"Wait a minute, wait a minute," Ariel waved her hands in the air. "He had those people murdered to stop the Nazis?"

I shook my head. "Only partly. He stored a lot of magical energy away to use when needed. Like you'd charge up a car battery."

"But how?"

"Oh, several ways. Gems are the best, the more perfect, the better. A magician can access the magic stored in a gem. Artifacts work, too; they're one of the main reasons the Nazis looted Paris. Gold and silver can be used, but only the purest and only if they're Shaped in such a way, like the gold filigree on a Fabergé egg, and so on and so forth."

"This job gets stranger and stranger," she muttered. "It sounds like the biggest conspiracy theory in the world."

"Sure it does; it's the world's biggest secret," I said. "The World Under, the unreal world, is far bigger, and far more dangerous, than you could ever imagine." I made a mental note to ask BB who handled her orientation. He or she needed a swift kick in the fundament.

Strength and iron resolve shone bright from her deep eyes. "How do you handle it? You've been doing this ten years." She cocked an eyebrow.

"Booze," I answered. "Booze and women. Lots and lots of both."

Maybe a minute passed as she calmly absorbed all the information I'd thrown at her. Another notch up, she was proving to be resilient. If she kept earning notches left and right I'd have to actually to consider her as something besides useless. "Why didn't they tell me during orientation?"

"They should have told you some of it—about some of the creatures of the World Under." She nodded. "Good. I have no clue why they didn't read you in on magicians; maybe they needed to see if you could hack it. Maybe somebody is screwing with you."

Ariel took a deep breath through her nose and her lips gave the tiniest quirk of amusement. "And what's the verdict?"

"You might avoid being a corpse for a while." There was hope.

"Gee thanks."

I couldn't tell if she was being sarcastic or not, but however she felt now I was at least reasonably certain she could watch my back without accidentally shooting me in the ass. There was some real mustard in that lady, a core of toughness and granite that you can't learn; you're born with it.

"Hello, Kal," came the buzzing voice from the tiny speakers in my Mac. I jumped, while Ariel's head nearly bumped the ceiling. "Oh, I hope I didn't startle you two?" Despite the concern expressed in the words, the tone remained flat, neutral.

"It's okay, Ghost. Glad you came. What have you got?" Out of the corner of my eye I saw Ariel stiffen up like a two-by-four. Curious.

"Kal, can you ask that woman to leave?" If I didn't know better, I could've sworn that Ghost sounded disdainful of our DEA transplant. Curiouser and curiouser. Without a word she stood, back ramrod straight, and huffed out of the office.

I kept my voice as neutral as Ghost's. "Not a way to make friends."

"I don't need friends like her." Cold, cold cold. I imagined I could see my breath steaming in the still air of the office. His voice became marginally warmer as he continued. "Kal, that was very clever addressing the inter-office email to 'Deus Ex Machina'. That is the first time anyone has ever done that. Obvious, though."

A compliment? Sort of, but I let it slide. "Did you get the autopsy reports I asked for?"

"Incoming to your printer right now." On cue, the printer dinged and began chugging out papers into the tray. The autopsy reports, complete with pictures. Funsville.

"Great. Thanks, Ghost."

"Kal," he buzzed.

"Yeah, Ghost?"

"That woman ..."

"Ariel?"

"Yes, that one. I don't like her." And with a soft click from the speakers he was gone.

Harsh words from electronic eidolon. What was it about Ariel that cheesed off the local genie?

"Green Pea!" I roared. "Get in here!"

Ariel stomped back into the office, her coffee with a hint of cream complexion tinged with red. Wordless, she took a seat.

"What's your gripe?" I asked, pulling a few photos from the printer and staring intently at them. One was of Krouse lying on his back on surgical steel autopsy table, torso cut open from crotch to throat, the sternum cracked open like a nut. Pink flesh the color of Hubba-Bubba bubble gum ridged the edges of the wound. Even with the grainy quality of the photo it was easy to see that the entire torso was hollow, scooped out like a melon. Pretty disgusting, but I've seen much, much worse.

"I ... don't like that ... *thing*." Icy revulsion laced her words.

I spoke softly, enough that she had to strain to hear. "There are a lot of things about this job that bite the big one. If you can't handle it, tell me now because if you *ever* allow yourself to be pushed around like that again by a Supernatural, I'll kick your behind so hard you'll be wearing your butt cheeks for earrings. Got me?"

She mumbled something unintelligible.

Once again I kept my voice soft, even though the anger inside boiled the liquid in my eyeballs. "I said 'got me?' and I expect an answer, so sound off like you know what a pair feels like."

"Got you." Her anger matched mine. Good. Anger I could use.

I stood and leaned over the desk, wagging a finger at her. "Always remember ... the World Under, the world below, or adjacent to, ours doesn't get to push us around. *We* do the pushing. *We* are the 800 lb gorilla, not them. Never, ever, forget that."

The nod she tipped me was almost imperceptible, but enough of a concession at that point, so I scooped up the rest of the report from the printer and motioned her to join me at the desk. I split the pile and handed her half. "Read. Tell me if you see anything unusual." After a moment of consideration, I added, "And by that, I mean 'stranger than usual in this case.' " She nodded quickly and we both dug in.

Reading the autopsy reports was a lesson in gruesome. Someone had expertly hollowed out all the victims' torsos like canoes with a knife, or in this case, a scalpel. Whoever had done the job most likely had medical training or had practiced with a blade often enough to become proficient. A bone saw was used to cut through ribs and sternum. Even more gruesome.

As I was flipping through the pictures, Ariel let out a hiss, the sound whistling through her nearly perfect teeth.

"What?" I asked, dropping the photos on the desk.

She handed me what looked to be the ME's notes on victim #2, one David Bellingham. "Look here, where it says 'Cause of Death.' Is this what you were looking for?"

My eyes swept back and forth as I read, my pulse hammering faster and faster as I grasped the implications. Bellingham had died of exsanguination—he'd been bled out like a hog at butchering time. His carotid artery had been severed with one clean slice by a horribly sharp blade and there wasn't an ounce of blood left in him. "Well, crap and fried eggs," I breathed. How could I have missed that? I cursed myself for twelve kinds of fool.

Ariel's smile became triumphant as she handed me the ME's report on victim #3, Arlo Doyle. Same cause of death. Same type of wound. Dry as a bone, not a drop left. I grabbed for the photos on my desk. My eyes widened as I laid the photos of all the victims in a row on my desk.

"Look here," I said excitedly, pointing at the ankles of victim #4, Henry McFadden. "At the ankles. See there, the marks? What do you make of that?"

She tapped a plum-colored fingernail against her front teeth. "Ligature marks."

"Yeah, ligature marks. But what do they tell you?"

"He was restrained. He's a big guy, a leg breaker according to records. He needed to be tied up."

I held up two photos. "Then look here. There are more marks around the victims' ankles than the wrists? Why, why are the bruises more severe around the ankles? And the slices to the carotid? Why there? Why not the brachial artery, or the femoral? Think … those facts … put them together."

Slowly understanding lit up her face and a sort of sick horror suffused her voice. "More marks, larger on the legs … throat cut … bled out … *oh damn!* He hung them up by the ankles and butchered them like … like …"

"Like hogs," I finished.

"Yeah, like hogs." She wobbled for a second, knees nearly giving way, but to her credit she remained upright. Score another point for the Pea.

"Okay, pop quiz, hotshot," I drawled. "Why would the Organ Donor kill his victims by draining them dry?"

"He needs the blood. Or he uses it." Her voice was barely above a whisper.

I nodded, slightly sick to my stomach. "He needs the blood." I ran my hands through my hair, resignation leeching through me. "We have a Renfield here."

"A what?" asked Ariel uncertainly.

"Jesus, lady, you were doing so well there for a while. Now I have to deduct a few points. Haven't you read *Dracula* or seen the movies? Even the crappy one with Keanu Reeves?"

"I don't watch movies and the only books I've read are nonfiction." Her look challenged me to smart off at her, which I felt might be a poor choice on my part.

Deep breaths. Two of them, filling the lungs, easing my frustration. "Renfield was a character in Bram Stoker's *Dracula*. An inmate in an asylum who ate bugs, birds, whatever he could get his hands on to try to absorb their life force. Dracula, you have heard of him?" At her nod I continued. "Dracula enters the asylum and offers the madman an endless supply of little beasties to eat in exchange for worship. Basically, Renfield becomes Dracula's slave. I believe the Organ Donor is a Renfield, a vampire's slave or servant."

Long, delicate fingers covered Ariel's mouth as she gagged for a second or two. "Oh lord, that's just *gross*. Stoker must have been insane when he wrote that."

I shook my head. "Not insane. He was a good agent who wrote a great book."

The sound of her jaw hitting the desk was priceless and I hid my grin behind my hand. "We got someone here collecting blood for a vampire. A Renfield." It was hard, but I kept my amusement at her discomfiture out of my voice. "I knew it was only a matter of time before the other shoe dropped."

"What?"

"Little while ago there was a zombie problem. Not a big one, but enough to bring the Bureau to Denver. But there is never just one Supernatural occurrence. If you see one, then you know more are coming. It's a domino effect. The World Under is funny that way."

She pulled at her lower lip, an adorable affectation that made me want ... hurriedly I derailed that thought. For me, that way led to madness. "Two questions, Kal. One: how do you know it's a Renfield and not just a lone vampire and Two: isn't this a permanent field office?"

"Good Lord," I groused. "Don't they teach you Peas anything anymore? With only 50 agents in the Bureau, and about the same in support staff, we go where the action is. The only permanent office is Warehouse in D.C., and to answer your first question: no, a lone vamp wouldn't be making this kind of media splash. They tend to keep to the shadows and nibble at the edges of society; they don't even think like humans. But when they employ a Renfield, it's usually someone crazier than a bedbug. Although this kind of attention is normally counter to their motives." I held up the photos. "I think this is plenty crazy, don't you?"

Before she could answer, there came a tap-tap-tapping at my

door. "Nevermore!" I called.

Alex popped through. "Very funny, Kal every time." Despite the sarcasm, he looked bright-eyed and bushy tailed.

"Wow … someone's feeling his oats today. I hope she let you sleep," I commented dryly.

He had the good grace to blush. "I had Ghost check all the police reports from the cities where the bodies were found and I think I've got something." He spared a wary glance at Ariel.

"It's okay, Alex, you can talk in front of the Pea."

Licking his lips, he continued. "The fourth victim was found on Arapahoe Road, in Englewood, one of the main arteries running through the Denver metro area. About a mile east of there a jewelry store reported a robbery."

My ears perked up and Alex gave me a knowing look. "That's right," he continued. "Three man-made rubies, 1.5 carats each, all three perfect."

Ariel pursed her lips. "And?"

"And a store not far from the first victim reported the robbery of a two-carat diamond, clarity I.F."

"I.F.?"

"Internally Flawless," I answered before Alex could open his mouth. He stared at me, eyes wide. "What? I know things." My return look contained a wealth of smugness.

"How come DPD or the feds never put these two things together?" Ariel asked.

"Because whoever took the original gems replaced them with very good replicas. So good that no one looked at them twice until customers showed interest," Alex replied excitedly. "The robberies were discovered almost a full week after the two murders."

I pursed my lips while an ugly idea nibbled at the edges of my mind. "Alex, those stores … were they local, part of a chain? Big? Small? Get me the details."

"What's going on?"

"I think the Organ Donor is a Renfield and, quite possibly, a magician." It almost hurt me to say it. If it were true, I could be facing a whole passel of trouble and would need backup. Yesterday.

Color drained from Alex's face. "Holy crap! A Renfield who's a magician? You think it's because of the stolen gems?"

"What else could it be? He or she is trying to store up a lot of energy for his or her master. A vampire/magician combo makes me sick to my stomach." A thought occurred to me. "Set up a call with BB; I need to talk to him."

"You got it." He left looking shaken ... not stirred.

"Couldn't the vampire be the magician?" Ariel's question startled me.

"Wha—? Oh, no. Vampires don't have the gene for magic. Their main advantage is being incredibly fast and strong."

Forget the *Twilight* movies or the *Lost Boys*. Heck, forget *Dracula*. First thing an agent learns about vamps is that they are a completely separate species from old Homo Sap. They resemble albino humans and are highly allergic to sunlight (however, they don't burst into flames; that's a myth) and have a literally insatiable thirst for blood. To them, human hemoglobin is prime rib, lobster thermidor, and fettuccine alfredo all rolled up into one. We are just meals-on-heels to them.

I put my head in my hands and rubbed my temples. "So our Renfield is a magician or is working with one. He's stealing rubies and diamonds so he can store magical energy. The question is, what for?"

Chapter Four

Shark Smiles

Before I could speculate further, a high-pitched wail split my eardrums, the sound cresting before falling silent, only to pierce the silence again less than a second later.

I bolted toward the door. "C'mon, follow me." Without a word, Ariel was at my heels as I raced full out to Comms, shouldering past my team members. When we reached the room all the walls were lit with split-screen displays, a dizzying array of visual information. Maps, charts, and what looked like a radar display, but my eyes fixed straight on a satellite map of the city. A red dot blinked on the west side.

From behind, Alex burst into the room and sent Ariel and Agent Sue Farris sprawling. Without bothering to apologize, he took a seat on the leather chair at the blond wood table and tapped a staccato rhythm on what looked like a knot. In front of him, a section of table darkened and a virtual keyboard came into view.

"Turn off the siren, Alex!" I bellowed, hands over my ears.

A few keystrokes and seconds later the ear-splitting screech died away. Everyone sighed in relief. "Thanks. Tell me what's going on," I commanded.

Alex deleted all the images on the screens except for the map of the city, which he enlarged until it occupied one whole wall. "Magical output. About .95 gigamerlin. Sudden, died off almost immediately. Location is Golden, Colorado."

"What's a gigamerlin?" I heard Ariel ask one of the other four agents in the room.

Without turning around, I answered. "A merlin is a unit of magical energy. A gigamerlin is a boatload of magical energy." I turned toward Alex. "What can that much do?"

He tapped the keyboard and the opposite wall flared into life with some esoteric equations that I couldn't make heads or tails of, even after ten years. "Please tell me this makes sense to someone."

"Got it, Kal," replied Alex. "With this much energy you could fly for six, maybe seven hours or raise four or five Class One demons."

Great. I hated demons. Class Ones were small and nasty … razor teeth and a bad attitude to match. "Anything else?"

"About three zombies or one ghoul."

That had the agents and me shifting uncomfortably. Zombies were nasty enough, but at least they were brainless. Ghouls, however, were like zombies with free will and extraordinary physical abilities. Nasty, smart and always hungry. Three guesses on what they liked to eat and the first two don't count.

"Okay, folks, put on your thinking caps," I announced. "We have a magician, theoretically the one that raised those zombies last month. Why is he doing so now? And in broad daylight?" I checked my watch. "It isn't even lunch and we have a crisis on our hands, so go ahead, hit me with your best shot." Agents Jeff Cresswell and Dom Rigione stared at the ground, lost in thought while Agents Sue Farris and Bryan Manus just looked uncomfortable. "Anyone?"

Nothing.

"Great. Okay, here's the plan: Bryan and Dom, since you both look like you're constipated, go ahead and check it out. Arm yourself for war. Wear your Jackets and carry federal badges, Homeland Security or ICE—I don't care which—but get me some answers." Both nodded and got gone.

I turned back to the map. "Alex, you got the location pinpointed?"

"Got it, sir."

"Don't call me 'sir.' Send it to Bryan's RediPad and make sure they keep in touch at all times."

"Kal, why don't you go?" BB's voice carried mild concern.

I turned around to face the other wall, lit with a floor to ceiling display of my boss, big enough to see every pore and follicle. Kinda gross, really. "Hiya, BB, I'm taking the Pea to the Denver Federal Building to dig up more intel on the Organ Donor case."

His watery gray eyes bored into mine. Up close I could see that the whites were slightly tinged with yellow. "Why? What have you found?"

I related my suspicions about what Ariel and I had found in the Organ Donor files and watched BB's eyes grow wide behind his wire rims.

"That's … quite something, Kal. All right, you go ahead. How do you want to proceed?"

I'd been working on the answer to that question for a while now. "The last victim, Krouse, has a thin jacket and no relatives. I can have Alex give him a federal sheet as an undercover agent with the ATF investigating gun running into L.A. and that will allow me to get close to the case—me being his case officer and all."

BB's lips thinned almost to invisibility as he thought about it. "All right," he said finally, looking as if he had swallowed a lemon, peel and all. "Go to it. I'll give Director Marsh at the ATF the heads up."

"Thanks, BB, I appreciate it." I let out a breath I didn't know I was holding. "You might want to clue in FBI Director Stilson. If my read on Special Agent Briegan is accurate, he'll call to complain soon enough."

"Do you expect trouble?" BB hated inter-agency pissing matches, but on the plus side, our stream was stronger and went farther.

It was my turn to thin my lips. "I always expect it."

He sighed. "Very well. Take Agent McMillan with you. Have Alex give her a badge and ID."

"Awww, boss," I whined. Taking her with me really put the rusty nails in my Cheerios.

For a fraction of a second his lips twitched. "You heard me."

The screen blanked.

Damn it.

"Okay, Alex, you heard the boss. Let's do it up right."

Ten minutes later Ariel and I were speeding down Highway 70 to I-25, where we would head south to the Denver offices of the FBI—just a hop, skip and jump from 6 flags Elitch Gardens.

I parked the car—not my Honda, but a shiny black Crown Vic with more power than a whole herd of Hondas and twice as smooth. If it hadn't been as big as my first apartment at the University of Nebraska and ugly as sin, I would've been in hog heaven.

Exiting the black beast, I noted that my Green Pea was still fuming. Alex had handed her an ATF ID that read 'Gertrude Finger.' If I hadn't been there, she probably would've throttled the poor kid.

"I don't understand!" he'd cried. "That wasn't the name I put in the computer, honest!" He'd looked so heartbroken I did the only thing I could do—laugh my ass off. If my suspicions were correct, Ghost had a lot more of a sense of humor than I'd given him credit for.

"Really, Kal! It's not my fault!" He started to back away from Ariel, who was staring at him and grinding her teeth. If looks could kill, he would've been a red smear on linoleum.

"Did you set me up?" demanded Ms. Finger as she rounded the Vic.

"Oh, hell no," I replied. "You would have had a worse name, if it was up to me."

That didn't earn me any love, just a glare and a 'harumph' of rage. Really, it could have been worse. My trainer in the Bureau stuck me with the name 'Phil Ashio' as a cover identity with the NSA. Once I got over it I actually saw the humor.

"Ease up, Gertrude," I admonished as I opened the Vic's trunk. "We have to shed most of our weapons. Don't want to explain to the FBI why we are walking arsenals." Quickly I divested two punch knives, a garrote, a .45 ACP, three shurikens (silver plated), and my Bowie knife.

"Where the hell did you get that monster and where did you hide it?" Ariel breathed as the Bowie *thunked* into the trunk. Nearly half a centimeter thick and fourteen inches long, it almost qualified as a sword.

"A gift from my Dad, custom made. As to where I keep it … well, that's personal," I answered with a grin. Actually, I had a sheath strapped to my back, the knife running parallel to my spine, hilt down. Got the idea from *Crocodile Dundee*. Bless you, Paul Hogan.

She harrumphed and unloaded her own store of weapons. "I feel kinda naked now," she remarked as the last throwing knife landed on the pile of sharp edged lethality.

I nodded. "I know, let's get this over with. Remember, we're looking for personal notes not put into the system. Don't disregard anything."

"Right."

Entering the four-story FBI building encased in 2,010 bulletproof glass panels proved to be the easiest part. Inside, even after showing our IDs, we were disarmed (my Lahti raised a few eyebrows and garnered a cash offer) and made to walk through a metal detector. At least security at the FBI building was much more pleasant than dealing with the TSA at Denver International Airport.

We walked to a bank of elevators and pushed the UP button. "How did the Bureau know about that magical energy?" Ariel whispered out of the corner of her mouth.

"We're not in a spy movie. You can speak in normally," I countered, much amused.

Her cheeks reddened slightly. "Okay, but how did we sense … whatdoyoucallit … merlins? … from across town?"

"The Bureau has sensors the size of a quarter on every cell tower in every major city in the U.S. of A." The doors opened and we entered, pushing the button for the fourth floor. "As long as a magician casts a spell over 100 Megamerlin above ground, we can get a read on it."

"How much is a Megamerlin?"

I considered a bit. "Enough to remotely start a car, or cast a disorienting spell."

"So 100 Megamerlin …"

"Can kill," I finished. For a moment an idea floated to the surface of my mind but sank almost immediately.

"Do most magicians and supernatural creatures know about the Bureau?"

"Yeah. We're the bogeymen to the Supernatural community."

"How do they know?" she asked.

I threw her a level stare. "We don't hide ourselves from the World Under. We have to rely on the fear of the Bureau to help keep the Supernatural population in check. I'm plenty okay with not killing them as long they behave themselves, but the second they cross the line, they're mine!" Even to me my voice was a little bitter. I coughed to cover my embarrassment.

" 'Ours', you mean, right?"

"What?"

"If they step out of line, there're *ours*, right?"

I blinked a few times, pretending puzzlement. "Yes of course. Why?"

She wasn't fooled, but she shook her head, letting it go. The elevator *pinged* and the doors opened, revealing a tall, thin man wearing a thousand dollar dark gray suit. He had a ridiculously cleft chin and immaculately coiffed hair.

"You must be D.P. Roberts," he drawled, holding out a finely manicured hand as we exited. His eyes glittered like shards of glass in moonlight; they threw out sparks as he measured me with equal parts malice and amusement.

"Yes," I acknowledged, taking his soft hand in mine. I bet he paid a hefty sum every month for mani pedis. "You must be Special Agent Briegan, BAU." Instead of shaking his hand, I gave it a little squeeze. I'd read his file. He'd played lacrosse at Baylor back in the day, but I'd been a red-shirt freshman wide receiver for the Huskers when they were champions; I had a good thirty pounds on him. His eyes widened in surprise and a little pain. Apparently his time at the FBI hadn't included any regular physical activity.

"Good to meet you," he gritted, keeping his sarky little smile in place, though it trembled around the edges. With the chest thumping done, I let go and he immediately turned to Ariel. "Agent Finger, a pleasure." This time his hand was extended a bit more cautiously, but Ariel dimpled at him and tossed out a toothy smile that would've done credit to a Great White. It must have touched a familiar nerve because he gave her one that was every bit as toothy and predatory. The mating ritual of the wild Fed: keep your hands and feet away from the water at all times.

I knew then what kind of man we faced. Most people who worked in law enforcement are good and hardworking—people who want to bring a modicum of order to the chaos of our existence. Like me, they are bulwarks against which the waves of the venal and evil rage. They hold fast and shelter those who rely on them. But Briegan, he was cut from different material, a polyester parasite. Men and women like him have always been there asking the same questions over and over again. *Who do I have to screw over to get ahead? What must I do so I can be more powerful?* Yet, no matter how many times they reach a new plateau of might, they are never satisfied. Like sharks questing eternally for food.

My palms itched with the need to lash out at this man, but I trampled the impulse ruthlessly, no matter how fulfilling it would be. There were more important things at stake than my petty pet peeves. People needed me, people I could save by exerting a modicum of self-control.

I interrupted him before he could summon up a trite and charming line. "Special Agent Briegan, Agent Finger and I would like to see what you have on the Organ Donor before we claim our man's body, if you don't mind."

His smile faltered, then settled into something slightly contemptuous. Nodding to Ariel, he started down a long, blue-carpeted hall with us at his heels. "I didn't know the ATF had a man undercover in Denver," he shot over his shoulder. "No offense, but your man Krouse looked more like the leg breaker he posed as than the agent he was."

"None taken," I replied neutrally. "But that's the point, *not* to look like an agent. And as for what he was doing in Denver, I'm not at liberty to divulge that information at this time." His reply was a small snort.

Briegan stopped at a doorway and motioned for us to enter. A rectangular room, one long glass wall that gave an excellent view of the Rockies and the clouds above them. A dark wood table, also rectangular, dominated the space, surrounded by an even dozen leather chairs. Other than that, the room was empty, sterile.

"*Okay, Kal, I'm here,*" Alex said, voice squeaky and a bit tinny from the earwigs planted deep in our auditory canals.

I tapped the gold band on my right ring finger. In the setting lay a black sapphire that was actually a powerful microphone/transmitter. Alex would be able to hear everything and assist with Briegan if necessary.

"There are a few questions I'd like to ask you, Agent Roberts." Briegan closed the door behind him.

"*Kal, Sue and Dom just reported in,*" Alex squeaked. "*The burst of magical energy we detected came from a cemetery. Seems someone stole a body from a chapel right before the viewing.*" Since normal humans can't feel magical energy unless it's directed at them, it was easy to assume that a magician entered the parlor, animated the corpse, and got out without anyone being the wiser. Pretty easy to steal a body if it walks out with you. "*The deceased was one Jacob Mueller, former Olympic wrestler.*"

Olympic wrestler?

"Currently we are not at liberty to answer those questions," I said tersely. Sometimes the vaguest answers are the safest.

"Listen—" Briegan began, voice cold and intense.

"We were told you'd cooperate, Special Agent Briegan," Ariel interrupted with equal chill.

"Who would promise that the FBI would give the ATF information on an ongoing investigation?"

"Taking care of it."

My smile was genuine. "Our director assured us that it would be no issue, Special Agent Briegan."

"It may not be an issue for him, but it is for me."

I pretended confusion. "Hmm … it was assumed your director would clear it."

He folded his arms and out of the corner of my eye I saw Ariel frown at him. Looked like the shine was wearing off Special Agent Briegan for the Pea. Good for her; that meant she was a halfway decent judge of character. "You know what they say about assuming, don't you, Agent Roberts."

"Taken care of, Kal."

As if on cue, Briegan's cell rang and he answered, a look of annoyance flitting across his face. "Yes?" His spine stiffened. "Yes sir, they're here. But … yes. Yes, sir, goodbye, sir." Looking up from his phone, he opened his mouth once or twice before snapping it shut and, with a very stiff spine, tramped out of the room.

"Gosh, he looks pissed." Ariel sounded amused.

"I think his director just jostled the stick up his ass."

Alex chuckled softly in my ear.

Ariel's grin matched mine. "More like a Sequoia than a stick."

We shared a laugh and sat.

"Alex, no one saw the magician or the dead guy leaving the parlor?"

"No one. Sorry, but I think the bad guys were long gone by the time we arrived on scene."

"Did they find out why the magician risked a daylight spell casting of such magnitude, and above ground at that?"

Ariel answered. "The corpse was of a former Olympic

Wrestler. If he's making a zombie, he's making a strong one."

"*With the magnitude of magical energy we detected, Agent McMillan, it would most likely be a ghoul. Much stronger and faster than a zombie. They also have some free will and the intelligence to use it.*" For some reason he sounded a little miffed. I guess Ghost wasn't the only one who disliked the Green Pea. "*An Olympic wrestler turned ghoul would be a fearsome thing,*" he concluded.

"Is this the same magician who raised the zombies Dom and I took out a while ago?"

"*Most likely, Kal, considering that raising the dead is a very rare skill. Such a spell Shape is difficult to create and cast.*"

Oh, my aching gut. "A vampire and a zombie raiser slash serial killer? Just freaking great."

"*Sounds like a nightmare walking.*"

Before I could reply, the door opened and Special Agent Stick-up-the-Butt came in carrying a file box. "Here you go," he said stiffly, dropping it with a loud *thud* onto the table.

Without preamble Ariel and I dove in, looking for any scrap of information that might aid in the investigation.

"Agent Roberts," began Briegan, "you don't dress like an agent, what with the polo shirt and khakis. And are those *penny loafers*?" He was trying to bait me, a dig after the failed attempt at a petty power play.

"I'm slumming," I replied, not bothering to look up. I could feel the disapproval radiating from him. The urge to snap at him became almost overpowering, but once again I controlled myself. Behaving like an adult could be frustrating.

I don't like that guy. Distain dripped from the earwig.

"Uh-huh," I mumbled, holding up a part of an autopsy report. Nothing I'd seen so far proved to be of any use. Everything in the box had already been translated into an electronic medium and pirated by Ghost.

"Agent Briegan," Ariel began, "I—"

"Special Agent," came the quick response.

"What?"

"It's 'Special Agent Briegan,' Agent Finger." Gone was any sort of playful predatory smile. I guess the bloom was off the rose for the Special Agent.

Ariel didn't miss a beat, although the tension around her eyes betrayed anger. "Right." A few seconds later. "What kind of profile do you have on the Organ Donor?"

Briegan pursed his lips. "White male, between the ages of thirty-five and forty-five, physically powerful and highly intelligent. Some medical training. Loner, keeps to himself. Very meticulous."

Sounded like almost every profile I'd ever heard of. I pulled a few more pieces of paper … nothing. A few more minutes and I concluded that there was nothing new to be had here.

"Nothing of use, Finger," I announced. "Let's go."

"What are you looking for?" Briegan asked, doing his best to loom over us. He needed more looming practice.

"Just a handle on the Donor." I picked up the box and thrust it back into his arms. "Nothing here helps."

"How do you know?"

"I know. We'll see ourselves out."

Ariel tossed one last piece of paper into the box in Briegan's arms, gave him a cheeky smile and exited without a word.

His words followed into the hall. "Hey, you find anything, you're obligated to let me know immediately! You hear me?"

I shook my head. "Sure will." My voice dripped insincerity. "Thank you, Special Agent." We got to the elevator and I pushed the down button.

"What a douchebag, Kal."

Ariel's laughter rang down the hallway as the elevator doors opened for us.

The drive back to the office was uneventful except for one thing.

"Kal, we got another big spike on the sensors." I could hear the

blah blah blah of the siren in the background. "*You want me to send Dom and Bryan out again?*"

I said an unkind word that would've shocked my mother had she heard it. "Yeah, might as well. Let me know if they find anything."

"*You got it.*"

"How long have you been a team leader?" Ariel asked, puzzled.

My eyebrows shot up. That question came out of nowhere. "I've been the Epsilon Team Leader for six years now. A lot of faces have changed, but the game remains the same." A few seconds passed. "I'll have the job until I die or someone better comes along."

"So BB trusts you?"

I nodded. "And I trust him. So does the President. In fact, I haven't met a President who didn't trust him."

"You've met the President?" For some reason, I was disappointed in the awe in her voice.

"The BSI Director and his three most senior field agents are all present when a new President is read in on our existence and the existence of the World Under."

"And how do they take it?"

"Well, I've only met two Presidents, but usually they laugh their ass off until they get proof. Then they look like they're going to throw up."

"Proof?"

"It isn't that hard to produce some hocus-pocus."

"Who does the hocus-pocusing?"

I glanced at her out of the corner of my eye, her face a study in neutral.

"What's with the twenty questions?"

She tossed over an innocent look, but something still struck me as off. "I just want to know how things work. Like how come there are only fifty of you at a time."

My lips thinned and I bit back a few choice words. "Last answer for the night, hotshot. There are only fifty of us because stuff like this, the World Under interfering with the really real world, doesn't happen as often as you'd think. Fifty agents, fifty support staff. That's all that's needed, how it has always been done."

By the time we made it back to the office, Bryan and Dom checked in with Alex.

"Same thing as before, but in Wheat Ridge this time," he reported. "Body of a forty-year-old bodybuilder went missing."

Ariel said, "That would make one bad-ass ghoul."

I snorted. "Like a former Olympic wrestler is a pushover? The worst thing about a ghoul besides its strength is its ability to unhinge its jaw and take *really* large chunks out of its victims."

She made a face. "Well, that just put me off my feed for about … forever."

The thought of multiple ghouls certainly didn't give me the warm fuzzies, considering that in order to kill one you either had to hammer it into jelly, cut it literally to pieces or slice its head off— which is hard to do because they have a series of bony plates that ring the neck. In my time with the Bureau I've faced two ghouls, and both times I was happy to have backup. They're very good ambush predators.

BweeeEEEEE … BweeeEEEEE!

"Oh, crap …" I muttered and headed back toward Comms. This time Alex beat me to the punch.

"Another one, same intensity," he yelled over the alarm. "In Lakewood." He killed the alarm just as the rest of the team hurried in.

"Three ghouls, really?" Ariel sounded scared. She'd be more scared if she actually met one. I hoped she'd never have that pleasure.

Dom, a short, muscular, pug-faced Italian who had more bristly black hair than a Wookie, chimed in. "Let me guess, boss. You want Bryan and me to go check it out." He sounded less than enthused.

I shook my head. "No, Sue and Jeff can do it this time. I want you two to help Alex with the Organ Donor thing. I need to find how many more gems this pinhead has stolen."

Sue, a compact blonde who looked better from the back than front, smiled. On most people, it would've been pleasant, but on her it was just plain scary. Despite her frightening features and air of over all bad-assness, she was as dependable and efficient as they come. "Thank god," she said, her voice a harsh whisper, thanks to an Amphisbaena (a kind of serpent with a head at each end) attack a year ago. "I get tired of hanging around with the fairy princess here."

That got a chuckle from all round. Dom had no problem with his sexuality and openly shared his conquests with anyone who would stand still long enough to listen. The Royal Canadian Mounted Police were not the only ones who always got their man.

"You're just jealous that I don't share all this magnificence with you," he replied, posing dramatically. That earned a few more laughs.

I'm a big fan of humor, but it wasn't the time. "Pipe down you louts and get busy. This thing stinks to high heaven." A moment's pause. "We got a Renfield who could be a magician raising ghouls, or a Renfield *and* a magician causing us grief. Either way we have to be on a war footing. Everyone wear your Kevlar and Faraday jackets from now on in case things get hairy." I tapped Alex on the shoulder. "Set the Pea up with a Faraday jacket, too."

Ariel looked confused. "What's a Faraday jacket?"

Alex fielded this one. "It's like a flak jacket made of cloth and silver mesh. Designed by Michael Faraday, possibly the greatest magician of the nineteenth century, it absorbs magical energy. It won't totally absorb a really strong spell, but it'll negate smaller ones, giving an agent time to react. The only downside is, the more magic it absorbs, the hotter it becomes, which is why the fabric is highly heat-resistant. Silver is great for storing energy, but not without consequences. Gold and platinum can hold much, much more."

"What about—"

Enough was enough. "We don't need a history lesson here, we need results. Get Jackets for everyone, including Pat." Rule number one in this job: you can *never* be too careful. While in charge I was going to do my damndest to keep everyone alive. After donning their jackets, Sue and Bryan left.

Surprisingly, BB didn't put in an appearance. Maybe he was in the middle of some inter-agency politicking. Or butt-kissing, which amounts to the same thing.

For some reason everyone was slow to move. I snarled, "What are you guys waiting for? Applause? Get to work!" That had them stepping and fetching. With nothing left to do but wait, I turned to Ariel. "Green Pea, come with me."

Back in my office, we began to pile though the files once again.

"What are we looking for?" Ariel sounded as frustrated as I felt.

"Something … damn, anything we might've missed." I shook my head. "There's always something. No such thing as a perfect murder and there's always a pattern. We just have to find it." However passionate my feelings on the matter, the file failed to yield any new information, anything that might say 'Lookee here, X marks the spot,' and 'Here Be Serial Killers.'

After an hour of fruitless searching I was ready to chew the walls.

There came a tap-tap-tapping on my office door. Too wound up for the usual joke, I yelled, "Come in."

When Alex entered, I knew something had gone pear-shaped and Ariel tensed.

A familiar feeling entered my gut. By the pricking of my thumbs … "Who?" I rasped.

Without a word he handed me a smart phone, which I accepted as if it were poisonous. Putting the cell to my ear, I licked my lips and said, "Report."

"Boss, it's Sue. Jeff's dead." Farris's voice was thick, like she was choking on motor oil. "It was a trap."

… Something wicked this way comes.

"What happened?" I sounded calm, but inside something was building.

"We got to the parlor. It was empty, at least we thought it was. Next thing we knew a disorientation spell hit us, but the jackets shrugged it off. Then the ghoul came out of the casket. Jeff got his arm ripped off before I could kill the thing with my sword." Most agents kept short swords, twenty-one inches of folded-steel death; they were perfect for dealing with hard-to-kill Supernaturals.

My throat tried to close, but I willed it open. "You okay?"

"I got knocked sideways a bit, but, yeah, I'm okay."

"I'm sending Dom and Bryan to help clean up. Take care of the body and they'll be there soon."

"Right, boss. I'm … I'm sorry." I'd never heard Sue cry and the sound of her hitching voice tore at my insides.

"Keep your 'sorrys' and stay alive," I ground out tonelessly. I turned to Alex. "You know what to do." He nodded and left, eyes shiny with unshed tears.

"Kal—" Ariel began.

"You know," I breathed, cutting her off and leaning back in my chair, my thoughts becoming sluggish as an old familiar feeling began to boil in my blood. "Jeff fought the Supernaturals like he was born to the job. He seemed to get off on it." Thicker and thicker, my throat started strangling my words. "When he first came here, he was possibly the most arrogant SOB I'd ever met. Acted like he knew everything about the World Under and how to deal with it. Pretty damn cocky for a two-year man."

Moisture bled from the corner of my eyes and I angrily wiped it away. "You know what a Myling is? No? It's a ghost of an unbaptized child, usually killed by violence. The child's soul is flung from its body at the moment of death as it cries out for its loved ones. It's flung so far that it becomes lost, which is not a big surprise 'cause it's just a kid. When someone happens to draw near to one, it latches on like a tick and demands to be taken to a cemetery, the only place it can go to rest in peace. The problem is, the nearer you get to the cemetery, the heavier the Myling becomes, until the victim can't move. Then the Myling transforms into a spirit of vengeance and kills the victim.

"I don't think that is what the Myling really wants to do, though. I think that the closer it gets to a cemetery, the weight of its pain and memories starts to manifest as a physical thing and the frustration of not being able to proceed to its rest drives it crazy.

"We had just taken out a Hob that had gone postal in Bettendorf, Iowa. In case you need a refresher, a Hob is a household spirit that helps around the house. A relative of the Brownie. We had stationed our team in an abandoned gas station and were waiting for the next set of supernatural events to occur. A week after we expelled the Hob, the body of a fifty-year-old mail carrier was found on Route 33, crushed to death. That night, we went to investigate, loaded for bear. I figured it could be a troll, in which case we had a fight on our hands.

"At the site of the carrier's death, Jeff got jumped immediately by what looked like a ghostly Pekingese, demanding, in a high pitched whisper, to be taken to a cemetery. We all laughed, fit to bust our sides because we knew what it was. Of all the ghosties out there, Mylings are the easiest for a team to deal with. So we bundled Jeff in the car, checked the navi system and made our way to the nearest cemetery."

A big breath. My throat hurt, but not from talking. The muscles at the corners of my jaw ached.

"For five miles Jeff pissed and moaned constantly. You'd have thought that it was my fault he had a spook on his back. By the time we were a few hundred yards away from the cemetery gates he was pressed heavily into the back seat. At fifty yards the back end of the car was starting to drag on the ground, spitting sparks, so we stopped and hauled him out. At this point the Myling, which was now the size of a St. Bernard, must have weighed about six hundred pounds. All this time Jeff cussed up a blue streak, and that little ghost held on like a limpet, urging him on, to go faster. Every few seconds it would say 'are we there yet?' " Laughter like a bubbling black cauldron of hate erupted from my mouth, spewing against Ariel's ears hard enough to make her wince. If I could have stopped, I would have, but an old familiar rage burning inside me forced itself out with each heave of my lungs.

While the fury mounted, I stared at the polished desktop and continued. "The whole team started carrying him so the Myling wouldn't transform into a malevolent spirit and when we reached the graveyard (by that time it felt like we were hauling a Greyhound bus), the thing went *poof* … gone."

A deep breath that hurt my lungs. "We laughed and teased him unmercifully, but he took it like an adult … like part of the team. He wasn't so cocky after that."

I brought eyes dead as Disco to stare at Ariel's soft brown ones. She wasn't a bad kid. She listened and followed orders pretty well, so she had a chance at living longer than the average Tsetse fly. For some reason tears coursed down her face but for the life of me I couldn't understand why.

My chest hurt. "Go," I rasped.

"Kal, I—"

"Go. Now." Was that my voice? It sounded so harsh, more like a growl. A red haze seemed to edge my vision.

Ariel got gone.

I stood, knuckles resting on the beautiful polished wood of my desk.

Tap. Flesh and wood coming together softly.

Damn it, Jeff, why?

Tap, tap. A little harder, my blood surging hotter.

Who did this to you?

Thock thock. Even harder.

My fault. I should have guessed something like this would happen.

Thud thud. Knuckles starting to hurt. I didn't care.

My Fault. I should have sent more agents.

Thump! Thump! A coppery smell, one I knew so well.

MY FAULT!

I didn't stop, even though my hands screamed and red drops sprayed across the room. It didn't hurt, not compared to the screaming of my heart. Wood shattered, and I didn't care, the only thing that mattered was the rage coursing through my soul. Another death, one more in a long line of men and women who tried so hard to stem the flood of horror caused by Supernaturals. Monsters like Iku Turso, who some think of as Cthulu. And that's where it all started, nearly twenty years ago on a small island off the coast of Finland.

My mind wandered away from that old, gangrenous wound, still sore and weeping its ichor into my life. Better to think on recent tragedies, better to think on the death of a man who had belonged to a brotherhood of which I was proud, so proud, to be a part of. God, my hands hurt so much but it didn't matter because I threw everything against the walls, oddly irritated that there was no glass in my office to shatter. I did my best to break everything I touched and my Mac did a good job of smashing through drywall.

A roar erupted from my throat, a berserker wail of pain and rage that everyone must have heard. But I didn't care, I just wanted to throw things and scream and scream and scream. This rage, this old friend, burned like acid in my veins, but it felt so good to let the beast out to eat its fill of violence. I could have controlled it, sent it back to the dark corners of my mind where it could be locked away safely, but a perverse part of me enjoyed the carnage I wreaked when it manifested.

Eventually I ran out of things to throw. My office wasn't that big so I just stood there panting, blood streaming from the burst skin of my knuckles, more scars to join others. Personal mementos of colleagues lost writ large on my skin.

The only sound left was my labored breathing and I wished I

could sit but my chair studded the wall in two pieces, my smart phone next to it like a period at the end of my self-indulgent tantrum. The only unbroken thing in the room was the toy Winnebago the Brownies lived in. But I had probably scared them so much they were halfway to Hoboken.

"Kal?" Alex tentatively inquired from beyond the door, sounding afraid. Why would he be afraid? He was one of the brotherhood.

I tried to make my voice work, but it felt broken, useless.

"Kal?" The door opened a fraction, partially blocked by shattered mahogany. A sharp nose poked in, followed by a geeky face. "Kal?"

Somehow I found the right gear for my throat and managed to clutch-start it. "Nevermore …" Damn, I sounded terrible. Like a saw blade against rotten wood.

A weak smile from our resident magician. "I brought Band-Aids—"

"Step aside, Alex." Pat barged in like a one-woman phalanx, gently shouldering the magician aside. In one muscular hand she carried a first aid kit. Kicking aside the remnants of my desk, she finally reached my side. "God, you screwed the pooch again," she remarked sternly.

I nodded dumbly.

"Alex, hon," Pat called over her shoulder as she took my hands in hers. "Clear an office. He'll need someplace to park his carcass soon. And call someone about this mess."

"On it, Pat," he blurted, practically running away. Through the door I caught of glimpse of Ariel as she discreetly peeked in. She looked horrified.

"Go away, honey." Pat's voice could have frozen the sun. "I got this." Ariel performed a credible disappearing act.

Hard hands began cleaning my knuckles with alcohol from the kit. Strangely enough, I didn't feel it. "You have to stop doing this, Kalevi." Her warm voice carried an ocean of concern.

I started. "Only my parents call me that."

"Stand still, you big oaf." A slather of antibacterial cream. "I'll call you what I damn well please. I swear, your hands are more scar than skin. Idiot."

What could I say, she was right.

"These fits of yours are getting worse, Kalevi. Usually you'd just punch a wall or two, maybe throw a chair. I've seen some pretty nasty stuff in Iraq, but this takes the taco."

"You were in the armed forces?"

"Marines."

"How come I didn't know that?" I usually know everything about everyone I work with. Gives me greater odds at keeping them alive.

"My file is sealed, dimwit. The only thing you have access to is what happened after I left the Corps." She started wrapping my hands in gauze.

For some reason that bothered me. "I should still know these things."

"God, you're an idiot. But we love you anyway."

Chapter Five

Ghoul of My Dreams

Coms. I'd left the lights off and a womb of silence and dark surrounded me, something to match my mood as I waited for the inevitable.

My thumbs caressed my piano tie as I slid the silk through my fingers. It had been found amidst the rubble of my office, hanging like a banner from a shard of desk. The penny-sized brown stain had been removed, and the fabric looked better than brand new. I'd told Alex to set milk out for the Brownies and some extra Oreos, Double Stuff. They deserved it. Hopefully they still resided in their toy Winnebago—now parked under the desk in my new office.

No thinking allowed. If I thought too much I would remember terrible things. Hard enough just staying alive in this job.

The wall in front of me flickered.

"In fine form again, Kal." BB's spectacled face appeared larger than life.

"Sorry, boss," I rasped, rubbing my chin with a gauzed hand.

"How are your knuckles?"

I held up both damaged paws. "More scars, but I'll be okay."

"Have Alex heal them."

"No. The scars will be a reminder of my screw-ups."

Exasperation edged his voice. "You can't keep doing this every time one of your team dies. It's what prompts the psych evals."

"I'm okay." What the good people of the Bureau never seemed to understand was that my rage—the dark, hot force of my violent passion—was often a comfort. They doubted my ability to control it, but I knew it existed for my use, that my will directed its ebb and flow.

"Really?" Amazing how that one word contained so much sarcasm. "First it was just punching holes in a wall, now it's destroying whole offices. You're getting worse."

"I can hack it," I rumbled with no conviction.

"One of these days you're going to go around the bend and not come back."

"I suppose." No use trying to deny it. BB would think I was shoveling something that smelled like what came between 1 and 3.

BB hunched forward like he was shouldering a massive burden. "Listen, Kal, maybe it's about time you quit fieldwork and come to work with me in D.C., okay?"

I shook my head. "You really see me fitting in with all the stuffed shirts in the capitol? Sooner or later I'd kill one." I fingered my Lahti. "Besides, I need to stay active."

The gesture wasn't lost on BB, who sighed heavily. "After you clear up Denver, you're on vacation. No ifs, ands, or buts." He sounded so much like Dad I nearly laughed. Then he hit me with the H-Bomb. "When you get back, it's time for another formal psych-eval."

"Oh, *hell* no!"

He leaned forward far enough so that his eyes filled the entire wall. "Your latest tantrum brought it on, Kal. I can't cover for you on this one, so it's got to be done. Check?"

I nodded to the screen.

"I'm sorry," he said sharply. "I didn't catch that. I said, 'check?'"

Trapped, I replied, "Check, boss."

He leaned back and smiled like the benevolent dictator he was. "Good. Now … how's the new Green Pea doing?"

"Surprisingly, not too incompetent."

"High praise from you."

I stretched my aching arms. "Yeah, well don't go doing any happy dances yet; she's still half an idiot. And that's the good half. However, she's got the rest of the DEA beat cold."

"Do you think she'll work out?"

It hurt to laugh, but I did and that's all the answer he got.

Disapproving eyes met mine. "Your disdain is noted."

Once again I held up my hands. "Hey, don't get me wrong, I don't have disdain for her … I nothing her. She's not even on my radar until she proves herself against a Supernatural. So don't take indifference for disdain."

"So how do I know when you are being disdainful?"

I raised an eyebrow toward my hairline.

"Got it," he commented dryly. "Imagine my enthusiasm … my best, most successful man looks like a Scandinavian linebacker, is scarred like a boxer and has the sarcastic bent of a political analyst."

"Wide receiver."

"What?"

"I was a wide receiver for the Huskers, not a linebacker. I may be big, but they're *really* big."

BB snorted once and shook his head. "Right. Clean up Denver, take a vacation, get your psych eval, in that order. Capiche?" Without waiting to see if I capiche-d or not, the wall blacked out.

Did I really have a choice?

Didn't think so.

Later, after I noshed on cream cheese and bagels, with some highly caffeinated diet soda, Ariel strode into my office treading as if the place was mined with Bouncing Bettys.

"Easy there, Tex," I drawled. "I'm not going to break anytime soon."

She produced a champion level look of disbelief.

"No, really. I'm done for the day. Besides, my hands are really starting to hurt."

"Well," she said. "I wasn't too sure. I heard this happens whenever one of your team dies."

I swear the office was filled with more loose lips than a political convention. "I have my moments, but for right now let's put it behind us. What we really need to do is figure out our next move."

Color heightened her cheeks. "About that ..."

Uh-oh. "You did something clever, didn't you? Should I be worried?"

"As a matter of fact, I contacted Detective Wilkes. We have an appointment with him."

"We do, do we?" I inquired, sounding a tad ruffled.

"Yes, we do." Lips pressed into a firm line, she continued, "I identified myself as Agent Finger of the ATF and told him we were having some trouble with Special Agent Briegan."

Interesting and interestinger. I stared hard at her.

She wilted only slightly. "Briegan is the kind of creep to cut Wilkes out of the loop entirely, even though he's still the lead on the Organ Donor case," she said defensively. "And I was right. When I told him of our deceased 'undercover agent' and Briegan's hostility, he was more than happy to offer up whatever he'd dug up on the case. As long as we buy him dinner."

"What's this 'we' crap, Kemosabe?"

She raised an eyebrow. Hmph ... I'm better at that trick. "Why should I pay?" she asked archly.

"You want to wear the grown-up pants and take some initiative, you pay the freight."

"Whatever." She tried not to sound pleased with herself, but I could tell.

I stood. "Good ... feeling a little hungry. Where are we going?"

"The Chop House."

My smile was predatory. "Good. I'm *real* hungry, Pea." I shrugged into my sport coat, only a little damaged from my earlier temper tantrum, and checked the Lahti. "You know what, Pea? That was a really good idea. Smart move, actually. I'm very impressed." She smiled, but it faded quickly as my face clouded up. "But if you do anything like that again without my authorization, you're fired."

The Chop House is located near LoDo, next to Coors Field,

home of the Rockies. All during the drive there Ariel regaled me with a record-breaking power sulk complete with outthrust lower lip and crossed arms.

That lower lip sure looked tasty.

Whoa … I jerked on my mental leash. Thinking like that can lead to Bad Things.

I parked the Vic in a handicapped spot (or is Physically Challenged? Disabled? I can't ever keep up with the latest PC crap) and waltzed in like I owned the place. It wasn't hard to spot Wilkes; he was the only guy there whose clothes and bearing screamed, 'Look at me! I'm a cop." Before the smiling twenty-something hostess could grab a menu, I brushed past her with a grin and strode up to the detective.

Even sitting down, he dominated the table, a big side of beef with shoulders that looked a yard across. His black hair had been cut in what I like to call Marine Formal, close to the bone on the sides and about a centimeter on top. It made my own short blond hair look like Shaggy's from Scooby Doo. He wasn't much in the looks department; his cheeks and nose had been used as a punching bag far too often to be called handsome. However, something about him was curiously familiar.

Ariel rushed past, holding out her hand. "Detective Lieutenant Wilkes? I'm Agent Finger." He rose from his chair and gripped her hand, obviously delighted to be greeted by such a succulent morsel.

"A pleasure, ma'am," he purred with a wide smile showing about four hundred teeth.

Up close, he was taller than my own six four by an inch or so and, despite the jokes about cops and donuts, didn't carry an ounce of flab. He looked as lean and mean as they come.

Ariel reluctantly released his hand, eyes a little starry. What did she see in him? It looked like she'd begin to slobber any second. Without taking her eyes from the hunk in front of her, she started to introduce the hunk behind. "This is Agent—"

"Kal Hakala!" he finished, dropping her hand and engulfing

mine in his big paw. It felt like gripping a bunch of bananas. "Haven't seen you fifteen years!"

"Huh?" Not my most brilliant comeback.

Never met anyone who knew you from before, Alex pattered in my ear. *This should be interesting, to say the least.*

"You don't remember me, do you?" Wilkes looked slightly disappointed, retrieving his banana fingers from my grasp.

"Fifteen years is a long time, Detective."

His grin was surprisingly boyish. "What were you doing fifteen years ago in October?"

"Easy, playing for Neb— Holy crap!" My mind wobbled a bit. "You're Big Buffalo, the guy who chased me around Folsum Field? Broke my arm in the fourth quarter? I missed the last three games of the season because of you!"

Laughing, he offered us both seats. "And you humiliated the Buffs with nine out of ten catches for over a hundred yards and three touchdowns." His eyes went to a place far away, the glory days when we were young and immortal. At least his did; I learned about mortality at the tender age of fifteen.

"Those were some good times, man." Switching to Ariel, "Back in the day, it was my job to cover him like a wet blanket, but he ran past me so fast it felt like I stood still." Her smile did little to cut through the testosterone infused air.

"So what happened to you after college?" I asked.

"Ahh … joined the army, became a Ranger and the rest is history. You?"

"Became a Fed right out of college."

We stopped for a moment to order from a perky brunette server with a killer body who didn't mind flirting with tall, blond, Scandinavian me. Ariel rolled her eyes and ordered the beef tips with mash while both of us He-Men settled for 19-ounce Delmonicos, mid rare with baked potatoes.

Ariel snorted. "It's like you guys are trying to prove machismo by what you eat."

I shook my head. "Nah, you're buying, remember? I wanted to order something nice and expensive." That earned me a glare from her and a muffled laugh from Wilkes.

He stared for a moment. "What did you do to your hands?" Gesturing toward my gauzed mitts.

"Cut myself shaving."

"Right. How silly of me not to have guessed." Shaking his head, Wilkes cocked an eyebrow at my Green Pea. "You said over the phone that Krouse was one of yours—an undercover man looking into arms smuggling, right?"

She nodded.

"And Briegan wouldn't cooperate with you?"

My turn to nod.

"So what makes you think I can help you?"

I gave Ariel the go ahead. "You're still lead on the Organ Donor case, even though Briegan's cut you out of the loop. But something tells me that you probably have an ace up your sleeve."

"More like a Jack. Of diamonds." Something about the way he said that unnerved me.

I pretended nonchalance. "What you do mean?"

"It means I've discovered robberies coinciding near or on the same days as the murders."

Now my ears pricked forward. "Really? What kind of robberies?"

"A jewelry store near where the second victim was dumped got hit for eighteen ounces of platinum and a nearly flawless emerald. Rings, Earrings, wire, the whole bit. Near the third victim, an aquamarine the size of my thumb was lifted and a fake put in its place. I went back and checked the store videos, but the recordings were blank for days."

"How the hell did he ... never mind. I'm on it, Kal." Alex was more than a little irritated that someone beat him to the punch. It matched my own irritation at not checking out the recordings.

"In-ter-est-ing." I drew the word out long and slow. "Whoever it was must have been casing the place for quite a while."

He wasn't fooled, some cop-ly sense was alerted by either my words or manner. His eyes narrowed. "This isn't news to you," he accused.

"*Uh-oh, Kal.*"

Next to me I felt Ariel tense. "What do you mean, Detective?" she asked mildly. She was no actress.

The glance he gave her, once filled with a good heaping of flirtiness, now contained only annoyance. "You know what I mean," he said, voice soft and low.

It was time for the truth. "You're right, Detective. During our initial investigation, one of our computer geeks tripped on the connection. We're still looking into it, but you helped connect the dots."

"No lie?"

"No lie."

Wilkes digested this for a moment, just long enough for our food to arrive so we began to digest that as well.

"So what now?" he asked after tucking in the last of his Delmonico, a tender bone-in rib eye named after the famous steakhouse in New York City.

I hid a belch. Damn, that was some good eats. "You tell us what you tried to show Briegan. The thing that he's ignoring for now."

"How do you know I have anything else of value to add to this investigation?"

"*Kal, I just confirmed the two other robberies. It looks like someone wants to make a lot of gem batteries. An aquamarine the size of your thumb—assuming almost no inclusions and the cut is perfect—could store nearly a teramerlin worth of energy, or you could Shape a Summoning spell to call up a class six demon.*"

Crap, a class six demon? One of the minor lords of the Pit. A Minor Lord could reduce Madison Square Garden to rubble. Thank god for the rarity of the magic gene, or we'd be swimming with magicians stealing gems left and right.

"Ghost just came back from checking the digital recordings on the other jewelers. Each one had a week's worth of recordings erased."

"Kal?"

Wilkes's voice brought me back. "Mmm ... what? Sorry, just thought of something."

"How do you know I have anything else to add to this investigation?"

Ariel jumped in. "Because you're a good cop, because you're not as closed-minded as Special Agent My-Crap-Don't-Stink Briegan. He only wants to stick to his profile, what he knows best."

Wilkes chewed on this for a few seconds. "Flattery will get you everywhere." He grinned with considerable wattage. It faded after a moment. "Okay, you win. Here's what I believe ... The Organ Donor is a woman."

I nearly fell out of my chair. Out of the corner of my eye, Ariel paled, open mouth ready to catch flies.

"Is this true?" I breathed. I wasn't talking to Wilkes.

"I don't know, Kal, I can only think of about five or six female serial killers in the entire twentieth century. Those that have been recorded, that is."

"You don't believe me?" No anger, only a kind of resignation in his voice.

"No, no, no ... I believe you," I assured him. "It's just..."

"Unexpected?"

"Quite."

"What sort of evidence?" Ariel inquired, eyes wide. "DNA? Fiber?"

He shook his head. "Nothing so CSI ... it was the first victim, the prostitute. She had bruising on the back of her neck. Examination showed it came from a fist, a small one. Too small for a man ... ergo, a woman."

Ariel shook her head. "How do you know she didn't get into a fight with another prostitute?"

"According to the ME, the bruising occurred shortly before her death."

"Accessing the autopsy report now." A few moments of silence. *"Damn, he's right, it's all there. We missed it."*

Why did our killer get physical with the first victim? If this Renfield was a magician, she could've just hit the victim with a minor spell, too small for our sensors to pick up, and render the prostitute unconscious. Unless ..."Detective, the first victim, what was she wearing when she died? Any jewelry? Gems?"

Wilkes scratched his head. "The other girls said she liked to wear a lot of metal. You know, necklaces, big earrings, etc."

"Silver, gold?"

"Good thinking!

"I guess, why?"

If the victim was wearing enough pure silver and/or gold, it certainly would interfere with a minor spell. Her own little Faraday jacket. When the spell didn't work, or only partially worked, the Renfield would probably have used brute force."

Shaking my head, I spared a glance toward Ariel who still looked a little dazed. "I dunno, something about this feels really weird." I'd love to tell Wilkes what I was thinking but he'd try to lock me up in the loony bin.

"Weird isn't the half of it. I tried to bring this to Briegan, but his holiness dismissed it. He can't see that a woman can be a killer."

"Then he's more stupid than I thought," Ariel rumbled, a dangerous glint in her eye.

Wilkes smiled.

The sun sets quickly on the Front Range, ducking behind the Rockies. It'd been a long time since I'd enjoyed a sunset, perhaps seven years previously on vacation in Las Vegas. Since then I'd never cared to look.

For some reason I found myself caring as I sipped an amaretto sour on my balcony and watched the light fade from the sky in shades of pink and gold. Maybe it was this state, maybe it was this case, but for whatever reason, I was enjoying the end of the day.

I had driven the Vic back to the office, dropping Ariel off at her rented Hyundai and made my way back to the apartment, belly pleasantly full from dinner. Wilkes turned out to be good company and our mutual distaste for Briegan fueled a budding friendship. One I couldn't really indulge. My job didn't lend itself to long-term relationships of any sort. Not even among co-workers. When the job in Denver was done, one more member of my team would retire, her contract over. I'd miss Sue—a good, tough agent and capable killer. But that's business as usual for the Bureau … always a new face.

When full dark fell, I re-entered my apartment, strangely discontent. Seeing Wilkes, reminiscing over glory days, reminded me there was more to this life than vengeance. But not for me.

I closed my eyes as a vision of Iku-Turso, the Thousand-Horned one, the Father of Diseases, swam in my mind's eye and a very familiar rage threatened my momentary peace. Another sip of amaretto sour helped me quell the feeling.

There came a tap-tap-tapping on my apartment door, breaking the spell.

Might as well. "Nevermore," I called.

The door burst open in a shower of splinters.

Leaping through, hideously long arms tipped with black razor nails, the ghoul grinned horribly at me through a mouthful of needle teeth. "I hate that poem," it said.

Chapter Six

Dead Man Walking

My Lahti lay on the dining room table, six feet away. It might as well have been six hundred feet; there was no way in hell I could grab it in time before the thing was on me. Instead, I reached behind my back under my sport coat for the handle of my Bowie.

Green skin, pebbly like a toad's, covered the creature, giving it a warty, scabby appearance. Translucent slime dripped from it, even from the needle-filled mouth, glistening in the harsh light of the hallway. Black on black eyes, as pitiless as a shark's, stared at me from under a shelf of bone thick enough to stop a bullet. Pale, knobby, bony plates circled its neck. Naked, it had all the anatomical accuracy of a Ken doll and the lethality of a Bengal tiger. Main difference was, a Bengal tiger can't talk while it eats you.

My hand found the handle of the Bowie.

It tensed, and I noticed a small ruby in its forehead, glowing softly.

Muscles flexing, I began to draw.

Its hands flexed, revealing a glowing ruby in each palm.

My testicles tried to draw up into my body. The Bowie cleared the sheath.

It jumped.

God, I'd never seen anything move so fast. Before I could bring the knife out from the sheath strapped to my back, I fell backward, praying I wouldn't impale myself.

Nails sharper than scalpels found my chest as it sailed over, shredding jacket and shirt as if they weren't there. So quick I didn't feel any pain, just a sort of dull heat that let me know I was hurt.

Crash, right through the sliding glass door to the balcony and over the rail out of sight. I had seconds, maybe less, to save my life.

I hit the floor. No pain, but plenty of adrenalin. My free hand grabbed at the phone on my belt and my thumb found the right button on reflex. "Dial Alex," I grunted and I sprung to my feet in time to see a warty hand rise and grasp the painted iron rail of my balcony. I couldn't help but feel impressed … my apartment was on the fifth floor. The smart phone hit the carpet as I began to move, a harsh buzz of anger threading through me.

One stride. Two.

Long needle teeth, hundreds of them, cleared the rail.

Lahti met my palm, a comforting cold weight. I prayed Alex would pick up.

Heavily muscled arms propelled the green body over the rail. It was on the balcony.

I brought the Lahti up.

Bang! Slightly wide, but the thing flinched.

Bang! A flower bloomed on its stomach and black blood oozed out like Karo syrup. It ignored the wound.

Bang! Another flower on its chest. I pulled the trigger as fast as I could and it came at me, not even noticing the glass tearing its feet.

Bang! Black blood erupted from its shoulder, but it kept coming, almost within range to use its claws and I knew that one good swipe and my head would say goodbye to my shoulders in quick order.

Bang! From three feet away I hit the ruby on its forehead and for the first time I get a reaction.

It screamed. If you've ever heard a traffic accident, the sound of brakes squealing, the brutal *thump* of collision followed by the screech of tortured metal, how it stabs into your ears like an ice pick … that's what it's like to hear a ghoul scream, only a hundred times worse.

One hand went to its head, the other slapped down on the table for support and, without even thinking, I slammed the Bowie down, down through flesh and bone, down through something harder than both and through the wood beneath. A scarlet flare erupted from where its palm met the table.

Once again my ears were assaulted by that hideous traffic accident scream and I was afraid that they would start to gush blood. The Bowie was a good weapon, but pounding it through three inches of ghoul and wood had rendered it useless, so I went for a backup.

My younger self would have been proud had he seen me vault the couch, landing square in front of the flat-screen. One sharp slap from my palm on the wall beneath and the hidden compartment I'd created over a month ago popped open. What smacked into my palm didn't look like a weapon anyone would recognize. Except a Bureau member. An amethyst the size of my thumbnail, winking purple in the artificial light of my apartment.

An amethyst is simply a variety of violet quartz, not very valuable, kind of pretty, but to a magician it's a valuable tool. Although it is not pure enough to hold complex spell Shapes (due to iron ions), it holds one simple Shape very well. Something we liked to call a Boom spell. Having a spell gem in my possession without logging it out of the Armory was against Bureau regs, but I wielded a certain amount of influence and sometimes did things that, if BB ever found out, would put me eyeball deep into a latrine.

When I'd told the Green Pea that gems could be used as magical batteries, I hadn't told her everything. They're able to store spells, but those spells can be used by anyone, as long as certain conditions are met. A magician could Shape a spell that had the equivalent of an 'if/then' statement, like a line of computer code. All that was needed for the spell to be cast was the conditions set forth by the 'if/then' statement to be fulfilled. The amethyst I found in my hand had a LOT of stored energy and the spell was as simple as could be. All I needed to do was fulfill the 'if/then' part of the spell.

If I said a certain word (called an 'activation' or 'trigger' word, chosen by the magician who Shaped the spell), then the amethyst would release all its energy in one burst after a one second delay.

Simple. It was also a good idea that the trigger word be something very uncommon, lest you cast the spell accidentally.

With a tearing sound, the ghoul ripped the Bowie out of the table, leaving a gout of black ichor behind to stain the lacquered wood. "I was going to kill you quick, Hakala," it burbled, its voice the bubbling of tar in a deep pit. Black soulless shark eyes stared out from under the inch deep hole where the ruby had been. It lurched toward me. "But now I'm going to kill you slow."

How it knew my name, I could only guess, but right then my stomach was trying to hide behind my liver and I nearly peed in fear. For some reason it had slowed down—maybe the hole in its forehead had something to do with that—but all I could do right then was pray to god that I didn't miss.

Bang! Another shot with no effect. I dropped the Lahti and cocked back my left arm. If I screwed this up, the ghoul wouldn't have to kill me; I'd be dead already.

My arm came forward, the amethyst missile leaving my palm. "*Eggloss,*" I screamed.

Straight and true at the ghoul's head flew the stone. It lifted its mangled hand and casually tried to slap the purple quartz away. Its torn palm smacked against the spinning gem.

Crack!

I felt myself lifted, weightless for one brief second, as a blinding blue-white flash stole my sight. Fortunately, I didn't travel far, just a couple of feet into the flat-screen behind me. Something went *crunch* at the back of my head and there was a sharp, piercing pain.

Then nothing.

Blood. It was in my mouth and I reflexively swallowed, the coppery liquid sliding easily down my throat. Another swallow. My tongue and teeth hurt and everything was quiet, eerily so. It took a couple of years, but I got my hands underneath me and pushed up off the floor. Bits of glass fell out of my hair and landed silently onto the floor.

My legs gave out, something was wrong with my balance, and I fell back to the floor. Two, three tries later and I was able to stand as long as I had the wall to my back. Black and gray spots swam before my eyes and I felt the Delmonico I'd eaten earlier trying to make a comeback.

I blinked once, twice, and saw a mouthful of needle teeth lunge toward me.

Savage pain in my left shoulder and something *tore*, sending a lance of sharp agony up my neck to the base of my skull.

All the strength left me and my legs sagged. I knew I was about to die as a goddamn ghoul ate its way through my shoulder. Before everything went black for the final time, I sent an apology to my sister Leena for my failure.

I fell, the ghoul on top of me, and I got a great look at a warty, green and slimy scalp before the head exploded in a shower of black and pink.

"Kal!" The voice came from far away, a dim sound ringing with panic. All I wanted to do was stay dead. It's quiet and peaceful when you're dead.

"Kal, can you hear me?" Of course I could hear, I wasn't deaf. Why couldn't that damn voice leave me alone?

"Kal, it's Alex, I need you awake! Kal! Kal!" The screaming was really annoying. I cracked an eye to tell Alex to shut the hell up.

"He's awake!" That geeky face swam into focus, looking relieved despite the pale complexion and the sweat dripping from his nose.

"?" I inquired.

Alex's face got bigger as he leaned closer. "Listen, Kal, you're hurt ... real bad, but I can't help you without your participation." Hands gripped my head above the ears. "Look at my eyes, help me help you." I wanted to laugh at his *Jerry Maguire* quote. He was about as far from Tom Cruise as you could get. "Blink twice if you understand me."

Hah … blink twice? With those boulders on my eyelids? Was he crazy? But the panic in his voice pulled at me, so it must have been pretty serious. Slowly I brought my eyelids down. Then again. God, that took a lot of effort!

He smiled in relief. "Good, Kal, here we go."

Warmth flooded my skull, pleasant, comforting. Nice … then a voice broke the peace.

Kal, you there?

Of course I am, you nitwit.

Good! You're hurt real bad and I need you to help me heal you. I can't do this alone. I don't have any charged gems or the energy reserves, but I can tap into yours if you let me.

Sure thing, Alex. Anything you want, old buddy. But what the hell is wrong with me?

Swimming up from the depths of our link came a bird's eye view of my half naked body. Somebody had taken off my jacket and shirt. Damn … I looked like hell! Four thin cuts to my chest that sluggishly leaked blood and there was a big red and white mess where my left shoulder used to be.

See? Bad news. Now Kal, this is going to hurt like you won't believe.

I could believe it. I'd been healed before and the rapid tissue regeneration always got the nerves singing like a Mariachi band. Looking at the damage—gray-white bone and torn flesh—this would be bad. Maybe it was better to be dead.

Ready, Kal?

Go ahead, Alex.

I won't bore you with the details. I screamed, I cried, I gibbered like a Rhesus monkey in a cosmetics testing lab as the flesh on my chest knit at warp speed and the bones in my shoulder shifted and popped, regenerating tissue uniting into something pink and whole. Muscle re-attached to bone, ligaments spooled back into reality … All this happened in a matter of minutes that felt like hours. Misery fired along every nerve in my body and sang into my brain. A small piece of flat-screen worked its way out of the back of my skull and the hole it left behind closed with a small dribble of blood and a feeling that someone had stuck an ice pick into the bone and swirled it around.

Not fun.

"Want another sandwich?" Wilkes asked, drinking one of my precious Tommyknocker cream sodas. I nodded and took the proffered roast beef and cheddar on wheat. One bite later and I closed my eyes in bliss … just the right amount of mayo. Yummy.

Wilkes made a face. "How can you Scandahoovians stand to eat that white crap?"

"What? Mayo? It's the miracle condiment, made by the gods themselves." I took another bite. Double yummy.

When I came to after the healing, it wasn't the sight of Alex that had greeted my weary, bloodshot eyes but Wilkes, big and ugly himself looking all wild and disheveled. Behind him Ariel stood with arms crossed, looking distinctly uneasy.

"What the—" I'd mumbled.

"You okay, Kal?" Alex's face came into view, pale and sweating. A shaky hand slicked back hair that had fallen in front of his eyes.

I patted my chest and shoulder. Faint ridges met my fingertips, four long, thin, scars running from collarbone to sternum. The memory of the ghoul's claws raking my chest came rushing back and I thanked my lucky stars the wound hadn't been deeper. My right hand touched left shoulder and felt a knot of gnarled tissue the size of my fist. I moved the shoulder experimentally. No pain. A little stiff, but whole. "The ghoul?" I croaked.

"Is that what that this was?" Wilkes asked wildly. "Is that what it was?" He paced back and forth, running his fingers through his flat top.

Ariel snorted. "Calm down, Detective."

"Calm down? Calm dawn?' His eyes were wide. "Did you see that freakin' thing?"

"I saw it."

"What happened?" My throat was dry. To Alex, "Water, please."

"Sure."

"And Alex ... thanks, man."

The smile that hit his face nearly cut it in half and he scampered off to fetch some water.

Wilkes leaned over. "Kal, what the hell is going on here?" He looked like he was about to cry. You would too if everything you believed about your safe little world got tossed into the trash bin.

It was a struggle to sit up, but I managed by leaning against the wall next to my busted flatscreen. "Green Pea, report. What happened?" Lord, my voice sounded like the crackle of tin foil. I held up a hand to shut Wilkes up.

Ariel stepped forward, arms still crossed. "I was nearby when I got the call. When I drove up, I heard what sounded like an explosion. I entered the building, Wilkes charging a few seconds behind. When I got to your doorway, that *thing* was on you, chewing on your shoulder. Detective Wilkes came up from behind me and blew its head apart with a gun as big as a house."

She took a deep breath and rubbed her full lips. "We rushed the room and pulled that slimy bastard off your body. You were cold and unresponsive. Alex came in a minute later and took over. Looking at the ghoul, I saw a ruby in its palm and cut it out for the magician to study." She spat on the floor. I'd read books where people did that, but this was the first time I'd seen it done.

"And then?"

"And then Alex fixed you up. Took about ten minutes. When he was done, I gave him the ruby." she hooked a finger at Wilkes. "He's been freaking out about this ever since he killed that monster."

I managed a small smile. "Detective, what kind of weapon did you use?"

He pulled his jacket aside and revealed a huge chrome-plated pistol. "Desert Eagle," he confirmed, eyes slightly glassy. I guess he was in information overload. Not that anyone could blame him.

I croaked, "Green Pea, take the good Detective to my office and read him into the Bureau."

"You think that's wise?" Her tone told me she thought I was an idiot.

My best glare shut her up and she reluctantly led him away.

"Here you go, Kal," Alex said, handing over a glass of water that tasted so good I closed my eyes in ecstasy.

When it was empty, I set it down and turned back to the magician. "Tell me."

"I got your call."

Good. "Go on."

"I heard the shots, the caller ID told me it was you, so I had Ghost put out an alert. I only came into the picture after the fight was over," Alex reported, speaking as if he were reading from a grocery list. "When I arrived, I did what I could to heal you, but you did the hard part by lending me the energy to get the job done. Oh, and speaking of magic, I've already placed an Interdiction on the Detective without him knowing, so he won't be talking."

"How did the Green Pea take it when she found out you're a magician?" If only I could've been awake for *that!*

For the first time since I woke, Alex smiled. "I thought she'd have an aneurysm."

My weak laughter quickly turned to coughing.

"Easy there, Kal. You need rest and food." As soon as he said it, I felt the gaping emptiness inside and I wondered where the Delmonico I'd eaten earlier had gone. "After the healing was done, I raided your fridge and waited for you to wake." He looked at the damage to the apartment. The explosion, while localized to six square feet, had pretty much trashed the place. "You're lucky. The explosion from the gem ripped the ghoul's arm off. It was injured pretty badly by the time the Detective showed up. Sue and Dom were next on the scene and took care of the body."

I looked toward where the front door used to be. Someone had tacked up a blanket. "What about the neighbors?" Agent Farris told them it was a party gone wild, followed by a minor gas explosion. A weak story, but they bought it. Detective Wilkes was kind enough to shoo away the local law enforcement when they showed up. Would have been somewhat dicey if they'd seen the ghoul."

Mention of the ghoul brought something to the surface of my mind. "Alex, that thing had three rubies embedded in it—one in each palm and one in the forehead—and it was stronger and faster than any other I've faced. It was as if it had been … energized or juiced by steroids. The ruby that agent McMillan gave you, can you get a read on the spell?"

"I tried, but the Shape was already gone, the spell cast," he said sadly, shaking his head. "As for being juiced, I don't know, I've never heard of anything like that. It might be possible. You said it was stronger?"

"Yeah, and faster."

"Then whoever raised it is a lot smarter, and more capable, than we realized."

"Oh, crap!" I yelled, trying hard to get to my feet. My legs wobbled and Alex had to hold me, but I made it upright. "We have to warn the others. There are two more ghouls out there that can be used against us. If they're juiced, we're in trouble." Bureau agents had never been singled out for assassination before, but it looked like that had changed.

"Already taken care of, boss. By now they're all back at the office safe and sound behind steel and concrete until this is over. BB is pulling strings so this never gets any press or mention anywhere and by this time tomorrow, contractors will be done fixing up this place."

SOP for the boss. You'd be surprised how much things get covered up in the name of Public Safety. "Good, good. Thanks

Alex." I pointed to the kitchen. "I need to go there. I'm *starving!*"

Eventually, after three bowls of Lucky Charms, Ariel finished with Wilkes and I sent her on her way back to the Bureau where she could join the others in relative safety. Before she left, she surprised me by giving me a gentle hug.

"Boy," she whispered. "You guys sure know how to party." Then she was gone before I could cudgel up a smartass remark.

Another bite of the roast beef. I chewed slowly, savoring the flavor for a change instead of gulping. Wilkes finished the cream soda and opened another.

"I hope you left me one," I grumbled.

"Nope." He punctuated the negative with a belch.

I cocked an eyebrow. "You pissed?"

He shook his head.

"Then what?"

"I dunno. It's my first ghoul."

"Yeah."

"A ghoul. Really? An undead that likes to eat people and corpses?"

"Sorta," I said, taking another big bite. My belly was starting to press on my belt. "They like live meat … people. They're Type Two demons who possess and animate a corpse."

It was his turn to cock an eyebrow. "Type Two demons, really?"

"Really really. They're malevolent spirits, forces of evil from the Pit. Most undead are really evil spirits inhabiting and reanimating corpses. Like zombies … the dead possessed by the spirits of mass murderers. They're not much physically, but if they get near you … watch out. There are worse things out there, too. Things that would give the creators of D&D the screaming willies. The World Under isn't a safe place."

"Why do you call it the World Under?"

"Because The World Next sounds stupid." The roast beef sat

comfortably in my stomach next to the sugary goodness of the Lucky Charms and I felt almost human again. Better, much better, but tired to the bone.

A long pause. "So, what kind of things?" he asked.

I stared out at nothing. "Every story, every fable, has some basis in truth, a starting point where legend is born. Monsters and beings from every mythology interact with this world. Most are malevolent, but there are a few that have learned how to co-exist peacefully. The Bureau leaves them alone as long as they toe the line. However, the common citizens are so egocentric that if they were attacked by a werewolf, they'd refuse to believe it."

"That's pretty cynical."

"It's true. People want to believe, but at the same time they don't, because if the things that go bump in the night ever became real for them, they'd go crazy trying to adjust. That's where the Bureau comes in."

Wilkes took a good pull of his cream soda. "Is the Bureau in every nation?"

"Most of them, but not by that name. In the U.K. it's called MI-7, and in Germany it's called something with a lot of hard consonants and glottal stops."

"Heh."

Bite bite chew. Next came the questions that had been eating at me. "Why did you come to my apartment? And how did you find me?"

He snorted. "Easy peasy, Kal. When you and that pretty little bit of an agent were in the parking lot outside of the Chop House, I made a call to Briegan to fill him in, maybe change his mind on the robbery angle of the Organ Donor case. Told him a big blond named Hakala and a pretty African-American named Finger were collaborating."

Crap, I should have known he was the kind of cop to keep helping even if his help wasn't wanted.

He continued, "Imagine my surprise when Briegan said, 'he

sounds like that ATF dickwad named D.P. Roberts who visited earlier.' "

He fetched a root beer this time, a plain old A&W instead of Tommyknockers. "Struck me as mighty odd, so I followed you."

"Harrumph. I didn't notice," I said, darkly angry that I'd never spotted the tail.

"Not my first rodeo, Kal. Got all the way to your apartment, then went down the street for a Coke, came back and heard the shots … you know the rest." He took another pull of root beer. "What does the D.P. stand for?"

"What?"

"The alias you gave Briegan, D.P. Roberts. What does the D.P. stand for?"

I tossed him a lopsided grin. "Dread Pirate."

"'No one is afraid of the Dread Pirate Wesley,'" he quoted, stifling a smile and making a sweeping gesture with one arm. "What the hell did that to your living room?"

"A gem."

"A gem? What kind of gem does this kinda localized damage? Looks like somebody set off a small shaped charge in here."

I examined the blast. The ghoul had been right next to the couch when the explosion had gone off, and a good chunk of leather and foam had been ripped away. From my vantage point, there was a three-foot circle of utter destruction. If I'd been holding the gem, it would've torn my arm off as well as pulped my internals. "A good sized amethyst with way too much magical energy stored inside of it." I examined bits of ghoul stuck in the wall and made a note to have Alex put a much smaller charge in the next gem I'd give him.

Wilkes made a face, clearly uncomfortable with the thought that there were more things in heaven and earth than dreamt of in his philosophy. I knew how he felt, having been in his shoes once upon a time.

"Kal?" The buzz cut through the air like a hacksaw.

Jumping to his feet and drawing that damn howitzer so fast I could barely see it, the Detective looked around for the source of that strange buzzing voice.

"Easy, Tex," I said slowly, laying a hand on his arm and forcing his weapon down. "Put that away before you shoot me in the ass."

He blinked. "What was that?" The pistol was holstered in one smooth motion. Meanwhile, I walked over to where I'd dropped my smart phone.

There on the floor, only partially covered in ghoul goo, lay the cell, a blinking picture of the Casper-like cartoon from *Ghostbusters* on the screen.

"Hiya, Ghost," I said, picking up the cell gingerly and wiping it on what I assumed was a piece of curtain. The mess was slimy, sticky, and smelled like rotten eggs and wet ass.

"Hello, Kal. Good to see that you are all right."

"Thanks tons." I held the cell up. "Ghost, say hello to Detective Lieutenant Wilkes."

Wilkes looked ready to bolt, all wide-eyed and sweaty. "Uh, hi."

"Good evening, Detective." Was that amusement I heard? Couldn't be.

"Jesus, Kal," he breathed. "A cell phone demon?"

A high-pitched squeal cut through the air and the cell vibrated so hard it almost leapt out of my hand. "Ghost! Ghost! Chill out," I yelled over the caterwauling cell. "He has no clue! He's new to this." Eventually I wrestled the cell into submission and the cacophony stopped.

Wilkes had the good grace to look abashed. "Uh, sorry, dude," he muttered.

"Ghost, he thought you might be a demon because of the ghoul."

The buzzing voice emerged with a tone of only mild annoyance. "Tell him I am no demon, I am a benign non-corporeal entity inhabiting the electron superhighway."

Wilkes looked puzzled. "What?"

"A ghost," I affirmed. "He haunts cyberspace and helps the Bureau out with data acquisitions."

"You got a spook helping you steal information? Really?"

"Crudely put," buzzed Ghost. "But accurate."

Wilkes stared at his A&W. "Got anything stronger?" Sweat beaded on his forehead.

"Cabinet above the fridge."

"You want one?" he asked over his shoulder.

"On duty, so no."

"It's eleven at night. How can you be on duty?"

I stared at the ruins of my apartment. "As long as there are things like this out there, I'm on duty."

Without a word he rejoined me at the table *sans* alcohol. At my questioning look he took another drink of his root beer and belched. "If you're on duty, so am I."

"How do you figure?"

"Way I see it, you came here and muddied around in my investigation. You need to find this Organ Donor gal and you aren't doing it without me."

He had a point and I reckoned that there was very little I could do, short of drugging and kidnapping him, to keep him out of my hair. I was more than a little bit tempted to disappear him for a while, but he'd proved himself to be smart and capable, not to mention the guy who helped save my life, so in my book he qualified as One Of The Good Guys.

"Okay." I stuck my hand out and he shook it. "You're in for a while." He gave it a little squeeze, which I returned with interest. Which led to him squeezing even harder, making me squeeze harder and so on.

"Got a good grip," he gasped through clenched teeth.

I prayed that my fingers wouldn't burst like sausages in a microwave. "You ... too."

As if by some unspoken agreement, we both let go at the same time. "Okay, Scandahoovian, riddle me this: How did you get into this chickensquat outfit?" He was shaking out his hand.

"Long story." I winced, trying to rub some feeling back into my fingers.

The cell buzzed and hummed. "Kal joined the Bureau so he could get revenge for the death of his sister."

"Ghost!" I yelled as my hands itched to smash the phone, anger flaring.

"Kal," the specter said reprovingly. "If Detective Lieutenant Wilkes is going to be working with us until the current situation is resolved, then he should know what everyone in the Bureau knows. Besides, he did save your life."

Rage reddened my vision but I clamped a lid on it and gave the matter some serious thought. My sister stood at the heart of a story that had troubled my life for the past twenty years and fed my nightmares on the darkest and most lonely nights. Iku-Turso ... the monster of my dreams, the eater of my soul.

"No one knows the whole story ..."

Ghost buzzed again. "Wrong, Kal. Most of the story is in the common files in Records, but the full file, the one BB has, is quite complete, down to the last detail."

I should have known. The Bureau was as close to all-powerful as could be in the United States. In some other countries, it was exactly that ... Russia for example. "You read BB's file on me," I accused the cell.

"Of course. I have read the files on everyone in the Bureau. I have just finished sifting through the various databases for information on Detective Wilkes, as well."

"The hell you say!" he exploded, glaring at the phone, his big ham hands clenched so tightly the knuckles were paper white.

"It is true," Ghost said smugly—or as smug as an electronic buzz could sound. "Percy Girard Wilkes, born 1975 in Boulder, Colorado, the only child of Jeremy and Shannon Wilkes. Both parents dead, the mother by ovarian cancer, and the father during a bank robbery in Colorado Springs. No attachments, no lovers, just a series of one-night stands and an impressive movie collection dominated by Humphrey Bogart, John Wayne, and Peter O'Toole. Favorite books: anything by John Sanford. Favorite ice cream: Ben & Jerry's Phish Food. Favorite music …."

"Enough," Wilkes said, sounding more tired than I felt. "I get it. You are the information genie."

I couldn't contain myself. "Percy Girard? Really? You gotta be kidding me."

"Yeah, yeah, laugh it up, *Kalevi.*"

"Hey, Kalevi is a perfectly normal and common Finnish name."

"Guess which country you're in now, *Kalevi.*"

Leaning back, I looked him square in the eye. "Hey, I know it's unusual in the U.S., but Percy Girard is unusual *everywhere.*" For the first time in I don't know how long I gave vent to an honest-to-goodness belly laugh, my anger at Ghost evaporating.

A minute or two later the humor finally worked its way through my system. I had to give him credit—he let me have my moment and waited patiently for what he wanted, what he felt he needed to hear.

Heart in my throat, I whispered, "I've never told this story to anyone, so you'll have to forgive me if I make a hash of it."

In my hand the cell vibrated. "Alex tells me that talking about something painful can help."

"Not always, Ghost. Not always."

Chapter Seven

Twenty Years Earlier
Iku-Turso

June 13, 1990 was the day the official dismantling of the Berlin Wall by the East German military began in Bernauer Straße. Along with the slow dissolution of the U.S.S.R., it was a defining moment in the history of Western civilization and I was spending it vacationing with my family in Finland.

The Renault sedan chugged steadily northwest along the highway from Helskinki, my Dad's big hands steady on the wheel and my mom in the passenger seat. My sister Leena dozed next to me, her serene ten-year-old face slack with sleep. Her ability to conk out in the car always made me a little envious, but not that day. It was too perfect. The light through the window ran fire through her fair hair and lit her skin with shards of gold. To me, she always smelled of summertime.

It was 72 degrees outside and partly cloudy, hardly a whisper of wind to rustle the needles on the fir trees that dotted the landscape. The clouds would slowly scud across the sky and every half hour or so dump ten minutes of rain that left a smell, a freshness that only comes when you're in the countryside far away from crowded humanity.

"How much farther, Dad?" I asked softly, careful not to wake Leena.

"We're coming up on Turku, so almost halfway, son," he replied quietly. In fact, everything he did, he did quietly. A trait common to most Fins, at least the sober ones.

I couldn't wait to get to Rauma because from there we would take a boat to the family island in the Gulf of Bothnia. Ten days of fishing, smoking what we caught and lazing about. The thought of eating some freshly smoked pike made my mouth water and my stomach rumble.

I put the headphones of my Walkman over my ears and popped in Sammy Hagar's *VOA*, cranking the volume. While Sammy shrieked about not wanting to drive 55, we putzed down the road at about that very speed. Dad was careful about keeping to the limit. Tickets in Finland were based on percentage of income, and if you were bucks up, you could see some serious coin flying away into the government's till.

Turku came and went and, as always, I was amazed how *clean* the city was. Even Helsinki sparkled compared to cities in the States. Clean as a whistle, almost antiseptic.

Some thirty kilometers outside of Turku a Saab pulled alongside and I got a peek at the woman driving. A thrill of adrenaline shot right through me as my eyes drank her in. Pale pale hair, white-blonde and bound in a long braid. Black sunglasses, the kind the Blues Brothers wore, wrapped around a face that was chiseled from the palest alabaster, cold and beautiful at the same time, an Ice Queen. As the Saab passed, she looked my way and threw me the tiniest of smiles, barely acknowledging my presence, but it sent a heat through me fiercer than staring at Megan Freeman's rack during P.E. For a half hour after she'd disappeared into the vanishing point I was still harder than Chinese math.

Fifteen minutes later, while Sammy let me know about the two sides of love, a green Mercedes pulled alongside and the customer who drove that sweet ride had the complete opposite effect on me from the Ice Queen. He also had chiseled features, but while hers were delicate, his were craggy—all planes and hard angles with a thin nose like a hatchet and shaggy black brows that met in the middle.

Then he looked at me and I felt a sudden stab of fear.

"Don't worry, Kalevi," Mom said, quiet and confident. "He's no danger to us."

I nodded, relieved. For as long as I could remember, my Mom had her feelings and her ability to suss a situation at a glance, talents that bordered on the uncanny. Dad called it her 'luck' or 'the sight.' Was it magic? Maybe, but I'd never seen her do anything besides have those feelings.

"Thanks, Mom," I said, relieved, popping out Sammy and replacing him with Golden Earring. Soon they were singing about how the bullet hit the bone.

Eventually we made it to Rauma, a medium-sized town that clung to life, thanks to the paper mill on its outskirts. Dad then pointed the Renault west and headed straight for the sea. A few short minutes later we parked the car in a small lot less than fifty feet from the gray/blue water.

Nudging my sister awake, I exited the vehicle and joined my parents in unloading. It still struck me as odd that I could finally see eye to eye with Dad. Football had started filling me out with some hard muscle, but my strength was a far cry from a grown-up's. Dad may have left the Green Berets the year before to get a job as an electrical engineer, but he still worked out and carried with him the air of ferocious power and competence that told you he could rip most people in half with his bare hands. At thirty-four, his blunt, round, peasant's face was still youthful and carefree.

Mom, on the other hand, couldn't be more the opposite of Dad if she tried. A little itty bitty waif-like Finn with long, frizzy, black hair, she looked like she'd blow away if you sneezed in her general direction. I had no idea how someone so petite—five feet if she stretched tippy-toe—could give birth to a big lout like myself. But that Oompa-Loompa-sized lady had a core of iron in her that shocked some and terrified the rest.

Loaded up with suitcases, Dad and I staggered toward the water to an ugly little fishing boat beached just above the high-tide mark. A short, black-haired man fiddled with the outboard. I immediately recognized him from the pictures in our family album as my father's cousin, Juha.

Our footsteps must have alerted him. "Pekka!" he shouted, running up and giving Dad a hug that caused him to '*oof* in surprise. Letting go, he stepped back. "You look good! I guess the American Marines have fed you well."

Dad's face was nearly cut in half at the sight of a man he hadn't seen in over fifteen years. "You look good, too," came the reply. He poked a finger in Juha's little potbelly. "Looks like you also get fed well."

Juha rubbed his belly. "Property of the Finnish government." He turned to me. "My goodness, who is this? Is this Kalevi?" Next thing I knew I was engulfed in a bear hug. His head barely came to my clavicle, but his arms had some hard strength. "You look so big," he muttered into my chest in broken English. "So big, a strong boy!" He stepped back, tears at the corners of his eyes.

I mustered up the rough Finnish I'd been practicing. "Good to be seeing you, Juha."

"Ha! Good boy!" he exclaimed, happy not to strain his limited English. "Big shoulders, too. You're papa tells me you play American football. I saw some on television. I don't understand why they wear pads; it looks like they might get in the way. Now rugby, there's a game you should play. It will grow hair on your chest!"

"Rugby no popular being in America," I replied in sloppy Finnish.

"All the more reason you should move to Finland." Before I could think of a snappy comeback, he turned his attention to Mom and Sis. "Terhi, my goodness you're still pretty as a picture." He kissed her cheeks. "And Leena, you're going to outshine the sun, I can tell." My sister had the good grace to blush at his heartfelt praise. To tell the truth, she was the prettiest one in the family.

The boat ride took a good while because the island was several miles out to sea, and during the trip the adults chatted away about old times. Sis and I contented ourselves by running our fingers through the cool water of the placid sea. It was our first trip to Finland and we were content just to drink in the experience. I was born in Minnesota shortly after Mom and Dad got their citizenship papers. A couple years later Dad joined the Marines after earning his degree and Mom gave birth to Leena shortly after.

"Look there, kids," Dad said, pointing at a dark blob on the horizon. "There it is."

We strained and squinted. "I see it," Leena shouted. "It's big!"

Dad smiled at her. "Sure is, sweetie. Your grandfather lived there after WWII. He built the cabin we'll be staying at and he added to it over the years."

Soon the island came into view. Two acres of rocky land, covered in pine, smack dab in the middle of miles and miles of miles and miles. Juha steered the boat to a crude dock made of rock and cement that jutted out thirty feet into the water. There he made fast.

The cabin my grandfather built lay behind a screen of pine on the island's highest point and was crafted of whole logs, as were the additions. Inside was one large room containing several beds, a kitchen and—through a door in the back—a bathroom. The whole thing smelled wonderfully of pitch and cedar.

"I want to be go fishing!" announced Leena excitedly in broken Finnish. "I want to be catch and eat a whole one pike!"

"We to be doing just that," Juha answered in English. "Come with I to the boat."

"C'mon, Kalevi," Leena urged, grabbing my hand.

Ruffling Leena's hair, I said, "Catch something big, kid. I want to warm up first."

With a smile, she followed Juha down to the boat, where they embarked on their fishing adventure.

Connected to, but not accessed through, the cabin was the one thing no Finnish family ever did without … a sauna. For a country that has a winter that lasts more than eight months, a sauna is not only a luxury, but also a necessity.

It was there I went once I'd unpacked. I lit the fire in the box under a tray of stones. It would take about twenty minutes for the little eight-by-ten room to reach 140° F, a temperature most non-

Scandinavians consider way too hot, but for us ... well, let's just say we usually ramp it up from there. We tolerate cold very well, but we'd rather be hot.

Ahhhh ... Just like at home, I thought as my butt hit the towel-covered bench, the heat immediately raising a sweat on my skin. The smell of cedar was almost overpowering, but when I ladled some water onto the hot stones, the steam chased the cedar out of my nose and cleared out my lungs.

Thoughts swirled about lazily in my head as I soaked in heat and extruded sweat. Football, Megan Freeman's amazing rack, the Ice Queen and the hard man that Mom said was one of the good guys, fishing in the chilly waters of the sea, and the pike I would eat. Time in a sauna was for perfect for reflection and sweating.

When the heat became too much for my parboiled flesh to stand, I ran outside into the mild summer air, which felt like winter to my red and sweaty skin. Running along the dock, I took a flying leap into the cool sea, the shock forcing the breath from my lungs with a bubbly *whoosh*. After my body recovered from the reversal of temperature, I floated there for a while, soaking up the sun and enjoying the peace and quiet before swimming out deeper into the sea, stretching my muscles. Most Finns would do the sauna and soak a few times to jumpstart the circulatory system, but the sea felt too good for me to give it up just yet.

Fifteen minutes later I slogged onto shore, tired and content. A few hundred feet away in the boat, fishing poles waved back and forth as Leena and Juha cast for pike. It looked like such a good idea that I decided to fetch my fishing pole. Dad always said that there was so much pike in the sea that you could catch your fill right off the dock. I meant to do just that.

A rumbling, so faint at first that I wasn't sure that I'd even heard it, came at me across the water as I walked uphill. Before I got to the screen of pine, I heard it plainly ... the sound of an outboard. Slewing around, I saw a boat, maybe a fifteen footer, powering straight toward the dock.

In Finland, there aren't many nudity taboos, but having grown up in America, I was acutely conscious of my less than clad condition. I raced to the cabin to put on a pair of shorts.

By the time I struggled into sandals and jean shorts and ran back to the dock, the boat had already been made fast, bobbing slightly in the sea's gentle swells. And there she was, standing regally as if holding court, wearing blue jeans, a green t-shirt and a dark blue windbreaker. The Ice Queen. For some reason, the arrogant look on her face gave me a huge case of the willies. Even dressed casually, right down to the white Reeboks, she projected an air of authority and power that took my breath away.

One pale arm rose, beckoning, and, like a good doggie, I went. A flick of her fingers stopped me before my feet touched the dark rock of the dock.

"Where is your sister?' she asked in voice like crystal chiming, her English perfect and neutral. Without a word I pointed toward the little fishing boat.

For the first and last time, she smiled, a wide, cold thing full of pellucid malice. Fingers twirling oddly, she pointed at me and I felt a *force*, a sort of shock, wash over me. I tried to move, to speak, but nothing happened, only a faint, disconsolate gurgling climbed out of my mouth.

Meanwhile the Ice Queen, ropy white-blond braid trailing down her back, walked to the end of the dock and raised an imperious hand into the air. Something was held between her thumb and forefinger. Something that winked in the afternoon light.

She began to chant, softly at first, then with growing volume until she was shouting at the sea in a language that was almost familiar, like Finnish, but the words had a strange cant to them, and weren't so sing-song as modern Finnish.

But then I recognized two words. A name she intoned over and over, pouring lust and excitement into the words as if filling them with unimaginable cupidity. Iku-Turso.

Almost every Finn knows the great epic poem, *The Kalevala*. We're raised with it. It's ingrained since childhood … a part of the Finnish genetic code. Like the *Odyssey* and the *Iliad* for the Greeks, it carries the richness and flavor of its people.

It's the story of the world's creation and of the hero/rogue/singer, Väinämöinen. The original Finnish is a pretty difficult slog and the American translation reads like *The Lord of the Rings*—if it had been written by a drunk, dyslexic, bipolar, Russian philosopher.

Iku-Turso was mentioned several times in the poem, sometimes as a bringer of disease, sometimes as a god of war, other times as the son of Old-Age, and finally as an ocean monster. One being, many hats, but one thing was for sure … it was not a name a Finn wanted to hear when facing the sea.

My belly made a bee-line for regions south as an azure glow emanated from whatever the Ice Queen was holding. *What the hell was going on?*

A moment later I found out.

From far out on the water my sister screamed as the sea around the little boat began to chop and surge, water fountaining all around. Thousands of pike and perch erupted into the air as if fleeing something, trying to fly through a medium not their own. Juha kept his head and, despite the boat's rocking, managed to climb over Leena to fire up the outboard.

The engine caught with a tubercular cough and he aimed the craft toward shore amidst the shower of panicked fish. Silently I urged the boat to move faster, while behind me I heard the door to the cabin slam and the thud of running feet.

Out of the corner of my eye (I couldn't move my head, but my peripheral vision was pretty good) I saw another boat, a racer, coming our way, a rooster tail of water flying high up behind. *What the hell?* I wondered dazedly.

The Ice Queen was screaming words so quickly that they blurred together without a break. Whatever was in her upraised hand blazed so bright that it hurt my eyes to look at it, as if she held a shard of the sun.

My father ran into my peripheral vision, screaming my sister's name and diving into the sea. Long swift strokes carried him toward the boat, which, for some reason, had stopped.

My mother shrieked, a sound so full of anguish it pierced me through like a spear.

The rooster tail neared and I could see a man standing, orange/red flowers bursting from his outthrust hand.

Behind Juha's boat, the sea swelled massively, pregnant with menace, humping into the sky.

Black spikes burst from the water.

The Ice Queen staggered, deep arterial red blossoming from her neck.

What was under the water rose to the surface in a spray of mud and fish.

Iku-Turso.

I can't describe the fiend, only my impressions of it. Whatever shape defined it was so fundamentally wrong my brain couldn't find a reference. Horns ... thousands of them ... tentacles, hundreds ... the face of an old old man, careworn and yet brutal, vicious, many shapes and none. It rose out of the water, an offense to nature, a thing so alien that even the universe flinched in revulsion.

The Ice Queen turned to the boat that sped toward her, more red erupting, this time from her chest. I could see the man who was shooting at her, standing on the prow of the speeder. What surprised me most wasn't the fact that he was able to shoot so accurately standing on a moving boat. What put the cherry on top of this nightmare sundae was that it was the hard-edged man; the one Mom said was one of the good guys. And no one drove the craft, another impossibility to be heaped on the growing pile.

Iku-Turso roared, a malignant sound that offended my sanity. A black, leathery tentacle/arm slammed down on Juha's boat, flipping it into the air like a quarter and flinging my sister shrieking straight up fifty feet. Juha disappeared in a vast plume of water that quickly turned red.

The speedboat hit the dock with a tremendous crash, the prow too low to clear the piled-high rocks, crushing fiberglass and hurling Mr. Hard-Edge up and over the Ice Queen, who an instant later was nearly sliced in half by the splintered wreckage that followed Mr. Hard-Edge as he skipped on the water like a flat stone about fifty feet before sinking out of sight. The massive force of the impact slapped to the ground hard and, for a brief moment, I realized paralysis no longer gripped me. It didn't matter, though; the impact rushed the air from my lungs, causing them to squeeze shut.

Dad yelled, "No!" The scream of a man whose heart was being torn slowly from his chest.

Leena's answering cry spiraled up and up and up, a painful wailing that carried a wealth of suffering. From where I lay, my cheek rubbed into soil, I saw that one of Iku-Turso's knurled tentacle arms held her aloft some fifty, sixty feet from the water, flinging her about like a rag doll, her arms crushed tight to her sides. Blood spewed from her mouth, cutting off her shrieks, before the monster dragged her under.

I tasted bile as grief and horror warred within me. My lungs finally shuddered and I drew in a puke-soaked breath. My sister, Leena, the girl who smelled like summertime, had been killed by something so foul, so offensive, that my mind still refused to comprehend what I had beheld.

I SEE YOU.

It buffeted my brain, that voice. A foul, gelatinous thing beating on the surface of my thoughts.

I SEE YOU, LITTLE ONE.

You bastard! I thought with a fiery rage newborn in my soul, a powerful force fed by hate. *You goddamn bastard!*

IT IS GOOD TO SEE THE CHILDREN OF SAMPSA PELLERVOINEN STILL THRIVE AND TASTE SO GOOD. YOU ARE STRONG, THAT IS GOOD, AND YOU WILL NEED THAT

STRENGTH TO SURVIVE YOUR OWN HATE. A deep hint of amusement thudded into me like the sound of a drum. Something glutinous and gross caressed my mind. Revulsion brought more bile from my cramped stomach.

It taunted me? This thing I couldn't stare at but for an instant before my eyes watered and wits rebelled taunted me? The newfound burst of rage consumed my fear and cleared my eyes for a fraction of an instant and, maybe for the first time in millennia, a human clearly *saw* Iku-Turso.

How do you give shape and meaning to a *thing* that defies both? It seemed impossible, but I did. I saw the thing for what it was and right then my young mind shattered, spraying the shards of my sanity far and wide, only to reform imperfectly as my sight once again became dazzled by its alien impossibility. All I can say now is that it had all shapes previously mentioned, The Thousand-Horned One, The Old Man, The Bringer Of Disease—but it still remained so foreign to human perception that any effort to contain it with words would prove futile. It's no wonder that the sight of it drove poor H.P. Lovecraft mad.

Snot and tears drooled off my chin as I cried, tortured lungs heaving in misery, my mind so abused by the brief sight of that *thing* that I couldn't move. My sister, my beautiful sister, was gone.

Mom wailed as Dad stumbled onto shore, and they fell into each other's arms, sinking to their knees, too numb with shock to say or do anything. They clung hard to each other, grief fusing them into a single component of sorrow. As for me, I stayed where I knelt, too overwhelmed to do anything but keen my sorrow into the wind. Above my wailing voice came the sound of a helicopter, its shadow crossing the island.

Not too much time passed before another shadow fell upon me. "Boy, we need to talk." It was Mr. Hard-Edge, one of the good guys, a little worse for wear from his boating adventure, soaking wet and bleeding from a broken nose. Two fingers on his right hand sprouted new joints that had the flesh swelling purple.

He lifted me with one arm and held on until my wobbly legs had the strength to move. Satisfied that I wouldn't collapse, he hauled me over to my parents, who enfolded me into their grieving arms. While we stared at this hard man, he spoke to us of the government organization he belonged to that didn't exist. He told us that we wouldn't be able to tell anyone of its existence.

The chopper landed and three more men, all with faces chiseled in stone, exited. All had the same black suit, white shirts, and black string ties, looking like extras from *The Matrix*. One of them, a smallish man with a wispy black moustache, laid his palms on our heads. I couldn't feel it then, but I know now we had been Interdicted.

"The Ice Queen," I sniffled at Mr. Hard-Edge in English. "What was she?"

His hard face became harder. "She is what we call a magician," he replied in the same language, his tone slightly nasal. "But to me she is a witch. And I've been tracking her for a while. She wanted to make supplication to an Old One, one who could grant her enough power to become immortal."

For the first time, Dad spoke. "How ... how does she do that?"

"Sacrifice," the man said bluntly. Mom shuddered and cried harder. "She offered a human sacrifice ... a virgin."

"But Mister, why here, why now?" My voice was plaintive, lost. "Why my sister?" It hurt to think about. It hurt to breathe. It just hurt.

"We believe she's been following Iku-Turso's movements, that she tracked him somehow to this general location. Your sister was very convenient for her." He went on to explain how the Finnish government would be informing the world that my sister had died in a freak boating accident that had also claimed the life of our cousin. The bodies, they would claim, could not be recovered.

I didn't ask the obvious ... what if we hadn't been on the island when Ice Queen had arrived? The answer was simple: there were hundreds of islands off the Finnish coast, there was bound to be someone, somewhere, she could have used to lure the monster in.

"Was that really Iku-Turso? From the *Kalevala*?"

Mr. Hard-Edge stared out to the uncaring sea. "You got a good look, didn't you?" he said with just a trace of pity. "The Old Ones are always different than what legends make them out to be, son."

He must have seen something in my face, something feral, because he handed me a thick white card. On it was a telephone number in bold black print, nothing else. "Call me if you need a job, kid. You might have the stones for this kind of work."

He left then, no goodbyes, no apologies for our loss. You might ask why those hard men didn't do a *Men in Black* red flashy thingy and erase our memories. I've come to find out that using magic to affect memory is like performing brain surgery with a hacksaw. Not something you want to do to someone you're trying to save.

Something had been born that day, maybe created by the monster. Something that had Shaped me, molded me into the efficient killing machine I would later become. The need, the lust for revenge … the rage.

Chapter Eight

Wednesday Full of Woe

Bzzzz … "That … not all that … was in BB's report," Ghost said, nonplussed.

Old grief clogged my throat. "Yeah, well, whoever made the report sure didn't live through it." It hurt like a son-of-a-gun, breaching old wounds like that, but the funny thing was, Ghost might have actually had a point. All that accumulated mental pus had drained from me somewhat and I felt better than I had in a long, long time. I hoped I wasn't getting soft in my old age.

Wilkes made a face. "Damn, Kal, I wouldn't have asked you for the story if I knew it was going to be like that." He seemed embarrassed. "One question though, who is that Sampson Pellivoynen character the monster mentioned?"

"Sampsa Pellervoinen," I corrected. "From the *Kalevala*, a sort of fertility god who planted all the forests during the world's creation. I guess you could consider him the complete opposite of Iku-Turso, who is a destroyer." I stood and stretched battered muscles, weary to the bone. "One thing, Wilkes … how far behind McMillan were you?"

"McMillan?"

"Agent Finger. Her real name is Ariel McMillan."

Annoyance twisted his mouth. "God, I hate covert BS." He rubbed his forehead in thought. "Maybe four, five seconds behind. She can move like the wind, that one."

Interesting. "Excuse me, I have to see a man about a dog." With that I made my way to the bedroom, where my four-poster crooned to me of dreamless nights. But I still had miles to go before giving into that gentle seduction.

A fresh change of clothes later and I almost felt human again. The rags that I had taken off fit nicely in the bathroom garbage can. The bandages that had wrapped my hands joined them a second later. Alex was pretty thorough in his healing.

Instead of a polo and khakis, I decided on boot-cut jeans, a *Police: 2007 Reunion Tour* t-shirt and a pair of white high tops. I finished it off with a generic version of a North Face jacket.

Looking in the mirror, I had to smile. "Well, hello 1985."

Moving the bedside table, I pushed on a section of hardwood floor and flipped up a small trap door, revealing a floor safe. Inside were a box, thirty thousand in cash, and my will. The cash went into my jacket along with the will. The box I opened. Inside lay a normal looking Citizen wristwatch with a chrome band and black face, a duplicate to the one on my wrist; both were backed with what looked like a half-dollar sized piece of crystal. The one on the new watch glowed faintly, as if phosphorescent, while the one on the old watch shone a dull dark gray. I made a mental note to have Alex charge it soon.

"C'mon, Percy," I said as I entered the living room, tossing him the keys to the Honda. "You're driving."

In the car, stopped at a red light a few blocks north of the office, Wilkes asked, "So how big is this Bureau of yours?"

"Fifty field agents and fifty support workers."

"So few?"

I rolled down the window, needing fresh air. "Think of policing the World Under as going to war. Wars don't happen all the time, but when they do, someone winds up dying. Any more people and most of us would be sitting around all day twiddling our thumbs. Sometimes the job's so boring I can't get a pause in edgewise."

"And where does that little mage guy Alex fit in? Is he support?"

"We call them magicians ... mage sounds too much like a role-playing game." A really freaking deadly role-playing game. "Alex is

Special Branch, one of the support officers."

"Doesn't sound like much." I cocked an eyebrow. "Yeah? Well, it helps to think of field agents like swords. We cut, we chop. Special Branch is the body behind the sword." And BB is the brain behind the body. "Without Special Branch we wouldn't have the tech, or the magic, to help us do our job. Trust me, they need us and we need them."

"So who's the boss?"

"Of the Denver mission? I am, as most senior field agent."

"Who's your boss?"

"I'll let him introduce himself. And when he does, be respectful. He's one of the most powerful men in the civilized world."

"That sounds a bit dramatic."

"It would be dramatic if I had exaggerated."

That shut him up for a while and we drove the rest of the way in a comfortable silence.

When we slogged into the lobby, I laid my hands on the desk and threw a tired smile to a concerned-looking Pat while Wilkes stood in the middle of the room and gaped.

"It looks like the 70s threw up," he muttered in awe. "Really, who's your interior decorator? The Brady Bunch?"

Pat's Mac dinged and she rushed around the desk to give what for her passes a worried hug. Most people would consider it affectionate assault with the intent to commit bodily harm.

She quickly disengaged, which was good because my vision had been clouding with the lack of oxygen. "You had me worried sick, Kal." That rich voice soothed my ego and bruised ribs at the same time. "You got luck, I'll give you that."

"The only way I want to die, Pat, is in your arms."

"Charmer." She gave me a once over before heading back behind the desk. "Who's this lug?" she uttered throatily, a slow smile teasing her face. "Mama likes."

I beckoned the bemused Detective over. "Wilkes, this is Pat, our Receptionist."

"Receptionist?" He had caught the capital R. "I didn't reckon the Bureau would need Receptionists."

"Well, what I mean by Receptionist is 'formidable first line of defense.' She can disembowel you with a paperclip and used chewing gum."

"And I don't need the gum," Pat said, no longer smiling. I noted that one hand rested below the level of the desk.

I smacked my head. "Oh dear me, Detective Lieutenant Wilkes, I plumb forgot. Put your hands on the desk right there and don't move or Pat will blow a hole in you big enough to drive a Smart Car through."

"What?"

The smile left my face. "And I'm not even kidding." Quickly, he did as asked.

"What the hell is going on here?" he growled out of the corner of his mouth.

Pat met his eyes. "My job is Security and I take my job very, very seriously." Something in her face had him nodding quickly.

Ping went the Mac.

Pat's eyes checked the screen for second. "He's clean. Fingerprints match recorded data." Her hand came up from under the desk and stroked the keyboard. "Do you wish to add Mr. Percy Girard Wilkes to the temporary duty roster?" she asked tonelessly.

I nodded, placing a hand on the desk and feeling the surface warm. "I, Kalevi Hakala, am authorizing temporary access to BIS Station Denver effective immediately to Detective Lieutenant Wilkes of the Denver Police Department. Authorization code Victor Kilo Foxtrot 646."

Pat finished. "Recorded and authorized." Two more keystrokes and I had new sidekick—a huge one. She spared him a glorious smile, which he returned with interest.

"I may have to leave you for this side of beefcake, Kal," she told me after opening the hidden door. As we went through, Wilkes stopped a moment to examine it.

"Drywall over steel?"

I nodded, not really impressed with his observational skills.

"A hidden door to a secret lair. A little *Get Smart,* don't you think?"

"'And Loving It," I quoted, nudging him down the hall. The gang was all there, watching TV in the break room and chatting away like it wasn't a hair past midnight.

"Kal, you made it," Sue exclaimed, shaking my hand hard enough to dislocate my shoulder. "Alex briefed us."

The rest of the team added their congratulations on my not death, and even the Green Pea looked happy. I acknowledged them all politely and introduced Wilkes.

"This is Percy," I said. He shot me a glare promising revenge and shook hands all around. In the back of the room stood a thickset Hispanic man I didn't know. I pointed to him. "You, new guy, in my office. Wilkes, you too."

I settled new guy and Wilkes into a couple of chairs and leaned back in my own. "You must be Jeff's replacement."

He made to stand, extending a hand for me to shake, but I waved him down. "Flew in an hour ago, sir. I'm Matt Alba," he said quietly, in a melodic voice that carried a hint of New Mexico. "It's an honor to meet you, sir."

It took an effort to put a sincere smile on my tired face. "I'm not a 'sir.' I work for a living. And the honor is mine. I heard about that Cihuateteo you took care of down in Truth or Consequences. Good job." He seemed capable. Thick, with no neck and shoulders, wider than he was tall, all under an egg-shaped head shaved bald. Looked like he lifted weights—trains, Buicks, etc.

He smiled, showing a beautiful set of perfect chompers, relieved that I wasn't going to leap over the desk and bite off a chunk. "For now you'll stick to Dom like ugly on an ape," I ordered. "Since this is the first time someone or something seems to have specifically targeted a Bureau agent, we are on lockdown until this situation is resolved."

"Check, boss."

"Good. Now, if you haven't been briefed on the situation, have Dom read you in, then help us find the bad guys. And I mean yesterday."

He went and got gone. I focused on Wilkes. "I know this sucks, but you'll be working with us on the Organ Donor. Believe me; you don't want anyone in the DPD finding that lady."

He rubbed his chin thoughtfully. "If I'm tasked here, that means Sherrod will be on it. The man's a dork, but he listens to authority. If someone high up says I'm seconded to the ATF or whatever, he won't say boo about it."

"You computer literate?"

"I can work that Mac you got there."

I snorted and ran my hand lovingly along the monitor. "This thing is related to a Mac like a wolf is related to a Chihuahua. There are armies of computer geeks, hackers, and NSA analysts who'd sell their left testicles and their grandmothers to spend fifteen minutes alone with this thing."

"So ... that's good?"

Obviously the man was a heathen. "That's good. With this you can collapse nations." I sighed. "Let one of the others help you mine whatever data you need or have Ghost do it."

He shook his head. "I'd rather not rely on spook power." I could tell something was eating at him so I let the conversation lapse until he couldn't take it anymore and spilled.

"Gotta ask you, Kal ... the Bureau has all this power. Heck, you got more power than most third world countries. Who watches the watchmen?"

Ahh ... the one question all the Green Peas ask. Everyone thinks that Bureau agents are power-mad James Bond types with poor impulse control. The truth is, we're picked because we're not only good at what we do, and we're also not the power-mad type. It's not just physical ability; it's our psych profile as well. "We are monitored at all times by means that are very hard to circumvent."

"Magical?"

"And technological. The Director and Special Branch keep a close eye on us agents."

"Sounds like Big Brother."

"When you think about it, there has to be a balance." I took a deep breath. "Go grab some coffee or something. I need a minute."

The Detective nodded and headed out, leaving me to finally face an issue I really didn't want to face.

Training Green Peas is an important process. We go through a lot of them. If you consider that maybe a third of who we recruit don't make it through SEAL training at Coronado and then that number is reduced further by practical experience, it's a wonder we had any agents at all.

Ariel McMillan was a good egg. In fact, she had turned out to be the only DEA agent I'd met I didn't want to shoot in the face five minutes after being introduced, but I couldn't let that sway me from my decision.

Wilkes was putting paid to some Eggos when I entered the break room. "Follow me," was all I said before turning around and leaving. Curious eyes tracked the two of us as we made our way to Comms. They knew it was only a matter of time before I had to check in with BB. We ran into Alex in the hall and I pointed to the little magician. "With me." He dutifully followed.

"Well, well …" Wilkes breathed as we entered the dark room. "Talk about a big screen. You get to watch Monday Night Football on these?"

"We get to watch everything." Alex sounded smug.

"Get BB, Alex." My voice had turned gray and grim.

"It's after 2 a.m., Kal."

"Try the office, he'll be there."

And he was.

"So this must be Detective Lieutenant Wilkes," BB drawled, voice still soft despite the late hour. "I trust you have been well treated, Detective?"

Wilkes nodded openmouthed at the enormous face on the screen. "Yes, thanks. Still adjusting, though."

That brought out a small smile. "Detective, not even I've adjusted fully to the World Under. You just have to learn a modicum of acceptance." BB's eyes focused on me. "I've been waiting for your call, so speak … you look like a man with something on his mind."

I wasted no time on pleasantries. "After much consideration, BB, I think I'm going to have to flunk Agent McMillan out. Sorry."

"Kal, it's been a little over a day …"

"Enough for me to know, boss. She doesn't have the sand for the job and I'm not taking responsibility for a Pea that can't hack it when we're on a war footing."

For a moment it looked like he tasted something sour. "I am very, very sorry to hear that, Kal."

"She's a good person. She's tough and open minded, but her skills would better be used in Special Branch rather than in field duty and it's my recommendation that she be utilized in that capacity."

His gray eyes met my baby blues. "Very well."

"You'll have my report ASAP. I know it sucks, but it's necessary."

"Thank you, Kal." He removed his glasses. "I'm very … pleased to see that you are well." For a moment he sounded … relieved? Couldn't be. Vulcans could teach BB things about emotion.

"Thanks, boss." I signaled Alex to cut transmission. "Wilkes, give Alex and me a few, would you?" He nodded quickly and left.

I planted a butt cheek on the table near the magician. "Okay, kid. Why doesn't Ghost like Ms. McMillan?"

"Kal?"

"Don't be coy. He's been sour on her from day one, including that 'Agent Finger' stunt. What gives?"

He sighed in defeat. "It has to do with her first day of orientation at Warehouse. She heard about him and made the comment that spooks weren't to be trusted and he heard it and you know how sensitive he is and …"

"Enough, enough," I implored. Pissing Ghost off on the first day? Not the smartest move for a Green Pea. Taking a deep breath, I mentally counted back from a hundred, psyching myself up for what I had to do.

A minute later I was ready. "Okay, Alex. Call Agent McMillan in here."

Moments passed far too slowly before Ariel walked into the room, arms across her chest in defensive posture, looking wary. She must have smelled something brewing.

I pointed to a chair. "Have a seat." To Alex, "Begin recording."

He nodded.

"What's going on, Kal?" she asked quietly, confused.

"Ariel, you're done."

As I figured, she shot up out of her chair, nearly achieving escape velocity. "You can't do that!"

"Actually, I can and I am."

"Why?" Low and soft, a sign of danger.

"Because I can't trust you …"

"Is it because I'm DEA? Because of your unfounded prejudice toward that fine institution and the dedicated people who serve in it? Is that the case?"

"Not at all."

"Answer the damn question!" Was she really indignant, or was it all an act?

"Actually, I couldn't give a tinker's damn about the DEA. No, the reason I'm letting you go is that you can't handle fieldwork. Your actions at my apartment proved my conclusion."

Her behind hit the chair and she nearly went backwards ass over teakettle, but saved herself at the last second. For a few moments she gaped at me, at a loss for words, but I reckoned that wouldn't last long. And I was right.

"But—"

"Sorry, my mind is made up."

While she did a credible job as a landed fish, I jumped into the breach before she could find her voice again. "Ariel," I began, voice soft and soothing. "I like you. Really. You've got to be one of the brightest, toughest people to come through the Bureau in a long, long time, but your hesitation at my apartment when you saw that ghoul makes you a liability in the field."

"You're wrong," Ariel snarled, hands curled into fists.

"Am I? Think about what happened when you first saw me being attacked by that ghoul. What did you do?"

She glared hot death at me.

"You did nothing, Ariel. Nothing. A civilian blew its head apart while you stood there and gawked. You hesitated, and in this business, hesitation means death."

"I can do better," she uttered through clenched teeth.

"I seriously doubt that."

"But—"

"Listen. Think. Do you have any siblings?"

"A brother."

"Imagine your brother being attacked by a ghoul and he's a moment away from death. Got that image fixed?" She nodded. "Good. Now imagine an agent standing there, gun in hand, for a precious three to five seconds. How does that make you feel?"

Her silence spoke volumes.

"For your safety and that of my team, you're done. I do, however, find that you're a good candidate for Special Branch and have made that recommendation to BB. But you'll never go out into the field. Alex, end recording."

"Recording ended."

Ariel frowned, eyes moist. "I won't stop here, Kal."

"Of course not. I don't expect you to. And that's part of what will make you great."

A hitching breath and she gathered herself quickly. "This isn't fair."

I sighed. "Of course it is. It's the job of team leaders to test their new agents." A painful memory surfaced. "You should have seen my testing, brutal has hell. Right BB?

The far wall came to life. "Absolutely, Kal." BB's solemnity dominated the room. "Agent McMillan, you are hereby relieved of your duties and will report to DC immediately for reallocation to Special Branch."

"Yes sir."

"Alex, the door," I said before Ariel could move. The door opened to reveal all the agents on the other side. If eavesdropping were an Olympic event, my team would've won the gold. "I need a volunteer to escort Ms. McMillan to the airport and arrange her transport to DC."

Pat shoved her way through. "I will." She took Ariel's arm in a soft yet steely grip. "It isn't your fault, hon, it's just the breaks."

I leaned in close to Ariel, who was sweating heavily despite the climate control. "Don't worry, kid, I'll make sure that this won't shine a bad light. You've got brains, and in this business, that counts over muscle any day. Give Special Branch a chance; they'll be lucky to have you." Her answering look contained only a resigned acceptance.

Later, when I felt less of a heel, Wilkes and I sat in my office drinking sodas. Caffeine free.

"That happen often?" he asked between sips.

"Often enough. The senior agent has to make final evaluations, for the good of the team. For the good of the Green Peas. Not pleasant when they wash out, but that's the breaks."

"That's sucks."

"Tell me about it. Back when I first started, you should have seen what they put *me* through to evaluate my sanity. If I had failed, we wouldn't be talking now."

"That hard?"

"More like excruciatingly painful with a side of agony."

"Can the Director countermand your decision?"

"Not really. As leader of Team Epsilon, I have final say on whom I allow on board. If the Director feels strongly about the wash out, he can re-allocate the Green Pea to a new team, but they have to start all over from scratch."

"He seemed to have your back on this."

"He has the backs of every agent and Special Branch officer."

"You were pretty calm back there, almost icy."

"Not my first rodeo, man."

"Jesus! And I thought being cop for DPD was bad."

We sat in silence for a while, sipping our sodas and feeling the weight of the day. A sort of deep, cloying weariness settled on me and I realized all I wanted was to sleep for about five years.

"Wilkes, head on out and get some shut-eye. They'll have a cot for you."

He got the hint and got gone.

Alone again and tired ... story of my life. How many times during the past ten years have I repeated this cycle? Again I thought about Robert Frost and *Stopping By Woods on a Snowy Evening*. That guy hit the nail on the head when it came to the feeling of almost hopeless fatigue.

I knew I was getting onto dangerous ground. Feeling sorry for yourself is the quickest way to catch a heaping dose of death in this business. My resolution needed a jumpstart.

Pulling my wallet out, I flipped it open and unzipped a waterproof compartment I had made special. Inside were two photos. One was of my sister, frozen forever at ten, hair flying out behind her as she rode her bike, a half smile quirked on her perfect face. Leena, my summertime muse.

The other was of a red-haired woman with a wealth of freckles staring at the camera; face open in a wide smile of surprise and delight. I had just asked her to marry me.

Chapter Nine

Minnesota, Eleven Years Earlier

Flash!

Carol blinked for a second, blinded by the camera's flash.

Way to go, Mom, I thought, sourly, a half-second before my girlfriend tackled me in a bear hug. I knew linebackers who didn't hit so hard.

"Is that a 'maybe'?" Dad asked, standing in the doorway to the kitchen, a bottle of champagne in one large hand.

Machine gun kisses started raining down on me from an over-enthusiastic redhead with more attitude and brains than any other woman I knew. Except Mom, of course.

"Yes, of course I'll marry you!" More machine gun kisses. I've heard of being kissed to death, but right then I feared it would come true.

"Air!" I gasped theatrically. "Air!"

"Don't you let up a hair, girl," encouraged Mom with a smile fit to slice her head in half, once again aiming the camera. "You give that boy an inch and he'll walk all over you." *Flash.*

Despite the mixed metaphor, I had to grin. Mom loved Carol like a daughter. A tall, leggy, redheaded daughter, who took no sass from anyone, but had plenty of her own to dish out. I felt privileged that she loved a schlub like me.

Dad's meaty hand clamped down hard on my shoulder. "You better ease up a bit there, girl. He hadn't been hit that hard since the Fiesta Bowl."

Grunting, I heaved and, with a little help from Dad, hauled Carol up and onto my shoulder. "Thank you very much folks." I grunted. "We'll be taking off now. Maybe we'll find someone who can appreciate a former Husker." I made to move toward the door and wound up spinning Carol round and round the living room.

"You beast!" she screamed, laughing and pummeling my back. There was enough muscle there to hurt.

"You got that right, woman!" I hollered.

All and all it was one of the happiest days of my life and I was thanking my lucky stars that my brainiac redhead had said 'yes.' It was Thanksgiving, 1999.

While most people were debating hotly over a seriously screwed up election or the President's fellatio infidelity, I was looking forward to finally getting on with my life. I was twenty-four and felt it was about damned time. It wouldn't have been that much of an issue had I not broken my back the start of my junior year, a football injury that nearly cost me my legs. And it hadn't even happened during a game, but in practice when some damn freshman speared me from behind, his helmet ruining my chances for a spot in the NFL and some big money.

Recovery ate two years of my life as multiple surgeries and painful physical therapy helped me walk again, but kept me out of school. During that time I made the acquaintance of a beautiful red-headed physics major, one who actually liked a certain surly Scandinavian. We started dating in between surgeries; she pushed my wheelchair and I pushed my luck by being a royal dick. But the gods must have been smiling on me because she stuck around and managed to staple a smile on my face.

It was Carol who talked me into going back to the University instead of wallowing in self-pity. It was Carol who recognized my talent for chemistry, who pointed me in the right direction. Despite my best efforts to the contrary, I earned a degree in Chemical Engineering, graduating near the top of my class.

Things were looking up, I had made contacts and I was off to the Texas oil fields to help one of our nation's multi-gazillion dollar corporations eke more black gold out of supposedly dry wells. My biggest worry was whether some genius would invent a car that ran on water, or pipe dreams, and put me out of a job. As for Carol, she graduated *magna cum laude* with a degree in Physics and probably would change the world by inventing anti-gravity or time travel.

"C'mon son," Dad laughed. "Put the young lady down before she gets sick. Your mom just cleaned this place up."

Fortunately Carol didn't puke and we wound up snuggling on the couch as we admired the rock I had placed on her finger. Mom finished cooking dinner while Dad sat and watched the Golden Gophers drop a home game. The ring wasn't anything special—four small princess-cut diamonds set in a braided gold band. When I started to make the big bucks, then I would spend some serious coin on a proper engagement ring.

Thanksgiving finished on a high note and it was my last day of peace.

Black Friday dawned bright and cheerful, an unusual occurrence in Minnesota where, like Finland, November sees more snow than sun.

Mom and Carol had decided to head into town early to try to take advantage of the busiest shopping day of the year while Dad reckoned it was time to start the day with a sauna. I knew he'd rotate going in and out for the next couple of hours, so I had some time to myself. I was determined to take a trip down memory lane by going through my old stuff that Mom had saved.

Dad had converted my bedroom into a home gym, complete with free weights and a Bowflex—the Nautilus for the suburban male. Mounted in one of the corners was a TV, because god forbid he'd miss watching his reruns of *Hill Street Blues* while he worked out.

The only thing that remained mine was the closet, filled with sports memorabilia and old jackets. On the top shelf, just under the bare bulb, was a Payless ShoeSource box, a container for all my most precious memories.

The room reeked of nostalgia as I opened the box and started sorting through the contents. An autographed picture of Tom

Osborne and me, a quiet man and a hell of a football coach. Torn ticket stubs to a George Thorogood concert. The last letter I'd ever received from my pal Marty Spencer before he died of leukemia.

My fingers found the corner of a thick piece of paper and I pulled out a business card, slightly yellowed with age.

The card from Mr. Hard-Edge.

My hands began to shake and I felt my breath hitch in my chest.

Leena.

Screams echoed in the chambers of my memories, weighty with the strains of madness. Leena. She would be twenty if she hadn't … My mind skittered away from the thought, but I forced it back on track and felt something that hadn't been part of my life since that day.

The rage.

It had hidden all these years in the shadowed, cobwebby corners of my mind, biding its time like a patient spider and now, with the card in hand, I felt it jitter through my veins as if chasing away my reason. Iku-Turso. That bastard killed my sister, crushing her to death in front of her parents, dragging her body to the icy depths of the Baltic. Her screams sang through my mind, helping to fuel the fury that flooded me like liquid lunacy.

How could I forget her? How could my happiness derail the memory of my sister?

Call me if you need a job, kid. You might have the stones for this kind of work.

Mr. Hard-Edge's words flooded back as if they had just been uttered. A tough guy, one of the good guys, Mom said. The Ice Queen and the thing that shined like the sun in her hand. The boat had sliced her nearly in half as it rammed the dock, sending splintered fiberglass flying.

Juha, his crushed body found an hour later, eyes open as if he'd witnessed his death coming at him like a freight train. The ponderous alien weight of the monster and the fish that jumped out of the water, trying to escape into the foreign world of air.

Iku-Turso.

The rage was upon me and I wanted to destroy the creature that had so wounded my fifteen-year-old self. The box lay at my feet, contents strewn across the floor, and the only thing that mattered right then, the only thing that I could see past the fury in my soul was the card in my hand. The name on the card was Ilmari Virtanen.

"Operator, I need to place an international call." I didn't remember picking up Mom's lavender princess phone, but it was at my ear. Focusing on the card, I rattled off the number and the operator made the connection in a surprisingly short amount of time.

"Hello, Mr. Hakala."

A chill gripped me, dampening the rage and causing my skin to break out in gooseflesh. "Uh, hi?"

"We know you have a lot of questions. We have the answers. Are you free to take a meeting?"

Take a meeting? How yuppie. "Sure. When?" I was astonished at how calm I sounded.

"This evening. There is a diner in Grand Rapids called The Sweet Spot. You are familiar with it, I presume?"

Of course I was. Everyone in town had eaten there at one time or another; it had the best pepper steak in Minnesota. I made my assurances to the mystery voice.

"Good. Be there at seven o'clock. Sit at the third booth to the right. Remember, we will answer all your questions. Bring the business card." *Click.*

Somewhere during the conversation the rage had oozed away, leaving me feeling vacant and worn-out. What the hell was going on here?

The bell above the door rang, announcing my entrance into the Sweet Spot. Third booth on the right ... check. I scooted my butt onto the red vinyl bench seat, nervous as hell, and waited. My hands shook like I had Parkinson's and my stomach flip-flopped like a fish on dry land. Despite the cold weather, I was sweating something terrible.

The Sweet Spot was a take on the old shiny-steel railroad car '50s diner, complete with the greasiest burgers imaginable and gravy fries. Mom called it the Heart Attack Hilton.

Tickety-tock went the clock and my contact was late. Or was I early? My watch said seven-oh-five. Where was he/she/it?

"Mr. Hakala, a pleasure," I jumped as a heavyset man took the bench opposite. As he settled into his seat, I took a good long look. Florid with a round Charlie Brown head that sprouted coarse black hair pulled back like a scream from a corrugated forehead and a small pug nose that hung like a stubby period over thin liver colored lips. Small brown eyes stared back kindly from sockets bracketed by smile lines. The whole package was stuffed into a snappy Saville Row suit. With a self-effacing grin he extended a large hand and I took it. Man, he had a grip.

"Hello," I said, dubious.

"Do you prefer Kal or Kalevi?" Surprisingly he pronounced it correctly. Kahl-eh-vee.

"Most people call me Kal. They butcher my full name."

"Fair enough." He placed a small piece of shiny quartz on the tabletop. "Think of it as a sound distortion device. It prevents eavesdropping."

I gave it a skeptical stare. "It's a rock."

Small white teeth appeared. Somewhere down the line he'd had them capped, leaving them set in a perfectly even row. "Trust me, Kal, this is quite effective."

"I was promised answers."

"And I will provide." We were interrupted by a pretty brunette in a pink uniform who came to take our order. "Hello, young lady." A big hand reached out and crossed her palm with something thick, green and crinkly. Her eyes grew wide. "Darling, we need some peace for a few minutes, if you don't mind."

"Mister, this buys you all the time in the world." She sauntered off with an extra sway to her hips, no doubt lost in visions of holiday shopping.

"Allow me to introduce myself; my name is David Merced." Again that level smile. "My Director has given me leave to discuss your recruitment to the Bureau of Supernatural Investigation."

"Supernatural."

"Yes."

"That's crazy." I leaned back against red vinyl, crossing my arms. This meeting was starting to look like a Bad Idea.

Kind eyes became hard. "You know differently, don't you? Almost ten years ago you saw something strange and awful, something beyond the pale."

Iku-Turso. I felt like vomiting.

"Okay, so you're from this Bureau. What about that man I met all those years ago, the one who killed the witch?"

"He belonged to the Finnish equivalent of the Bureau. Most major governments have one to guard against things that go bump in the night. To protect the average citizens from the World Under."

I heard the capitals. "The World Under?"

"Yes."

"What is that?"

"That, my dear Kal Hakala, is the $64,000 question. Magicians and agents have been pondering that since the Roman Empire. Some believe that the Supernaturals inhabit this world with us, hiding, many in plain sight. Others believe that there is another world, a parallel Earth that is inhabited by nothing but Supernaturals, that, at certain times, the barrier between our worlds becomes thin enough for Supernaturals to ... oh, *bleed* through and cause havoc in ours. There have been many names for this world: Tir-Na-Nog, Avalon, Asgard, Olympus, El Dorado, Cibola, Atlantis, and even Middle-Earth."

"Hmm. What do you believe?"

"I believe that it doesn't matter. We have to protect our citizens. If that means killing every Supernatural that sets foot in the light of day, so be it."

My brain felt pummeled by absurdities. "This is heavy, man."

He steepled his fingers. "Kal, may I ask you a question?" I nodded. "How do you feel?"

"What?"

"It's a simple question. How do you feel?"

How did I feel? For a good long while I'd felt great. I'd graduated, found a wonderful woman, and my future looked pretty damn bright. But all that tasted like ashes in my mouth.

"Angry. Full of rage, hate and spite." That didn't seem like enough. My temples pounded. "I want to kill something with my bare hands. That's how I feel."

"Why do you think that is?"

"Because some damn monster killed my kid sister!" I realized I was shouting and killed the noise, making apologetic motions to the staring patrons.

Merced shook his head. "Easy there, young man. This crystal keeps others from understanding what we're saying, but it doesn't have volume control."

"Sorry."

"No need. Now, Kal, my guess is that you were feeling just fine. In fact, life seemed pretty normal and then you picked up the business card given to you by my Finnish counterpart. Is that correct?"

"Yah."

"May I have it please?"

I fished it out of my wallet and handed it over.

"Thank you." He teased one tattered corner with a nail, parting the layers of paper. "The first thing you must know is that magic exists. The second thing is, so do magical beings, what we call the Supernaturals." Delicately, like a surgeon, he managed to fully split one corner. "Third thing is, we can use magic, those with the gene to do so. We call them, of course, magicians. Ahh … there we go." Carefully, he pulled the layers apart.

Sandwiched within the card was silver tracery, which looked like a cross between a circuit board and Celtic knot work on crack. The silvery threads glinted in the fluorescent light, incredibly fine. "What the hell?" I breathed.

"What you see here, young Kal, is part of a spell."

"A spell? A spell for what?"

"The spell was designed to negate a spell that had been cast on you. Simply put, when you touch the card, the spell reads your aura. Upon sensing a certain level of maturity, it releases a spell that removes a subtle, but benign, spell that had been cast on you years ago. Like a white blood cell attacking foreign bacteria."

"What the … how does it do that?"

"The closest analogy is a line of computer code, an 'if/then' statement. Are you familiar with that?"

"Yeah, learned a little programming in college."

"Well, there you go then."

I rubbed my face. "How can magic last indefinitely?"

"That depends on what you cast spells on. High quality gems store magic and spells for a long, long time … we're talking centuries, maybe even millenia. The lower the quality, however, the quicker the charge is depleted. Metals like silver, gold and platinum also can hold a magical charge, but not as long as their gem counterparts." He tapped the card on the table. "See here, the lines and whatnot? Pure silver that is. Holds a small charge for a decent amount of time and the purer the metal, the longer the charge lasts. In this case, if you don't paw the card all the time, it can hold a charge for up to twenty years before it's depleted. The knotwork and circuit board pattern here, see that?" I nodded. "That is the Shape of the counterspell. You can also have a gem hold energy and the Shape of the spell, depending on quality, but obviously you can't stick a gem inside a card."

Something he had just said hit hard. "Twenty years?"

Merced nodded. "Yes, and long term spells—like curses, hexes, or benign ones like the Interdiction you and your folks have been under—are fueled by the person's body. We all produce energy, be it in the form of heat or electrochemical. Spells can tap into that. Strong spells can weaken the body dramatically while mild ones have no ill effects at all."

"I need a drink," I grunted.

Smiling, the Merced pulled a silver flask out of his suit jacket and held it out. I gratefully accepted and took a swig of the finest vodka I'd ever tasted. No hint of flavor and the right amount of burn as it traveled down my gullet.

"Damn, that's good," I commented, taking another hit.

Merced took the flask back and downed a swallow. "I thought you might be needing this."

Now that I had some heat in my belly, I struggled to gather my thoughts. "You said there was a spell on me and that the card took it away when it 'sensed' I had a certain level of maturity. What kind of spell? And why all this ... this ... whatever this is?"

He handed the flask back and I took another swig. "The agent you met in Finland saw something in you and had you tagged," he explained. "Sort of like tagging animals so scientists can track them in the wild. Except he had it done magically when the Interdiction was laid on you and your family. Interdiction is what we call the Compulsion spell; it prevents you from blabbing about the World Under or the agencies that police it. Part of the tagging was to lay a kind of ... filter on the experience."

"A filter? What kind of filter."

Merced's voice became quiet, calm. The kind of voice you'd use when talking to a dangerous animal that was sizing you up for a midday snack. "You have to realize that you were a very young man who just witnessed something that could have easily twisted your mind had there been no intervention. Without that filter, you likely would have become insane, thus ruining any chance you had of leading a happy, productive life. The filter blankets strong emotions and fuzzes the memory so they have much fewer effects than they normally would have."

Bitter laughter leapt from my throat. "So that guy gave me rose-colored glasses?"

He nodded. "In a manner of speaking."

Once again the rage poured through me, igniting my blood and making my temples pulse to the beat of my heart. Merced must have seen some indication because he reached out and placed a comforting hand on mine.

Instantly the rage was gone, like it had never been there. "Wh—"

"Feel better?'

"Did you just … just …"

"Yes, I put a spell on you, a minor one to calm you down."

"It worked." I thought a moment, savoring the clarity of mind. "How … you're a mage?"

"We call them magicians, but yes, I am. What I did was Shape a spell in my mind and thrust it upon you, dampening your rage. Now imagine a fifteen-year-old boy feeling that kind of fury. What do you think would happen to that boy? Your parents needed no such assistance; they were judged to be able to handle the situation."

"That boy would go crazier than an outhouse rat," I admitted.

"Right."

"What do you mean by 'Shape' a spell?"

Merced took a deep breath. "Hard to explain, kid. Like explaining color to a person who has been blind since birth." He took another swig of booze. "When a magician wants to cast a spell, or create one, he thinks about the desired effect, the amount of energy required, area of effect, the time to cast the spell, and how long it will last. All down to the smallest detail. He or she holds all that information in mind at one time and then wills energy from his or her body, or an outside source, into the those variables. That energy feels like the first rush of alcohol on an empty stomach, only much more intense. If the magician can juggle all that, he then uses magic to *push* the spell outwards toward a person, a gem, or carefully crafted artifact."

"Sounds ... complicated."

"Tell me about it. It's sort of like shooting an arrow at a target while drunk, blindfolded and riding a merry-go-round."

I gave that a few moments consideration. "So now what?"

"Kal, we've had our eye on you for quite a while. Your aptitude tests are stratospheric and you meet all the physical requirements. The Bureau would like to offer you a job."

"You mean I get to fight those things that go bump in the night?"

"Exactly.

By the pricking of my thumbs ... "What's the catch?"

Those brown eyes drilled into me with relentless intensity. "The average lifespan of a field agent is less than three years."

...something wicked this way comes. Cold gripped my insides, my guts rendered into ice. "You mean most *die* in three years?"

"Those that don't retire."

"What do you mean 'retire'? How can you retire in less than three years?"

Then he told me how much field agents get paid. After picking my jaw up off the table, I conceded that you could retire after three years.

"Are you an agent?" I asked.

He shook his head. "No. I used to be a team magician, but I got too old for field work and now spend my time with recruitment and R&D."

"R&D?"

"Trying to develop new spell Shapes and artifacts."

"Wow ..."

"Yeah, 'wow' is right. You got an answer for me, Kal?"

I gave the matter some hard thought. Merced waited patiently for me to finish, or to catch a whiff of something burning.

"What do I have to do?" I asked suddenly. "This doesn't seem like a job you just jump into."

"No, it isn't. Usually we recruit from one of the alphabet agencies or the military, but there are a few special exceptions. If you want in, there will be a training period. Two months in marine boot camp in Parris Island, then the 25-week SEAL training at the Naval Special Warfare Center at Coronado, California. Then there is a one-month course at our DC office so you know how to recognize and deal with the most common forms of Supernaturals. After that you'll be assigned to a team as what they call a Green Pea, a probationary agent."

"Jesus!"

"We expect the best, so we pay the most."

He had a point. Then he said something that put the rusty nails in my Cheerios.

"One thing, however. No wives, no girlfriends, no boyfriends. No permanent relationships at all while in service."

"What?" The prospect of telling Carol I had to postpone our wedding for a couple of years made me want to run away screaming. That red hair of hers was a serious warning to the rest of the world. "What do you mean 'no permanent relationships'?"

Merced leaned closer. "We want our agents focused on the task at hand, not on their partners. That is a non-negotiable point. You'll be traveling a lot, moving from hot spot to hot spot. In between you'll be training, honing your skills so you don't get a case of dead. If you want to work Special Branch, there are a few stable positions, but they are much sought after and usually granted to senior personnel." He leaned back. "If you do decide to get married or have a girlfriend while in service, you'll be retired immediately. That's the job. Always has been, always will be."

Could I handle staying away from Carol for all that time? Three years seemed like forever and a day. Would she wait? If she did, would we still feel the same way about each other?

"What about my parents?"

"Parents we don't mind. Most agents tend to be loners who can handle very limited contact with their parents. Your mother and father, however, are in a somewhat unique situation. Due to the incident in Finland, they are already aware of our existence, if only peripherally. Most parents are told their children are entering military service, but I don't see the problem with revealing the truth to yours, considering that they, like you, are already under Interdiction.

"One other thing to think about," he continued. "Let's say you join up and survive for the next three years or so. You will be under observation all that time. Wielding the kind of power you will have requires a lot of checks and balances. You will be investigated and evaluated time and time again. It's part of the job and another reason for the big paycheck." With that he touched my hand lightly and the rage came surging back like a tsunami.

He sure knew how to hit the right button. And how could he not? I'd been 'tagged,' right? Despite the fact that I knew I was being played like Charlie Daniels's fiddle, I didn't care.

Iku-Turso. I wanted that monster dead in the worst way.

Two days later, after Carol flew home to Nebraska to personally tell her parents the good news, I sat down with mine and spilled the beans about the job offer.

"You can't do that to the girl, son." Dad blurted, shocked that I'd actually consider the idea of postponing my marriage. "This will tear her heart out."

Mom's eyes flickered briefly to her husband's before settling on mine. "Do it, son," she ground out. "Anything to find out how to kill that monster."

"Terhi—" Dad began.

"No!" Her pale face had become bright red and her eyes flashed the fire of her hate. "It killed our little girl! She was only ten and it took her!" Tears clogged her throat, but never reached her eyes. "I think this is a sign from God. I *feel* it."

For a moment he looked like he would argue, but his broad

shoulders slumped and he bowed his head in defeat. "I worry about Carol. She will be hurt by this."

"For nearly eleven years I've lived with the idea that our beautiful daughter died in terror and pain," she declared thickly, staring at Dad, whose face was slack with anguish. "That deserves an answer. If anyone can destroy that *thing* it's Kalevi. I know it. This secret place will give him the tools, will teach him how to be the person to kill Iku-Turso. And then our daughter will rest in peace."

For the first time I got a glimpse of the anger Mom had lived with all these years, a mirror to my own. And looking at Dad, well … he may not have been enraged, but his anguish was real and seeing it so naked on his face fueled my fury.

He looked into my eyes and winced. Whether he saw my rage or determination—I don't know—but he nodded sadly.

David Merced had given me precise instructions on how to proceed if I accepted his offer.

"I have to pack."

And miles to go before I sleep.

The most cowardly thing I've ever done in my life happened an hour later. I broke up with Carol over the phone.

What could I tell her? That I'd been recruited by an ultra-secret government organization dedicated to stopping the forces of magic and supernatural evil from threatening the world? I knew that if I even dropped hints about the Bureau, the Interdiction would swell my throat shut.

So I told her that I had joined the military, which was, at its heart a lie that tore at my soul like shards of ragged glass. I told her I was heading out to Parris Island to train as a marine and then to Coronado for SEAL training, which was the truth. Telling her that it was something I felt I had to do for my country seared my conscience with hypocrisy. The meat of my mission to join the Bureau was revenge, plain and simple, but how could I inform the woman I loved that all I wanted to was kill, kill, kill? That the need burned through me stronger than my devotion to her? I loved her, desperately, but the rage … the rage was far stronger than any other emotion I could possess.

Less than five minutes later, after calling me a coward with cold feet and declaring that I had never loved her, she hung up on me.

Tears choked my heart as I settled the phone in its cradle. In my gut, I knew she'd never call, never write, never even contact my parents to check on me.

She was gone.

Chapter Ten

It's Good to be a Bad Ass

"Kal ... Kal! Wake up!"

Head on arms. Arms on desk. Spit dribbling from mouth to form a puddle under my chin. What the hell?

"Kal, wake up?" the voice insisted.

I silently promised death, lots and lots of death, to the bearer of that voice. "What the heck," I ground out, slowly easing out of the land of oblivion.

"Kal, we got a situation in LoDo!" Alex grabbed my arm and shook me hard.

"Wha-what kind of situation?" Was that my breath? Ugh ... smelled as if I'd been kissing the wrong end of a goat.

"Ghouls!"

Okay, that woke me up quick. Strange how the little things motivate you.

My feet hit the hall before Alex knew what had happened. I waited patiently for the little guy to catch up. "In Comms," he said, leading the way.

Everyone crowded the room, most looking as disheveled and sleep-deprived as I felt. "What time is it?"

Sue looked at her watch. "Three thirty-five a.m."

Wonderful. A whole three hours of sleep, just enough to make me feel worse than when I went to bed. Bryan, looking no better than I, handed me a cup of coffee. Taking a sip, I sent a prayer of thanks winging to the caffeine gods.

Everyone stared at the far wall, a grainy black and white showing a street view of downtown Denver. "Traffic cams," I surmised.

"Got it in one, Kal," Alex said quietly, hands on the virtual keyboard. "The computer has been running periodic checks for suspicious behavior ever since we started on the Organ Donor case using the local cams. A couple of minutes ago it alerted me."

"And?" Another sip. Just a few more gallons of that heavenly fluid and I might feel human again. Might.

"Hold on ... they're moving fast ... trying to locate them again ..."

"Locate who?" Wilkes cut in.

I shushed him. "Let the man work."

"Got it!" The magician's finger stabbed toward the screen.

On screen two indistinct figures carried a third. Both moved with an odd sort of grace, despite being burdened. "Is this what you saw? Can you clean that up a bit, Alex?"

"Way ahead of you, Kal." His fingers danced over the keyboard. Computer magic happened and the image clarified.

"Holy crap!" Sue breathed. The others nodded.

"That's exactly right. We got ghouls," I breathed through teeth bared in a grimace of loathing.

The ghouls stopped and laid their burden on the street next to the curb and I felt a sick dread ... They were positioning a naked body out onto the gutter. The Organ Donor corpse delivery system—thirty minutes or less, or your cadaver is free.

"Okay, everybody," I barked. "Time to open the Armory."

"Heck yeah!" shouted Dom, pumping a fist into the air.

One thing that will always shoot straight to the heart of every field agent is the Armory. A lethal blend of *Willy Wonka and the Chocolate Factory* and *Rambo*, it had enough potential for destruction to take out the Latin American country of your choice. Every deployed team had an Armory, just in case the feces impacted into the rotary oscillator.

To the left and down the hall from my office was what looked like a wooden door bearing a little black plaque that read, of course, 'Armory.' My palm slapped the wood above the plaque and the

Shaped gold wire embedded there warmed under my fingertips like an affirmation.

Only the team leader can open the Armory and, thanks to aura reading, only when not under duress. A click sounded from deep within, and I gave the door a gentle nudge. Lights came on, illuminating a room the size of a generous walk-in closet.

"Holy moley," Wilkes breathed from behind.

"You got that right." I would've loved to linger, but time was of the essence. It's always that way on the job.

Black cases contained various explosives, egg-shaped polystyrene containers held spell gems that glowed with furious energies, a rack of black dusters made of something that superficially looked like leather, drawers of body armor, helmets, eyewear, tasers, ammunition and, of course, guns, guns, guns! Assault rifles, pistols, revolvers, and even a Thompson submachine gun. Anything you needed for widespread mayhem.

"Back off, people!" I shouted as the team rushed forward. "You know the drill. I do the handouts; you wait your turn." Groans and muttering answered me. You'd have thought I was docking their pay.

Body armor first. Just enough for everyone.

Wilkes's eyes did their best to pop out on springs. "You gotta be kidding me!" He held the black chitonous breastplate and leggings reverently.

Dom threw him a smirk. "A former Bureau agent was one of the producers of *Batman Begins*," he explained.

"You want to be a superhero?" I asked. "We got the product to make you one. Try it on; it should fit."

Next came the Faraday Coats, the much bigger, and heavier, brother to the standard model Faraday Jacket. Like their little brothers, they tended to overheat when deflecting an overabundance of magic. They had two major problems: they were heavy enough to restrict movement, which can be fatal if you needed to move fast, and each one cost the government more than a

Cadillac Escalade due the fact that platinum, not silver, was used in their construction. Along with the coats I handed out some touks, or knitted winter hats. At least, that's what they looked like. Made of wool over a titanium cap and mesh, they were the closest things to a helmet without looking like one.

"Dom, you get the .338 Lapua." I handed the weapon into eager hands.

"Boss, I love you." The Italian lovingly stroked the rifle like a child. "Baby, come to papa."

Sue grimaced. "That's just too disturbing for words."

"Ain't it, though? At least he can shoot. Here, Wilkes, a .44 revolver to go with that Eagle you're not bringing with you. Don't look at me like that; these are clean guns so no one can match ballistics. Here, take some explosive rounds; they'll put a hole in a brick wall. That make you happy?" He was happy, lovingly holding the gun and the box of ammo to his chest. I tossed over a speed loader. "Just so you know, these are Silenced weapons." He looked up, catching the capital letter. "So don't be surprised when you fire and don't hear anything."

Next came the gems. "Only one each! I don't have to remind you what you are carrying there, do I? Wilkes, you don't get one; you haven't qualified yet. These are set spells, usable by anyone. Handle them wrong and they'll likely kill you or turn you into a hermit crab." Each polystyrene egg case had a tab that could be pulled, exposing the trigger word for the spell gem inside. On the side of each case was a pictogram depicting the spell. For myself I chose only one, snagging two silvery vials with wax-coated stoppers—a spell so dangerous that it took five magicians to cast. Only the team leader had the authorization.

Everyone received a pair of sunglasses. Our sterling Detective shot me an inquiring look. "Night-vision," I explained.

"Harrumph," he snorted. "They look like Oakleys."

The amusement in Dom's voice was thick enough to cut. "We are not without a sense of style, dear boy."

And, last but not least, communications. Wilkes held up a little round, flesh colored Band-Aid the size of a dime. "What the heck?"

"Throat mic," Sue replied, applying one to said area. "Only transmits subvocal. One tap turns it on. One tap turns it off."

Earwigs went in and ring mics were slipped onto fingers. We were ready.

"Okay, folks. Sue rides with Dom, Matt and Bryan, you two will partner up, and that leaves me and Wilkes." I threw him a cocked eyebrow. He wasn't impressed. "You, Detective, stay on my six like you're glued there. Alex will coordinate and keep the locals off our backs." The little magician nodded and scampered off to Comms.

"You know the rules: Stay alert, stay alive."

"There weren't as many fully automatic weapons in the Armory," Wilkes grumphed as he drove down 225 toward I-25, taking us downtown. Thanks to Alex, our three cars sped along at nearly a 100 mph, not a cruiser in sight.

"We do try to keep a low profile," I replied.

He tapped his black, ridged body armor. "You call this low profile?"

"Button up your coat and you'll be fine."

"Damn thing's a furnace."

"Better a furnace than a microwave spell."

"You're kidding, right?"

"Nope. Invented in the eighties by a little Puerto Rican magician who left reality far, far behind when he caught his wife cheating with another man. Back then the team that took him out lost three people. Had to scrape them off the walls. So far no one has been able to replicate the spell, thank god."

That cooled that line of inquiry as he considered the imagery. At least he buttoned his coat.

Once we got to the canyons of LoDo, all dark and mysterious with steam billowing out the manhole covers, we made our way to

Wynkoop, the street where the body was located, parking our Crown Vics so they blocked access. The remains were within spitting distance of Morton's Steakhouse. Fortunately, the only things moving were the members of my team.

We fanned out around the body. "Bryan, take pics and see if can get an ID." The victim was a tall slender man, soft … no hard muscle. No tattoos, at least not on his back or legs. I briefly wondered what kind of bad man he used to be. "We need to be out of here soon. Sue, roll the corpse over, see if you can spot anything, then reposition the body. We'll let DPD handle him. He isn't going anywhere."

"Alex, keep checking those traffic cams. I want those ghouls found yesterday."

"*On it, boss.*"

It was only a matter of time before some midnight wanderer or partygoer stumbled onto the scene and started to freak out. Witnesses were such an inconvenience.

"Hurry up, guys. Time is a-wasting." I kept my eyes peeled for pedestrians and runaway ghouls.

"Holy Batman and peanut butter, Kal, you gotta see this." Wilkes sounded shaken, as if he'd been gut-punched.

My ears pricked up and I whirled around. Bryan had turned the body over on its back so that I had a clear look at its face.

Briegan.

"Crap and fried eggs," I whispered. Gone were the arrogant sneer and the lines of annoyance on his brow. Instead he looked like some poor bastard that got himself hollowed out and dumped. I never liked the guy, but I wouldn't have wished that fate on anyone.

Adrenaline kicked in. "Folks, finish this up now, then flip him over. We are out of here in one minute."

Longest minute of my life. I tried to think of the motive behind this murder, but my brain seemed to be out to lunch. Instead, my skull began to pound with the beginnings of a migraine.

"*Kal, got something. Parking garage two blocks due south of your location."*

"C'mon folks, let's head out." My spine tingled with a surge of excitement. Action, actually doing something … killing the monsters that dared to inhabit my universe … what a rush. I needed this. It was my drug and it left no needle marks. Was it wrong, feeling jazzed like this, getting off like an adrenaline junkie? Does killing for the sheer pleasure of watching those evil bastards die make me a psychopath? I don't know, but the thought sure didn't deter me.

There was no parking on the street, but an alleyway next to the parking garage turned out to be a good place to stow the Vics.

"Pretty sure they're in there, Kal. Don't know which story."

The garage had four levels plus a roof. A lot of territory to cover chasing undead on steroids.

I smelled a trap.

"Careful guys, this stinks to high heaven," I announced, my tiny throat mic carrying my words across the ether before we exited the Vics. "Sue and Bryan take floors three and four. Wilkes and I will cover one and two. Dom, I want you to get to the roof of the building across the street and cover us with the .338. Matt, you're on his six. Keep him alive. And everybody, if these ghouls are like the one in my apartment, they're faster that you can believe. If you see a gem imbedded in their flesh, shoot it. Now, don your glasses. Check?"

Five throats subvocaled, "*Check.*"

"Good."

Except for Wilkes, we all had gone through the same training and could move like ghosts when needed, silent and virtually unseen. Surprisingly, he managed to be fairly quiet as well, his time as a Ranger serving him well. Not too shabby. Crap by SEAL standards, but passable.

Sue and Bryan passed me as we entered the front entrance, heading toward the stairs.

"You realize we look like extras from a Wachowski Brothers'

movie," Wilkes said.

"They were Special Branch," I replied. "Now, can the chatter."

Slowly we made our way around Audis, Hyundais, Fords and Buicks, breezing our way through the first floor. Most people would have been scared spitless, but I grew more excited, more confident with every step. Trap or not, I was going to kill me a monster.

The faint smell of rot reached me, meat left out too long.

By the pricking of my thumbs …

A flash of movement up to my left under a Ford truck, almost too fast to be seen, sent my nerves screaming. A skittering noise drawing away, claws on concrete raising the hair on the back of my neck. Almost without thinking I followed, with the Detective close behind.

"*Boss,*" Dom sent. "*Got a bogey on the rooftop moving too fast for me to hit.*"

"Keep on it," I replied. "Got the other one. Sue, Bryan, would you be so nice as to kill that ghoul for me?"

"*Check, boss.*"

Metal tore, the sound reverbing through the garage and scraping my nerves like a file. We approached warily, only to find a Camry with a shredded passenger door. No ghoul.

"Wilkes, it's screwing with us."

"*I got that, Kal.*"

"Keep a lookout behind. Something is wrong here."

"*Check.*"

The Camry exploded in a ball of orange fire and I was flung across the garage, tumbling ass over teakettle across the floor, Faraday coat shredding across concrete until I came to rest against the quarter panel of a white SUV. My vision fuzzed as my titanium clad skull slapped into the pliable metal.

When my vision finally cleared, I realized that my night-vision glasses had been lost. Good thing there was a Camry on fire to provide fitful illumination. I tasted blood in my mouth, and that just pissed me off.

"Boss!" The words were frantic.

"I'm okay, Dom. Wilkes, can you read me?"

"Urgh … that hurt. I'm okay." He didn't sound it, but I let it slide.

A hand like an iron vise clamped around my ankle, grinding the bones together. Pain shot up my leg all the way to my groin and I had to chew back the scream that threatened to burst free from my throat.

The ghoul slid bonelessly out from under the SUV, hand still locked around my leg. Before it could stand, my Lahti silently roared, burying three slugs into its shoulder.

A horrible needle grin split its vile, warty face. "A waste of bullets, human. I thought you were good."

My own vicious grin gave it answer. "Wait for it." A half-heartbeat later, "PEANUTBUTTERFROG!"

Sounds weird, huh? Not quite 'I'll be back' or 'Go ahead, make my day!' but then again, Schwarzenegger and Eastwood weren't trying to activate tiny quarter carat diamonds imbedded deep in the shoulder of a rampaging undead.

When I had opened the door to the Armory and those lights came on, my eyes went straight to a specialty item that Alex had worked out for me a couple of years before and had become the rage among the field agents.

What the bloody little genius had done was to take small diamonds and imbed them into bullets, which, when entering a the enemy, tended to fragment into shrapnel that caused further damage to the body in which they had been forcibly implanted.

The diamonds were much harder than the lead surrounding them and they stayed whole when they hit soft, soft flesh. So imagine that those little gems had been charged with as much magical energy as they could hold. All you had to do then was say the word that activated the spell—a word that no one would stumble on by accident. Ergo: Peanutbutterfrog.

Boomx3.

If it had been a Hollywood movie, the ghoul's arm would have separated from its body in beautiful slo-mo, with little bits flying hither and yon in an orgy of special effects gore. What happened wasn't Hollywood, but it was close.

It spun away, a chattering rattle erupting from its throat, right into fire from Wilke's .44. Unfortunately, the Detective hit it only once in the chest, the explosive round leaving a softball sized hole that oozed odious black ichor. If he had hit the sucker with more than one, the fight would've been over right then and there. Instead, the monster blurred forward, the claws of its remaining hand slashing. More metal tore and Wilkes flew off to the side, .44 clattering to concrete.

My Lahti belched fire five more times, but the ghoul was ready, dodging as if it were performing some graceful undead ballet … the Damned *Swan Lake*. All five shots missed. It straightened from its last dodge to see a polystyrene egg case roll three feet from its toes.

I bellowed the command word written on the side of the egg. "SNOWDIRT!"

The egg case burst like a paper party popper. A Marquise cut sapphire the size of my pinky nail, glowing with a harsh blue radiance, spun madly into the air to a height of about three feet. Hair thin lines of azure light erupted from the facets, extending some six feet.

The gem spun faster, the radiant blue lines crisscrossing the ghoul hundreds of times in less than a second. This lasted for a brief moment before abruptly winking out and *tinking* to the floor of the garage.

I stared at the ghoul. It stared at me.

Then it toppled. And fragmented … an avalanche of ghoul spreading itself thin along the cement in thousands of pieces.

Cool beans.

That was Alex's version of a Bouncing Betty.

I vowed to get him a raise.

"Holy, moley ... that hurt." Wilkes groaned into his throat mic.

"You okay?" I asked.

"I just said that hurt ... of course I'm not all right." Two grunts and a few groans later, he staggered out from between a couple of pick-up trucks. A ginormous hole had been torn in his Faraday Jacket, exposing the shining armor underneath, which bore four parallel, jagged claw marks.

"Kal, you all right?" Alex sounded frantic.

"Scratch one ghoul, Alex. We're okay. Keep the cops off our backs ... There's been excitement."

"So I hear. Don't worry; they've got other things to worry about now."

"Good. By the way, the Bouncing Betty worked great. Out." With my ringing endorsement for his toy echoing in the ether, I picked up the sapphire. It still amazed me that such a small gemstone could be the focus of so much destruction. Thank god.

Then a really disgusting thought ran through my mind.

Wilkes said out loud, "What's wrong? You look like you stepped in something nasty."

"No, not *stepped* in." My gaze lingered on the ghoul tartare at my feet. Before I could lose my nerve, my hands plunged in.

"Oh, that's not right ..." Gagging noises from the Detective.

I did a bit of gagging myself. "Oh, and I thought they were smelly and disgusting on the outside." Slippery, glutinous fluid slimed my hands as my fingers thrust deep among the folds of waxy flesh, sending shivers of revulsion down my spine.

"What the hell, what the hell ...." Wilkes moaned over and over. Finally he couldn't take it anymore and puked so hard I thought his shoes would come up.

Found it. In my slime and gore covered hand, between thumb and forefinger, I held a two-carat diamond.

"You done puking?" I asked.

More barfing.

"Guess not. When you're done, let's get to the roof, Detective."

I went subvocal. "*Team, check in.*"

Sue's voice broke in hard. "*Can't talk, boss … fighting dead guys.*"

"Fair enough."

"*Boss, they need you,*" Dom sent. "*I can hardly get a bead on the ghoul they're fighting. Too fast!*"

"On it. Out." To Wilkes, "Come on, barf boy, we got to go." I grabbed his arm and pulled the puking wonder after me to the stairs.

FROM THE DEBRIEF OF AGENTS SUSAN H. FARRIS AND BRYAN T. MANUS BY SENIOR AGENT KALEVI HAKALA:

"*See anything?*" Even subvocal, Sue's voice was tight.

"*Negative. Just some Toyotas,*" Bryan sent back.

Her night-vision glasses rendered everything in shades of black and white, much better than what the military used, all green and gross. She smiled, feeling a familiar frisson. Three parts fear and one part anticipation in a chemical cocktail that had her blood fizzing. However, a little slice of her mind remained separate from the excitement, as if someone else looked through her eyes, enjoying the experience like a 3D movie. It disconcerted her slightly, but she paid it no heed … She had monsters to kill.

"*Boss,*" Dom sent. "*Got a bogey on the rooftop moving too fast for me to hit.*"

"Keep on it," Kal replied and, as usual, his voice held nothing but crystal cold competence. "Got the other one. Sue, Bryan, would you be so nice as to kill that ghoul for me?"

"*Check, boss,*" Bryan sent back. With a couple of shaky grins they headed toward the stairs to the roof.

"*Dom, where is it in relation to the stairs?*" Bryan's subvocal voice carried nothing of the fear that slicked his skin in a sheen of cold sweat.

"About sixty feet, crouched behind a BMW. I still can't get a bead on it, Bryan. But I got your back."

"Check. Out."

"You ready?" Bryan asked. A drop of sweat stung his eye. Angrily, he wiped at the moisture. Little butterflies tortured his stomach and bile tickled his throat.

Sue licked her lips, ignoring the chatter between Kal and the big guy with broad shoulders, Wilkes. "Yeah, I'm ready."

Nodding, the two burst onto the roof, pistols at the ready. Sue with two handguns (a snub nosed .38 and a 9mm Baretta) and Bryan with his .45 ACP and a Roman style short sword sharpened to a razors edge.

Dom sent, *"It's moved. Looks like it's ready to charge."*

Spider-like, the ghoul skittered under various cars, drawing nearer to the two agents, who crouched, trying to angle for a look under the vehicles.

"Eleven o'clock," Bryan said. Sue shifted her stance, aiming her weapons to where he indicated.

Skitter skitter.

"Damn, it's gone! How does a ghoul move so fast?" Bryan sounded panicky.

Sue wasted no time replying. "Gems imbedded in its flesh, like Kal's report said. Magical steroids."

"Look out!"

It was a credit to Dom's skill that he even managed to hit the ghoul as it launched off the hood of a Volvo at the two agents.

The bullet tore its way through the monster's ribcage under its left arm at 3,340 feet per second, tearing away bone and tissue as if it wasn't there, exiting the other side through the armpit in a shower of bilious black blood, bone and flesh.

It didn't even slow down, landing next to the agents amidst a hail of gunfire. Sue had time to shoot twice with the .38, the explosive rounds tearing out great gouts of foul flesh from the ghoul's midsection, while her Baretta silently chattered six rounds at its skull. Three missed, two impacted on the heavy bone plate of its brow and were deflected while one drilled through a black shark eye, spraying dark ichor down a slimy, warty cheek as the round hammered through its skull to no effect.

A slime-covered green arm arced around with blinding speed to pound against Sue's chest, crumpling a titanium armor plate and snapping ribs like rotten sticks. She flew through the air, limp and breathless, to land sprawling near the stairwell door.

While chunks of ghoul flew from the monster from Sue's explosive rounds, Bryan's .45 flared, two rounds pulping a kneecap, followed by a sword strike to the right arm of the beast, shearing it off at the elbow.

The arm that hurled Sue fifteen feet swept back around, razor nails neatly slicing through soft flesh, cartilage, and bone, almost severing Bryan face from his skull in a shower of blood and shattering his night-vision glasses. Knees buckling, he collapsed, hands to ruined face, blood streaming from between his trembling fingers.

Below, the sound of an explosion reached the combatants.

The ghoul *laughed.*

Despite the pain, the blood, the sound drilled into Bryan's consciousness, a sound so horrifying that he lost control of his bladder.

Another explosion from deep within the garage.

The ghoul lunged, arm flashing wickedly toward Bryan's crotch.

A round from a .338 Lapua took the ghoul in the other knee, pulverizing bone and knocking the monster off its feet, its keen-edged claw missing Bryan's crotch my millimeters. The agent feel backwards, legs kicking frantically as he tried to escape the gibbering ghoul.

Still grinning horribly, it crawled toward Bryan, claws eating into concrete, flaking up gray particles, a horrific smile frozen on its slimy face.

"One ghoul down. Team, check in."

Sue's .38 flared from where she lay, spitting bullets until the hammer went *click* and more rotten tissue ripped free from the crawling monster, including a lower jaw. Needle teeth sprayed everywhere, like shards of malignancy. *"Can't talk, boss … fighting dead guys,"* she sent. Lungs still agonizingly laboring for breath, she stood on trembling legs and started for the monster.

Leaving a trail of black slime, the ghoul flipped itself over with its one remaining arm and rolled quickly under a minivan and out of sight.

"Boss, they need you," Dom sent. *"I can hardly get a bead on the ghoul they're fighting. Too fast!"*

"On it. Out."

* * *

Despite the period of vomiting and the protesting of his gut muscles, the Detective managed to keep up with me as we raced up the stairs toward the roof. We were moving so fast it nearly got us killed.

Blue-black fluid splashed toward my boots when I placed them on the landing between floors three and four. It was Wilkes's quick reflexes that saved us. A hand grasped the collar of my jacket and hauled me back, my feet trying to head off without me. Fortunately, my reflexes weren't bad, either, and I grabbed the rail before my spine could find out how hard the stairs were.

"What the hell is that?" Wilkes exclaimed through my earwig, pointing at the puddle of malignant liquid that rippled unnaturally toward us, questing to and fro.

"Oh, lord," I replied. "Don't let it touch you, not even your clothes!" My feet beat a hasty retreat as I dragged Wilkes back with me down the stairs.

The liquid, thick, almost gelid dark mercury seemed to move with a purpose, as if it was alive. I knew, however, that wasn't the case.

"Dom, my ETA just flew out the door. We got zombies on the stairs."

"God, boss, you need help?"

"Negative, keep doing what you can for Bryan and Sue."

"Kal, this is Sue. I'm hurt and Bry is seriously messed up. We're good for now; the bogey is in hiding under a minivan, hurt badly. But we need to evac soon."

We continued to back down the stairs, the fluid following.

"On it. Out."

Crap. Two of my team down, if not out, and a raging puddle of ugly had me stepping and fetching. The familiar anger bubbled up, but I put a tight lid on it.

"Kal, mind telling me what that stuff is?" Wilkes sweated heavily, looking more afraid than when we fought the ghoul. Understandable … the ghoul he could shoot.

"We call it Zombie Puke. Think of it as liquid evil. Zombies spit it at their victims. If it touches you, it turns you into one of them. Zombies may be slow shamblers, but this stuff is what makes them so dangerous."

"You guys need a raise."

A chorus of 'hell yeah' and 'you got that right' answered that remark. Even Alex chimed in.

No time for that. *"Cut the chatter, folks. Out."*

My eyes never left the questing liquid and after three more steps it started to steam and fade from view. "Good," I said aloud. "The zombies are about twenty five feet away." At the Detective's questioning look, I explained. "Zombie Puke can't exist outside the host body for long, only a few minutes, and maximum range from the host is about twenty-five feet."

"That's just sick." He sounded as if he would upchuck again.

I had a thought. "Sue, if it's still under the minivan, toss your gem at it and get out of there."

"Boss, all I got is an acid bomb. It'll leave a hell of a mess." She sounded almost concerned. The acid bomb was inspired by the movie *Alien*, a gem that released the most toxic, corrosive acid ever imagined in a twenty-foot radius. Because of the potential for

damage, it was usually saved as a last resort.

I thought this qualified. *"Use it and get out. You're more important than private property. Out."*

To Wilkes, "Get ready, they're coming. This time aim for the head and make sure you're using explosive rounds."

"Check."

Just as a massive *crump* sounded from above, two decaying, shambling figures appeared above us on the landing, drooling and spitting blue-black malevolence. They looked like what they were, two swiftly rotting corpses with a seriously bad attitudes. Our handguns barked without sound and two heads exploded, spraying black gore across the stairwell walls. Done and done.

"Sitrep!" I barked.

"On our way," Sue sent. *"Scratch one bogey."*

Dom: *"Ready to go."*

"Get to the Vics and get to Alex for a heal, Wilkes and I have cleanup duty. Out."

"Let's go."

"What about the bodies?"

God, my head hurt so much I had trouble forming a coherent thought. "Just corpses now, I'll disappear them."

Wilkes frowned. "Don't know how to feel about that."

Smiling wearily through the pounding in my skull, I gave him a friendly pat. "Look at it this way … you're alive. Go down, I'll be with you shortly." The Detective got himself scarce and I waited for the other members of my team. Soon, a grunting Sue stumbled down the stairs, leading a wailing Bryan, bloodied hands holding the torn shreds of his face in place against his skull, crimson rivulets flowing down his throat.

"Jesus, Sue, let me give you a hand," I gasped in horror, moving to assist.

She shook her head. "Naw, boss. I got it. You handle the cleanup." A fey light glinted in her eyes that stopped me in my tracks. Did she blame me? I nodded and she headed down, gently maneuvering Bryan.

Pulling a silvery vial from my web belt, I peeled the wax seal with a thumbnail. There came the soft *hiss* of air entering the vial and I quickly unscrewed the stopper and set it carefully next to the zombie remains. *"One thousand one,"* I counted. *"One thousand two, one thousand three ..."* Four seconds later I was through the metal door to garage level 1. Safe.

Wilkes was standing next to the pile of ghoul cutlets. "Don't throw up again," I said.

"No promises, but there's nothing left in my stomach," Wilkes replied shakily. "I think I even hurked up future lunches."

"Pretty. I could've gone all year not hearing that." I reached into a pocket and removed another vial. "Back up," I told him and he nodded, biting his lip.

From underneath the door to the stairwell, a bright blue/white light flashed for an instant. Wilkes shot me a look and I just shook my head, too exhausted to explain what I knew of the Bureau's most dangerous spell.

I knelt down by the soggy mess of ghoul chops, wrinkling my nose at the fetid smell. I thanked my lucky stars that my stomach was still empty.

Something hissed and groaned from a few feet away.

Wilkes brought up his .44. "What's that?"

A ten-foot circular section roof that was the level 2-garage floor began to sweat little droplets that steamed and sizzled when they hit concrete. Groaning like a tortured beast, the roof began to sag and steam a malodorous gray vapor.

"Acid. Let's get going." Another vial came out of my web belt and I teased the wax seal off.

"What the hell kind of acid does that?" He sounded dubious.

"Our kind, the kind that can eat through ten feet of concrete," I replied, rising quickly. "Let's go and don't look back."

"But—"

"Trust me. This will take care of everything." I went subvocal:

"Alex, in a half hour, see if you can set off the alarms in every jewelry store and wholesaler in a five mile radius of this garage."

"Got it, Kal."

I opened the door to the Vic—the others were long gone—and belted myself in. Behind us, in the garage, there was another flash of blue/white light, then silence.

Chapter Eleven

The New Job

The man in the white polo shirt stretched tight across his massive chest held a large white card that read, 'K. Hakala' written in bold black marker. He stood above the crowd like an elephant among zebras. He was that big. And scary looking, with a nose that had been on the wrong side of fist more than once and skin roughened by years of being generally naughty.

"That's me," I told him, easing my duffel to the floor and extending a hand.

Brown eyes bored into mine for a brief moment and, from his sneer, found me wanting. "I guess so. Grab your kit and follow me." So I did, entering the bright September sunshine outside of Ronald Reagan Washington National Airport. Instantly the tingle of smog in my nose made it itch and my eyes watered enough that I nearly bumped into Gigantor as he pulled to a halt in front of a shiny black Crown Victoria that all but screamed 'Fed!'

He fished around in the pocket of his perfectly pressed chinos and pulled out the keys. "You drive," he said blandly as he tossed them over.

I protested. "This is my first time in DC." Somehow I felt that my tour of the Smithsonian would be postponed indefinitely.

"Then you better learn how to follow directions."

The retort that heated my tongue cooled off quickly as I came to the belated realization that Bigfoot here had probably gone through the exact same training at Coronado that I had just finished. Which made him a very dangerous giant. One that outweighed me by a good sixty pounds. I jumped into the front seat and pulled out into traffic.

Every big city has industrial parks and the DC area was no exception. Not too far from the airport lay the Springfield Industrial Park where I found myself pulling to a stop in front of a warehouse painted a dirty white. A glass door labeled 'McClennan Statistical Analysis' proved to be the only entrance besides four large loading bays closed tight.

"Is this it?" I asked, tossing the keys back to Tall, Dark, and Scary and hoisting my duffel.

"What?" he scoffed "You expecting something like the Hoover building?" If his disdain got any thicker it would've cemented me into place.

"It's a little Bond. You know, 'Universal Export'."

"That's MI-7's bailiwick, not ours."

It seems the Brits are not without a sense of humor.

Inside the door was a lobby decorated in hospital and prison chic, a mishmash of industrial beige, teal, and bilious yellow that made my eyeballs spin in their sockets like a cartoon character's. A pretty blonde with long frizzy hair and hooker-red lipstick manned a large brown desk set against the far wall.

"This the new Green Pea, Thomas?" the frizzy blonde inquired of my surly companion.

Thomas the Ugly Giant grunted.

Hands on desk, my aura was read, palm prints analyzed and electrochemical and heat signatures recorded. Wham bam, thank you ma'am. The frizzy blonde stared at me with eyes like frozen marbles, left hand under the desk and zero expression on her lovely face.

Once I passed muster, a hidden door (steel faced with drywall) opened and Thomas the Enormous led me into the building.

A hallway. A really long hallway painted pale apple, a kind of faded Golden Delicious that I thought of as Institutional Ugly. I hadn't been expecting a hike.

"Afraid of a walk?" The big man's tone challenged me.

The look of disdain I shot him failed to impress and we both set off on shanks mare. After a couple dozen yards we came to a door on the right, also pale apple, with the word 'Combat' stenciled in black at eye level. On the wall to the right of the knob was an 8 x 10 shiny black plate. Thomas ignored the door and kept walking.

Once again, after a couple dozen yards, came another identical door with black plate, this one labeled 'R&D.' More doors appeared at regular intervals, all the same, all with shiny plates: Medical, Dormitory, Records, and Admin. It was at this last door where the giant laid one big hairy paw on the shiny plate and turned the knob with the other.

Another lobby, much more tastefully decorated in warm brown tones and dark woods, certainly less punishing on the eyes. A mahogany desk wrapped around another hard-eyed Receptionist dominated the area.

"Thank you, Thomas," said the Receptionist, a thin woman with brown hair permed into a kinky halo and a high, thin voice. She had an aura of cheer lacking in the first Receptionist. "I'll take the Pea from here." Thomas turned around and left without a word, but not before tossing me a speculative look.

"Pea?" I asked the lady, trying on my best smile at full wattage.

She wasn't impressed. I must've been losing my touch. "Short for Green Pea. All questions will be explained soon. Have a seat, the Director will see you shortly." Her tone told me she was already bored with my presence.

I placed my rump on one of those chairs you expect to find in a dentist's office … cloth wrapped over steel, the kind that helped induce hemorrhoids. Magazines such as *People* and *Newsweek* overflowed kitchy little wooden racks, the kind you buy at Wal-Mart. All in all, the feeling was less than welcoming.

While at Coronado, I learned to catch winks whenever and wherever I could, and I developed the ability to nap with my eyes open. I decided to exercise that skill and drifted off into a pleasant nothingness where thinking was not only optional, but frowned upon.

"Mr. Hakala, the Director will see you now," the Receptionist's thin voice suddenly broke into my consciousness. I was on my feet instantly, duffel in hand, internal clock telling me that a half-hour had passed.

"Hrrm … where do I go, ma'am?" I beamed, trying another full-power grin. It bounced right off her sallow skin.

She pointed. "Down the end of the hall, go right. End of that hall, left, and it's the door at the end labeled 'Director.' " She spoke slowly, as to a six-year-old.

Once again I flashed my pearlies and trotted off. When I made it to the Director's door I had the near overwhelming urge to rap out 'Shave-and-a-haircut', but resisted the temptation manfully. Instead I settled for a polite tap-tap-tapping.

"Nevermore!" came a low smooth voice. I smiled as I entered, amused at the literary reference.

Wow.

And I mean … *wow.*

Big office…the kind of big you can park a semi in. Beautiful wool and silk carpeting done in dark blue and green, a long, dark wooden table surrounded by luxuriously appointed leather chairs so comfortable-looking that I grew drowsy just looking at them. And way down at the end, almost too far away to see, a huge oak desk that ought to have been donated to science fiction. It wouldn't have been out of place on the starship Enterprise.

"C'mon in, Mr. Hakala. Don't worry, it strikes everyone like that." The man striding toward me appeared to be Dad's age, with perfectly groomed, thick, brown hair graying at the temples. The way he moved told me he knew how to take care of himself and, as he drew nearer, I realized that he topped my six-three by at least a couple of inches. His suit, a Caraceni, draped him like a lover, accentuating his wide shoulders. Not an ounce of bureaucrat flab marred his waistline and close up I saw the fine scars on his cheeks and chin, long healed badges of honor. He had the coarse, weathered look of a man who spent a lot of time in the sun and wind. A roughhouse sailor playing corporate dress-up.

The hand he extended engulfed my own in a grip both powerful and controlled. I realized that I faced a suit who was also a trained killer. "It is a pleasure, Mr. Hakala, a real pleasure." He sounded like he meant it and his smile equaled mine, watt for watt.

"Thank you, Director."

"Come, let's get you squared. Drop your duffel there. You can pick it up later." That done, we headed off toward his desk and I wondered if I had the strength to make the trek.

He seated me in a soft leather chair that did its best to absorb me into its plush depths. Heroically, I kept my eyes open and somehow cudgeled my brain into order.

"So, Mr. Hakala. May I call you Kal? Or do you prefer Kalevi?" Surprisingly, he didn't butcher the Finnish.

"Kal is fine." I pronounced it 'Call.'

"Call?"

"Kal with a k."

His grin took ten years off. "I'm glad I don't have to speak Finnish. Might tear my throat to shreds."

"It's not so bad, Director. At least there's not any irregular verbs," I smiled. "Of course, there aren't any *regular* ones, either."

His smile at my weak joke was genuine. "Kal, then. Now is the time when all good men must make up their minds."

"Sir?"

"Your contract. Now is the time you have to decide on a two, three or four year term of service."

Ah. The answer sprung into mind easily. It wasn't like I had a girlfriend anymore. "Four years, sir."

His eyebrows shot up. "Four? That confident?"

"Committed, sir."

For a moment his warm hazel eyes became icier than a politician's heart, then the smile crinkles at the corners of his eyes came back. "Kal, you know we have a rather large dossier on you?"

"So Agent Merced told me, sir."

"You're in this for revenge, aren't you?"

Lying wasn't an option; neither was denying the rage that flooded my body. "Yes, sir," I affirmed thickly, swiftly caging the wrath that heated my veins.

The Director nodded. "Honesty. That's good. I applaud that. Many men and women join for many different reasons, but the motive that worries me most is revenge. It can cloud your judgment, put other agents at risk. *That* I won't tolerate. Ever."

In for a penny, in for a pound. "I'm not trying to take down all the Supernaturals in the World Under, sir." I bared my teeth in what wasn't a smile. "Just one."

A fat file was produced from a drawer hidden somewhere in that enormous high-tech desk with its built-in monitors and geegaws. "Everything I'd ever want to know about Kalevi Hakala." Flip, flip, flip. "The only man in over sixty years who saw a Class Five Supernatural."

"Class Five?" I heard the capitals. They were categorizing them? How very ... bureaucratic.

"Yes, Class Five. 'A being of Mythic or god-like proportions.'"

Funny, I certainly didn't think the beast was god-like at the time. My face must have betrayed my feelings.

"Believe me, Kal, we categorize them not because of some sense of order, but to bring them to a level we can understand. Too many of them are so alien from what we can comprehend that this is the only way we can deal, to be effective.

"Yet you stood five hundred feet from one of the most alien, most incomprehensible monsters in all creation and weren't driven completely crazy by the experience. Your parents, too, retained their sanity when 99 percent of humanity would have been reduced to gibbering idiots.

"Do you know how rare, how special that makes you? You and yours impressed the hell out of the Finnish agent and he tagged you right then and there as one to watch." Flip, flip, flip. The pages of my life laid out on white, multi-purpose paper. "Your test scores are impressively high and you handled SEAL training like you've done it before." He closed the file and speared me with a look. "All this scares the living daylights out of me."

"Sir?"

"You are either going to be the best agent this Bureau has ever seen, or you are going to sink spectacularly, sucking good agents down with you. I don't know which."

"I can hack it, sir." I had to. As the saying goes, failure was not an option.

"I'm caught in the crosshairs of a quandry, Kal. I'd half-hoped you'd wash out of Coronado, like over sixty percent of trainees do, but that didn't happen, so now I have to make a decision. Keep you, or let you go."

My voice roughened as panic tore at me. "I can't go back, sir. I gave up too much for this opportunity." Carol's smile flashed into my mind's eye before fading like a sob.

"I know, Kal. And that's part of what bothers me, the fact that you'd give up a woman like Carol Stuart. Why? Is it *just* revenge?"

The words came tumbling out before I could stop them. "But I have promises to keep. And miles to go before I sleep. And miles to go before I sleep." Even to me they sounded trite.

The Director's eyes did their best to travel to the back of his skull. "Robert Frost?"

"Yessir. I made a promise, Director. I have, no ... I *must* keep it." If he bounced me, I didn't know what I would do. The possibility threatened to undermine the gutrock of my reality.

"We are the hollow men, we are the stuffed men," he began.

"*Leaning together, headpiece filled with straw,*" I finished. T.S. Elliot had always been a personal favorite.

He snorted, a smile hitting his lips. "Very nice. Now if you can quote Whitman—"

"Oh Captain, My Captain! Our fearful trip is done—"

"Okay, okay ... as far as literature is concerned, you're well grounded." The Director stared at me, scarred face becoming blank.

The seconds stretched ... became a minute ... became two. A tickle of unease vibrated through me, but I tried to bury it under resolute will. However, something intervened, a force that fanned the unease, allowing it to become part of the rage that had awoken within me the past year, fueled me, aided me through my trials at Coronado and Parris Island. It grew, pulsing behind my eyes and I *let it*, reveling in heated exhilaration. I felt empowered and the blood roared in my veins.

The intervening force withdrew, gone like the memory of a warm breeze, and I put the rage away, contained it, almost fainting with release.

The whole thing lasted for a few brief moments as we stared at each other.

"Your rage is a big thing," the Director said softly, dropping his eyes to his desk.

"Huge," I confirmed.

"I didn't think you would be able to keep it under control, but you did. I'm impressed."

My heart beat hard in my chest. "You did that? You did something?"

Once again that small smile. "No. It's the chair. A small gem in the back holds the power and silver thread in the arm rests gives shape to the spell. It exposes the singular weakness in whoever sits in it, and sends the data to my desk. The words 'well rounded' activated the spell."

Getting angry again seemed counterproductive, so I nodded, the muscles at the corners of my jaw bunching and unbunching.

The smile he tossed me seemed genuine and had some warmth to it. "I wasn't sure if you'd jump me or just storm around the room. Good to see you can keep all that anger on a leash. Good for you. You're in."

I let out the breath I didn't know I was holding.

"Team Epsilon just lost a man to a pack of Hellhounds two months ago and needs a replacement. Their leader is a five-year man, my best. In fact, I'm looking to hang up my spurs in a year or two and he's the front-runner to replace me. If anyone can channel that rage of yours, it will be him."

"Thank you, sir."

A well-manicured finger touched a flat-screen keyboard and an ominous hum began in that massive desk. Only a few seconds passed before a section to his left tilted up and a small pile of paper was ejected. I wondered if there were Supernaturals in the damn thing doing all the dirty work. A desk like that must have cost more than my parents' house.

He handed me a pen and turned the stack around so I could read. My contract with the Bureau. "Standard stuff. Initial where it says initial and sign and date at the end. Most of it is a non-disclosure form, in case you get around the Interdiction, which no one has. Last page discloses your salary."

My eyes made the attempt at a Loony Tunes classic ... popping out on springs. I hadn't seen so many zeros in all my life. A two-year agent got paid better than an All-Star Lineman in the NFL. A three-year could easily retire after the contract date. My four-year pay plan would give Trump a heart attack. Then I reminded myself that there were as many belowground retirees as there were above. Scribble, scribble and done.

"Go back down the hall to the Dormitory. You've been approved to access all areas of the building except R&D; that's where the Magic happens. When you get there, tell Epsilon you're the FNG. They're the only team in-house right now."

I rose. "Thank you, sir. You won't be disappointed."

"I know." He paused. "Kal, you realize that if you find a way to kill that monster of yours, the Finnish government might not let you? It has cruised all over the planet, but most of the time it stays in the Baltic."

The thought had occurred to me. One thing at a time, though. "No worries. If I can find a way to kill it, then I can find a way to make the Finnish government say yes."

"All right. Welcome aboard, then." A dismissal.

I trekked toward the door that would let me escape the aircraft hanger the Director called an office and made my way to the Dormitory, slapping a hand on the black plate. I warmed up under my skin and the knob turned.

Inside, the dormitory was almost as big as the Director's office and separated into twenty smallish bedrooms along a long hall and one big living room with a flatscreen TV the size of an RV. Seven dark brown leather Lazy Boy recliners were arranged in an arc in front. Looked like a great way to watch the Vikings on a Monday night. Off to the right of the TV stood a fridge, all stainless steel, that would've made Wolfgang Puck weep with envy and beyond that, two foosball tables and an air hockey table. I caught a glimpse of thinning hair in the center-most recliner. The TV clicked off.

"You must be the FNG," came a smooth, urbane voice. I guess announcing myself was off the table.

"I must be," I replied, closing the door and dropping the duffel. "You must be part of team Epsilon."

"I am the team leader." A slim, balding man with short dark hair extricated himself from the recliner. Rushing forward, I extended a hand. Although smaller than me by at least six inches and fifty pounds, his grip matched mine ounce for ounce. I felt unusual calluses under my palm.

"Sir, good to meet you. I'm Kal Hakala."

"Sit down." Without waiting to see if I would, he took his own self back to his recently vacated seat.

That little antenna that warns me of danger just picked up a signal that put my whole body on alert as I eased into a recliner.

"Listen up, Green Pea, from now on, you are a waste of protoplasm ..."

So began The Speech. Well practiced, he must have delivered it a hundred times. Somewhere along in the middle of what I was sure was a heroic rant, my brain mercifully switched off and I faded from reality.

"You got me, Green Pea?" The question, delivered in a tone that could have cut glass, snapped me back to reality. My internal clock said at least ten minutes had passed. Not bad.

"Yessir." Safest response. Ever.

"Good." Watery little eyes drilled into mine. "Go to room six; that'll be yours. Rest for a while, you'll need it, Pea."

"Yes, sir. Thank you, sir."

As I made my way down the hall to room number six, his cultured voice floated along with me. "I'm not a 'sir'; I work for a living. You can call me BB."

Room 6: Twelve by ten. Nice blue cut-pile carpeting. An oak armoire for my gear and a bed. A beautiful, comfortable looking queen-sized bed. My shoes never made it off my feet before I flopped into its welcoming embrace. *Flights of angels* and all that stuff ….

"Wakey wakey, Green Pea." Somebody wanted to die.

My brain tried to remain in the 'off' position, but months of training had the volume up to 11 before I knew it and pushed me out of my self-induced coma.

"Gah!" I exploded.

"Aww … you musta got all of six hours sleep, Pea. It's time to get up and pay for your stay."

"I thought the Fed was paying my way," I grumbled, trying to burrow deeper into the mattress. I realized my mouth tasted like a goat's pen. Only worse.

"On your feet, Pea. It's chow time."

Sleep fled, chased off by my stomach. "We got a mess hall?"

"We got a kitchen and a well stocked pantry and fridge. We make our own grub here."

The thought of eating something other than camp chow and MREs appealed to me on a visceral level and levered me to my feet. Standing in the doorway was a wide, flat-faced Native American, complete with long black hair and a turquoise, squash-blossom necklace. Faded jeans, a coarse blue button-down shirt and cowboy boots completed the ensemble. A grin creased his leathery face, exposing even white teeth. There must have been a hundred of them.

"Name's Canton Alsate, Pea." He held out a broad, rough hand, which I took.

"Kal Hakala." I removed my hand before he could fuse the fingers together.

"Interesting name."

"Finnish."

"Harrumph. They grow them big up north, I see. And pale. You are the whitest white boy I've ever seen. Well, I'm your tour guide and combat trainer. Come with me." He turned and headed down the dorm's long hallway.

"I swear I just went through training." The words bounced off his back. I realized that sleeping in my clothes did nothing to enhance a clean, fresh scent. In fact, I smelled like a gym locker.

"You did, but you haven't gone through *my* training."

I mulled this over as I followed. Eventually the hall opened up into a large room—a kitchen big enough to feed my hometown. Canton approached a sizeable stainless steel vault door with a large mechanical latch. With a grunt, he wrestled it open to reveal a walk-in freezer blowing frosted air through a plastic strip curtain. Bravely, he plunged into its depths and soon emerged with two white paper-wrapped packages.

"How do you like your steak?" he asked.

My stomach rumbled. "Still moo-ing."

The packages flew at me and I fielded them like I still played for Nebraska.

"Good!" His smile nearly blinded me. "Make mine med-rare and don't screw it up."

I looked for a broiler and found it, turning on the gas. A combo of charcoal and mesquite was the best, but considering what I'd had to eat in the past 33 weeks, my stomach ached for steak, so I wasn't going to be picky. I laid the two-inch thick, beautifully marbled meat onto the grill and smiled rapturously at the sizzle. Soon the smell of beef char filled the air and set my salivary glands at 'waterfall.'

Steak done, Canton and I ate in silence, savoring the flavor. From the marbling and texture, I reckoned it was prime bone-out rib eye. The kind you'd expect to pay forty dollars for in a fancy-schmancy restaurant. Fresh-tasting apple juice chased the steak to my stomach.

"Not bad, white boy. You can sure cook." Canton let out a medium-sized belch.

My stomach strained against the fabric of my jeans. "One thing I know is how to treat a steak."

Canton wiped his mouth with a napkin, finished his apple juice and levered himself to his feet. "Tomorrow I see how good you are with a knife, what you learned at Coronado. Then comes orientation. As for now, you have to face Mace."

I groaned. "What's a mace?"

"Not a 'what,' pale face, but a 'he.' Mace is our team's unarmed combat champ. He wants to see what you're made of."

"Let me save him some time. I'm bone and meat, like everyone else."

"Funny guy. C'mon." He started toward the exit.

Crap. Facing some hand-to-hand expert and me with a solid wall of steak in my stomach. It was insane to fight with a full ... Waitaminute.

I may be slow, but I get there. I smelled rodent. "Canton!"

His voice was sardonic. "Just figured it out? You're faster than most."

Double crap.

I followed, wondering if there was a head on the way where I could barf and lighten the load.

Canton must have been psychic. "Don't even think about it, white boy."

Triple crap.

The long hallway again, tramping on down to the door that read: 'Combat.' Canton placed a hand on the black plate and opened the door.

Big room, wrestling mats on the floor here and there, the ceiling far above a maze of catwalks and structural supports. Along the walls stood racks of just about every non-projectile weapon known to man: swords, spears, halberds, etc. There was also an array of punching bags, wing chun wooden dummies, and even a boxing ring.

"You need to loosen up?" Canton asked quietly.

My stomach tried to tie itself into a knot, but the rib eye prevented that. "No."

"Well then, take your shoes and shirt off. The gang will be here shortly."

They were. And what he meant by 'gang' was everyone in the whole damn building.

Of course, to top it all off, the Director put in an appearance, in a pair of blue jeans so new they were almost black and a salmon-colored polo. Hard muscle writhed like oiled serpents under his tan, scarred skin. I guess he didn't want to get blood on his $4,000 suit.

"No offence, Kal, but this is what we live for. New recruits are always a source of excitement," the Director laughed as his perfect white teeth came close to blinding me.

I hid nervous jitters behind sarcasm. "Glad to be of service."

His smirk said he read me like a book, but he clapped me on the shoulder and joined the throng of about twenty spectators.

I raised my voice. "Canton, got a question for you."

The Native American sauntered over from where he was chatting up the frizzy-haired receptionist. "Whatcha need, white boy?"

"You said this Mace character is your best unarmed combat guy. What's his specialty? Muay Thai? What?"

"Krav Maga."

Well that just put another condiment on crap sandwich. Krav Maga translates from the Hebrew 'contact combat,' an Israeli martial art used by their Special Forces and commandos. The whole purpose behind it is to inflict the maximum damage in the minimum amount of time. SEAL training used it, along with Brazilian Jiu-Jitsu, and Muay Thai, but I was far from expert. The idea came to me that abject cowardice might be the better part of valor.

"By the way, who are those characters?" I whispered, waving to a posse of nerds. Men and women stereotypically complete with birth control glasses and pocket protectors in white lab coats. All of them had the kind of smile reserved for those who *really* enjoyed blood sport.

"That's the squad from R&D. Magicians and physicists, mostly."

"Cool. I get to be killed in front of the Geek Squad. My parents would be so proud." It was about then that things really became pear-shaped.

"There he is," Canton enthused, pointing a stubby finger at a figure in the doorway to the endless hall.

I squinted. Something seemed to be subtly wrong with the proportions until I realized that the doorway wasn't small, it was that the guy standing in it filled it up. All the way up.

Thomas. The man who picked me up from the airport. Gigantor.

That sucked big time.

Thomas walked straight to the boxing ring and vaulted the ropes with ease. Without touching them. If that demonstration was designed to intimidate me, it worked all too well. "Canton, tell me again why the hell I'm here."

"Easy peasy, white boy, to prove how tough you are. It's a rite of passage we all take."

"And why would you do something so incredibly stupid?" Maybe I could appeal to logic and scram with my tail between my legs. Better than having my head pounded down so far below my shoulder blades I'd be able to taste navel lint.

Logic wasn't going to help me here. "Because, white boy, we gotta see what kind of iron you got. Don't try to wuss out."

I didn't have the heart to tell him that my iron spine had rusted through the second I found out that I'd be fighting Thomas Mace. Instead of proclaiming my cowardice to one and all, I eked my way to the ring, steak-filled stomach plummeting lower and lower with each step. Thomas had taken off his shirt, showing massive amounts of scarred skin and great slabs of muscle. So much that I thought he might be part Silverback gorilla.

As I climbed through the ropes I had a desperate idea. If logic and sanity wouldn't work on this crowd, maybe pride would. That plus a whole heap of sarcasm.

"Thomas, good to see you again." I said with a wide smile, extending my hand. The big dope grinned sardonically and said nothing, not even bothering to shake.

"You're the team's unarmed combat champ, right?"

Nod. Obviously a man of few words.

"Quick question, then. I hear you specialize in Krav Maga, correct?"

A frown, but he nodded.

Hoping I lived to see tomorrow, I raised my voice. "What kind of wussy setup is this, then?"

Everyone got quiet. I fancied I could hear tumbleweeds rolling by.

"I said, what kind of wussy setup is this? You all speak English, right? Your mother tongue, I believe."

The big man rumbled. "You think this hasn't been tried before?"

Uh-oh. Plan B.

I leaned in close. "That right?"

His misshapen nose lowered to within an inch of mine. "Yeah."

Quick as I could, I grabbed his crotch and squeezed. Hard.

Thomas made a whooshing, whistling noise right before a fist the size of Iowa clocked me under the left eye. I dimly heard Roger Rabbit comment from deep within my subconscious, '*Look Raul ... Stars!*'

When I was able to open my eyes without it hurting, I saw Thomas bent over himself, clutching his happy place and grunting in agony. So far so good ... I wasn't dead yet. Getting to my feet proved far more difficult than I'd imagined, but I finally found myself upright. Score two points for the home team.

One thing any combat expert will tell you is never kick your opponent. It's giving the enemy your leg to use however they wish, and when that happens you might as well update your will. I knew it and Thomas knew it. Heck, even the gaggling herd of geeks knew it. So I kicked him.

The heel of my foot connected with his oft-battered nose, splaying it across that pug-ugly face. Blood geysered and the giant toppled with a crash that shook the ring. A shooting pain in my foot interrupted my triumphant yell.

Jumping up and down in anguish blinded me to the monster climbing to his feet, a snarl of hate on his damaged visage. Before I could react to the presence I felt at my back, a truck parked itself on my face.

Agony in my mouth, blood gushing down my throat, teeth buried deep in my tongue and an incredible *pressure* constricted my chest. He was on me, on my back with a knee buried in my spine, wrenching my arm back, twisting. Something tore sickeningly and a scream raked my throat with shards of bone.

A dark, hot thing woke inside me, rearing its rough head. The Director feared my rage, feared that it would consume me, make me a threat to those nearby. The truth was far worse than he could've possibly imagined. Instead of an emotion that would devour others, or me, it was the bestial part of myself that had only one mission: kill the enemy. No other outcome could or would be allowed.

As my shoulder dislocated, I rolled under Thomas's vast weight, ribs bending, a couple breaking, his knee tearing at the skin of my spine, flopping onto my back so I could stare into the giant's maddened eyes. What he saw there gave him pause.

That was enough for me. One, two, three swift hammer blows with the arm not in his grasp. Three impacts: one to cheek, one to crushed nose, one to the throat that rocked his head back.

Gagging, he dropped my arm, hands shielding his battered throat, giving me the opening I needed. Instantly my hand, my elbow, forearm, drove into the slabs of muscle at his side and washboard stomach. Before he could squirm away or strike back, I was on top of him, pounding away at anything I could hurt, rage fueling my blows.

His hands fell from his throat as his eyes rolled back in their sockets and I had my shot, a perfect strike to the larynx that would end the battle once and for all. Dimly I heard someone thunder my name from the group of appalled spectators, but I paid no mind. Only one objective remained: kill. From the far places of my mind, I knew satisfaction and willed myself to *stop*.

I stood, swaying, the rage emptied from the broken vessel of my body. A few dozen eyes gazed at me in wonder and not a little bit of terror. The Director stood in the forefront, hands on the ropes with Canton at his side, a wicked looking knife in his hand. A part of me knew I could kill him before he could throw it, despite the arm that hung useless at my side. Next to him stood BB, Glock in hand, not quite pointed at me. A much more effective weapon. I couldn't dodge bullets. Maybe someday.

"Well, Director … did I pass your test?" I slurred before passing out.

Chapter Twelve

DNA and Elephants

I woke up on a cot this time, not my desk. Much more comfortable and a lot less drool to worry about.

It came to me vaguely that the knocking that woke me still continued. Mouth full of cotton, I hollered for the sadist to enter.

Sue stuck her homely face in. "Kal?"

"Yah. What's left of me. What time is it?"

"A little after eight."

"Oh, for the love of Pete, tell me it's p.m."

"A.m." she responded, entering and closing the door.

"What's wrong, Sue?" My back gave out a series of sharp pops as I bent over. The spot between my shoulder blades screamed as the flesh stretched, bruised from where I'd been flung by the car bomb.

"You … you gotta talk to Bryan," she said woefully.

Alarm bells jangled. "What's wrong?"

"You gotta talk to Bryan," she repeated, shaking her head.

"How bad is it?" His face had been torn to ribbons, blood everywhere. Alex had grabbed the biggest, most power-filled gem he could lay his hands on for a healing, but there had been so much ripped and ragged flesh. The bones of his skull had been visible through the cage of his fingers.

She must have been taking mind-reading classes. "It's not his face."

I rubbed my eyes, in no mood for cryptic colleagues. "Okay, where is he?"

"In his office."

"Why isn't he asleep?"

"Says he can't."

"Go, then. I'll be along shortly." I knew it was urgent, but I needed a few moments to reboot my brain. When she got gone, I stood and stretched, trying to work the kinks out and coax some oil into the rusted bits. No matter how much I cudgeled my mind, it refused to get into any gear besides neutral.

Out of the corner of my eye I saw my Faraday Coat folded neatly on my desk. Puzzling because, if memory served, I'd only checked in the offensive items back in the Armory, preferring to keep the defensive ones out in case of emergency, and I was pretty sure that I'd dropped the darn thing on the floor, too tired to care about being neat.

Curious, I picked the coat up, holding it out and turning it this way and that. Perfect. Not a smudge, not a tear. When we had arrived back from LoDo … it had been trashed, torn up one side and down the other. This … this coat showed no signs of wear and tear.

I crouched down to look at the Winnebago under the desk, happy my little Brownies were still with me. "Thanks, guys," I whispered gratefully. "I didn't know you were capable of such things." My temper tantrum yesterday might have scared them a little, but they had stuck around, showing more loyalty than I deserved. At that moment things became just a little brighter in my universe. From the Winnebago came the theme from *Hawaii 5-O*, by the Ventures.

I needed coffee. Lots and lots of coffee. The thought made my mouth water and even fired an extra synapse or two. In the lounge, I caught Dom putting paid to what looked like his bodyweight in donuts.

"Really?" I asked, incredulous. He must have been thirty percent sugar.

"We're cops," he mumbled around a mouthful of bear claw. "Ultra-secret bad-ass super cops, but cops nonetheless. Might as well act like it."

"You are one bona-fide one hundred percent disgusting human being, Dom. I mean that."

His smile literally dripped with sweetness. "That's why you love me."

Hot, aromatic Kona coffee went into my personal Kliban Cat mug. My knees almost buckled in olfactory delight. "I love you because you are the best sniper I've ever seen and you love to kill Supernaturals."

"Aww … you flatterer."

A long slow sip. The scalding liquid flowed over my taste buds and trickled down my throat. I imagined I could feel the caffeine enter my bloodstream. Sitting down, I snagged a donut from the pile and took a bite. "God, that's gross."

"Tastes great, huh?"

"Yeah." Another sip to wash the sugary pastry down. "Who's got Comms?"

"I do. Alex was too wiped after healing Bryan, Sue and the Detective. Gonna be out for a while, I think. Matt's shagged out, too."

"Let Alex sleep, then. He deserves it. Any chatter yet?"

Dom took down a long john in one bite. "Just the FBI scrambling like roaches." He took a sip of his own coffee. "They have officially taken over the case. Their Director wants all the data we have on the Organ Donor. Was waiting for your okay."

"Send it to him, but with a note telling him that if his people do manage to corner this bastard, they should call us. We have to take her … him … *whatever* down. They're not equipped to handle a Renfield, much less a magician."

"This ain't gonna thrill him none."

"I don't care. Make sure you keep BB in the loop. Maybe his weight will cool the FBI's jets." I took another bite. The sugar rush mixed with the caffeine was beginning to jump start my system; however, I felt the telltale beginnings of another headache. "Dom, did that feel like a trap to you? Those ghouls?"

He thought a moment before replying. "Kinda yes, kinda no. If someone wanted to trap us they would've used more ghouls, although they were faster and stronger than any others I've heard about. And forget about the zombies; they're no real threat except to the Straights."

"That's what I thought. This morning wasn't a trap. Someone was testing us. I'll bet you my college jersey that we were being watched."

"Why?"

"I don't know. Maybe to see who we were, to get our identities."

"Man, that hurts to think about."

I stared into his soft brown eyes. "Dom, there's someone out there who killed Jeff, tried to kill me and now has drawn us to a spot where they could observe us. This has *never* happened before, not to any team I've heard of. You?"

He shook his head. "Never. Usually we roll into town, kick the bad guy's butt, then roll out. Business as usual. This … this is …"

"Premeditated?"

Dom's eyes grew wide. "Yeah …"

The words didn't want to come, but I had to let them out. "We're being hunted. Dom, get a message to BB, I want another team here ASAP. An extra magician would be nice, too."

"Two teams? There's never been a need before."

"Bureau teams have never been hunted before. We're in a whole new territory here, Dom. Get it done." Damn, but my head ached. Lack of sleep maybe, but it was becoming harder and harder to think.

Leaving Dom to his donuts and duties, I made my way toward Bryan's office, curious, worn-out, and truly afraid for the first time in years. Something, *someone*, had us in the crosshairs and I had no clue why. I was used to fighting lethal Supernaturals, but none that had this kind of … deliberation.

Coffee in hand, I reached Bryan's door and knocked.

"Come in," came the listless response.

I did and was greeted by the sight of Bryan, elbows on his desk, head in his hands. I took a seat and a sip.

"What's going on, Bry?" I asked casually.

"Did Sue send you?" he asked in a voice roughened with misery.

I saw no reason to deny it. "Yeah."

"Thought she would've waited longer."

"She's worried about you, you idiot."

"I know, I know," he moaned through his fingers. "Didn't want to talk to you about what's been eating me until this op was over. Should've kept my mouth shut."

My curiosity bump itched furiously and it needed to be scratched. "Talk to me about what?" I said softly.

From the safety of his palms, he mumbled, "I seen the Elephant, Kal."

Little micey feet scurried up and down my arms, raising gooseflesh. "Aww, Bryan …" I began.

"No, it's true, Kal. I done seen the Elephant. Seen it long time ago, but I've been trying to gut through it for the past few months." His sounded whipped, beaten.

'Seeing the Elephant' dated back to the California gold rush era, around 1849. It once symbolized the Great Adventure, the wonder and glory of trekking across the country to reach California in hopes of finding gold. In the Bureau, however, 'seeing the elephant' meant you were done. You'd found your mortality, your fear. 'Seeing the elephant' was a sure-fire way to earn a one-way ticket out of a job. An agent who saw the elephant was not only a danger to himself, but to his fellow agents.

I licked suddenly dry lips. "Bryan, you've almost reached three years. You faced down and beat a Mara in Texas. Since you've been on this team, your performance has been exemplary. What changed?"

"The Mara was just the beginning, boss, but I shoulda had that ghoul. It got to me because my fear made me slow." He raised his head, showing me his face.

In ten years I'd seen a lot of things. Firbolgs, Paasselkä devils, Duergar, giant spiders and even a Banshee or two—all of them ugly, all could curdle your blood, but nothing prepared me for the sight of Bryan's mangled features.

Five long scars ran raggedly in a diagonal from temple to the corner of his jaw, covering the length and breadth of his face. Instead of a nose, he had a weeping raw pit, and a once-generous set of lips was now a tattered ruin like shredded cloth. Each scar was about a centimeter wide, leaving very little territory unscathed. Donut and coffee tried to make a re-appearance.

"Look at me, Kal," he moaned brokenly. "I'm a mess. Alex said the ghouls did something to me, something that interfered with his healing. He couldn't regenerate the lost tissue, only heal what was there and only by a fraction of what he should've been able to do." Tears flowed from his perfect, untouched green eyes. "After fighting monsters all this time, now I've become one."

"Listen," I retorted. "I've worked with a lot of agents in the past ten years and I can honestly say you're one of the best. Ain't no one I'd rather have on my six, you got me? You're still an agent, one of the good guys, no matter what you look like."

"But I can't go on like this, Kal," he cried. "It ain't my face … I'm just too afraid."

Thoughts tumbled like dice in my skull and came up craps. "You are going back to DC; there you will head to Medical where they can patch you up. Alex is good, but healing isn't his forte. We'll get you to the right people who can make you good as new." I prayed that I spoke the truth. I had no clue if magic could fix his face.

Bryan looked bleak, but he nodded anyway. I could tell that whatever might happen in the future, fixed face or not, here before me sat a broken man. I holstered my rage before it could burgeon, the emotion useless to me at that moment.

"I'll make the arrangements. You get ready to leave. Check?"

"Check, boss."

"And I'll talk to BB about a Special Branch position if that's what you want."

He nodded without enthusiasm. "Thanks, Kal."

At Comms, I told Dom to have a plane ready to transport Bryan back to DC before noon. He tossed off a nod and got to work.

After Comms, I hit the gym. Off of the lounge, it consisted of a Nautilus and a treadmill with a unisex shower the size of a small closet. It was there that I unleashed the beast within, utilizing its power for a workout, hammering the weights until my muscles burned with fatigue.

It might've been an hour, maybe longer, before Dom summoned me to Comms, slick with sweat and smelling like the inside of a sneaker.

"What's going on?" I asked, wiping myself off with a towel. Dom's face scrunched up as he typed furiously at the keyboard. Wilkes, Matt and Sue stared at what looked to be a police report made large on one wall monitor. "Where's Bryan? He take off?"

"He should be in the air about now, on his way to DC," Sue stated, relief thick as tar in her voice. "But look at this report.'

"Go ahead and give me the *Reader's Digest* version."

Wilkes cut in. "This is a police report on a robbery earlier this morning, shortly after the Organ Donor called in." He smiled predatorily. "Turns out one of the silent alarms Alex set off was to a place called Frost, a ritzy diamond store near LoDo. Police surprised someone exiting the building. Somebody opened fire with what looks to be a .45, hitting one officer in the knee. The other officer got of a couple of rounds before falling to the ground, paralyzed."

"Please, oh *please*, tell me they killed the perp." I had my fingers crossed.

Sue shook her head. "No, but a daylight search revealed blood on a sidewalk leading to an alley, where the trail disappeared."

"And let me guess, in a couple of hours the paralyzed officer suddenly found himself mobile again." Most paralysis spell effects were short term.

"Got it in one, Kal."

"Matt, I want that blood. Get me a sample. We can have the DNA sequenced faster than any conventional lab. I don't care what you have to do to get it, just get it."

"Check, boss." He made himself scarce.

"How fast can you get that DNA analyzed?" Wilkes inquired.

Dom took that one. "Alex will probably have it done in forty-five minutes."

The look of incredulity on the Detective's face was priceless. "Jesus, that's unbelievable."

I snorted. "We just fought zombies and ghouls and you find *this* unbelievable?"

"Good point," he conceded.

"Alex is fast," Dom put in. "But the thing that's going to take time are the databases. Could take a while to get a match."

I smiled. "Got it covered."

Three hours later, Alex emerged from what we laughingly referred to as our lab. Insanely advanced by normal standards, woefully inadequate by the Bureau's. Despite the hours of sleep, he still looked like five miles of bad road as he staggered into my office, a cup of steaming coffee in hand.

"Okay, Kal ... now it's up to the computer," he commented softly.

"You're tired, kid. You're missing the obvious." I held my phone up.

Face contracted in puzzlement, he shook his head. "Still not getting it, Kal."

I dialed his cell. When it began to ring, I told him not to answer and said into the phone, "Ghost, you there? We need you on something important."

Alex muttered in disbelief, "I must be clean out of my mind to forget him."

"You've had a long couple of days, Alex," came the buzz from the cell. "Who can blame you?"

I smiled. "Hi, Ghost."

"Hello, Kal. I see you are still alive."

"Thanks loads, Ghost. I have a favor to ask. Alex is doing a DNA search … can you speed the process up?"

"I am already on it. I will have an answer in a few minutes."

"Thanks, Ghost."

"You're welcome, Kal."

Cell back in its holster, I flashed Alex a smile and leaned back in my chair.

He sat down. "You deserve that smug smile plastered on your face, Kal."

"Yes," I drawled, rolling the syllables around in my mouth like candy. "I do." Slowly, the conceit leeched away as I remembered an earlier conversation. "Alex, what interfered with Bryan's healing? A spell? What?"

"I'm not sure." Worry etched into his face. "I'm not a healer by trade—my specialty is energy storage and the development of combat spells—but putting Bryan to rights felt like walking through tar. Someone or something put that tar in my way so I couldn't heal him efficiently."

"Do you think it was something in the ghoul's claws? A poison or something?

"No … didn't feel like poison. Felt like a spell."

I felt sick. "An anti-healing spell … cast by a ghoul?"

Alex shook his head. "Ghouls *are* magic; they don't do magic."

A sudden thought hit me with the force of a gut punch. "Whoever is raising these things … could they use the gems implanted in the ghouls to cast spells? The one that attacked me had three gems in it. One I shot with my Lahti, one I destroyed when I pinned its hand to the table. The last you have. Could one of those gems have held an anti-healing spell?"

Sweat started to bead on the young magician's face. "I don't know. I haven't heard of anyone giving a ghoul the ability to cast a spell. That's just foul … really foul."

"We're dealing with a psychopath that drains his or her victims dry, presumably for a vampire, then scoops their insides out to give to the police—all while robbing jewelry merchants. This case has been foul from day one."

Buzzzzz-ing from my cell, so I freed it from its holster. "Yeah, Ghost?"

"Sorry, Kal, but this DNA does not match any criminal in any database."

Disappointment tasted bitter. "Thanks, Ghost."

Alex piped up. "Hey, Ghost, can you access the systems of our sister organizations overseas?"

"They have heavy encryption, but nothing I cannot hack."

That put some chills in my gut.

"Can you check their databases for magicians who have specialized in raising the dead and spells that interfere with healing?" asked Alex. I saw the light bulb go on over his head. "Also, check for magicians who are, or were, experimenting with physical enhancement spells."

"On it." *Bzzzzz* and gone.

My head hit the desk, several times. It was so obvious; I couldn't see the forest because the trees were in the way. I should've considered that avenue of thought earlier. Instead of alarming the kid further by putting my skull through the desk, I asked, "Alex, if the ghoul who attacked me had the same ability, how come you were able to heal me?"

"The cuts on your chest were very shallow. It sliced your clothes more than it did you. And you'd already destroyed two of the rubies. One of those might have held the spell that would have prevented healing."

"One for super-steroids, one for anti-healing … what would the third one have been for?" I needed more coffee to still my aching head, so I signaled Alex to follow me to the lounge.

"I don't know, Kal," he mused. "It tagged you but good. However, nothing bad has happened to you since."

Fear stabbed into my chest hard enough to constrict my lungs. "What did you say?" Thoughts of coffee fled, screaming.

"I said he tagged you but good."

Oh crap. Of course! Maybe I was suffering from early onset Alzheimer's. I'd dropped the ball so many times now that I should've been benched. "God, Alex. *Tagged*. The damn thing could've tagged me!"

He did a credible gaping fish routine before grabbing my shoulders and spinning me around to face him. "Hold on," he snapped, placing his hands on my skull.

Warmth flooded my head as his eyes captured mine, drawing me in and down, down, where I couldn't move and wouldn't if I could. I trusted this young man; he'd saved my life once already. Hell, I trusted all my team members implicitly.

"What the—" he gasped, shocked. Grinding his teeth, he gripped my skull much harder. "Hold on, boss," grated, sweat starting on his upper lip. "Hold on."

I held. One second, two, then three before the pain came. A low hiss in my mind followed by a wire of agony. It built and built, overloading nerves with its searing virulence, but I didn't care because I had something that was stronger than the pain, stronger than any magic I've ever faced.

I had the rage.

Slowly, I opened the box in my mind, freed the little strand of fury and used it to fight the pain that threatened to buckle my knees.

Alex groaned, "God, Kal ... oh god, Kal."

A little more oozed out of the box and I let it. Something spidery, something knotted out of hundreds of black threads resolved itself in my mind, attacking the fury I had unleashed, but it was too strong and, one by one, the threads began to snap. Slowly, inexorably, the agony began to recede and a small smile of victory twisted my lips like a rictus. I was winning. Then I sensed something else, like a sword or bar of emerald light that also attacked the spidery thread-thing, surgically burning each strand into curling nothingness.

Gone. The pain … suddenly and completely gone because in its place was magic, magic pouring into me like a flood, quenching the need for the heat of my rage.

The floor slammed into my knees, sending a spike of pain right to my hips, but I didn't care. All I knew was that I knelt on the floor, the pain and rage snuffed out. "What happened?" I breathed torturously.

Alex wasn't on his knees; he was on his side, curled up into a ball of misery. "Oh lord … that was rank … so rank."

I pulled him into my arms, alarmed. "What, what's wrong?" No response. "Alex!" I shouted.

Wilkes ran in, alerted by my cry, and his knees joined mine on the linoleum. "What the hell happened?"

"I wish I knew. He was doing some mojo and it knocked him sideways."

"Jesus, what kind of magic was he doing?"

"I was removing a spell, a nasty one, too," Alex whispered brokenly. Weakly shrugging us off, he managed to plant his legs under him, swaying slightly as he stood. "You won't believe what I found."

"Believe me, kid. I'm keen to find out."

Wilkes added, "Me, too."

"You were right, Kal, you had a spell cast on you. The spell was wrapped around your brain like a spider web. Deep, too. That pain you felt was me cutting the threads, so to speak." He took a deep breath. "There was an evil, evil thing your head."

"I'm surprised there was *anything* in there," Wilkes joked. I shot him a malicious look, which he found less than impressive.

"That thing, those threads … possibly one of the most elegant and horrible spells I've ever encountered," Alex continued shakily. "A spell designed to degrade you mentally. By the look of it, you would have been a drooling idiot by sometime next week."

"And that would have been different how?" the Detective sniffed.

That was two I owed him. Fortunately, thanks to Alex, I had the wherewithal for a serious case of revenge. Leaning in, I whispered into the young magician's ear, "Thanks, kid, I owe you one." He nodded, exhausted.

Before I could move, his hand clamped onto my bicep. "Wait, boss … I have to ask, what was that thing in there fighting the spell with me? Was it you? I've … I've … never felt anything like it. So angry, so hot and focused on destruction."

Gently, I disengaged. "Comms, now, everyone. We may have a problem." Alex had my trust, but the rage is something I shared with no one and at that moment, I had other things to think about. Hopefully, I was wrong about what rolled through my now-freed mind. If I was right … things could get very interesting. And not in a good way.

With everyone assembled promptly, I had Alex check everyone for spells. Nada. Relief flooded me for just a nanosecond before the other shoe dropped right onto my noggin.

Bryan … he wasn't there to be checked. Instead, he would be in DC soon.

Oh crap.

Bzzzzzz ….The invisible member of our team checked in. "Kal, there's some news."

"Don't keep me waiting, Ghost."

"England, 1994. A magician named Margaret Whitcombe of MI-7 attempted to create performance enhancement spells for their agents."

"Did it work?" Dom asked.

"All too well. The agents who volunteered for the program experienced greater speed and strength, but suffered for their gain."

"Let me guess—stress fractures, torn muscles, and such, right?"

"Yes, Kal, exactly, some of the damage proved to be quite severe and required extensive healing. The program was scrapped. Whitcombe continued her work in research before she drowned in a boating accident off the shore of Ipswich in 1995. No body was recovered and no one has taken up the reins of her research."

The spell web must have affected my brain more than I thought because now my mind was moving at warp speed. "Ghost, check to see if they have her research on performance enhancements."

"Checking … Sorry, Kal. There is no trace of her research in their database. The only reference to it is in her personnel file."

"Toss her pic on the wall, if you would."

The screen flickered for a moment before a photograph of a woman of indeterminate age appeared. Curly, kinky red hair, green eyes, pretty in a severe sort of way. I felt my testicles try to escape into my body. "Well, this ain't good," I muttered.

Everyone stared, but I said nothing just yet. I was too busy connecting the dots and forming a picture that looked like Armageddon on a stick. "Ghost, run that DNA sequence through the BIS mainframe, if you please."

From the widening of his eyes, Dom figured it out. A few seconds later the rest did too. By the pricking of my thumbs …

Our answer didn't take long in arriving. On the screen there flickered another picture of a slightly older Margaret Whitcombe with hair buzzed short to her skull. She looked somewhat different … harsher, more careworn, but it was her. Only, I knew her as Winifred Keener, a former agent with the BSI.

Something wicked this way comes …

Yeah, things had gotten interesting all right.

Chapter Thirteen

Ten Years Earlier
Vampires Suck

"How did you know?"

BB sat at the foot of my bed, staring intently. He did staring very well. Had I known him better, I might have been intimidated. As it was, after a healing and a good night's rest, I felt too good, too comfortable in my bed, to care.

BB had come to personally check on me. After the fight, I reckoned what was left of me looked like what the chimps at the zoo throw at each other. Torn muscles, dislocated shoulder, and a broken foot would normally have laid me out for a few weeks. Thank god for magic.

"Say what, boss?" I asked, feigning ignorance.

BB was having none of it. "You heard me. How did you know it was another test?"

I tossed off a smug little smirk. "Nobody was betting. When people get together for something like a fight, someone always takes bets. Everyone was more interested to see what would happen than to place a bet. From that, I smelled a rodent. All that talk of it being something the Green Peas had to go through was just that … talk. A smokescreen to hide the Director's agenda."

He snorted in amusement and stood. "Not too bad for a Cornhusker. Good job, Green Pea. He had to be sure, you understand. We depend on each other."

"Got it. No problem, boss." The thing was, I understood perfectly the need for certainty, to know that the person on your six was not only capable, but willing to risk all to protect you, just as you would them. Stretching and groaning, I levered myself out of bed, stretching this way and that. Joints popped and muscles protested, but I felt *good*. Hungry, though. Pawing through my duffel, I took out some clean boxers, a pair of chinos, and a faded denim shirt.

"Come on, Pea, let's meet the rest of the team," BB announced once I was presentable.

Sometime overnight another team came in from the field and made themselves cozy in the kitchen, plowing through enough food to satisfy a battalion. Canton and the rest of Epsilon were putting paid to sausages, eggs, flapjacks and what looked like fresh squeezed OJ. My mouth instantly started to water.

"Hey, white boy," Canton shouted, jumping to his feet and pummeling me on the back hard enough to bruise bone. "I ain't never seen anyone take Mace down before. You got some Apache in you, I bet."

"Nah, just a whole lot of stubborn ass Finn," I replied.

BB chimed in, "You obviously know Canton. He's our blade man. He'll train you in hand-held weapons and help you find what suits you. You know Thomas." The big man nodded from where he was murdering some biscuits and gravy, nose showing none of the damage I'd inflicted. "That one over there is Will, our sniper." A lean, medium-sized man with spiky blond hair and blue eyes tossed me a lopsided smile, showing a wealth of dimples. "And here is our resident magician, Winnie."

Winnie turned out to be a lean, tallish lady with very short red hair and enough freckles to be continued on the next person. She had a narrow, almost gaunt face with high cheekbones and lively green eyes that sparkled in an otherwise severe face. "Howdy, Green Pea," she drawled, a west Texas dialect warming her words. "Good fight. You got a powerful way about you, boy." She took my hand, shaking it with a firm, calloused grip. "If you get a moment, I'd like to hear about that Class Five you saw in Finland."

All conversation in the room halted abruptly as twenty-two eyes stared at me expectantly.

"Winnie, how did you hear that?" BB asked without a hint of emotion.

"Well, shoot, BB, it's all in his jacket. I always look up the file on new team members."

"Be that as it may, let the Green Pea eat. He must be starving."

Free from the need to talk, I helped myself to OJ and began to hunt for some cereal. In the cupboard to the right of the fridge I found a box of Lucky Charms. I was in heaven; somebody up there must have been looking out for me.

Two bowls later, I cocked an eyebrow at BB. "So it was a test. I trust I passed."

BB smiled slightly. "Of course. If you had failed, we would have put you somewhere else. Outside the Bureau, that is. Can't let all that valuable training go to waste."

"So, no more testing?"

That was met with a dry chuckle. "Everything is a test, Green Pea. All the time. It's part of the Bureau experience."

I could live with that, as long as I got to kill the Bad Things and move closer to my goal, which was to kill the Biggest Bad Thing. "What's with the other team?" I inquired.

"That is Team Theta. They just returned from a month in the Appalachians taking care of some Garmrs and a local witch who was causing a bit of a stir."

My eyebrows did their best to join my hairline. "A witch? Garmr?"

"What we call an untrained magician who uses magic to raise the dead, cast curses and the like. A Garmr is a giant, ravenous hound. You can understand why they need to be stopped. With extreme prejudice."

"How many teams are there?"

"Ten, Alpha through Kappa. There are always five teams deployed somewhere, spread around the largest cities. Right now the World Under is a bit quiet, so we should see some more teams coming in soon." He leaned in, eyes grave. "Understand this, Pea:

you won't be working with the same people for long. A lot of agents only take a two-year stint. It's the most dangerous job in the world. Sometimes a team is torn apart by Supernaturals and the survivors absorbed into other teams. The point is, don't become too emotionally attached to your teammates."

Easy to say, hard as hell to do.

I learned that the big warehouse was home for both BIS Agents and Special Branch. It was huge, comfortable and had all the amenities, but for me it would never be home, only a place I stayed when not deployed. Some people could easily deal with it, comfortable in their skins, not caring where they lay their heads. Me, well … it would take a while before the tug of longing for Minnesota and my parents became a weak ache I could easily cope with.

Soon more teams rotated in: Alpha, Kappa, and Zeta. Theta was deployed overseas to England to cross-train with MI-7. It was not uncommon for our teams to meet and train with their Bureau equivalents. I was told that the following year my team, Epsilon, would go to Israel. Apparently the Mossad also took care of Supernaturals.

During my stay in DC, I was allowed one phone call to Mom and Dad. Under supervision, of course. Mom told me how proud she was and Dad asked where he could send a care package. I gave him the address of Camp Lejeune, knowing that the package would be re-routed.

The next fifteen days became a lesson in pain and humiliation as Canton whipped me up one side and down the other in close quarters weapons combat. If you can name a weapon that lets you near enough to an opponent to see the life drain from their eyes, I've probably swung it. From war hammers to short swords, to hand axes and cestus, I learned the basics of how to deal death, nice and personal like. On the thirteenth day, Canton announced that I seemed to have proficiency with shorter, bladed weapons. Didn't matter to me, as long as I got to kill something.

After weapons training BB taught me about many of the more common kinds of Supernaturals. The most prevalent were the undead. Zombies, ghouls, ghosts, wights, skeletons, banshees, etcetera, etcetera *ad nauseum*. The dangerous ones were created, or summoned, while the harmless haunts usually couldn't find the path to what lay beyond this Earth, what the magicians called the Infinite. Having seen what I'd seen, experienced the most heinous truths that this world has to offer, belief in the afterlife was no great stretch.

I just lacked faith.

Sixteen days later, Epsilon received its next assignment. A vampire hunt.

"For you, with the exception of Mr. Mace and myself, this will be your first time facing vampires," BB intoned solemnly. The meeting room in Records had a corporate boardroom feel, all earth tones with the smell of Pledge and leather hanging thick in the air. We sat in slightly uncomfortable leather chairs (to help keep us awake, no doubt) at a table that could have comfortably seated a football team, while our fearless leader paced back and forth in front of an 8x10 wall screen.

"So," he continued in his funereal voice. "Let us do some background, shall we?" The screen lit up with a top-down autopsy photo of what looked to be a very tall, very slender albino man with stringy, long white hair. His torso had been surgically opened, exposing some very interesting and disturbing as hell skeletal and muscular details.

Will made a face, his surfer's features warped in disgust. "That's just gross, boss."

Winnie leaned toward the screen, eyes glistening avidly. "You say *gross*, I say fascinating. Look at those bones, they look like they're densely honeycombed."

"That they are," affirmed BB. "This honeycomb structure gives them great stiffness relative to weight. And look at the muscles, notice anything?"

"They're … striated somehow …" she murmured.

"The muscles are more like carbon fiber than human muscle tissue. The same goes for the tendons. Combine this muscle with that bone and you have one seriously strong Supernatural. Add to this an ability to regenerate quickly, even severed limbs.

"Vampires are severely allergic to sunlight, but you can forget garlic, crosses, holy water, silver and the bible. No effect whatsoever. The only physical banes that correlate to the legends are blackthorn and rosewood, to which they are also highly allergic. Thus no rapid regeneration from wounds inflicted by those substances. It seems that their flesh becomes more plastic when encountering those kinds of wood, so if you can pound a stake made of blackthorn or rosewood through a vampire's heart, it dies."

I raised my hand. "What about other abilities, like flying and mesmerism?"

"All folklore and fairytale, except for one. The most powerful vampires, the eldest, the leader of a nest, can disincorporealize."

"Uh, boss, you seriously lost me." Canton looked as puzzled as I felt.

BB gave the Native American a rare smile. "They can phase out of our current reality."

"Huh?"

"They can become ethereal, Mr. Alsate."

"Double huh?"

In my best stage voice I whispered, "They can turn into mist."

Canton frowned. "Why didn't he say that?"

"Him use heap big white man words only him understands," I intoned, deadpan.

"Oh, cool."

BB threw us a good glare. "You two done?"

We nodded and he continued. "They can only disincorporealize for a short period of time. Apparently the energy usage is phenomenal, so if they disincorporealize for more than three minutes or four separate instances, they must feed or go mad with hunger, leading to a berserker rage they cannot control."

Will raised his hand. "Is it true they are immortal?"

"No, but research shows that with their fantastic regenerative abilities, they most likely can live for several centuries.

"Very little else is known about these monsters, except that they were never human and cannot create more vampires by biting a human and having that human drink its blood. That is pure fiction. Like I said, forget the folklore."

A new photo appeared showing the vamp corpse with its mouth pried open. Every tooth appeared to be a canine, no molars. "Note the teeth, people. There are twenty-two and every one sharp enough to easily pierce skin. Also, their saliva contains a fast-acting paralytic, onset time within five seconds. Anyone bitten is unable to move for at least two hours. So stay away from a vampire's mouth. "

"That's it?" I asked, looking nervously at Winnie, who still stared raptly at the autopsy photo.

"That's it," he said. "Any other questions?"

Thomas crossed massive arms, each bicep as big as one of my thighs. "What's the Op, boss?"

The photo faded from the flat-screen, replaced by a map of Texas. "San Antonio." Another photo, this time of a bloated body floating in water. From the crowd in the background and the shops and restaurants, I knew it to be the famous River Walk. "This is the body of Anton Marks, dead for over a week. You can't see it from this photograph, but his wrists were slashed." Another photo, this time of Marks on an autopsy table. Pasty white and lumpy, the corpse was barely recognizable as human. I felt my stomach churn with acid.

"This is a post-autopsy photograph," BB lectured. "As you can tell from the Y incision on the torso." The photo minimized by half, making room for a document of some sort. "According to this autopsy report, cause of death was exsanguination."

"Something tells me it wasn't a suicide," I stated, trying not to barf.

"Our Green Pea is correct. Either our vampire lost control, or its Renfield couldn't reason with it. We know this because of what happened to the victim's throat." The photo of the body disappeared, replaced by a close-up of the victim's throat. Someone had done quite a job, savaging the poor man with—judging from the clean edges—a very sharp knife, exposing the faded waxy pink tissue underneath. "The coroner came to the conclusion that every one of you must have arrived at already; the damage was caused by a razor sharp blade, the tissue literally dug up. The Police believe it was done in a fit of rage. What alerted us was this." Yet another photo, another close-up. Small arcs had been gouged into the flesh, as if something had been scooped away.

"Is that a bite mark?" Winnie enthused, completely fascinated. For me, I manfully struggled to appear bland, no matter how sickening the pics were.

"We believe so. We also believe that whoever mangled the throat tried to disguise, or cut away, the bite mark, but was not entirely successful. The evidence is inconclusive. Or would be if not for this." Three more photos appeared, side-by-side. One was of a cow, throat slit and lying on a patch of desiccated yellow grass; one was of a pair of Black Labs, throats also slit. The last showed a young girl of perhaps ten, half buried in chalky dirt, dark rings of mud around her wrists.

All of us took in the sight of the little girl in a kind of horrified silence, rocking back where we sat. Everyone except Winnie, who had risen and moved slowly toward the flat-screen, studying the photos intently, almost hungrily. I couldn't help but be a little troubled by her fascination.

"The cow was killed two weeks ago, also drained of blood. Look at the surrounding grass—no spray, no bloody mud, nothing. The two dogs were killed five days later. The little girl ..." For once BB's legendary cool slipped, his voice harshening. He clenched one hand so tightly the knuckles had turned white. "She was killed shortly after. Wrists slashed like Mr. Marks. It has been estimated that her death preceded our last victim's by two days."

"Too much blood." Thomas sounded sick. Hell, I felt sick.

"What do you mean, Mr. Mace?"

"There's too much blood spilled for one vampire. A cow, two dogs and two humans … all within, what? Two, three weeks? One vampire doesn't drink *that* much."

"The Director has reached the same conclusion. According to the amount of blood theoretically harvested from each victim, we can look for three vampires."

Pins dropping would have made more noise. *Three vampires?*

"Yes, three vampires," BB intoned softly. "And possibly a Renfield. But even with those deaths, all that blood missing, there wasn't enough evidence. It could be ritualists, cultivating blood for some dark purpose. But there is more." A new picture popped up, a map of the North America. A glowing crimson spot appeared at Atlanta, Georgia, and a red line ran from there, connecting to Montgomery, Alabama, where it ignited another glowing crimson spot. From there, the line headed to Jackson, Mississippi, then south to Shreveport, Louisiana, before crawling along to San Antonio.

"Team Gamma took on a large nest of perhaps twenty vampires in Atlanta. They thought they had executed all of them and were going to investigate further, but were distracted by an outbreak of Indus Worms." We nodded; the domino effect of Supernatural events was well known.

"After the suspicious deaths in San Antonio, the Director decided to dig deeper and found similar deaths in the highlighted cities, along with very minor, mostly benign Supernatural activity. These vampires are heading west. We just don't know what their ultimate destination might be. However, we *will* stop them in San Antonio."

"All right, Winnie," I said. "I understand that magicians can Shape a spell in their minds," I stared out the window of the Gulfstream, "and gold and silver can be used to give a spell their

'Shapes', but how can a gem retain a spell's Shape?"

It was my first time aboard a private jet and the Gulfstream 550 fell into the category of indecent luxury. Not that I felt indecent. Quite the opposite, I could get used to traveling in such style. Every seat proved to be hideously comfortable; the lambskin leather contoured itself to my body like a lover and the two couches in the back of the cabin were—if the sound of snoring was any indication—soft enough for Canton and Thomas to fall blissfully asleep.

Winnie sipped her diet cola. "Look, Pea, magic isn't an exact science, at least not yet. All that most magicians know is that the higher quality, or purity, of the gem used, the more energy and spell complexity can be employed. Other than that, it's still a mystery to me."

I turned and wiggled into my seat, leaning back and closing my eyes. "So what happens to the spell 'Shape' when the energy is gone? Is it retained in the stone so you can put more energy in without imprinting a new spell?"

"The process of casting the spell erases the Shape, so the stone once again becomes a blank slate, good for re-use."

"Damn," I muttered sleepily. "Too complex for this old Scandahoovian. Hey, BB, I know what I want for Christmas; just wrap a big bow on this jet and park it under the tree."

"Sounds good to me, brother," mumbled Will. He, too, sounded as if he was ready to drop off into dreamland.

BB, though, sounded as calm and collected as ever—no sign of fatigue in his voice, not even a little bit. I wondered if he was a new kind of Supernatural hired by the Bureau for its ability to stay awake. Forever. "Maybe if you survive the next few years, Pea. These planes won't be on the market until 2003, by which time we will have much better aircraft at our disposal."

I didn't know about that. It felt plenty damn 'better' to me.

"BB, I been thinking," said Will.

"Oh? Are you sure that's wise?"

"Ha-Ha. But, seriously, why San Antonio? If'n these vamps are all allergic and such to sunlight, why the heck would they go to one of the sunniest places in the U.S. of A.?"

"I'm sure I have no idea, William. Vampires may look like albino humans right down to their pink eyes, but they don't think like humans. *Cogito Ergo Sum*—'I Think, Therefore I Am.' Words that define us, given voice by Descartes, words that describe the way we think." He paused, as if considering the vast differences between our species. "Vampires, however, use different words to define their thought processes; perhaps 'I Feed, Therefore I Am'. A way of thinking that is so alien to us humans that we have very little chance of comprehending. We are more likely to learn how a centipede thinks than a vampire."

"That is so damn spooky," Will slurred as he fell asleep.

The last thing I heard before succumbing to slumber was Winnie's voice. "But it's so fascinating …"

When the Gulfstream's wheels hit the runway, the jolt was slight, but enough to bring me to full consciousness in an instant as months of training violently kicked in.

Everyone woke, everyone except BB, who had simply been sitting, reading a book—*The Plague* by Camus. A good read, if a bit depressing.

"Oh, good, Pea, you're up. I wanted to give you something before we landed, but this book was too fine a read to put down." So saying, he marked his place and reached under his seat, hauling out a brown paper wrapped package a little bigger than a shoebox. He handed it over with a small smile.

"Dang, it's heavy," I observed as my fingers tore into the wrapping. Under that brown grocery paper rested a thickly lacquered, pale pine box with a bright silver clasp. Oh lordy … could it be? A little thrill ran through me as the last shred of paper exposed a carved letter *H* the size of a silver dollar on the lid.

"What is it, Green Pea?" Thomas asked from over my shoulder, causing me to jump in surprise.

"Don't sneak up on me like that!" I said irritably. "It's something that's been in my family for a while. At least, I hope it's what I think it is."

Canton made an appearance in jeans and a grubby wife-beater t-shirt, exposing his thickly muscled, dark-skinned arms and corded shoulders. "Now you have me curious." Will came up from the seat behind and stared over my other shoulder.

I popped the clasp and slowly lifted the lid, holding my breath. Inside lay a cream colored piece of paper folded in half, which I removed and read:

Son:

As you probably guessed by the box, this is your grandfather's weapon. You are out there, risking your life, doing good works for the people of our adopted country and I think he would want you to have it. I am hoping, considering your line of work, that it might prove useful.

Treat this weapon well, and it will keep you safe. Also, I have left you a little something under the velvet. I had it made special for you.

Love,
Dad

"Is that what I think it is?" Will uttered reverently, voice barely above a whisper, staring at a pistol nestled in a bed of crushed red velvet.

Thomas snorted. "What, a Luger?"

"Heathen," I said quietly, eyes stinging with unshed tears. "It's a—"

"Lahti L35," finished the sniper. He raised a reverent hand. "May I? Please?"

I wanted to bite his hand off at the wrist, but viciously curbed the impulse. "Go ahead," I muttered grudgingly.

He gently lifted the pistol out of its velvet nest. "Oh man oh man. A Lahti L35, designed in 1935 by Finnish arms designer Aimo Lahti. Only 9,000 were ever made. Fires a 9mm parabellum with 8 round magazine and is heavy as hell at two-and-three-quarter pounds unloaded. It has a bolt accelerator that improves reliability in cold weather. In the hands of someone who appreciates it, accuracy is guaranteed and the reliability is outstanding. Oh god … it has the loaded chamber indicator!" His expression became rapt, as if he were beholding a lost religious relic, and the words tumbled out of his mouth like a prayer. "How much do you want for it? I've been looking, but haven't found one for sale, just a bunch of crappy Swedish m40s."

I quickly plucked it out of his hand. "Not for sale at any price."

His face fell far enough to bounce and I felt like I'd just kicked a puppy, but there was no way he'd get his hands on my grandfather's pistol. I placed it on the seat next to me and removed the velvet lining.

"Now *that's* what I'm talking about!" Canton shouted, startling us all.

Will rounded on him. "Don't *do* that, you bonehead!"

"You have to admit … it's impressive," Thomas grunted in admiration.

There, at the bottom of the box, gleaming in the light streaming through the windows, lay a knife. And what a knife! Fourteen inches of blade, six inches of mahogany handle and sharpened to perfection. A Bowie knife, long edge curved to a needle point and sharpened on the back from the tip to about a third of its length. Jim Bowie never dreamed of greased murder like that knife.

"Hey, white boy, I want to come to your house for Christmas," declared the Native American. "Your parents know all the right presents to give!"

Winnie rolled her eyes. "Boys and their toys."

I smiled. "You bet your sweet bippy."

Later, in an old office building rented and prepped by Special Branch, we set up in our personal offices and headed toward Comms.

"We find ourselves in fortunate circumstances, people," BB commented as he paced in front of a map of San Antonio displayed large on a wall screen. "If we dot the kills ..." Glowing spots appeared on the map. "We see that all incidents stretch from the Riverwalk to the north, outside the city. We can safely conclude that the vampires are somewhere out there, north of the city.

"We all have rooms in the Mariott Rivercenter." Lots of whistles and high-fives and I resolved to raid the mini bar. "Calm down, people. The following agents will stay here: Mr. Alsate, the Green Pea, and Winnie. The rest of us will enjoy ourselves at the Marriott. Mr Mace, if you don't mind, please refrain from urinating in the pool this time."

Chapter Fourteen

Strange Revelations

"I ... am understandably surprised." BB's face belied his words. One day I may see him actually do more than twitch a muscle or two on his face and then my life will be complete.

"Alex, send the file," I said. Two taps of the keyboard and it was on its way. "Here's everything we've got. Now that I believe Bryan has been tagged; he could lead Winnie ... Margaret ... straight to the Warehouse. It's changed locations, what, three times since she disappeared?"

"Indeed. The Warehouse is the one of the most secure places on the planet with state-of-the-art tech and magic. She won't get in. Bryan can come in and Medical will repair his face and remove the tagging."

"Boss, she's been killing people and taking their life energy. Half a dozen people can power a hundred gemstones. She's got enough power to animate an army of ghouls, or a boatload of ghouls, and amp them up with her magical steroids. Bryan has to be diverted for his own good. I'm absolutely sure she's got it in for all of us, especially you and me, boss. You know why."

For a moment he almost looked concerned, but it passed quickly. "There are four teams here, Kal, plus six magicians in R&D and three in Medical, not to mention other Special Branch support staff, including our rather formidable Receptionists. We can handle ourselves. I will have everyone armed and armored."

I wanted to reach through the screen and throttle him, but instead I settled for a few inappropriate curses.

"Feel better?" he asked.

"You going to divert Bryan?"

"No."

"Then I don't feel better." I spent a few anxious moments pacing. "I think it's time we closed up shop here, boss. We're coming home." Before he could reply, I reached around Alex and cut communications.

"Awww … Look at that, guys," I pouted insincerely. "Comms are down. Oh well, time to go home."

The whole team stood there, jaws clanging off their chests. "What? Go! Move! We're closing shop." Still they stared. What? They never witnessed BB getting hung up on before? "Now! Move!" I shouted.

They scrambled. They fled. An amber light on the table told me someone was attempting to dial in. I powered the system down, then headed out to collect cell phones. If he couldn't contact us, he couldn't order us to stay.

"What's the play, Kal?" Pat asked, startling me as I stuffed the last of the cells into my jacket pockets.

"Closing up shop, Pat."

"What do we do when we get to Warehouse?"

I shook my head. "Either save the day or not."

"If the day doesn't need saving?"

"Then I take the heat."

"*We* take the heat."

"No, just me. No one in the Bureau has ever been reprimanded for following orders. You and the rest of the team will be fine."

"And you?"

"Just out of a job, not dead. I'll be fine." My face remained neutral, hard, while she smiled slightly—telling me I'd fooled no one—and headed off to pack.

A heavy hand landed on my shoulder. "What now, Kal?" inquired Wilkes, taking a swig from a can of Coke.

"We leave, you stay."

"So that's it? You just head out after stirring the pot?" He didn't sound angry, but he sure as hell wasn't happy.

I sighed. "What do you want us to do, Wilkes? The Organ Donor is gone, out of your hair. Special Branch will pick up Krouse's body and head out, leaving the case in the capable hands of the FBI. Eventually, when there are no more victims, they'll leave and the Donor will go down in history with the other great unsolved mysteries like Jack the Ripper and such."

"That doesn't work for me."

"Why?" I asked as my feet pointed toward the Armory.

He moved quickly to catch up. "Because she's out there, the killer of the people I've sworn to protect, and I want her."

My palm hit the pad and moments later the Armory door opened. "She was one of us; we'll take care of her." I entered.

He followed. "I swore an oath. I have to do this."

I spun and leaned in close, coming nose to nose with him. "What the hell are you about? You saw what we fight, and I let you come along because you've got skills, but you would've died in that damn garage without me. Where we're going, I can't guarantee your safety and I won't have you in harm's way. So go home."

"No."

Opening a drawer, I pulled out a couple of duffels. "Fine, you don't have to go home, but you can't come with us."

"Now wait a min—" he began.

"No, *you* wait," I interrupted hotly, loading a duffel with body armor. "I want you to come, but you can't." His face fell and I felt like I'd smacked a kitten. "Crap," I snarled. Fishing in my jacket, I pulled out a thick, white card. "Here, take this. You ever think you need something different, come look me up. I think you got the stones to do this job." The Detective took the card, his face grave and sullen. With one last nod, he left. I both hoped and dreaded that I'd see him again.

Packing up the Armory took less time than I thought and in a short hour we had loaded the Crown Vics and were motoring toward Colorado Springs. Minus one Detective Wilkes, who had taken my Honda.

"Boss, why are you going south? DIA is north and east," Alex transmitted through my earwig. The whole team wore them, and throat mics, just in case.

"BB will have alerted the TSA to keep a lookout for us. We'll take the Colorado Springs Airport. He won't expect us there."

"But how are we going to get out? The Bureau doesn't have a plane there."

"Don't worry, Alex. I have a cunning plan."

He didn't reply. Probably got busy. Yeah, that's it.

A tap shut off the throat mic and a push of a button powered up my cell. I had six messages and I was pretty darn sure I didn't want to hear them.

Most cells have chips that can be tracked by the authorities. Ours were different in the fact that we could turn those chips off. My cell was the only one still in use and I made sure the chip wasn't active. As far as BB was concerned, we were headed to DIA.

"Ghost, you there?"

Bzzzzz …. "I was wondering when you would get around to me, Kal."

"Sorry, Ghost, we've been packing."

"So I've heard. BB has been heating up cyberspace looking for you."

"That's part of what I want to talk to you about. Can you do something to the traffic cams? I don't need Big Brother using them to find us."

"You should listen to BB, Kal."

Uh-oh. If Ghost wasn't with us, we were executively screwed. "Ghost, listen … you know the bad guys are after BB, and the Warehouse isn't safe anymore. We have to get to DC or they're gonna eat his liver with some fava beans and a nice Chianti."

A long pause. Almost too long. "What makes you think you can do what those teams at the Warehouse can't?"

"Because I'm the only one left alive who's worked with Winnie besides BB, and I'm the most experienced agent the Bureau's got.

He needs me, he needs my team … the only team to face a superghoul. If I'm wrong he can fire me. If I'm right, and I am, then I can tell BB 'I told you so.' "

An even longer pause. I felt a drop of sweat trickle down my temple as my anxiety mounted. "All right, Kal. Every traffic cam in the state is down."

I let out a breath I didn't know I was holding. "Thanks, Ghost. One more thing; I'd like you to commandeer a private plane at the Colorado Springs airport, something fast. Use whatever story you want, but make sure it is fueled and ready to go. Be certain everything is ironclad and under the aegis of whatever agency has the most pull. Will you do that for me?"

Bzzzz … "I think it is customary to say at this point 'You will owe me one.' "

"Do this and we're even, all books closed. How's that?"

"Done." Click.

I holstered the cell. Okay, Ghost on board … the weight of the world had just lessened a tad. Then that weight doubled in an instant when we reached the Colorado Springs city limit.

A thump. A click. A barrel of a gun at the back of my head. "Touch your throat mic and you're dead." Sue's voice had more ice than a lawyer's heart, but, somehow, it wasn't Sue's voice. A strange crackling and popping reached my ears.

By the pricking of my thumbs …

"That you, Winnie? Or should I say, 'Margaret'?

"Winnie will do just fine; let's not stray from the familiar."

"Nice choice of words that. Is Pat alive?"

"I think so. I gave her quite the shot to the skull."

My mind raced furiously. I risked a quick glance in the rearview mirror and saw Pat's head lolling bonelessly to one side, blood dripping from the corner of her bruised mouth. A cold, hard pounding started behind my eyes as my old friend, rage, began to make itself known. I flicked my eyes to Sue.

I've seen a lot of eerie things in my time, from undead centaurs to squids that sang like angels, but what I saw in her face hit me right between the eyes and threatened to send my brain home, screaming to mama.

Sue's face, broad and unlovely, slowly *shifted* as her eyes, changing from color to color, stared insectlike at me. The crackling and popping noises I'd heard were the bones of her face re-aligning. *Pop, pop*, new cheekbones. *Snapcrunch*, the whole jaw flexed obscenely to new proportions. To make matters more stomach churning, then they shifted back, only to start all over again. It was a face in flux and, although Winnie's dispassionate gaze showed no pain, I was willing to bet everything I had that poor Sue was in desperate agony. Fury boiled the acid in my stomach.

"Like what you see, handsome?"

"Possession, huh? Of a live human being? Everybody thought it was impossible. I gotta hand it to you; you proved them wrong."

The gun barrel jabbed harshly against the back of my skull. "Of course. No one knows more about spells and the Shape of magic than I do. I've raided two of the greatest databases in the world." Once again that barrel ground into me. "But enough talking, Kal. Keep heading toward the airport. And don't try to be a hero or everyone in this car dies. You know I'm quite capable."

"Absolutely, Winnie, but isn't it customary for the evil genius to monologue a little and reveal how her dastardly plan came together for the edification and dismay of the handsome hero?"

Once again the barrel smacked down hard and a trickle of blood ran into my collar. That was going to leave a scar. "You always did have a smart mouth, Kal."

"We've got a couple more minutes before we're there, Winnie, so just spill."

Silence for a few seconds, then, "Okay, I'll consider it your last request *and keep the goddamn speed below fifty!*" The shriek flensed my ears like shards of glass and I took my foot off the accelerator.

"Try that again and the last thing you'll see is the windshield getting splattered with your brains. Check?"

"Check," I affirmed, grinding my teeth.

"Good. Now, as for the possession spell ... no good. That one will follow me to the grave."

Soon ... I prayed, looking into those weirdly shifting eyes.

"As for the rest ... I think you figured it out already. You're a smart one, Kal."

"I have a theory ..."

"Oooo ... do tell, big boy!"

The throbbing behind my eyes intensified, but I noticed a slight stir from the backseat and hastily started my own monologue. "You're the magician who created the zombies that brought my team to Denver in the first place. You're also the Organ Donor, cutting open bad guys and scooping out their insides. All that gruesomeness was a way to hide the fact that you were really after their blood and their life energy. How am I doing?"

"Very good, Kal. Soon you'll be the smartest corpse around. Continue."

"You staged the bodies for maximum effect and called the cops to come pick up the organs for two reasons. One: to hide that you were stealing high-quality gems and replacing them with replicas and Two: You just like screwing with the authorities. You get off on it." That earned me another hit and for a second the pain painted everything bright white. I imagined that the back of my skull was becoming mush.

"Ow! Okay, okay ... ease up on the gat, Win. Let's see ... it was you and a ghoul who ambushed Sue and Jeff at the funeral parlor. The ghoul took out Jeff and you got Sue from behind. Under the cover of silver mesh so we wouldn't be able to sense the spell, you tagged Sue and laid on a possession—all without her knowing— then adjusted her memories a tad, not enough to really mess with her mind, just enough to match the events she described. My guess is the spell not only allows possession, but you can rifle her mind and see through her eyes without her knowing about it, right?" If only the glass hadn't been pimp-tinted, the others driving behind could have seen the gun at the back of my head.

The smile that flashed through teeth that rolled like Chiclets in her mouth sent a chill down my spine, causing my rage to flare. She must have seen the expression on my face because she wagged a finger at me. "Now, now … control that temper of yours. Yes, you are absolutely correct so far."

"Those spells, the ghoul-makers, were there to draw us out, to see who I had on my team … and to mess with us."

"Check."

"From Sue's mind, you got the location of my apartment and sent that super-soldier ghoul to attack me. I'm not sure if you hoped to kill me or set me up with the mental deterioration spell."

"Killing you would have been optimal, but it's good to have backup. I must say, you never fail to impress." Her voice began to take on an East Anglian dialect. "You defeated my ghoul one on one, just like that vampire in San Antonio."

"How do the ghouls cast those spells?"

"A simple 'if/then' … If the ghoul pierces flesh, then the spell activates."

"Very interesting." I risked a glance in the rear view to see one of Pat's eyes open and close slightly in a lugubrious wink. I prayed Win would keep her focus on me. "You had the ghouls dump Briegan's body. You killed him because you knew I'd talked to him, so you wanted to mess with my head a bit. Then you made sure we would find those ghouls in the parking garage along with those two zombies. You didn't want to kill us, but you wanted at least one tagged with that anti-healing spell. You wanted me dead—that's why the car bomb—but you should have used C4 instead of gas in the tank."

"I didn't have any, love."

I gritted my teeth. "You knew Bryan would be sent to DC, to where Medical would try to patch him up because you needed Warehouse's location; it had changed a couple of times since 2000."

Her lips tickled my ear. "You are sooooo good, love. You have *almost* all of it figured out."

"You plan on taking over Bryan when he gets to Warehouse because when the ghoul hit him, not only did the gems it must have swallowed cast an anti-healing spell, they laid on a possession. You'll kill everyone you can and disarm security. All to get BB." *Hurry up, Pat*, I urged silently, praying that the maniacal magician would keep her ever-changing eyes focused on me.

"You know why," Winnie/Margaret screamed in my ear. The face in the rear view mirror was almost totally devoid of Sue.

I winced as my ears rang. "Okay, Winnie. I get it. But one last thing ... how did Margaret Whitcombe disappear from MI-7 only to reappear in the U.S. and join the Bureau without getting twigged?"

"Don't miss this next right ... good. Remember, not too fast," she directed. After making sure I wasn't trying to pull a fast one with the Vic, she continued. "Disappearing was easy. What wasn't included in my file was the debris from my boat coming to shore near Dover, a nice touch to seal the deal. To MI-7, I am so much fish food at the bottom of the channel. As for traveling to America, when you are a magician, it's easy if you know how to keep a low profile and have the use of a Faraday Cage.

"The rest proved to be simplicity itself ... I am rather brilliant with a computer and I managed to create a foolproof cover for myself as a widow living in Odessa, Texas." She shuddered. "Horrid place. Then all I had to do was cast one or two harmless spells— amateur magic really—and the Bureau showed up in a few short hours. You know how quickly people cycle through the Bureau, so anyone who had cross-trained with MI-7—who might have recognized me—were long gone. And thanks to paranoia, there is no easy access to other agency's files. I was safe."

"Not anymore, honey." A fist, small but hard, hammered into Sue/Winnie/Margaret's jaw with a *crack* that even I felt. Almost without thinking my head ducked just a fraction before a 9mm round parted the air where the back of my skull had been.

I slammed on the brakes, feeling the weight of two female bodies impact on the back of my seat—pushing it forward—and my head into the center of the steering wheel. Ow … Shaking away stars, I wrenched the wheel to the right and the Vic slewed, jittering and shuddering, to a stop.

Out of the car, fast … the rage had me now … Pat was in danger … My hand found the handle to the rear driver's side door and gave it a yank. My arms dove inside for Sue and there she was, snarling, shifting face crackling and popping, teeth flashing and biting …

My hands gripped the lapels of her white silk blouse, now spattered with the blood flowing from a bite on my left wrist. "Don't do that, Winnie," I snarled into her ravaged face as I dragged her from the Vic, Pat following behind. Shaking Winnie like a rat finally calmed her down.

The second Vic had screeched to a stop only a few short feet away, the guys tumbling out, pointing their pistols at Sue's head. "Boss, what's going on?" Dom bellowed, arm steady on the top of the car, the barrel of the .44 in his ham fist looking like a tunnel to hell.

"This ain't Sue," I hollered back. "Margaret Whitcombe is possessing her."

Winnie/Sue/Margaret bared her bloody teeth in a hateful smile. "Not anymore."

Her head exploded.

Brain, blood and bone liberally mixed with skin and short, blond hair sprayed out in a five foot circle, dousing me in a shower of gore. As if from far away, as I stood there stunned, holding on to Sue's headless body, I heard the sound of several people being violently sick. I have no idea why I didn't join them. Maybe the rage kept me from joining the upchuck festival, kept me at an emotional distance from the horror of Sue's grisly death.

Whatever the reason, I levered her body into the Vic, moving it out of sight while those not losing everything they'd eaten in the last decade stood around, blocking the view from passersby. While I knelt on the hot asphalt, someone produced a cotton t-shirt and a gallon jug of windshield wiper fluid.

"Boss," whispered Dom. "Let me wash you and Pat down. We can't let you go to the airport like this." I nodded and stripped off jacket, tie, and shirt.

Pungent washer fluid, warm from the trunk of the Vic, splashed over my head and onto my back, stinging my eyes. The white cotton T came away red as I used it to wipe off chunks of flesh and ribbons of blood. The damn fluid got up my nose and stung like hell, but I didn't care; at least it blotted out the smell of Sue's brains.

Behind me came the most chilling sound I'd heard in a while ... Pat was crying. She had been with the team as our Receptionist for three years now, and in all that time, through all the death, the sorrow, and the horror, she had remained steadfast and diamond hard.

Crap ... I started to feel a stinging in my eyes. Instantly I reached for the rage and felt it warm my insides. The sting and the stench of the washer fluid vanished and all that was left was a desire to kill. A splinter of bone fell from the tangle of my hair.

Knowing there were no more silvery vials, I had to think of a way to dispose of damning evidence. "Alex, the acid bomb spell, can it be detonated remotely?"

A few seconds later he answered, "Sure, all you need is a cell."

"Dom, get yours out of the trunk."

"Check."

"Pat, when you're done, get in the other car. I'll take this one."

"Check, boss," she hiccoughed.

Boss? She's never called me that. I risked a glance and saw a face blank with shock and wet with tears. Another thing I owed Winnie for.

"Someone got a shirt?" A lavender silk number was thrust into my hands.

"One of mine," Dom said.

Shrugging it on, I noticed that my chinos were a mess, caked with gore, and I used the rest of the windshield wiper fluid to wash off the worst. I still looked like I'd been wading hip deep in a slaughterhouse, but there was nothing to do about it unless I wanted to walk on the tarmac in my boxers. "Let's go. When we get there, you go in and check on the arrangements. I want us in the air yesterday." I noticed that Pat had raided Sue's luggage and was dressed in a jeans and a t-shirt that were far too generous in hip and shoulder. At least she didn't look like a walking bloody bandage.

"Check."

"Dom, got the phone?"

"Check, boss." He passed over a slim affair that Apple hadn't slated for sale yet and I tossed it on the front seat after turning it on. Unholstering my own, I dialed BB ... Nothing, just a recording for Maxine's Data Storage.

"Crap!" I yelled, furious.

A lot of curious stares piled up and threatened to topple onto me. "No one's answering. I reckon Bryan's already at the Warehouse. Let's go."

Time to fly.

Chapter Fifteen

Ten years Earlier
Down Dark and Dirty

"Okay, white boy, someone coming at you with Recon 1 or K-bar is gonna have more hand speed than you because this pig-sticker is so heavy. Your best defense is its longer blade. You can make short sweeping motions to keep them at bay, but don't ever let them get too close; you're at a disadvantage." Canton held his own knife up for me to see, a Recon 1 Tanto. It had a blade length of four inches and came to a chisel point. Made with Japanese Aus 8A stainless steel for strength and durability, it had a strong G-10 handle that could withstand 200lbs of pressure without breaking. I'd trained with them at Coronado and knew that in the right hands they were cold-steel death.

"I love that blade you got there," he continued. "Looks like it was made out of an industrial file, and those are good, high carbon steel. You learn to wield that with any sort of speed and you're going to be near unstoppable." His calloused finger rippled along the Bowie's diagonal file grooves.

BB's office was the biggest, so we had pushed his oak desk in the corner, threw the chairs out into the hall and used the space for sparring practice. We knew BB wouldn't mind because training was the key to survival in the Bureau. Besides, he was back at the Marriott sawing logs.

Forty-five minutes of me being tossed around more than a dodgeball, Canton called it quits. Good thing he did, too … I might have bled on his Dockers. I'd never seen a man move so fast or wield a knife with such impeccable skill. It was almost a religious experience.

"Keep training, white boy, you're going to be greased slaughter some day with that thing. Assuming you live long enough," he panted, wiping the sweat from his face with a towel.

I sat there, back against the wall in BB's office and nodded, too tired to think. After a second, he joined me on the floor.

"You mind if I ask you a question, white boy?"

"Why don't you call me Green Pea, or Pea, like everyone else?" I grunted.

"Because you are the whitest white boy I ever saw. I mean, *damn*, you don't ever tan, do you?"

"Some, but only after I burn real good."

He snorted his laughter.

I stared out the window at the night sky, stars bled away by light pollution. So very different from our place outside of Grand Rapids, Minnesota. My parents' house was remote enough that cell phones were useless and the nearest neighbor was three miles away. There, in the secluded countryside near the Chippewa National Forest, you could see the Milky Way clear as anything and shooting stars were a common sight. Sometimes I'd drive out to Chase Lake and take Dad's boat out on the clear, frigid waters and lie back and stare at the sky for hours on end. Out there, as the boat rocked gently under me, I felt comfortable, peaceful, haunted by nothing.

"What I wanted to ask you, Kal, was about the Class Five." His use of my name startled me. I looked over and found his obsidian eyes fixed on mine.

"You must've read the file," I yawned. "It's all in there."

"I read the file, but it ain't all there." His glittering eyes, so much like polished marbles slicked with oil, became even more intense. "There's always more."

"Dude, do you get the idea that this might be painful for me? That talking about my sister's death might be somewhat traumatic? I'm not ready yet." Keeping my voice steady took an incredible effort of will.

He pursed his lips, lost in thought.

"Canton, I'd like to tell you, but until I find some way to kill that monster—" His head whipped around, eyes flying wide. "What?"

"What makes you think they'll let you kill it?" he asked quietly.

My temples throbbed. "Because it's a Supernatural and we kill Supernaturals. Especially those that kill people, like my sister or those people on the Estonian ferry it sank in 1994."

"Listen to me, Kal," he ground out in a whisper. "The Finnish government will never let you kill that thing, no matter how many Estonian ferries it sinks. That thing is a validation for the Kalevala—proof of the rich magic and history of a small nation. You try to kill it, their government's Bureau will shut you down so hard your *descendants* will feel it."

My cheeks grew hot as anger thrummed through my veins. "Damn it! You're telling me they're gonna let that thing keep on *murdering* people?" I shouted, slamming a fist against the floor. "Because of a sense of *history?*" The rage started to build, but I savagely held it back.

"Don't knock history. All countries thrive on history, it's what helps bind a people together and gives them a sense of pride. I read up on you Finns. Not a single war won. Too few soldiers, but every country that has gone up against your people has come out *much* worse for wear. The Finns always inflict terrible casualties on their enemies, but they get beat by sheer numbers."

"We call it *sisu*," I ground out. "Finns have it ... kind of like guts, or *chutzpah*, or ferocious tenacity. There's no direct translation, but it's a combination of all three."

"Well, from what I read that's certainly true, and you got it in spades, but however much of that *seesoo* stuff you got, it ain't gonna help you."

"*Sisu*," I corrected. "If you're going to say it, don't butcher it." The anger-high was starting to fade as his words sunk in. We Finns are a quiet, proud people and it made a perverse sort of sense that we'd seek to preserve something that killed children to retain a sense of national unity.

"Hey, white boy, you want a beer? I want a beer." He turned his potential energy into kinetic and bounded out of the office. I followed a second later.

"What the hell? We're on shift," I protested.

"BB doesn't mind," Canton said, pulling a couple of cold ones from the lounge fridge. "As long as it's only one." Cold wet glass slapped my palm and I twisted the cap off.

Damn that tasted good. The beer cooled the hot bite of my anger and aided in calming the beast, which made me feel almost relaxed. Better living through chemistry: the motto of the twenty-first century male.

A long, heavy belch rumbled up and out of my gut. " 'Scuse me. I needed that."

Canton tossed me an even look. "Yeah, I figured."

"You did?"

He nodded. "I read your psych profile, white boy. Everyone has. You can read each of ours as well; we have no secrets. Keeps us honest." He pointed to me with his bottle. "But your profile ... I see the rage in you, especially when I mention the Class Five. You should see your face. Your cheeks get bright red and your eyes, white boy, your eyes *change* from that pale blue to a dark, dark blue that's almost black. I wanted to see that anger in your spirit. It's why I asked about the Class Five."

"You saw it when I fought Thomas," I protested.

"That was from twenty feet away, not close enough. I needed front row seats to your concert of fury." After a small burp, he took another swig. "The Director and BB may be satisfied that you can control yourself, but I gotta stand shoulder-to-shoulder with you and I want to *know*."

If I'd been in his situation, I'd have done the same thing. How can you be sure of a man who's supposed to have your back when he might have some loose screws?

He smiled knowingly. "Yeah, you know what I mean, don't

you? I had to know, man. And I saw that thing inside you, that heat that changes what you are, and I've come to the conclusion that you're okay. You use it; it doesn't use you, and I'm fine with that." With one long pull he finished his beer. It found the trash from a distance of eight feet. "Score one for me. And consider the beer congratulatory."

Laughter bubbled out of me from I don't know where, but it felt good, real good.

Later, in Comms, monitoring the local media and police chatter, Canton said, "You know, white boy, if you ever do find an end round the Finnish government and hunt that beast, you let me know. I'd be real interested in seeing that bastard up close."

"You don't want that," I replied distantly. "I was a few hundred feet away and it nearly drove me mad by just *being*."

"White boy, that thing ain't never seen an Apache with his full anger on."

Once again clean laughter rolled out. Something about Canton touched a chord within me, maybe a similarity of spirit. "Hey, I just realized, you called me 'Kal' instead of white boy a while ago."

"Yeah, well ... don't let it go to your head. If you tell the others, I'll just deny it."

"Jerk."

"And proud of it, white boy. Proud of it."

False dawn started to light the sky and I flipped through endless cable news channels, bored to tears by the talking heads spewing recycled news and local pap. A lot of what I saw seemed created to scare the crap out of a community of middle class parents—sensational drivel that meant nothing except ratings for the media vultures to feed on. The perfectly manicured and coiffed heads put on masks of concern or restrained sorrow as they doled out what mushrooms grew in.

One talking head caught my attention, a pretty blonde with a vacant expression that mirrored the inside of her skull. "The Cascade Caverns claimed another life today as workers found the body of the second guide to be killed in less than a week. The young man had been trapped under several hundred pounds of fallen rock, in the third, and largest, cave-in in the past month." Cut to a shot of a gurney decked with a black body bag being hoisted into an ambulance by two burly EMTs. "The cavern owners have cited recent rains, applying stress to already weakened limestone. The caverns have been closed until geologists and work crews can assess the damage and estimate when if ever they can be repaired." Back to the head, face contorted into a semblance of distress. The Stepford News Anchors.

By the pricking of my thumbs …

"Canton," I yelled over my shoulder. "I think we just got lucky…"

When I filled him in on the cavern story, he squinted at me, rubbing his chin in thought. "White boy, you think that some vampire and a Renfield are sitting on their fundaments in a bloody tourist attraction? Something that's visited by thousands of tourists a year?"

"You think a vampire is strong enough to weaken rock? Cause cave-ins?"

"Hell, Mace is strong enough, I reckon."

"Just think ... Instead of tourists coming through all the time, you only have to worry about a couple of geologists and a few workers checking out the situation. Lot less people, a whole mess of caves to hide in. They probably did it to be left alone."

"Hmmm …" he mused, then smiled brilliantly. "Oh, I believe it, white boy. I just wanted to hear the pitch you're going to give BB."

"Me?"

"Your find, your pitch. Let's call the boss."

"You've given me much to consider, Kal. Thank you." BB stood, looking awfully dapper for a guy who'd had only a few hours sleep. His white Le Tigre polo stretched tight across hard, ropy muscle. He gestured toward the office door. "Stick around. I'll get back to you shortly with a decision."

It didn't take long before BB entered my office as I put paid to roast beef sandwich. "Gear up, Pea, we're going spelunking."

For the first time I saw an Armory and, let me tell you, Christmas came early for me. "Oh, I am a happy man!" I exclaimed, staring at rows upon rows of deadly instruments.

"Keep your Bowie," Canton said, "It's a great close-in weapon. But for a real vamp hunt, you want pure firepower supplied by Uncle Sam himself. No not SMGs—too close in the caverns for those—but grab that Glock and take three or four mags of rosewood rounds." He stared at a collection of revolvers and pulled down a .44. "These are great for explosive rounds, but take some armor-penetrating ones as well."

"Really? Armor-penetrating rounds?"

"Yep. Depleted uranium core surrounded by lead. The lead flattens and strips off while the uranium punches right through vamp bone. They might regenerate, but this will give them pause for the cause. Just be careful where you aim, though. These rounds will go through steel. Also, the weapons we'll be using will be Silenced."

I heard the capital S. "Magic, I take it."

He nodded, grinning. "If only the Apache had something like that, eh, white boy? Where would you be then?"

"In Finland, drinking beer and doing blondes with fine porcelain skin, feeling sorry for the savage red man."

A hard knuckle thumped me in the breadbasket. "Wise guy."

I loaded the .44, found a holster and planted it under my jacket. "Anything else?"

He nodded. "You'll be wearing body armor, some really fantastic titanium and Kevlar stuff, but here ..." He handed over a collar covered in some sort of black material. "This is basically a gorget—something to protect your throat if a vamp triees to go for the jugular. It connects solidly with the armor." Canton picked up a little clear plastic box filled with what looked like two-inch-long band-aids. He pulled one out and stuck it onto my Adams Apple. "Subvocal mic. Tap the center once to activate, once to deactivate. We'll be able to hear you with earwigs when you go subvocal, but the smart chip doesn't transmit when you speak normally."

"That is beyond cool." The mic fit comfortably, the adhesive strong enough not to peel off when I moved my neck. "Why go into the caves now? Why can't we wait until dark and catch them when they come out?"

"We do a daylight entry because they're logy and listless during the day. We want to catch them napping so we can nap them permanently." He smiled. "At night they're faster, have more energy. Not the kind of vamp we want to face."

Okay, got the picture. Hyper vamps bad, sleepy vamps good. "Can I get something with a lot of punch? Something magical to at least spice things up?"

"We'd give you gems, but you ain't rated, white boy. You really gotta be careful how you use magic or else you'll wind up killing yourself as well as the bad guys."

Crap. Getting some magic would've come in handy. Smirking at the look on my face, he passed me a brace of wooden stakes. "Use these if you can. Rosewood and blackthorn ... stab stab no regeneration. Get it in the heart and the vamp is fish food."

Fish food. The thought was encouraging and I really needed a bad guy to kill, needed it like an addict craved his next fix. All the training in the world never really fed the beast inside me and I knew I had to let him out once in a while to feed, if only for a little bit. Did that make me a monster? I didn't know, but as long as I left the Straights alone and kept my eyes, and my guns, trained on the Supernaturals, I thought my being a monster would be all right.

"You got that look, white boy. Your eyes, they're darker now."

My smile would've sent my mother screaming from the room. "I'm ready to get down and dirty today, compadre. Down and dirty."

His smile answered mine, nastiness for nastiness. "Oh yeah!"

Two black SUVs rambled north toward Boeme, Texas, the home of Cascade Caverns. Why black? All Fed vehicles seemed to be black. At least we fit the stereotype.

"Remember," BB buzzed through my earwig as the SUVs parked near a low-slung building in the middle of twisted scrub trees. A small sign declared it to be the Cascade Caverns' gift shop/ticket office and, for some reason, a bright green T-Rex dinosaur stood nearby in the middle of a cactus patch. Weird and weirder. "We are Federal Marshals after a fugitive named George Bixel. Our story is that a source claims Bixel is in the area. We are here to check the caves out. I will enter the building with Mr. Mace and evacuate anyone who might be here. The rest of you check to make sure that everyone leaves and keep a look out for someone who could possibly be the Renfield. Check?"

Everyone affirmed and BB headed to the building with Thomas. The door was locked but several seconds of pounding brought out a janitor who took one look at BB's U.S. Marshal outfit and beckoned the two in. They entered and came back shortly, followed by the janitor, who took off in an old Chevy Prism.

"We are in luck. Only one person left ... a security guard near the cavern entrance, which is out back."

BB and Thomas took off their U.S. Marshal flak jackets and replaced them with the insect-like titanium/Kevlar armor that we all wore. When done, BB handed out what looked like diving goggles faced with smoked glass. "Night-vision," he said to me. "And don't worry about flashes. Built-in filters will keep you from becoming blinded by bright light."

"God likes me," I muttered with a smile. "He really, *really* likes me."

Bringing up the rear right behind Winnie, I followed the team around the ticket office to the trail behind the building that led to the caverns. Cheery wooden signs bearing historical facts pointed us in the right direction.

"Green Pea, you better not shoot me in the butt," Winnie

growled, eyes flicking to the .44 in my hand.

"If I shoot you, Winnie, it won't be in the butt."

"That's telling her, white boy," Canton grinned back at me, throwing Winnie a lurid wink.

"If you children would pipe down," BB said from the lead as he rounded a tree and started down a long set of concrete steps, descending the side of an enormous sinkhole. "We should see the security guard any second."

Down the stairs to the floor of the sinkhole we went, the trail a concrete ribbon winding through grass, low shrubs and under an arch of stone that soared thirty feet over our heads. After a few dozen yards the ribbon led to small opening in the wall of the sinkhole, a large slab of stone jutting over like a brooding brow. A webbing of yellow tape crisscrossed the entrance, bearing the words "DANGER! DO NOT ENTER" in bold black.

Will's voice startled us. "Boss, where the hell is the security guard? Shouldn't he be around here somewhere?"

"Should be," replied BB, pulling out a revolver that made my .44 look like a popgun and gave me a serious case of pistol envy.

A few more steps provided a clue as to the guard's whereabouts.

Blood. A small patch, the size of a quarter, but fresh and sticky in the bright Texas sunshine. Drops and drips trailed toward the entrance to the cavern—the trail of a man's life left in crimson.

"Boss," Canton whispered. "I think the Renfield just served up lunch for a vamp or two."

Thomas Mace grimaced. "Which means there could be at least one vampire who is awake in there." He spat off into some prickly pear.

BB spoke without taking his eyes off the cave entrance. "We either go in and take our chances or we wait out here and try to pick them off at night." His face lifted to the clear blue sky. "Either way this gets solved today before anyone else dies. I am calling a vote; what say you?"

"Go in now," rumbled Thomas. "Night is their time."

Will shook his head. "Shoot, boss … I'm a sniper. I reckon I can pick them off as they come up and you all can finish them off."

"I'm just magic support, boss," Winnie drawled. "I ain't trained for close quarters combat. You know that."

Canton took a deep breath. "I want to go in … down and dirty in the dark is the only way to fly." The smile in his voice was evident to all.

Silence. It was only a few heartbeats before everyone but BB turned to look at me. "You're the tie-breaker, white boy," Canton muttered, softly enough so only I could hear.

A warm rush filled me. Oh yeah, life just keeps on handing me gifts. My smile startled the hell out of Winnie. I took a deep breath through my nose. "Time to get dirty, folks."

BB nodded. "Okay. Will, you stay up here and keep watch. Shoot anything that isn't us. We will let you know if you are needed."

"Check, boss."

My smile was filled with seething nasty. Time to play.

Chapter Sixteen

The Warehouse Blues

Of the six teams still in the field, two were offline on an op, one was in Australia training with their Bureau equivalent and the three remaining were on the way from cities closer to DC than Denver. I gave instructions to stay put and meet us at the airport. I had a feeling we might be outnumbered.

The Homeland Security cock-and-bull story Ghost drummed up for us acquired a Citation Encore, easily one of the nicest jets I'd ever flown in. Once on board, I checked on Bryan's flight and found out that he'd landed an hour before Winnie had taken over Sue's body.

I reckoned she was already in DC. Hell, she might have skipped the moment she'd been wounded, preferring to wait for the spelled agent to come to her. Either way, it indicated she hadn't been severely wounded and was able to travel at a moment's notice. Everything she did was well thought out, well planned. Which made sense. After all, the Bureau had trained her.

Before takeoff, I unholstered my phone. "This'll work?" I asked Alex.

"Should, Kal … Listen … I …" He faltered.

"You couldn't have twigged onto Winnie's spells," I told him woodenly. "She was one of the best and something like this has never happened to a team before." Raising a hand to cut off his objection, I continued, "You have talent like I've never seen before, Alex, but she has experience and a wealth of knowledge from two countries."

With a whipped-puppy look, he went back to his contoured leather seat while I held up the phone and dialed Dom's number. If things went as planned, his cell's ring tone would be the trigger word for the small sapphire sitting on Sue's headless body, which would explode in a ball of boiling acid that would reduce her, the entire Vic, and a good section of tarmac into a steaming puddle of foul-smelling black goo. The phone rang twice before the line went dead.

God, she deserved so much more, the least of which was a burial in Arlington with honors. Instead she had received an acid bath and a one-way trip to a toxic landfill. A little black star with her name in the center, mounted on the wall of the Warehouse's Records Room would provide the only epitaph, seen by a select few.

Damn. Pain throbbed through my skull, sending a red haze, a cloud of fury, through my vision, coloring everything around me shades of scarlet. Cursing, I rose to my feet, the onset of a full-blown crap attack coming my way like an out of control freight train, devastating everything in its way.

The door to the lavatory slammed shut against my back and the rage crashed through me, while in the mirror I saw my eyes darken into something frightening, feral. For a moment the rage was everything, everywhere, carrying with it Leena's clean summertime scent.

Sudden and shocking—like a hard slap to the face—the rage passed as if it had never been. I watched as my eyes faded to sky blue and an aching emptiness filled the space where the fury had been born.

I started to cry. For the first time in years, perhaps twenty, tears coursed unabated down my face and racking sobs shook my body. Coughing and hacking, I fell to the cramped floor, muscles quivering like jelly, useless. Some small part of my brain, far in the back amid the stacks of trivia, wondered if the floor had been cleaned recently, reflected that it would be pretty gross if I were lying on a carpet of dried urine and fecal particles. The things we think of when stressed, huh?

Hands over my mouth, I sobbed, the loss of my agents, the loss of Carol, the loss of my innocence finally surging through my tired mind, unhampered by my customary fury. Emotional walls I had built over the years had crumbled under the strain of time and fatigue. Eventually, the silent sobs quit and I lay there, quiet and spent, empty of purpose and volition.

Five, ten minutes later, with eyes fever red, I wobbled to my feet, turned on the tap and washed the snot and dried tears from my face.

"What's wrong with me," I mumbled through the tepid water. "What is going on?"

The walk to my seat lasted four days as I passed those who pretended not to notice my disheveled appearance and bloodshot eyes, pretended not to be aware that I'd been bawling myself sick in the bathroom for the last few minutes.

When the back of my lap hit the seat and the plane began to taxi for a takeoff, I tried BB's office again from a satphone. Still, nothing but the answering machine.

"Nothing on BB's end?" Pat's voice had a raspy, guttural quality heard in those who spent some time screaming. She flopped down on the seat next to mine. By the color of her eyes, she'd had her own bout of the weepies.

"Just the answering machine. Doesn't mean anything." A lie. It meant that something was terribly wrong and we both knew who was responsible.

Pat laid her head against my arm, a gesture of solidarity or the need for comfort? Maybe both?

"You okay, kid?" I asked, laying my cheek on the top of her head. Her hair smelled of lavender and mist.

"Who you calling kid, old man?" she joked sadly.

"I am officially the oldest cat here, so everyone is a kid."

"Harrumph."

"Don't 'harrumph' me. I'm the old man. Not a man jack one of you has hit 30 yet. You're only—"

She broke in. "A young girl still and never mind about my

age!"

"So 'kid' is actually a compliment." I may have looked like hell, but my tone was light and playful.

We shared a long silence until the jet reached thirty thousand feet. With a sigh, she rolled her head away. "I've seen a lot of bad things in my life, both in and out of the Bureau, but that … that was a something out of a nightmare, her head exploding like that."

Nightmare, or a scene from *Scanners*. "Yeah, it was bad." Once again I felt the patter of shredded bone against my skin.

More silence. More memories of blood and death. "Can I tell you something, Kal?"

"Of course."

A long, indrawn breath. "I've worked with Special Branch for six years now, worked with five different teams. All good people, all people of character, but you, Mr. Kalevi Hakala, the Ferocious Finn, are my favorite."

" 'Ferocious Finn'?"

She looked at me curiously. "You didn't know?"

"I never bothered to ask."

Her hand rubbed my shoulder. "You always have this shell around you, stronger than any armor. You smile and joke and say the right things, all the things a normal person would say and do, but it's just an act, Kal."

A normal person? Since when were the people in the Bureau normal?

She must have read my silence as an affirmation. "The only time I see you, the real you, is when you rage, when you lose control. That's the damaged part of you coming through to roar its pain to the world. A beast and a wounded child at the same time."

"Thank you Doctor Phil," I remarked dryly.

An iron hard finger poked me in the side hard enough to hurt. "There you go again, jerkwad, throwing up a glib remark to deflect a serious conversation. It's been your M.O. for as long as even BB remembers."

"You talk to BB about me?"

"I'm Special Branch. I'm not only a Receptionist, but I also have an M.A. in Psychology and do psych-evals on all team members, just like all the other Receptionists."

I scratched my head in puzzlement. "You've never done a psych-eval on me."

"Not a formal one. When you've had an eval done in the past, it was always at Warehouse or while being investigated, right?"

"Right."

"It was a Bureau Receptionist who did it. Just like you, Kal, so blinded by your revenge you didn't even know it was the Receptionists who head-shrunk you."

It was? My mind filed back to the countless evals I'd had in the past. Same dumb questions, same bs answers ... *scritch scritch scritch* went a pen on pad as every one of the Special Branch evaluators wrote down how I felt—my 'feelings' being of special interest to the Bureau. Can't have any budding psychos running around with the power of a Bureau agent, can we? And Pat was right, all the docs were ladies, dressed to kill, with minds sharper than razors—those keen intellects cutting deep into my brain and scooping out the damaged bits for scrutiny.

And boy was I ever damaged—a haunted soul bleeding rage and pain whenever hurt. But this was old news to the Bureau. As long as I could focus my fury on the Supernaturals without hurting others, I was aces.

"No," I muttered when the pause became too long. "I never noticed. Why the hell are you talking to me about this?"

When she looked at me, the force of her gaze rocked me back. "Because this is the first time I've seen you experience an intense emotion that wasn't anger. Do you have any idea what this means?"

"No. I'm not a psychologist."

Another poke in the same spot. It was going to leave a mark, I knew it. We Finns bruise like bananas.

"You're doing it again, you big idiot," she growled. "What it means is that you're starting to break. A crack has finally appeared in that invulnerable armor of yours. And just when I'd given up on you being human, too."

"Cute."

"What it also means is that if you don't seek professional help soon, on a regular basis, you could have a serious emotional crisis."

My laughter, when it came, carried enough bitterness to corrode the strongest metal. "Oh, Pat, you don't get it." More caustic mirth bubbled out of me. "Maybe no one does. I *know* I'm deeply damaged, like one of those hoarders you see on TV, their sickness displayed for all the world to see, but unable to do anything about it. I have that same kind of obsession. Instead of being unable to stop my actions, I *want* to continue this path toward my self-destruction."

Her look of dismay was like a slap.

"Why am I still an agent?"

No words, just a shake of her head as tears gathered in her eyes.

"Why am I granted so much latitude? Why haven't I been officially reprimanded for my drinking during an op? Why haven't I been benched for destroying my office? I have the worst morale of any agent in the Bureau, but instead of a room with rubber walls, I am still issued a team and given license to kill Supernaturals as I see fit."

"I don't know." The words might have been a prayer, they were so soft and sorrowful.

"The reason isn't hard to fathom, Pat. BB doesn't want me to be sane, to shed my obsession like dry skin. The crazier I am, the more effective, and right now I'm very effective indeed. *That's* why my leash is long and loose. There is one thing I can be absolutely sure of … as long as I pose no threat to the team or Straights, the Bureau will use me until I'm empty and useless."

Silence. Pat stared toward the front of the plane, eyes set and glassy.

"Of course, you knew that already. I think everyone with half a brain knew."

She nodded.

"It's okay, Pat, I don't mind. I've been living with this … thing in my heart for so long, it's no longer a burden. I may be a bit friable right now, but I'll pull through like I always do."

Perhaps a minute went by before I felt warm lips brush my ear. "I love you, you big dope," she whispered. "And I don't want to see you hurt or in pain." That said, she rose and sashayed her way to the back of the cabin. The back of her front carried a lot of appeal.

One nap later we entered DC airspace and after an apple juice we landed. Before the jet could taxi to a stop, black Vics and SUVs surrounded us, federal cop chic.

Teams Delta, Iota and Beta spilled out of the vehicles, a sinister version of the clown car trick. The team leaders surrounded me as my feet hit the tarmac: Ayre Grossman, tall, rail thin and no sense of humor. Malcolm Czerny, short, balding and strong as an ox. Audrey Washington, a dark haired stiletto of a woman with almond eyes and midnight hair. All of them deferred to me as the senior man in the field. Not sure if that was a good thing.

Audrey, a three-year agent, looked me up and down, focusing on my gore-stained chinos. "Kal, you look like hell." She offered no warmth and would welcome none.

"I feel worse." Not far from the truth.

"What's the play?" Ayre asked solemnly. Everything he did was with heaping doses of solemn.

"You all got the update, so the rest is easy. We suit up, hit the Warehouse with everything we've got and save the day."

Ayre's hairy eyebrows shot up. "That's it?"

I gritted my teeth. "Yah, that's it. Except, if you see a skinny red-haired witch, shoot to kill. No ifs, ands, or buts."

Audrey smiled, a sight that would scare most people. "Good. I like it."

Malcolm's voice rumbled up from some deep pit. "We brought

an extra SUV for your team."

I turned to my people lined in an arc behind me. "Suit up, load up and let's roll."

Agents die in the field, but the Warehouse has always stood resolute amidst the carnage of war with Supernaturals. A good dollop of paranoia saw the Bureau office shift from location to location every few years, in case some clever Supernatural came a-calling, a policy that had worked since the Warehouse had been established in 1866. My palms grew clammy on the drive to Arlington, heat building up behind my eyes as I became more and more excited at the prospect of a good dust-up.

Tires squealed as we rounded the corner into the Warehouse parking lot. Low rent Dodges, Hondas and Fords were parked in the employees' spaces—nothing flashy, nothing that would draw a second look. Another ordinary day at Maxine's Data Storage (don't ask, I don't know, either) where the good guys fight the good fight.

Everything seemed normal as we pulled to a jittery stop, SUVs and Vics leaving smoky black streaks on the pavement. Before I knew it I found myself running toward the single point of entrance, a glass (actually panes of wurtzite boron nitride, 58% stronger than diamond) and carbon steel door with the cheesy company name stenciled in white.

I risked a quick glance inside before jinking my head back out of sight from within. What I'd seen had soured my stomach. "Delta, go round back to the door marked 'Exit.' Three feet to the right and three up is a hidden panel. Push and it will reveal a keypad."

"What the hell is it?" Arye asked, voice dead as Disco.

"Director's escape route in case something like this happens. Access code is Whiskey Foxtrot Tango 113. That'll get you in the back. Keep in touch. Check?"

"How the hell do you know that?"

"Friends in low places. Now get gone."

"Check, boss." Delta team made themselves scarce.

"Everyone else, follow me. Magicians in the middle. Stay

frosty, people, you're not going to like what you see."

The lobby looked the same as the last time I'd seen it, with the exception of a spray of red and pink against the puke-yellow wall behind the Receptionist's desk. I knew exactly what I'd find and wasn't disappointed. Kim, a two-year, lay on the floor behind the faux-wood desk, a neat little hole between her eyes. Somebody had used a high velocity round to redecorate the wall behind her. I checked the shotgun mounted under her desk. Not a round fired. Bryan/Winnie's handiwork was my guess. A ghoul would've just torn her to shreds. How the hell did Bryan/Winnie get past the outer defenses?

A tap on a button and the panel door popped a couple of inches. The Lahti preceded me into the long hallway, the others filing close behind.

Arye's somber voice sounded over the earwig. "*You weren't kidding about a hatch. It's barely bigger than a body can get through. Going in now. Out.*"

My skin felt tight as a scream across the bones of my skull as I reached the first door, the Combat room, its black lock plate charred and still smoking slightly, the acrid smell of burning wire and insulation irritating my nose.

I pushed the door open with the toe of my boot, revealing black with a good dose of deep dark. Quickly, I slipped on my night-vision glasses, and the cavernous combat room revealed itself in glorious shades of black and white. Infrared would've been useless. Zombies and ghouls tended toward room temp.

Two steps in and it hit me. The smell ... blood, bowels, and piss, the smell of violent death along with the acrid stink of fear. Somebody had died ... check that, a *lot* of somebodies had died.

Six steps, seven. More blood smell. Eight, nine and I spotted it ... or them ... the bodies, a whole mess of them, two or three teams worth. Not that they were recognizable, I was going by sheer volume of bits and pieces. They had been literally ripped limb from limb and then stuffed into the weapons racks in a macabre display of horrific humor, blood dripping blackly to the floor.

Dripping? This had just happened!

Too late I turned my attention upwards where ghouls dropped like spiders into our midst. The Lahti silently spoke twice before a slimy, warty body hit mine, razor claws flashing, tearing at my body armor.

"Brasssalmon!" I grunted as I bounced off a wrestling mat. Twin *booms* from the explosive rounds nearly tore the ghoul in half as it raked another claw across my chest, shredding Kevlar and leaving deep grooves in titanium. I cursed myself for not leading with the .44 and dug my hands into the thing's putrid, slick innards. Setting my shoulders, my biceps, I *heaved*, tearing the monster in half, finishing what the explosive rounds started. Thick, dark, foul fluid sprayed across my face. I nearly lost what I'd eaten for the past two decades as the putrid stuff entered my nostrils. The legs and lower torso landed next to me, twitching, while the upper body flipped end over end to land flopping and gnashing at Matt's feet. Two explosive rounds from his .44 into the thing's head ended the monster.

Six more ghouls jumped like jackrabbits around the room, and the teams, clustered together, were firing back to back in a tight group, keeping each other safe in the eye of a storm of bullets.

Another ghoul sped toward me, almost too fast to see. I managed to draw my own .44 and get a round off, which took the creature in the knee, blowing the joint apart, causing it to stumble and fall wetly onto the mat. More explosive rounds tore it to bite-sized pieces.

Four more went down, shredded in a hail of exploding bullets, and I felt like we might come through this battle unscathed, but the sight of two agents down, writhing in agony in the center of the group, brought my rage surging to the fore.

One more ghoul, dodging bullets and whirling across the floor like a dervish—a blur of undead wrath—came at me at speeds I couldn't fathom. The fury that powered me was easily up to the task. The .44 fell to the mat, but the Bowie appeared as if by magic, and I ducked and swung, slicing clean through its arm. A gurgly shriek came from its armored throat as it passed and turned *so quickly* that the laws of physics might have been made of rubber. Again it rushed me, but I spun, Bowie flicking out to catch it above the knee, half severing its leg. The monster tumbled to the ground, and I was on it as its shriek ripped through the air—the sound of metal being shredded—but that didn't matter because my hands grabbed both sides of its slimy head and *wrenched!*

Panting, I finally came to myself, holding a ghoul's head in my hands, watching its mouth open and close spastically.

"I ain't never seen nothing like that," someone breathed in awe.

"Then you ain't never worked with Kal," said Dom, sounding proud.

I dropped the head and wiped slime off my hands. "What the hell are you two talking about? We have agents hurt."

"It's okay, Kal," Alex interjected wearily as he wobbled to his feet. Two other magicians had their hands on the downed agents who now seemed to be asleep. "Me, Carl and Ilena have them in hand. They'll be fine after a little nap."

A nap. A nap sounded good, real good. I hadn't had a decent night's sleep in days, but I still had miles to go … "Any anti-healing, possession or tagging spells?" He shook his head. "Good job then. You, too, Ilena, Carl." They tipped me a nod each.

Malcolm broke free from the bunch and trotted over while I retrieved the Lahti from a pool of translucent ghoul goo. "How did you do that?" he demanded.

"Do what?" A pant leg became the resting place for more slime.

"Move like that, man. No way was that normal!"

Fury still had a hold on me and it showed in my eyes when they met his. He blanched and backed off, muttering an apology. "I need two volunteers to escort the wounded to the cars. The rest come with me," I said tonelessly, keeping my gaze fixed on Malcolm. It was a little Alpha Male of me, but we were in a bad situation and couldn't afford dissention in the ranks.

Pat bulled forward from the group. "What the hell is this, Kal? These things didn't stand a chance. Why would this Winnie person waste them this way?"

Arye broke in, "*Everyone okay, boss? We heard fighting.*"

"Fine. Gimme a sitrep."

"*In the BB's office, waiting for you.*"

"Stay put. We'll be there. Check?"

"*Check.*"

"I have an idea why, Pat," I growled. "But we have some housecleaning to do." Storming past, my blood up, I signaled the rest to follow. Next down the hall was R&D, a Special Branch room. I paused, readying my glasses in case that room proved to be dark, too.

Alex stepped up, whisper low and harsh, features uncommonly tense. "Kal, you ever been inside R&D?"

I shook my head. "That's where the geeks go to die, not me."

"The walls are lined with Lexan cubicles, about twenty-five of them. Ten by ten, but that's not the issue. It's the gem locker."

"The what?"

"Gem locker, a safe mounted into the floor … state-of-the-art electronic/magical lock. If this Winnie managed to open the safe, well … there's about twenty million in spell gems in there."

"*Jesus … Twenty million?*"

"Yeah. And at least two hundred class-one gemstones."

I didn't need this right now, but I had to ask. "Class one?"

He leaned in close. "Max quality gems of all kinds, the purest an unlimited budget can procure."

Wasn't that a comforting thought? "Just great," I muttered. "It's a wonder I don't have ulcers." Pissed, I kicked the door in.

Nothing.

Well, not *nothing*. If you had plopped a tornado inside the room the damage wouldn't come close to what we found in there. In the black-and-white world of night-vision, broken sheets of polycarbonate resin lay scattered everywhere, along with what I reckoned used to be some very expensive electronic equipment. Add to that enough body parts to have come from at least six victims as well as enough blood to warm the heart of any die-hard Cronenberg fan.

Including one ghoul.

Its head had been literally crushed to a fetid black pulp. The weapon had been a large microscope, judging from the ghoul ichor liberally coating its base. The wielder of the fatal microscope lay next to the ghoul she had killed.

"Oh, crap … Ariel!" Suddenly the rage vanished as it had never been and I found Ariel in my arms, her body still warm. Through the torn remains of her left sleeve, I could see the shredded flesh of her arm, still sluggishly oozing blood.

"Alex!"

"On it, boss," the little magician breathed, falling to his knees next to me, hands cupping Ariel's unblemished cheeks, closing his eyes. A few incredibly long, agonizing seconds passed before his lids fluttered open. "She's alive, just barely. Ilena, Carl, help me." The other two magicians stumbled forward. "Boss, move."

I moved. I waited. I fretted and paced as the trio laid their hands on the woman I had come to admire but had needed to bounce from the team. Her flesh began to knit and regenerate right before my eyes, blood drying, flaking off her chocolate skin to land on the floor as fine, rust-colored dust. Alex rose from the group and staggered to me, face older by at least ten years. "She'll be okay, boss, but she needs fluids, lots and lots of fluids. I'll have someone take her outside."

My hand found his shoulder. "Thanks, Alex," I said, voice thick with emotion.

He nodded. "She wants to talk to you."

All I needed to hear. Shouldering the other two magicians to the side, I knelt at Ariel's side, staring into her pale, pale face. Her head was cushioned by her carefully folded jacket. A moment later, her eyes fluttered open.

"Hi, Kal," she sighed.

"Hi, yourself," I answered gently.

"You were right, you know."

"About what?"

Slowly her face crumpled. "I hesitated …

"Ariel—"

She wailed, "I hesitated and three magicians died in less than five seconds!" Sobs racked her body.

Carefully I drew her into my arms and she clutched at me with the singular power of her despair. "It's okay," I crooned as if to a child.

"No! It's not, Kal! You were so right about me."

"Ariel, Ariel … shhhh. I know, kid. But the important thing is you're all right."

No response.

"Ariel?" Still no response. "Ariel!"

"Boss, she's unconscious." Alex's small hands gently pulled at me, and I let Ariel go. The two other magicians converged on her supine form, hands fluttering over her cheeks and neck. "Don't worry, Kal. They'll take care of her."

I nodded. Emotions warred within and for a split second I didn't trust myself to speak. Eventually, though, I shrugged off such distractions, willing the doors to my heart to swing shut. "Alex, check the gem locker. Matt, you and I will cover."

"Check."

From a hip pocket the little magician produced a one-carat diamond that shone with a soft green glow. It held it hard in his fist and stepped into the room, careful of the rubble. Matt and I followed, weapons at the ready. Forty-nine agonizing steps later the young magician reached his destination and knelt.

I placed a hand on his shoulder. "Wait a second, Alex. Check for bugs."

"What?"

"Humor me."

"Check, boss." A hand dipped into another pocket and rooted around for a second, producing a topaz the size of my pinky nail. Holding the gem in one hand, he closed his eyes and sighed.

Suddenly the stone glowed yellow through his fingers, outlining the bones of his hand, and something went *pop* behind and to the right of me. I whirled, ready to face a reasonable facsimile of hell, but there was nothing, only a wisp of grayish-black smoke. Three more small reports sounded a second later.

"Got to hand it to you, Kal," Alex uttered aloud, trembling slightly. "Four cams, three tech, one magical."

"Good job, kid. Carry on." *Clever, Winnie, real clever,* I thought.

Nodding, he turned his attention to the floor, running a hand over a section of short-pile carpet. A strip separated from the rest and found the magician's fingers. He pulled and a three by three square came loose, exposing plain gray concrete. Almost lovingly, he set the diamond on the hard surface and stood.

He said, "Better back up a little."

Easy enough to do when magic is involved.

Alert for ghoulish intervention, I kept my eyes peeled and tried to grow a couple in the back of my head. From the hole in the carpet came a soft white glow, accompanied by a gentle whine. The whine and the glow remained steady for about thirty seconds before abruptly cutting off.

"Looks like no one has opened the safe," announced Alex, back on his knees next to the hole.

I took a quick look. No concrete and no evidence there ever had been, only a dark steel door with a keypad and rotating handle. "How can you tell?"

"Locking spell is still in place," he replied while he punched the star key. A yellow light blinked four times. "No one has entered the combination recently, at least not in the past four hours."

I nodded and pointed to the charred remains of the spyeyes. "She wanted to see where we hid the locker and the combination."

Alex produced another diamond and set it on the safe. More glowing and whining and—*voilà!*—the slab of cement was back in place. A trick most contractors would sell their grandmothers to learn.

"Kal, something has been eating at me," Alex said as he drew close.

"You're wondering how she disabled our spyeyes, defensive spells and lockdown protocols."

"How did—"

For the first time in the last few hours, something like a smile touched my face, but couldn't find a grip. "As senior field agent, I've been read in on all Warehouse defensive protocols—magical and otherwise. The answer is simple. Just like you killed the spyeyes, she disabled the Warehouse defenses by using magic."

"Do you have any idea how much magical energy it takes to do *that*?"

"By your horrified expression, I'd say a metric ton."

"Not funny, boss. It would take a couple hundred magicians working in concert to pull it off, and even then it would be problematic!"

I felt the beginnings of a major league headache coming on. What was Winnie up to? How did she get that kind of power? Some terrified part of my lizard brain didn't want to know.

First things first. "Arye, we're on our way."

"*Check, boss.*"

"Audrey, you and yours take Medical. Mal, check out Records, then both of you check the Dormitory."

"What's going on, Kal?" Audrey asked, stone-faced. Malcolm glowered over her shoulder like a protective golem.

"This was a waste of time. She knew a few prepared teams would take out her pets." My voice grew hoarse. "This evil twist wanted to delay us so she could get away. I'll bet you serious money there's spyeyes in every room. She wanted to find the gem locker."

"That it?"

"No, that's not it," I answered, staring hard into her eyes. After a moment she dropped hers. "She wants BB and may have him. And ... she wants to send me a message."

"What message?" Malcolm grated.

What message indeed? It took about two seconds to come up with an answer. Snarling, I snapped, "Go on, get to Records, the Dorm and Medical. When you're done, get to Admin."

Both nodded and followed in my furious wake as I spouted out orders. "Have your magicians check for spyeyes and listeners and burn them out. Alex, you and Matt go to Combat and sterilize that, too. And, Alex, find out what happened to the defensive protocols, if they were dispelled, burned out or circumvented. And don't forget the ghouls; they probably have gems we can use, most likely in their stomachs."

"Check, boss."

The rest of Epsilon followed me down the hall to Admin, where Arye and his group waited patiently, weapons at the ready. At their feet lay the headless body of a sturdy looking man. The walls were covered in a patina of blood, bones and brains. It was Bryan; I could tell by his shoes.

Damn her.

"Stand down, everybody," I announced, heading toward BB's office, a good case of mad building up.

BB's office wasn't as big as the previous Director's, but a few families could live inside and still have room for privacy. The old, clunky science fiction desk had gone the way of the DoDo and BB's sleek, blacktopped mahogany number had plenty of tricks built in; they were just less obvious. Touching the polished surface, I was rewarded with ... nothing. No icons or virtual keyboards popped into existence.

I pulled the plush leather chair to the side and crawled under, rooting around for the desk's CPU. Nothing. Gone. Gone, too, were the two 500 terabyte hard drives.

"Damn it," I muttered.

Dom bent over to look where I was crouching. "What, boss?"

Scrambling out, I started to remove my armor, setting the Lahti and .44 on the desk along with my Bowie. "Might as well stand down, Dom. I finally got the full picture here." Soon the bulky breastplate and leggings joined my weapons on the desk.

"What's it about, then?"

Instead of answering, I looked around. *Where would she put it?* I wondered. Not in the corners of the room; that wasn't elegant enough for her. No, she wanted me to find it, but where?

The portrait of the President, slim and dapper in a dove-gray suit, his soulful brown eyes staring with great compassion and intelligence, hung a few short feet away from the desk.

Of course.

Striding up to the portrait, I stared into those soft, brown orbs. "Okay, Winnie, what do you want?" I asked tersely, broadcasting my ire through my eyes.

My phone vibrated in its holster. I answered with a snarly, "What?"

"You're much better than I expected, Kal. I'm glad you resisted my effort to kill you."

"You weren't trying to kill me, Winnie. You wanted my mind going in a hundred different directions."

Her laugh made me gnash my teeth. "Don't frown, darling; you'll wrinkle so. And don't even think about trying to back-trace this call. I am magically and technologically shielded from detection."

I tried for the heart shot. "You missed BB, didn't you? He's safe and out of reach and you are screwed, Win."

"I didn't miss anything, you impudent ass. He's right here, and if you want him back alive, you'll do exactly what I say." Hate roughened her voice and her East Anglian dialect started to show, her west Texas drawl slipping away like the tide.

"You know the drill, then. Proof of life. Now. Or I hang up and you can go pound sand."

"Listen you little—"

"No!" I shouted into the phone, spit flying. "You give me proof of life or all bets are off and I will spend my life hunting you down! So don't dick me around, bitch!"

Silence. A long one and I began to wonder if I had just killed BB. Arye, no slouch, stood in the doorway, normally deadpan face slack with shock.

"Kal?"

My temples throbbed. "BB?"

"Whatever she wants, don't—"

"There you go, Kal," Winnie cut in. "You have your proof."

"What do you want, Win?" I had a good idea and I prayed to god I was wrong.

"The keys to the kingdom, dear Kal. I want you to give me the keys."

The phone's plastic casing cracked in my hand and I eased my grip. "BB wouldn't give them up. What makes you think I will?"

Once again that laugh that made me want to hurl. "How about this?" Next came the unmistakable sound of flesh hitting flesh and Win's voice demanded gruffly, "Speak! Now!"

By the pricking of my thumbs ...

"Kalevi?"

My heart hit rock bottom. "Dad?" I whispered. "Are you okay?" Tears began to well.

Winnie's voice returned, triumphant. "He's fine, Kal."

"How did ... when did you ..." My throat closed.

"Imagine my surprise when I found out you were still in the Bureau when you came to kill my zombies in Denver. It was a simple matter to quietly avoid Bureau watchdog programs and Google your family. It cost me a couple of my nicer gems, but the men I hired to kidnap your father did a splendid job. Too bad they didn't live long enough to spend their pay. And don't worry about your mother. She's just fine. As far as she knows he had to go out of town for work. He's been making regular calls home. You see, *Kalevi*," she turned my name into a curse. "After you killed the first ghoul, I thought that maybe a little insurance would be an intelligent move on my part."

It took a few moments, but I finally found my voice. "Damn you, Winnie."

"Damn me? Damn *you*, Kal, you and BB. Because of you I've suffered what no human being should ever have to suffer! So you are going to give me the access codes to BB's computer and then your father can go home."

I'd been around the block enough times to know a lie when I heard it. "You hate me because of San Antonio, I understand that, but my father has nothing to do with that. Promise me you'll let him go. Let me hear the words."

"Of course. I promise, Kal."

Still lying. "Okay, Winnie, anything you want. Where and when?"

So she told me.

Angrily I agreed, then had Arye's magician burn the spyeye to char.

A few minutes later found me outside, phone in hand, furiously dialing Alex's number as Dom looked on in consternation. "C'mon, Ghost … answer. Ghost?"

Bzzz …"I'm here, Kal. What can I do for you?"

"I need a favor, Ghost. The biggest mother of all favors."

"What is it?"

I filled him in on the day's events.

Bzzz … "Anything you want, Kal. She must be stopped."

"Ghost, she said we couldn't back trace her, that she was magically and technologically protected. But can you do it?"

Buzzcracklecracklecracke! I'd never heard the Ghost make that kind of noise before. A few seconds passed before I realized he was *laughing.* "She may be sly, but so am I," was all he said before disconnecting.

Minutes later, Alex and the rest of the magicians joined me outside. "Every camera, spyeye, defensive spell, alarm spell, and weapons emplacement have been disabled, dispelled or destroyed." He shook his head in wonder while the other magicians looked stunned and at a loss. "The power needed to do that is off the charts, Kal." His world had been rocked and now he was trying to make sense of the chaos.

I shook my head. "I don't know how she did it, Alex, but it was just her, her and her ghouls. She's not the type to share power; she wants it all to herself."

"How, then?"

I shrugged. "Dunno. Right now the question is, how much silver wire can we lay our hands on?"

"How much do you need?"

My eyebrow tried to reach my hairline and he smiled. "The defensive spell over the roof the Warehouse is Shaped by silver wire," he explained. "A lot of it. It's how we can sense a Supernatural from over a mile away. All we have to do is dig under some gravel and roofing tar."

"Good." I grinned nastily. "Let's head in. I have a plan."

Chapter Seventeen

Ten Years Earlier
Cascade Cavern Combat

I followed the team and the concrete ribbon down, down steep inclines that switchbacked through the naked gut rock of Texas. Shortly after we had passed under the big slab of rock overhanging the entrance, we came upon a light switch. Unfortunately the power had been deliberately cut off so we were forced to use the night-vision goggles.

"I've never used night-vision like this," I sent quietly, in awe at the clarity of sight.

"That's because it's not just magic, it's tech, too, white boy."

BB's voice somehow transformed the dry rasp of subvocals into a lecturing tone. *"Enough chatter, you two."*

"Check, boss."

"Check."

"Sending HUD to your goggles … now," BB announced.

Winking into existence in the upper right-hand corner of my goggles came a map of the caverns, rendered in thin white lines. Long and snake-like, they stretched off to the northeast for hundreds of feet, widening and narrowing at points before opening into an enormous cave roughly two-hundred-fifty feet long and nearly a hundred wide. Little side tunnels dotted the map—perfect ambush sites for an enterprising vamp.

The slope steepened and turned, steepened and turned. All the while the humidity rose and the temperature dropped until it reached a comfortable 68°F. The only sounds were the barely noticeable scuffing of our rubber-soled boots and the slow, regular drip, drip, drip of water.

If a hard, vicious thrill hadn't been searing through my veins I would've been in awe of the wonders around me: limestone carved by countless centuries of ponderous erosion, dripstone deposits forming extraordinary displays of stalactites and stalagmites, pillars of time curiously formed to appear almost organic and soft as they stretched toward one another.

The ceiling began to rise as we descended into the first cave, over a hundred feet long, the walls and ceiling hung with lichen-covered stone that looked as if it had been melted and then re-shaped by gravity.

The path wound round humped rock and shallow pits, pools of mineral-rich water and strange looking protrusions on the walls. Soon, about seventy feet in, we came to the cave-that the talking head on TV had been blathering about, where the tunnel began to narrow. Jagged-edged rock created a large, treacherous mound that humped its way ten feet into the air—an ugly assault on the beauty of the cave.

"*What now, boss?*" Canton asked, staring at the mass of rubble blocking the way.

BB turned his goggled gaze to the magician. "*Win, can you do something?*"

"*I got it, boss.*" She pulled off a glove and dug around in a pocket for a gemstone, walking slowly toward the cave-in. The gem, a garnet, glowed white in night-vision while she placed a hand on a skull-sized piece of limestone. A few seconds of concentration and she gave a brief nod, the garnet winking out. "*That should do it, boss. It'll hold for about five minutes.*"

"*Good,*" he sent. "*Everyone over and mind your step.*"

I don't know what kind of spell she used, but even the smallest rock remained steady, as if cemented in place. Navigation was still dicey, however; the dripstone was slick with moisture and with one slip, any of us could have easily twisted or broken an ankle.

On the other side, some twenty feet from the end of the fall, the cave split in three—one right, one left and the cement path running straight ahead down the middle. BB signaled Canton, Win and me to stay by the fall and stay ready.

Signaling Thomas to take the right-hand corridor, BB took the left. Our HUDs indicated that the corridors on either side were short, only a couple dozen feet long. "*Light bomb, Thomas,*" he said.

"*Check.*"

Light bomb?

I found out real quick what that entailed.

Each of them pulled out a gem from their web belts and softly whispered into their fists before hurling them into their respective corridors.

If I had been wearing military grade night-vision goggles, they would've overloaded from the actinic glare that flooded like liquid light from those corridors. Five, six, seven seconds of blinding whiteness later and the light died as if a switch had been thrown.

BB nodded to Thomas as both entered their respective corridors. They came out seconds later and slowly continued up the center passage. "*All clear,*" BB sent.

"*Cool, eh, white boy?*"

I couldn't help but grin. "*Friggin' awesome.*"

Fifty feet farther down and the concrete ribbon became a catwalk, iron railings on either side protecting tourists from a steep dropoff to either side where hundreds stalagmites waited to impale the unwary. According to my HUD, this section of the caverns ran on for roughly a hundred fifty feet.

More protrusions resembling melted wax jutted from the walls while stalactites loomed above. I began to get the feeling that we walked within the bowels of an immense, stony beast.

Sccccchh ... The sound was so soft that it almost wasn't, but the hyper-alert part of me took note and spun my body around, the Bowie already in my hand coming up and it ...

Shunnk ... plunged wetly into the stomach of a young man, a child really, eyes wide in fright and confusion ... mouth gaping, a trickle of blood drooling from his lower lip. Horrified, I stood there, staring, taking in the thin, pinched face and the long, greasy hair, the black and white of night-vision rendering him into smears of gray.

"Oh, god," I whispered, agonized as he stared at the knife in his gut, my hand frozen on the handle. "I'm so *sorry!*" A kid, just a kid, no more than sixteen and I had gutted him like a trout.

Suddenly a hole appeared in his throat spewing blood while gore shot out the back of his neck and his legs gave way, gravity sliding his body off the Bowie to land in a heap at my feet. My head swiveled to see Canton lowering his pistol, a frown on his normally inscrutable flat face.

"What the—" I began.

"Shut up!" He interrupted. "*Keep it subvocal, Green Pea!*"

I nodded. "*Sorry, Canton.*" My eyes traveled to the lump of bone and meat at my feet. "*Look what I did, man. Just a kid ...*"

"*Look closer, white boy,*" Even through the earwig his voice was sad. "*Look at his wrists, his neck.*"

I knelt at the kid's side and plucked a slack arm. Heavy gauze covered his entire forearm from wrist to elbow, as did the other arm. Next to the body lay a wicked little knife, a dagger actually, the type with a nine-inch triangular blade called a misericorde. "What the hell?"

"*Vampire lunch box.*" Thomas announced, staring impassively at the corpse. "*Five will get you ten that that's the Renfield. Looks like he was sneaking up on you, Pea. Wanted to take you from behind.*"

"*But why?*" Relief flooded me that I hadn't committed cold-blooded murder on an innocent kid. Renfields usually were vamp lovers who enjoyed doing their master's dirty work. My mind flashed to the photo of the murdered girl and I felt a brief moment of satisfaction. Moments ago I'd considered the kid I'd killed an innocent victim, but now he belonged at the head of a long list of monsters I longed kill. One down ...

"*Renfields are tasked by their vamp masters for protection. Just be happy he didn't have a gun.*" Thomas sounded immutable as a rock.

Right. Good thought that. With a brutal smile that hurt my cheeks, I stoked the flames of my wrath, certain that I'd need it soon.

Curious as to where the kid came from, I stepped over his cooling body and backtracked until a knot of black caught my eye. A dark nylon rope wrapped around the base of one of the iron railing uprights led down over the side of the catwalk into the depths of the stalagmite forest below. Somehow the kid had held onto the rope long enough for us to pass and then had quietly climbed up, pulled the misericorde and snuck up on me. The kid had skills. Grimacing, I looked over the side into the darkness below.

And into the snarling face of a vampire hoisting itself up at me, a hiss of rage steam kettle whistling from its throat.

I raised my arms in time to catch the freight train that slammed into my chest. It threw me back against the opposite railing, bending me backwards and sending the Bowie and .44 clattering off into the darkness. It was my first vampire and it was everything I didn't want it to be.

Bone white skin stretched taut over obscenely protruding cheekbones and lips like flatworms parted to reveal a mouthful of pale spikes. Insanely strong hands gripped my shoulders and *bent* the titanium armor plates. My lungs rebelled at the strange snaky smell of it as flecks of saliva from its open mouth spattered against the skin of my face, deadening sensation. I knew it was only a matter of moments before its teeth found me and bit my face off.

Like an animal lashing against the bars of its cage, the rage struggled to be set free, so I opened the door.

The monster's progress toward my face halted as the rush reached my muscles and a look of incomprehension etched its way onto the whiteness of the creature's face. A tight smile on mine answered it. Roaring, I heaved myself up from railing and whirled, slamming the vamp against cold iron. Then, again and again, hammering at the railing with the monster's flailing body, summoning every ounce of strength that I could leech from the fury that boiled within. The repetitive pounding against that railing became my whole world, my whole reason for existing at that moment and I felt *good*.

"Green Pea…"

Again and again, trying to obliterate that hateful face, each impact ringing against the metal.

"Green Pea!"

The face, that terrible face with its pink eyes now slick with some sort of viscous fluid, but I didn't care, I kept slamming and slamming…

"Green Pea!"

Hands grabbed at me, my upper arms and shoulders, but that didn't matter, the beast inside wanted to feed because this *thing*, this *monster*, had to die, they *all* had to die so there were no more Leenas for me to mourn. My gloved hands found either side of its head and I *twisted!*

"Holy Mary mother of god," someone whimpered.

"*Kal!*" My name, so urgently called through the earwig, finally brought me back to myself, pulling the plug and draining the rage from my flesh.

"What?" I gasped aloud, panting and sweating in the humid air.

"*Kal, are you all right?*" BB sent, sounding like he was talking to a dangerous animal.

"*What?*" I sent back stupidly, not understanding the question.

"*White boy, look at your hands.*" Canton sounded scared.

"*I don't know about you guys,*" Thomas interjected coolly, "*but I've never seen the like.*"

Winnie silently crossed herself.

Uncertain, I looked down and saw that I gripped the vampire's skull by its thin white hair, its blood, quite black in my night-vision, pattered down onto the concrete. Its body lay in a widening pool at my feet.

"Oh," I grunted, dropping the dripping head. It landed with a hollow *thunk*.

" 'Oh,' *you say? 'Oh'?*" Thomas said, a faint hint of sarcasm leeching through my earwig. "*You just killed a vamp bare-handed and popped its head off like a champagne cork. That's never been done before.*"

"*Well then, I guess I'm not a Green Pea anymore.*"

Canton's smile shone bright and fierce. "*You got that right, white boy.*"

With a snort, I looked for my weapons and found them a few short feet away. As I rose, Bowie and .44 in hand, there came a *thump!* and BB flew past me, arms flailing, to land with a crash ten feet beyond.

Another vampire was among us, hands clawing. Thomas grabbed an arm in an attempt to throw the creature to the ground, but the vampire heaved the big man right off his feet with one arm as if he were a child and threw him over the side of the catwalk to fall among the stalagmites below.

Canton fired, wooden bullets stitching up the front of the monster's button-down oxford shirt, but strangely the vamp smiled and *blurred* forward, fist smashing into the Native American's chest. He flew backwards right into Winnie, connecting with bone-breaking force. Both landed and lay very still.

The .44 roared silently in my hand, two explosive rounds hitting its left bicep, blowing the arm clean off. Another steam-kettle shriek split the air. I raised the Bowie in a mocking salute. "Come on, ugly, let's do this." My smile was as potent as a shout. It looked at its truncated arm for a second before raising its pink eyes to meet mine.

Its answering grin nearly tore its face in half and, for the life of me, I couldn't meet its gaze. That just pissed in my Wheaties.

We charged each other, the vamp reaching speeds I couldn't hope to match, but it was up against my sheer bulk … the unstoppable force meeting the pissed off object. The impact knocked the wind out of my sails and set both of us landing on the back of our laps.

Despite the shriek of agony from my lungs and the pain in my ribs, I snagged the iron railing, levering myself upright. The vamp came at me and, instinctively, I stabbed with the Bowie, catching the beast in the stomach. It felt like stabbing half-dried cement, the knife entering almost two inches before stopping.

The vamp smiled toothily and smashed me in the in chest with a forearm like an iron rebar. Ribs groaned under titanium and I thanked my lucky stars I didn't have any air in my lungs to lose.

With a hiss the vamp grabbed my skull with one obscenely long-fingered hand and began to squeeze. Those damn digits nearly encircled my head.

Raw pain exploded behind my eyes in the biggest migraine of my life. So I did the only thing I could … I let go of the Bowie, pulled my Glock, and jammed the barrel in its mouth right through its razor teeth, knocking a couple down its gullet. Before it could react I pulled the trigger. Twice.

The muzzle flash lit the inside of its maw as wooden bullets tore through the back of its head. The screech that flew from its throat sent knives of agony through my ears. Convulsing, it fell to the ground while cool air rushed into my starved lungs and I finally felt like I had a chance.

A couple of seconds of relief were all I could count on, for the vamp was thrashing like a broke back snake. I knelt on the thing's chest and tore the oxford button-down shirt down the middle, exposing the Kevlar vest underneath. No wonder Canton's bullets hadn't hurt it. Pulling the Bowie from its stomach, I sliced a hole in the tough fabric. I unclipped a rosewood stake from my belt and, in an incredibly Van Helsing moment, plunged it between its ribs and into the monster's putrid heart.

It stopped thrashing and the high-pitched scream cut off abruptly, bringing blessed relief to my already abused skull.

"*White boy, you are one hundred percent greased murder, you know that?*"

"*Get off me, you big idiot,*" Winnie cut in. "*I think my wrist is broken.*"

I thought fast. "*Win, heal yourself. Canton, check on BB, see if he's okay. I'm going to check on Thomas.*"

"*Listen … to the Green Pea … giving orders,*" Thomas grunted laboriously.

"*You're okay!*" I sent.

"*Define 'okay.' I'm … wedged between these stalagmites … and I think I have … some broken ribs. One … of my arms is pinned, too.*"

"*Win, how's your wrist?*"

"*Five more minutes, Kal. I'll be right as rain.*"

During those incredibly long five minutes, I located Thomas, his body wedged in the V of several stalagmites. "*Canton, I'll need help with the big guy. He looks wedged in pretty solid. Will, come on down, but be careful of the cave-in.*"

"*Check, Kal.*"

Kal … not Green Pea. Yep, if the situation weren't so dire, things would have been looking up. "*Win, how's the boss?*"

"*BB's back is broken. He needs some major healing. That thing must have kicked him.*" Win produced a brightly glowing diamond like a lone star in the dark. "*Going to take more than just a few minutes.*"

Crap. The third vamp would have to wait. "*Looks like you and I have a date with the next vamp, Canton.*"

"*You really know how to sweet-talk me, white boy.*"

"*No way you two—*" Thomas protested.

"*Can it, Mace,*" Canton sent. "*You and BB are out of the picture and that leaves me in charge. Besides,*" he slapped me on the back, "*I got me a genuine vamp-slaying fool here, so don't you worry about me.*"

What Thomas said next was damn near unprintable.

Canton nodded. "*I'll take that as a 'yes, boss.' *"

We were joined shortly by Will, gingerly climbing his way up and down the cave-in. He looked at the bodies and tipped me a wink. "Good job, kid," he said aloud, producing a length of rope, and we proceeded to go fishing for Thomas. Eventually we managed to get the big man unstuck from between the stalagmites cradling him.

What came up that rope looked half dead, and that was the good half. Battered and bruised, Thomas's arm had an extra elbow and he had so much blood leaking from so many places that he looked like a bloody human sieve.

Winnie produced another gem—a sapphire—and, after setting the big guy's arm, went to work on the rest of him. It kinda weirded me out seeing flesh knit so quickly, like God had hit the Fast Forward button. Within a few minutes Thomas was able to stand on his own.

"*Stay safe you guys*," he muttered owlishly. "And kill that damn thing."

Canton and I nodded.

Winnie pronounced BB able to be moved and his snores echoed through the cavern like an affirmation. "*He's okay*," she said, worn-down and pale. "*I've put him in a healing sleep. A nuclear blast wouldn't wake him.*"

After that Thomas and Will, who carried the snoozing BB in his arms, left with Win in tow while Canton and I continued down the cavern, ready to bag us a fang-faced monstrosity.

Slowly following the ribbon of concrete, we came upon five smaller caves at various points along the route. At each opening, Canton produced an aquamarine and, after whispering the activation word *Frogcheese*, tossed it in. Each exploded into a ball of brilliant light that lasted for nearly a minute. Each cave turned out to be a dead end. Thanks to Thomas and BB, though, we had plenty more aquamarines.

Our HUDs led the way to the largest cavern yet, the Cathedral Room. If I hadn't been so scared that a vamp would jump out and bite me in the ass, I would've marveled at the arched ceiling, the enormous humped formations along one wall like giants frozen in the act of rising and the long pool, dark and mysterious, fed by a waterfall that spanned thirty feet.

"Jesus, Canton. That thing could be hiding anywhere. It'd take us years to find it."

He grunted, dug into a pocket and handed me two aquamarines. *"You take the trail above the pool; I'll take the middle. One at a time. I'll go first. If you can retrieve them, do so."*

Slowly I eased down the path, .44 in one hand, blackthorn stake in the other, nerves a-jangling. I was halfway along the edge of the pool and twenty feet above when Canton told me to stop.

A hundred fifty feet away, he dropped a gem behind him and I averted my eyes. The harsh light lit the cavern in a stunning display of brilliance, washing over every geological feature. For a full minute we twisted and turned, waiting for a steam whistle howl of pain. Nada.

"I was sure it'd be here," he sent, bewildered.

"So was I. It's a perfect place to hide out. Close to the exit tunnel and plenty of water ..." I looked down at the pool. No way ... could it?

Holstering the .44, I lifted an aquamarine, whispered the trigger, and dropped it into the pool. White light illuminated the crystal depths. Something deep down moved with eerie speed.

Then a geyser of water erupted from the pool's placid surface, a vampire at its head, clawing its way up from the light. Amazingly, it reached the ceiling of the Cathedral and hung there like a spider, hissing in pain, fingers and toes literally imbedded in limestone. It ratcheted its head around, its pink eyes finding my goggled face, and hissed.

It was a female.

And very pregnant.

Stunned, I stared. Maternity jeans, loose blouse, distended belly and white hair hanging down at least five feet. My hand wanted to grab the .44, but a *girl*. A bloodsucking, albino fiend of a girl, but a girl nonetheless. How could I kill a girl, and a pregnant one at that? Could I turn myself into that kind of monster?

That decision was taken from me. Its back exploded with four holes, thick black blood spraying into the water. Shrieking, it launched at me, stone splintering behind as Canton missed with two more shots.

As she/it flew at me, I knelt almost by reflex, sweeping the blackthorn stake up in a savage arc to punch into the vamps chest. Those honeycomb ribs, normally so hard, so resilient, gave sickeningly to the wood, allowing it easy access to the dark heart within.

The thing impacted my shoulder, spinning me around and knocking me down before slamming into the cave wall behind, bones snapping.

"Kal! You okay?"

"Did you see that? DID YOU SEE THAT?" It's impossible to shout subvocally, but I gave it a damn good try.

"I saw it, white boy … Still can't believe it, but I saw it."

"A freakin' pregnant vampire? Did you know that was possible?"

The wiry Native American knelt over the body and drove a rosewood stake into it. I guess just to be sure.

"Hell of a shot, Canton. Hell of a shot."

"Thanks, white boy. It looks like we bagged our limit. Let's round up the bodies. There's a spell that will get rid of the evidence."

"Oh god …" I moaned out loud, horrified, pointing at the body.

"What?" asked Canton, turning around. His eyes followed my finger. "Holy crap …"

The body was moving.

Or, at least, part of it was. The belly—that distended, pregnant belly—heaved and billowed like a sheet in the wind. Something was moving inside that female vamp and we both knew what it must be.

Canton put a hand to his mouth. "This can't be happening, this just can't be happening," he babbled, horrified.

The sound of rotten cloth ripping came from the corpse, followed by a spot of blood that appeared on the belly of its blouse. Something was coming. Something was *eating* its way out of the female.

I reloaded the Glock with more rosewood bullets and emptied it into the belly of the monster. Then did it again. And again.

Canton vomited into the pond. Whatever was inside the female stopped moving.

Without a word we each took an end and carried the damned thing down the tunnel to the bodies of the other vamps and the Renfield. Canton produced a wax-sealed silvery vial and opened it, setting it near the corpses. Dragging me into a side tunnel, we waited there until a blue/white flash came. He explained that the spell worked only on organic material and had a range of thirty feet. After the flash we gathered what bits of metal and plastic that remained and headed out, tired and numb from the horrors we had witnessed.

"Not bad for your first mission," he said, as the sun hit our faces. "Let's not do that again."

Done up in gold and burgundy, the Presidential suite embodied opulence, decadence and elegance. With a few more 'ences' thrown in. This was the scene for our rager of a party where champagne and bourbon flowed and somewhere, somehow, Canton managed to get us hot and cold running babes. Not to mention a few good-looking guys for Winnie to drool over.

Everyone was having a fine old time, except for BB, who remained at the office preparing the report for the Director, confident that we had a brief respite until the next Supernatural occurrence.

"You did good today, Kal," Thomas remarked drunkenly, a giggly brunette hanging on one massive arm. "Real good."

"So no more Green Pea?" I asked from the comfort of an overstuffed couch. By the looks of it, I was the only sober one in the suite. A can of Coke kept me company, even though a couple of girls who were *way* too young for me had offered to cure my loneliness, making the animal part of my hindbrain stand on its back legs and howl.

A momentary look of sobriety passed over his face. "Seriously, Kal, that was fine work. Welcome to the team."

"Thanks, man. I appreciate it."

The big man nodded and led the giggling girl away. Over at the piano, Win started up a merry little tune, *Camptown Races*. Stephen Foster would have been proud of her skill. A young man with more muscles than brains sat next to her on the bench, tongue lolling in near unrestrained lust.

Eventually couples drifted away to do what came naturally while I watched *ESPN* amid the odds and ends of the party lifestyle: empty beer cans, champagne bottles, and greasy pizza boxes. All in all, a good time.

Sometime around 2 a.m., BB came back, looking like death warmed over, and went directly to his bedroom (kicking Winnie and her boy-toy out). Smirking, I took a pull from a can of Mr. Pibb and continued my channel surfing.

"Whatcha dooin'?" slurred Win as she came up from behind, *sans* boy-toy.

"Can't sleep, too keyed up."

Her forearms thumped against the back of the couch as she brought her head level with mine. "How did you do that?" Her beer-soaked breath shriveled my lung tissue and I resisted the urge to retch.

"Do what, Winnie?" I asked patiently.

"Move so fast. And you tore that vamp's head clean off! How did you do that?"

How did I do that? All I remembered was the fury and the terrible need to kill, to harm before I could be harmed. Rage and need fueling the machine that was my desire for revenge.

"I dunno," I said finally.

"You don't know?" she mumbled. "You don't know? Well, kid, we sure as hell should know. We need to get you *tested* and right away."

That put me on my feet fast. "You nuts? Really? There's no way I'm gonna get tested by anybody."

A vague mist filled the space behind Win, who still leaned over the couch staring drunkenly at me. All I could do for a second was cock my head to the side and think, *What the heck?*

Maybe I was tired, maybe confused or maybe just inexperienced, but that one second of hesitation cost us.

When the vampire sprang into being from whatever dimension it used to phase in and out of our reality, I saw that it wore new, almost black, jeans, a dun colored button-down shirt and a long tan leather duster, the ensemble topped off by a brown fedora. If Indiana Jones had come from the bottom most depths of the abyss, he'd look like that thing.

Before I could move, it grabbed Win from behind and grinned at me, tipping me a pink-eyed wink. I never wanted to see that kind of smile again. It spoke of things dark and damned, of shrieking madness.

I'm never far from a weapon, one of the things drilled into my head during weeks of training. Win barely had time to scream before the Lahti was in my hand. Only problem was, no wooden bullets, and she was in the way.

Win's scream cut off as it tightened its grip around her throat. Staring at me with eyes full of liquid hate, it spoke in a voice like broken glass in a blender, "You took mine; I take yours."

It must have heard something, a scuff, a whisper of breath or even the beating of another heart because it took a long step backwards and swiveled slightly, eyes darting to the side.

"You got him, Kal?" BB asked softly.

Somehow I kept my voice steady. "Yeah, I got him."

It hissed and raised Win higher, her feet dangling inches from the floor.

"Kal, I still have blackthorn."

Okay, I admit it took me a second to get his meaning, but when I did, my stomach tied itself into knots. But I didn't hesitate, not with a monster in the room. Two shots, center mass, and Win went limp in the creature's arms, bleeding like a stuck pig. Startled, it dropped her.

Three shots in rapid succession from BB's revolver. Three blackthorn bullets raced toward a target that was no longer there. Instead, the bullets passed harmlessly through a grayish something that looked like the mist I'd seen earlier and buried themselves in the drywall.

It rematerialized in time to catch two from the Lahti, but phased out—or whatever you called it—when BB fired again. It *knew*. It knew who had the wooden bullets and it knew who to fear.

It should've feared me.

When it phased back, my first punch took it in the nose, which broke with a loud *snap*. Before my next punch could connect, it had already begun to heal. That didn't matter; I kept at it, maintaining my distance, kicking and punching, keeping it occupied so BB could reload.

One punch in the throat took. It bent under my knuckles and I started to feel the rush, the frisson in my blood that accompanied my rage. Faster and faster I punched and kicked while it futilely tried to defend itself against me.

It retreated, first one step then two, then a third. I grinned savagely in anticipation of beating it to death.

It lashed out—a kick that shouldn't have connected—but it was so fast that, even though my reflexes were heightened, its size-ten cowboy boot smacked me solidly on the hip, sending me flying across the suite. Fortunately, drywall stopped me from going too far. By the time I rose unsteadily to my feet, it had grabbed Win's wrist as she lay moaning on the floor. Meanwhile BB peppered it with shots from his .45, the wounds healing almost before any of its turgid blood could flow. BB must have run out of blackthorn.

Pushing myself from the wall, I started for it—intending to deal some world record damage—when it misted again, this time taking Win with it. The mist sank out of sight through the floor.

Thomas burst into the room, still drunk and only half dressed, as I rounded on BB. "Did you know they could do that? Take people with them?" I yelled, still under a full steam of mad.

"What happened?" Thomas asked blearily.

"No, I didn't," BB replied, mouth set in a grim line. "We don't have time for this. Thomas, go back to bed. Kal, come with me." He ran for the door and I followed, determined to catch up with the thing that had taken Win.

But they were long gone.

Chapter Eighteen

Thursday and Far to Go

Past midnight by a few minutes and there was a chill in the air, a cool breeze coming in from the north. It felt sorta nice, considering my full getup of Faraday Coat and body armor.

Ghost had followed Win's call to a suburban track house, a two-story early '90s building that looked like every other house in the neighborhood except for the color of the brick facing. The kind of place where the middle-class go to die … the Great Suburbanite Graveyard.

Shortly after the sun went down, my team, including the other team leaders, were in place outside the six-foot fence that circled the back half of the house, ready to storm the battlements at my signal. However, I had to be sure of my Dad's safety.

No subvocals, no radio transmissions, hand signals only for the moment. Nothing for Win to pick up on should she be ready for us.

Her voice spooled through my memory like poor quality audiotape:

"All right, Kal, I have an idea where we can make the exchange.

"What did you have in mind?" I had asked, clutching the phone so hard the casing creaked.

"Tomorrow morning, 10 a.m. The Library of Congress."

"Are you out of your damn mind? Why there?"

"It offers a nice variety of victims in case you decide to be … naughty. Meet me in front of the Library Shop. Alone, and I cannot stress that point enough. If I even catch the faintest whiff of another agent, BB and your father will become my next ghoul minions. Understand?"

"I understand." The words were gall in my mouth.

"Good. Bring the contents of the gem locker and the passwords. After I verify that the passwords work, I will set your father free."

"It won't work, Win. The passwords are useless to you now."

"Don't you mess with me, boy, your father is coming close to losing an ear."

I deliberately put some panic into my next words. "Win … things have changed in the past ten years, really! I'm not messing with you. There is only one place on earth the CPU you stole will work and that's in BB's desk and when you took it, you wiped all the hard drives. The passwords for the CPU and the files are useless."

"You lie!" she hissed.

"C'mon, Win, you know the Bureau, the paranoia. Confirm with BB. What you have is a hunk of junk."

A long pause. I began to sweat. "Very well, say goodbye to your father."

No! "Wait, Win, I know what you want. I can give it to you!"

"You know nothing, Kal. You're just a soldier."

"I know you want the list." I held my breath.

"What … do you know of the list?"

"The list of the 150 most powerful magical artifacts on the planet and their locations. That's the list you want, isn't it?"

I could hear her harsh breathing over the line. "If you are playing an angle here, Kal—"

"I'm not!" I blurted. "This is my dad. You know I wouldn't risk his life."

"How did you know about the list, Kal? It's not something agents have access to."

"Ten years, Win. Ten years in the field. I'm not the usual agent, you should know that."

"Yes, Kal, you are a most unusual agent. I remember San

Antonio like it was yesterday. Very well. Ten o'clock … Library of Congress. Please don't disappoint."

There was one thing for sure: no way would I produce the list for Win. For one thing, I didn't have it and couldn't get it. If I did have it, I still wouldn't give it to her, not even in exchange for my father. Those artifacts, scattered around the globe, had been deliberately kept under lock and key in a magical version of nuclear disarmament. As for the list, it was an urban legend in the Bureau, like Bigfoot, but much more mysterious.

When I discovered the missing CPU and hard drives, I knew the list had been the target, because only the President and the Director were privy to that secret, and where else was BB going to keep such a secret? As for Win, the story I fed her about BB's desk was true—once the hard drives and CPU were removed all you had was silicon garbage—but I needed her to believe I could produce the list or my Dad was dead.

I looked through my binoculars. No movement in the house. Not that that meant anything. Win could be asleep or watching TV in the dark. But it was time to take it to the next level.

I had to hand it to Win, she could pick 'em: an innocuous, middle–class area, no doubt with a neighborhood watch (sometimes more effective than Brinks) and a six-foot privacy fence that was easy to police. My main concern besides Dad and BB was for the owners. Had she killed them or was she squatting while they were on vacation? I couldn't help but fear the worst.

Going in through the front door was a no-go, so praying she didn't have watchdogs (or watchghouls), I pulled a smooth up and over and found myself on the lawn inside the fence, crouched low to the ground.

The average motion sensor is an effective tool if you don't know about it, but if you suspect that they are there, they can be circumvented. The best way to beat a motion sensor is simply to move *slowly*, mere inches per minute. I estimated the distance from the fence to the house and figured on an hour or so until I'd reach the porch.

Wonderful.

Low and slow, a snake in dark armor slithering through the new summer grass, the sweet smell tickling my nose. Every nerve jangled with the fear of discovery, tension that mounted with every inch taken. It was an effort to keep my breathing slow and even— discipline versus the animal instinct of fight or flight.

Besides my iron will, calling up every ounce of training I'd ever had, regrets accompanied me on that trip. More so than any other time since I'd joined the Bureau. Maybe the erosion of my defensive emotional wall was to blame or just too many damn losses in my life, too many names recorded as stars on the wall in Records. And names that never would be recorded there. I had plenty of time to ponder those regrets and the mistakes I'd made in the past ten years.

Carol came first—the woman I'd loved and asked to marry me. The woman I'd ultimately failed in that love, the specter of my sister a barrier rising tall between us. Next came my sister; the only regret was not finding a way to kill the thing that had taken her. Mom and Dad, who had waited ten years, and still waited, for a son to finish a quest that could prove futile. All the agents who had died under my command, men and women who had put their trust in an obsessed leader, their names written onto the pages of my mind with ink darker than midnight.

My fingers touched metal. Galvanized steel, the lip of a window well. A thick iron grate covered the top, restricting access. Slowly I unclipped a borescope from my web belt (which I like to think of as the Bat Belt), and carefully, gently, fed the flexible tube through the grate. Three feet later I maneuvered the 'scope to get a glimpse of the basement window, the feeble moonlight providing just enough illumination to see through the glass. Wood. The basement window had been boarded up.

If one was boarded, it made sense that the others would be as well. Time to hit the back door. Five minutes later I was there, two gems in hand, a topaz and a grayish diamond that retailers identify as 'champagne' in an effort to glorify crap goods. Both held low level spells, well under 100 megamerlin, low enough that whatever sensors she might have wouldn't be triggered. I hoped.

I breathed an activation word and the diamond glowed faintly, a dirty green-white. The glow never intensified, but little pinhead motes separated themselves from the center and floated toward the door lock, disappearing inside the keyhole. *Click.*

I set the topaz in the middle of the 4x4 concrete slab that was the back porch. It glowed only briefly when I uttered the trigger word before winking out. I started a mental countdown … *three-hundred, two-hundred ninety-nine, two-hundred ninety-eight.* Everything was ready.

Easing through the back door, I found myself in a room too dark to see much besides vague black humps and bumps. Night-vision put paid to the dark and the bizarre world of black and white came into view. Kitchen tile cool under my feet with an island four feet away and an LG stainless side by side on the opposite wall. In fact, all the appliances were stainless with pots and pans hanging on a half-moon rack over the island. Toaster, coffeemaker, butcher-block cutting board, salt and pepper mills, Shun knives, and a food processor were laid decoratively around the dark granite countertop. The whole thing looked like an ad from Williams-Sonoma.

To my left, an archway led to a dining room, while straight ahead another led to what I supposed was the living room. I decided on the dining room first. That contained an expensive looking oak table covered in an intricate teak inlay with six chairs surrounding. A wood and glass faced hutch looked to be crammed with antique plates and crystal stemware. Whoever owned this house had spared no expense on furnishings. Even my yearly salary would be hard-pressed to finance such understated trappings.

From the dining room, I could see half of the living area, blond hardwood floor covered by a genuine Persian rug, an antique grandfather clock, and a wood and cushion settee. The rosewood coffee table with its scattering of magazines cost more than my Dad made in a year. I began to suspect that this might be Win's house, her bolt-hole right near the Bureau.

Quietly, I ghosted into the other room.

Thanks to a Silencer spell, I didn't hear Win's shotgun go off, but I sure felt the result.

The floor found my butt as quickly as the deer slug found my ribs under my right arm. The Kevlar and titanium stopped the round, but the full force of its awesome kinetic energy was transferred to my ribs, breaking at least one and shooting the air out of my lungs.

Agony became the word of the day as I writhed on Winnie's expensive hardwood floor, fighting to get air into my burning chest. Every attempt to cudgel my paralyzed diaphragm resulted in a needle-sharp stab of pain from my abused ribs.

"You know," came the hateful voice, all traces of her slow west Texas drawl gone, replaced by pure Anglican. "I detected that cyber-spook sniffing around, looking for me. In fact, I expected it."

All I could do was perfect my landed fish routine.

Winnie … no, Margaret Whitcombe, came into view as I thrashed, a Mossburg 930 SPX shotgun cradled in one arm. Where Winnie held herself loosely, as if her bones were connected by rubber bands, this woman was strung tighter than piano wire—hard, lean and ready to explode in an instant.

Her thin lips twisted into what a psychopath might call a smile. "You are so predictable, Kal." She prodded me with a foot, which did my ribs no good. "When you can breathe again, please take off your coat and all your armor." Sneering, she left my field of vision.

Suddenly my diaphragm unclenched and I almost sobbed in release and shrieked in pain at the same time as my broken rib strenuously objected to the pumping of my lungs. "Damn it!" I hissed, black spots swimming in my vision.

"Off with your clothes, Kal. And please … use only two fingers when removing your weapons. I know how well you shoot." This last delivered with a metric ton of acid.

"Not … well … enough," I gasped, sitting up and shrugging out of my Faraday coat. "Not near … well enough."

I half-expected a shot, but none came. "You are such a funny boy, Kal. I just bet your dying words are going to be a scream."

A part of me was sure she was right.

When my lungs stopped their frantic swelling for air, I was finally able to focus on Margaret as she lounged at the bottom of a stairway to the second floor. Jeans, cowboy boots, red checked flannel shirt, short ginger hair, three diamond stud earrings, freckles and a shotgun (pointed at an area just south of my navel). Yep, all there and ready to scare.

Then I spied with my little eye something that almost caused me to lose twenty pounds, all brown.

Not three feet from her right hand stood a little side table, a Chinese looking thing with stylized flowers and ivy delicately painted on the body. But what lay on its black granite top gave me the galloping willies.

A cylinder, perhaps two-and-a-half feet tall, rested on a circular base about six inches wider than the cylinder's diameter. Coiled round and round the base and twisting up the cylinder itself was a length of very thin silvery wire, completely encasing every inch. Here and there on the cylinder small diamonds glittered and glowed, maybe a half-carat each, and the silvery wire seemed to run *through* them. A length of wire trailed from the base for about eighteen inches, wrapping twice around a pair of diamonds the size of my thumb that glowed blue and green respectively. The other end of the wire on top of the cylinder led to a large ruby that rested on a silvery block of metal about two inches thick and six high. The wire wrapped twice around the ruby as well. Next to this bizarre contraption was a black RediPad, its screen glowing dimly.

There are defining moments in life where the paradigm shifts and takes you in directions you're not sure you want to go. They either lead to Good Things or Bad Things. My encounter with Iku-Torso was a Bad Thing. That contraption in Margaret's possession was another one.

A Tesla coil ... a *magical* Tesla coil.

Crap.

Tesla Coils are devices that generate high voltage, high current, and high frequency alternating current electricity. They create impressive electrical arcs and lighting effects. The Bureau had been trying to produce a working magical Tesla coil since the early 1900s, with no success. It was considered the holy grail of every Bureau-like agency in the world; whoever developed it would have access to a much greater amount of magical energy—like having the A-bomb while everyone else had slingshots. The last time someone had tried to fabricate a working magical Tesla coil, all that had been left of the developer was a pile of greenish goo that resembled lime Jell-O.

Somehow, maybe by raiding the databases of the two most powerful Bureaus in the world, Margaret had managed to produce one. It certainly explained how she'd breached the Warehouse's defenses. Sheer raw magical power.

We were neck deep in the latrine for sure.

Her echoing laughter was pure liquid mean. "I see you understand the situation now. And if you're wondering ... yes, it works."

My armor came loose and *thunked* to the floor. Just a t-shirt and leg armor left. I stood slowly so I could remove the leggings. "You lured the team to Denver because you were finished with the ... coil. You still had some gems to steal, but you wanted to get to BB so you could get the list." The pieces fit together neatly, so neatly that it made me sick. "I thought it was about the gems, the vampire, but it was about the list. It was always about the list, once you completed the coil."

The shotgun never wavered as I stripped off my leggings and dropped them to the floor. Now all that protected the family jewels was my Far Side boxers. "Nice to see you're not a tighty whitey man," she remarked blandly. "But if you must know, it was about *both* the coil and the artifacts. Imagine the energy this coil could produce by harnessing the power of, oh ... let's say ... the First Tablet of Babylon, the Spear of Longinus, or the Grail. Imagine the force that could be unleashed with Excalibur!" Her eyes went to a far off place where only loonies dared to tread.

"You're not really going to let my Dad go, are you?" I glared hot death at her.

She remained unfazed. With one hand she touched the RediPad, fingers flying over its virtual keyboard. From my vantage point, I couldn't see what was on the screen of the little 8x10 inch flat pc. Keeping an eye on both the pad and me, she laid a hand on the gem glowing red on top of the coil. After a few seconds her mouth thinned and she seemed to strain with internal effort. Finally, she grunted and smiled. "There."

I shrugged, feigning nonchalance. "What?"

"You and your team are very clever, but you didn't catch the spyeyes I had installed in the trees *outside* of this property, both tech and magical. I spotted you and yours ages ago, dear boy, and have now rendered them unconscious, despite those gorgeous Faraday Coats."

My stomach did a little flip-floppy thing.

She raised the shotgun, pointing the barrel directly between my eyes. "And to answer your question: yes, your father will be freed once I have the artifact list. Alas, dear boy, you will not. Nor will BB."

My mental clock counted down ... *forty-five* ... *forty-four* ... "You win then, Margaret. I know why you want me dead, but tell me this: how did you survive with two bullets in your left lung?"

She hung a twisted grin on her face that sent a spike of fear into my heart. "One thing about vampires is true ... their blood does have regenerative properties."

Thirty-three, thirty-two. "You know why I did it, don't you? I couldn't let it use you to get to us. Better dead than food, right?"

"You don't know what the hell you're talking about!" she screamed, voice shrill and face turning a mottled red. Her mind was obviously taking a walk off the map. "Do you know what I've had to do in the last few years to stay alive? The degradation? The horrors I've seen? A master vampire, you idiot! They know of more evil than you could possibly *imagine.*"

Twenty-one. "Win, I—"

"I've been to Hell, boy! A Hell you know nothing about, one you can't even *conceive of!*"

Fifteen, fourteen. The need to keep her talking twisted through me. "I'm so sorry, Win, I really am ..."

Two strides forward and the shotgun rested under my chin. "You will be sorry," she snarled, dripping hate. "But first the list. NOW!"

Seven, six "All right ... no problem." *Four.* "I have a printout in my web belt." *Two.* "Let me get it." *One.*

Margaret held up a hand while keeping the shotgun jutted under my chin. "Wait ... back up *slowly,* I'll get it."

Zero ... negative one ... negative two ... What had happened? Something should have happened! Where did I—

BOOM!

"Okay, Kal," Alex had whispered earlier at the Warehouse, holding two gems in his palm. One was a grayish diamond, the other a topaz. "These are poor quality, but will do the trick."

I stared at the little gems and flicked the diamond with a pinky. "One of these is the lockpick, right?" He nodded toward the diamond. "Good. What does the other one do?"

Alex smiled like a proud papa. "This topaz is a distraction device. Has the kick of an M80, but with twice the light and noise. It'll definitely get someone's attention."

"What's so special about that?"

"When activated, it has a five minute delay … like a fuse. If you repeat the activation word, it will deactivate. I call it the Yellow Grenade."

I smiled. "Now that's what I'm talking about, kid!"

A 'distraction,' he called it. Might as well have called it 'the loudest freakin' noise you've ever heard in your life'. Margaret flinched in surprise and it was enough.

My hand batted the Mossberg to one side and I stepped in, throwing a punch to her ribs. Had my own been in good shape it would've caused real damage, but a stab of agony from a broken rib robbed the strike of force. It was enough, however, to drive her back a couple of steps so she could pull the trigger. The deer slug stirred the air by my left ear, a brutal reminder that I wasn't bulletproof.

I stepped in again, throwing an overhand left and she dropped the Mossberg. At that point, it would only get in the way. She blocked the left and countered with stiffened fingers to my broken rib. Breath left my lungs in a wheeze, but I followed through with a head butt that *crunched* her nose but good, spewing blood from both nostrils. She fell back toward the stairs, broken nose bent to the left, and I followed, ready to end it.

Too cocky. With a mushmouthed mutter, her diamond earrings glowed.

Uh-oh. Heart and stomach bounced off the floor.

Faster than human, she was on me, peppering me with blows I couldn't avoid. Mike Tyson-caliber punches that broke my jaw and had me on my knees in an instant retching blood.

"You … always were clever, Kal," she gasped with a mouth full of blood while stumbling toward the Tesla coil,. "Too damn clever for your own good." Her hand found the gem on top. "I don't even care much about the list anymore. I'll find some those artifacts on my own." She stroked the ruby. "With this, I can do almost anything." Eyes blazing, she grimaced at me through the film of blood on her lips.

I reached for it and it was there, the rage ... a deep and abiding well, ready to be tapped. So tap it I did. My pummeled and broken ribs hollered at me in a voice as loud as the world, but I was deaf. My jaw pulsed something fierce, but I didn't feel it. All I heard was the singing of my blood; all I could feel was the heat in my veins.

First step ... hands outstretched.

Her eyes narrowed.

Second step ... and I froze.

She smiled.

Something warmed on my chest and belly ... *Third step.*

Eyes widening in disbelief, she mouthed words I couldn't hear through the singing.

Once again I froze fast in the grip of a paralysis spell that hit like a Peterbuilt. Something sizzled on the skin of my chest and I smelled burnt hair. The Shape of my rage inside the cage of my stilled flesh fought the spell effects but was not enough. Desperately I reached for more, dug deep into the well of my soul and did what I'd always feared to do ... let it all out, let it run free without shackles, without restraint.

Shrieking through my soul like a cacophony of the damned, the Shape of it crashed against the spell with a sound only I heard, crashed and won. My savage smile grew ever wider as the spell crumbled, ignoring it much like I ignored my wracked body.

Fourth step ... Brownish black spots grew on the chest of my t-shirt as the coils of silver wire wrapped round and round and round my torso heated to almost red-hot after absorbing the energy that had slipped past the rage.

Dom stared as Alex wrapped my torso and upper arms in silver wire. "Are you crazy, boss? Is that your problem?"

"Crazy like a fox, Dom," Alex smiled as he made another circuit with the wire. "This much silver wire will absorb a lot of magic. With the amount we're using here, it will be more effective than a Faraday Jacket. The only problem is when it absorbs too much, it will begin to overheat."

I grunted. "That prostitute in Denver wore silver, Dom. Absorbed enough of Winnie's spell that she had to resort to getting her hands dirty. The first real clue Wilkes twigged to."

"A skintight Faraday jacket," chuckled Dom. "Or should I say, a Faraday t-shirt. But why? It'll be difficult for you to move."

My eyebrow headed north. "Just in case, Dom. Just in case."

A fist to her face, all my power behind it, snapping her head back hard enough that it bounced off the wall, leaving a small dent in the drywall. A kick to the ribs that raised her two feet into the air, and I could *feel* her bones break under my foot. Two more kicks, stomach and hip, had her virtually senseless at my feet, eyes rolled to the back of her head.

Groaning, I ripped off the smoking t-shirt and stumbled into the kitchen. I hit the cold-water nozzle for the sink and pulled out the dish hose from its mount next to the faucet. Icy water sizzled and steamed as I showered myself, shuddering at the ferocious burning ache and the burnt pork smell of charred skin. Three, four minutes later I stumbled painfully back into the living room, silver wire fused into my melted flesh. Margaret lay moaning and twitching in a bloody heap on the floor amid the remains of her teeth, so I turned my attention to the coil.

Up close, something about the coil hurt my head and no matter what angle I chose, the pattern of diamonds studding the cylinder blurred my vision. From the pile of clothes, I found my smart phone. Scrolling through the icons, I selected VIDEO and hit RECORD. Thirty seconds were more than enough.

"You get that, Ghost?" My voice emerged as mushy wet rattle.

Bzzzz ..."Yes, Kal, I've got it."

"Good. You know what to do."

"Good luck, Kal." Click.

Time to end this farce, I though. I'd had enough. More than enough. Sue, Bryan, all those agents in the Warehouse, her victims in Denver. There had to be an accounting. The books must be balanced. And I had just the tool for the job.

The Mossberg was surprisingly light and felt like the well crafted, precision instrument of death it was designed to be. One good swing reduced the coil to a bundle of matchsticks and platinum wire, garbage for the heap. I then brought the business end around and pointed it at Margaret's face.

She didn't flinch as the barrel touched her forehead; her half-open eyes stared at me with a blend of hate and resignation. "You're dead, Kal," she gurgled through shredded lips and a throat full of blood. "You just don't know it."

My laughter was a brittle thing, made of regret and misery. "Of course I know it. I've been dead for twenty years."

The Mossberg roared silently.

"Boss! Boss!" Whoever was speaking sure sounded worried. "Please boss, wake up!"

It had been so long since I had a decent night's sleep. What day was it? Wednesday? Thursday? So hard to remember. Yeah, Thursday morning, I think. Gee, last good sleep was two days ago. Only two days? That wasn't right … so much had happened since I stumbled hung-over into the office on Monday.

"Boss!" Cool water passed my teeth and trickled down my throat. So good. My lips hungrily pursed for more.

"That's it, boss. Drink up."

"How is he?" Something told me I should've known the second voice. The thump of many feet vibrated the floor beneath me and with it came the buzz of many whispers.

"Looks like ten miles of rough road," said the first voice as I gulped more sweet liquid. "Broken jaw, nose and god knows what else. Plus major burns on his torso, more than I want to look at. Seems like he was right about the silver, but pulling it off will peel a lot of skin off with it."

"Damn, what a mess." I felt someone come close. "I'm gonna fix you up right, Kal. Okay?"

"Okay, Alex," I mumbled through the blood and water in my mouth. My eyes opened, Dom and Alex coming into blurry view. "But first … Dad and BB … the basement." God, it hurt *so much* to talk. The pain from my broken jaw was tearing my skull apart.

Dom's eyes widened. "You sure, boss?"

I nodded. "She knew we were coming … would want to keep them close … kill them in front of me just to torture me." A tooth wiggled loose and I spat it out. "Careful … may be a booby trap or two."

Dom and two others left to check the basement while Alex pulled out a sapphire and laid a hand on my forehead. "Just relax, Kal. You're less beat up than when you fought that ghoul in your apartment."

"Wait, kid …"

"What?"

"Grab a couple of those diamonds from that smashed coil over there … we're gonna need them."

He left for a few seconds and came back. "Done, boss." The sapphire found my forehead again. "Now can I heal you?"

Sighing, I surrendered to the magic.

Golden warmth flowed through me, a relaxing, soothing feeling … much better than anything I've felt in, well, better than anything … even drawing four aces in Texas Hold 'em at the Bellagio.

"Son, are you okay?"

Aw, Dad … let me sleep.

"Son, you have to wake now."

But I feel so *good*.

A different voice cut in. "Get up, Kal, it's time to go. Come on, soldier, up and at 'em."

Soldier? Time to go? Really … awww … that sucked. I cracked

open one eye to see Dad's round peasant face hovering over me. "Just one more hour, Dad. I'm *tired*." How many times this week had I woken like this? Far too many, it seemed.

His face split into a wide smile. "Good to see you awake, boy. Your man Alex tells me you took quite a knock-about."

Alex? Oh yeah ... Alex ... Margaret ... the shotgun and the skull blowing apart like a watermelon hurled at pavement. "Urgh ... help me up, will you, Dad?"

Strong hands gently assisted me to my feet, where I swayed a few moments before discovering equilibrium. Dad's hand stayed on my shoulder the entire time, a pillar of steadiness.

Raising my head and opening my eyes wide, I took stock of my surroundings. The place was empty, wiped clean with typical Bureau efficiency. Only the holes from the deer slugs remained and I was willing to bet my last paycheck that they would be gone very soon.

Belatedly, I realized I wore nothing but my boxers. My hands caressed the tight skin of my chest, feeling the slight ridges of scar tissue from the touch of burning silver, a melty line that went round and round my torso and upper arms. At least it didn't hurt anymore.

"Everything's been disposed of," BB remarked offhandedly, a bright shiner painting his left eye in glorious purple. "Alex just left and the rest of your team is waiting for us in the van." He ran a long finger up my shoulder. "He did a great job on you, Kal. A lot less scarring that I thought."

"The Tesla coil?" I kept my voice casual.

"Smashed to bits in your struggle."

Aw darn. "Too bad."

The look he tossed my way told me he was saving plenty of questions for later. Then, slowly, like the sun coming out from behind a cloud, he smiled. I almost passed out from shock.

"Good job, Kal." His hand found mine and pumped it hard. "Damn good job."

Dad leaned close. 'Thanks, son."

I pasted a tired grin on my worn out face. "No problem, Dad."

To BB, "Boss, my contract's up in five months. I quit."

Chapter Nineteen

Five and a Half Years Earlier
Deep in the Machine

"We still don't know where it's from, how it got there or how to get rid of it." BB's face betrayed no hint of worry or apprehension. No surprise there.

I took a sip of vodka, savoring the clean taste and smiling at the pleasant burn as it trickled down my throat. Blue Ice, distilled in Rigby Idaho and made with potatoes, like a vodka should be. BB always did stock the good stuff.

He'd called me in shortly after I'd returned from an alligator hunt. The New York City sewers were notorious for the things and every time you killed one, another took its place, just like roaches. This last gator measured nearly thirty feet and had skin whiter than a Klan member's sheets. Fortunately for me, it wasn't bulletproof.

The team and I had stuck around the Big Apple for the next event, confident in the 'where there's one, there's another' law of Supernatural occurrences. Turned out that a troublesome troll came up from the World Under to take up residence under the Brooklyn Bridge. It had eaten two cars and their passengers before we finally managed to dispatch the armor-skinned beastie with an anti-tank weapon. I had been cleaning bits of troll out of my hair when the Director called.

Now BB wanted to talk about some spook that inhabited the Bureau's computer system. "Are you sure it's not just some genius-level hacker?"

BB swirled the cognac in his snifter before answering. "Special Branch is pretty sure. They've tried an exorcism, but without its true name there's nothing they can do."

"Well, you didn't bring me here and serve me your best vodka just for a chin wag, BB. What do you want?"

"Must you always be blunt?"

"Blunt is good. I like blunt, blunt works for me. I'll leave subtle to the politicians."

"To the point then. Special Branch's focus does not lend itself to … investigation. In fact, they don't know diddly on how to go about it. I need you to see what you can find out about this ghost in our machine."

Cute. Since it showed up six months ago the spook had been the talk of the Warehouse, a cybernetic spirit that had Special Branch scratching their heads in wonder and confusion. What could I do that they couldn't? Then it hit me. "You want me to find out its true name, don't you? How the hell can I get that? It's not like the spook's going to tell me."

BB slowly inhaled from his snifter and took another sip Louis XIII cognac. At $1,600 a bottle, it was the only vice I'd ever seen him indulge. "If it was easy, it would have been done by now. You've got eight weeks to find something out. Start by talking to the new Special Branch member, Alex Dumont. He might be of some help."

"The new *uber*kid from MIT? Heard he was smarter than a sack of Einsteins."

"That he is. I think between you two you might achieve a desired result. As an added bonus, your team members will have rotating vacations while you're gone. If you succeed, you'll get an extra week for yourself."

Two weeks vacation? Sure I'd be monitored, observed the whole time, but *two weeks?* I felt like I'd hit the Lotto.

BB almost smiled at the look on my face. "I see we have a deal, then."

We did.

Cornering Alex took a while. Seems he made his home in R&D and rarely left, surfacing only for Twinkies and Jolt Cola. It was during one of his infrequent breaks that I managed to trap the elusive geek.

"You should check your email and answer your phone, kid," I remarked, while pulling up a chair and planting my fundament. A Hot Pocket disappeared down his gullet faster than money into a politician's bank account. He spared me only a cursory glance from his iPad before gulping down a full can of soda and letting loose a resounding belch.

"Mmm ..." Was all he said.

Crack! My hand hit the aluminum tabletop hard, sending soda and Hot Pockets flying, decorating the young man with Jolt. "Now kid," I smiled sweetly as he gaped at me through cola dripping from his lank hair. "It's only polite to answer someone fully when they address you. Didn't your mama ever teach you manners?"

He continued to stare at me, mouth half-open, an unfinished bit of Hot Pocket in one cheek like a chaw of tobacco. "Um ..."

"Um? Strange word that. Usually employed by idiots and halfwits. Which one are you?"

Face flushing crimson, he shook his head, caramel droplets flying. "Neither, sir."

My smile was beatific. "Ahh ... two words strung together coherently. Very nice. But I'm not a 'sir,' I work for a living." Leaning forward, I extended my hand. "Agent Kal Hakala."

"A-Alex Dumont, sir!" A smile pasted itself on his face. "Hey, you're the agent who saw the Class Five!"

Yippee. Another one who wanted to hear that story. My smile faded at the edges. "Before you ask ... no. Just read about it."

He looked so hurt ... like I told him there was no Santa Claus.

Keeping my tone conciliatory, I said, "Alex, they tell me you're the best thing to come along since sliced bread and I need to pick your brain."

He threw me a puzzled look and removed his birth control glasses, wiping the lenses with a corner of his cola splattered shirt. "About what?"

"The Director seems to think that between the two of us we can figure out how to get rid of that cyberspace spook."

"Did you know that I'm working on the source of magic?" he said quickly, picking up his iPad (slated for release in 2010), scrolling through his notes until he found the one he wanted. With a nervous smile, he showed me a screen filled with equations that instantly put me into snore mode. "I have a theory that magic is really just Dark Energy, which permeates all of space. Dark Energy currently accounts for 74% of the mass-energy of the universe! Isn't that amazing?"

The kid probably couldn't play poker to save his life. I'd spooked him bad. Holding up my hands, I said, "You had me at The Force, Luke."

"Not quite," he commented with something like pity in his voice.

"Oh really? Dark Energy surrounds us, permeating us and binding the galaxy together. Right?"

"Right."

"Well for such a smart guy, you don't know your movies that well. Obi-Wan said that in the first *Star Wars*."

"Ummm …"

"Your sparkling wit never ceases to impress, kid."

It started slow, but built up until it burst forth fresh and joyful, infecting me with its purity. Minutes passed as we laughed, drawing amused looks from passing agents grabbing coffee or something to eat.

"Oh, damn, sir. You're right." He wiped his eyes. The kid looked a lot less stressed and nerdy when he smiled. "You're really quite right. It does sound like The Force."

"It's okay, Alex. When Lucas left Special Branch in 1970, the money he earned helped him fund *THX 1138*. Which, of course, led him to *American Graffiti* and then *Star Wars*. Hey, kid, close your mouth. You're catching flies."

The poor sap hunched over the table, looking like he'd been

sucker punched. I don't think he would have been more surprised if I had told him Christ was secretly into S&M. All traces of the mirth had evaporated ... zero to serious in six seconds flat. "But ... but ... Dark Energy was discovered in 1998 at the Lawrence Berkeley National Laboratory and the Australian National University. How could Lucas ... but ..."

"Don't worry, kid," I soothed. "Lucas was just trying to find God or a connection with all living things." Inside I laughed and laughed. Had I ever been that young?

"Oh thank god!" He moaned in relief. "I thought you were saying that I was decades behind the times here. Research wise."

"Listen, I know you probably signed up for the cool toys and research, but did you opt for basic at Parris Island?"

"Yes."

Hmm ... that surprised me. He looked like he'd blow away in a gentle breeze. "Then get on a team as soon as you can. You magicians in Special Branch need to see what the front lines are like."

"Why?"

Taking a few calming breaths, I resisted the urge to shake him. "Look, you research guys are great. Don't get me wrong. What you do is important and a lot of times saves lives, but when you're out in the field, you see what's needed to improve *our* ability to save lives. Not to mention our own. You also develop a deeper appreciation of the value of human life when you see it ripped to shreds firsthand. It's so safe and insulated in R&D and reading our reports is a crappy way to see how the World Under works."

I rose and headed out, a little hot under the collar, leaving him to ponder my words. I'd come on a little strong, but the subject had been a sore spot for agents for a long time. It's easy to view the world from an ivory tower, but that vantage doesn't let you see the dangers that lurk in the underbrush.

Okay ... It was time to chill a little and concentrate on what the kid *didn't* say. He'd changed the subject pretty damn quick when I mentioned the ghost.

We all have a 'Duh!' moment, and mine kicked in right then, stopping me in my tracks. As my dad would say, "The wheel is spinning, but the hamster's dead." BB, however, had no such lifeless rodent issues. He knew there was a connection between Alex and the spook and he threw me at the kid to find out. He'd needed a blunt object and blunt is what I do best.

Time to go back to school.

Driving a Crown Vic is like wearing a fur coat … you're a little embarrassed, but the feeling is awesome. The Vic sailed across the New Jersey Turnpike, the I-95, and the Massachusetts Turnpike smoothly, almost stately, with plenty of power to keep me firmly rooted in the fast lane.

MIT was a good 450 miles from Warehouse and, although some might think me nuts, driving all the way seemed to be the safest route, considering I was investigating a spirit who could plunge into any computer on the planet and wreak untold damage if upset. Besides, it had been *years* since I drove just for the pleasure of it and BB hadn't given me a deadline.

Paying cash for gas and food kept me off the radar in case the spirit suspected I had my nose in its business, which I figured, by Alex's reaction, was the case. It didn't take a genius to figure things out; Alex and the spook showed up at the Bureau at roughly the same time, so the probability of those two events being connected was high.

Six hours and one pit stop later, I parked the Vic in the lot of the biggest and best brain factory in the world. MIT had been affiliated with fifty National Medal of Science recipients and seventy-five Nobel Laureates. It received billions in endowments and the aggregated revenues of companies founded by MIT grads would equal the seventeenth largest economy in the world.

Yeah, stepping onto those grounds, I felt like a hick from the sticks.

How do you find the registrar's office in a place that extends over one mile along the northern bank of the Charles River Basin, has five schools, one college and a total of thirty-two academic departments? Easy, tuck your pride down someplace deep inside and ask. Several times. Then proceed to get lost and ask for more directions from smirky, sarky students who, if they knew what you did for a living, would pee their pants and run home crying into their pocket protectors.

"You lost?" The pretty girl had straight blond hair and cornflower blue eyes, artfully ripped jeans, Converse sneakers, and a black Pogues t-shirt. But that's not what made her stand out in a crowd, not what made her unique in my eyes. She had to be at least six-two, barely two inches shorter than my own six-four, the only girl I'd ever met I didn't have to stare down at.

I hit her with my pearlies at full wattage. "Is it that obvious?"

"Only to the sighted," She said, dimpling irresistibly.

"I need to find the registrar, Miss—?"

"Stephenson. Juliet Stephenson, Mr.—?

Smiling, I pulled my FBI badge out of the inside pocket of my charcoal suit. "Hakala. Special Agent Kal Hakala."

Juliet gave my badge and ID close scrutiny. "You don't look like a fed. More like a football jock." No trace of disdain in her voice.

"Used to be, about a thousand years ago, but I grew up and joined the really real world."

She laughed, a full hearty sound. "The really real world? What's that?"

"A world of responsibility, of finding your place and making the most of it."

"So you've found your place?" she asked, face serious. "That's a rarity."

I decided to be truthful. "Not sure if I found my place ... I think it's more like I found something I feel passionate about."

Those dimples again. "What makes you think that's not

finding your place?"

Damn. My heart started doing the Rumba. I covered it with a chuckle. "I'd love to continue this philosophical chitchat with you, Miss Juliet, but I need to get to the registrar. Can you give me directions?"

A slow sway later and she took my arm. "I'm going that way, cowboy, come with me." Her long fingers intertwined perfectly with mine and I felt a gentle heat from our contact. This was no party girl at a rage, tarted up in a short skirt with 'screw me' pumps on, a one-night stand that satisfies physically yet leaves you empty. No, she was something special—a tender, yet strong, woman whose warmth I felt down to my bones.

How was it that a girl I'd just met had such an effect on me? I don't know, but something about that tall drink of water woke a small part of me that I thought had been stowed away for good. *Danger, Will Robinson, Danger! Here be dragons ...*

Some things are best left alone.

Maybe she saw something in my face. "What's wrong, Special Agent Kal Hakala?"

" '*I have miles to go before I sleep,*' " I quoted quietly, filled with quiet regret.

" '*And I have miles to go before I sleep,*' she repeated. Robert Frost ... one of the saddest poems I've ever read."

I nodded, not wanting to reach for the warmth she offered. Instead I shifted the topic to inconsequential things and she rode with it without batting an eye.

Juliet walked me as far as the registrar's office before patting my arm and, with a small sad smile, leaving. She didn't know why I'd pulled away, but she respected the decision.

A kindly but slightly harried middle-aged woman with curly gray and brown hair gave me a smile. "What can I do for you, sir?" She and a few other women manned the office, pecking away at PCs and scurrying here and there with reams of files.

I hate being called 'sir.' Makes me feel like I don't earn my money honestly. I flipped her my badge and ID. "Special Agent Hakala, ma'am. I need information on one of your graduates, a Mr. Alexander Dumont."

She peered at the ID suspiciously through a pair of half-moon reading glasses she kept on a silvery chain around her neck. "Well, Special Agent Hakala," she commented with a bit of frost. "I cannot let you access student records without a warrant."

Once again I broke out the high-wattage smile. "Ma'am, I'm not here to dig into his student records. This is more of a background check." The frost began to melt. "Can you give me the name of his Faculty Advisor, please?"

Mollified that I wasn't there to raid her database, she looked down at her PC. "Spell his name, please." After typing it in, she looked up at me over her cheaters. "You'll want to see Professor Martin at the Plasma Science and Fusion Center."

"Don't suppose you have a map."

Without a word she handled me a pamphlet. "Have a nice day," she said, already returning to her work.

Opening the pamphlet, I looked at a map inside. M.C. Escher couldn't have made heads or tails of it.

Wonderful.

"That's a name I expected to be mentioned in the same breath as 'Nobel,' " Professor Martin beamed at me, a slightly graying man somewhere in his fifties. Small and lean, he looked like a physically fit Mr. Rogers but had the forceful personality of a drill instructor. I took to him right away.

The mention of Alex's name and the sight of my badge brought out a small, conspiratorial smile. Clearing a stack of files off a chair afforded me a place to rest the back of my front.

Steepling his fingers, he continued to grin. "So what can I do for you, Special Agent?"

I decided to forgo the false charm and hit him straight between the eyes. "Background check on your former student. It seems that during the mandatory Polygraph Test, he became evasive regarding his last year at MIT and I've been sent to find out why."

"His last year?" he asked dispassionately.

"Yes. Did he suffer some sort of trauma you might know about?"

Where do professors learn the cynical, inquisitive stare? Is there a handbook? If so, I wanted one. I found myself facing the full brunt of his hazel eyes. "Is he in trouble?" he asked quietly and I could hear his mental defenses rising.

"Hardly. If he won't come clean on why he's so evasive or if I can't find out why, he merely loses the opportunity at a position with a very high clearance level."

"How high?"

"Stratospheric."

He tried to think of some objection, some way to rationalize not telling me what he knew, but couldn't find any. "Alex seemed shaken up after Christmas break," he said, sounding resigned. "Had trouble concentrating, focusing and was generally on edge."

Ding ding ding ... we have a winner. "Any idea why?"

He shook his head, and I felt a twinge of disappointment.

I stood and extended a hand. "Well, thank you then, Professor. I appreciate the effort."

Hard calluses met mine. "You're welcome, Agent Hakala. Sorry I couldn't provide you with more information, but I think I know who can."

I threw him a raised eyebrow and he smiled in amusement. "Check out his roommate, Jamie Schenk. They shared a place close by."

"Oh, please don't tell me it's on campus!" I groaned. I'd had to ask three different students to find Professor Martin and I'd still managed to get lost. Twice.

"Don't worry, young man," he laughed. "It's a house off-campus. I was there once, checking up on him during that bleak period I mentioned. Let me give you the address."

Better and betterer. Every clue seemed to lead to another clue, but it felt like progress. Once I got the address I shut the door on the cluttered office with its several jillion books and HP desktop and files and files and files everywhere.

Finding the Vic, hell ... finding the *parking lot* took the better part of a half-hour, but I managed to leave MIT with all body parts and sanity intact.

Thanks to a portable GPS, I finally found the little run down two-storey house less than three miles away. The neighborhood looked crappy enough that I didn't want to park the Vic on the street, but I didn't have a choice. A battered white Neon squatted in the center of the house's cracked and overgrown driveway.

Any redeeming qualities the place might have possessed a hundred years ago had long since become extinct. Not only was the paint a dim memory, but mold, rot and rust had taken over where it left off. Just standing at the front door made me want to get a tetanus shot, but I knocked on the bilious yellow wood anyway. No answer. So I knocked harder.

"Go away," came a faint, high-pitched male voice.

"Open the damn door or I'll set the place of fire," I hollered, too tired to put up with any BS.

A few moments later, "Okay, dude ... door's open."

Did I really have to touch the knob? It looked ... *infected* somehow, as if the metal were a living, gangrenous thing. I put a hand in my jacket pocket and buffered the touch of the knob with linen. I made a mental note to burn the jacket.

Inside, the house told me a different story. The door opened into a cave-like interior that made me wish for night-vision. When my eyes finally adjusted, I found myself in an empty room barely the size of a small walk-in closet with stairs to my right leading to the second story. Directly in front was a white wooden door covering loud roaring noises and a bright light coming from the space beneath.

"Hello?" I called.

"In here, dude," came from beyond the door.

The leather soles of my dress shoes clacked off of what I realized was a very nice, dark hardwood floor and the white door that led deeper into the house didn't look scuzzy at all, a vast improvement over the diseased appearance of the front door. What the hell was this? On the other side, I had my answer.

Well, well, well … a large … *very* large living room dominated by a 64-inch flat-screen showing a computer animated fantasy show. A fat kid in an overstuffed beige leather chair sat directly in front. All the way on the other end was a kitchenette with a fairly fancy black Frigidaire. Between the two extremes stood an impressive desk arrangement that reminded me of BB's, but without the interactive surface. Instead, twin Alienware desktops sat humming under dual 24-inch flat-screen monitors. Everything in the room sparkled and had that just-waxed lemony scent that made me nauseous. I was starting to get creeped out.

As for the fat kid, he didn't look up once as I entered, his focus solely on the huge flat-screen, his fingers flying over a keyboard on his lap. His curly brown hair was cut short and his clothes looked new—from the white Air Jordans to the blue Tommy Hilfiger polo stretched tight across his wide belly. The standard set of geek birth-control glasses perched high on his pug nose.

"Kid, this is strange on so many levels. How come the exterior of your house looks like crap?"

"You kidding?" he asked, not looking away from the TV. "You see the neighborhood out there? I got over twenty grand worth of stuff in here. No way I'm going to get it stolen."

"You Schenk?"

"Who wants to know?"

Was this kid for real? I laid my badge in front of his face.

"Hey, dude! You made me die! Now I gotta start this quest all over again!" He finally looked at me, his mouth curled into a pout.

Enough. I was tired and needed a drink or seven. "Listen, Schenk, I'm here because of your former roommate Alex Dumont and what happened over Christmas break." I played the hunch with a straight face, hoping for the best.

It didn't work. The kids face closed up faster than a miser's purse and he went back to his game. "Don't know anything, mister."

Was helping the authorities such a bad thing? "Kid, do you want me to take you to Boston? I can question you there. Right now I'm doing things all nice and mellow. Please don't make me pull out the stops."

The kid smirked. "You can try, mister FBI dude, but you'd buy yourself a whole lot of trouble."

Well … time to take a different tack. Strolling over to the PC station, I wigged the mouse and the monitors came to life. "Hey!" the kid protested, struggling to raise his bulk out of the chair.

"Sit your butt down, chunk style." I let my voice go harsh and mean and he flopped back into the chair as if his strings had been cut. "You spoiled rich kids are all alike, but I got you pegged." Ahh, he'd left his mailbox open. Nice. "You got into MIT, but you gained admittance with your parent's money." I moved the cursor to GET MAIL. "You weren't good enough to stay in. Your grades started slipping and you let Alex stay here on the cheap in exchange for tutoring, or help with your homework." I scrolled through his old messages. One from Mom and Dad … how sweet. They were going to the Hamptons and had invited him. "Tell me if I'm getting warm."

Silence from Mr. Chunky.

"I'll take your lack of reply as an affirmative."

"Dude, wait till I tell my dad …"

"You're not going to do anything, kid. You wouldn't want me to tell him how you're floundering here, would you? Ahhh …" Looks like someone from caseypotrey@hotmail.com had sent an email with a good-sized attachment. I hit DOWNLOAD and watched the file open. Pages upon pages of what looked to be computer code, but I didn't have a Hacker-to-English dictionary handy, so it remained so much gobbledygook. Then came pages of mathematical equations. Stuff that was light years above my head. Jackpot. "Lookie here, kid, how about I flush Casey's email? You wouldn't mind that, would you?" His stricken look said he would mind very much.

"Dude, what do you want?" he asked brokenly.

"What happened over Christmas break, kid?"

"Dude ..."

"Spill it or I hit DELETE."

"No! No! Wait!" He took a deep breath. "My parents got a cabin in the Adirondacks. Alex and my other roommate Casey borrowed it from time to time when my folks weren't using it."

"For what? Were they hooking up?"

"Nah, dude, they're not gay. It's a great place to get chicks. There are rich girls by the ton out there. They'd party, smoke a little grass, get laid, have a great time. That's all."

Who would have thought? Alex Dumont, loooove machine. "Go on."

"Well, last Christmas break Alex comes back alone, says that Casey decided not to go back to school, wanted to travel and see the world."

I looked at the email. Dated a week ago. Casey still wrote ... or did he?

"But you think different, don't you?"

"Dude, all I know is I get a call from my parents a few weeks later saying there was a weird burn mark on the floor and that it was coming out my allowance."

Burn mark? Curious and curiouser. I considered the email. "What did Casey do at MIT? What was his passion?

"He was a programmer, dude. One of the best hackers I ever met, too. He set up my whole system."

Interesting. "He's still doing your homework. How do you keep in touch?"

"Just by his Hotmail account."

"You have anything of his?"

"Yeah … he asked me to keep his things. Go upstairs. The second door on the left. His room's the same as he left it."

I grabbed him by the ear lobe. "Show me."

Casey's room looked like any young man's, only cleaner. The spotless quality of the house told me that Jamie had a neat streak (judging by how lazy he seemed, doubtful) or a maid, (much more likely).

Not a big bedroom, but not small, either. A twin bed with a red tartan comforter, a plain pressboard desk and an equally plain chest of drawers. "Everything the same?" I asked.

"Yeah. Except for his laptop. Alex took that."

Didn't look like much—kind of drab and spartan. No posters, pictures, nothing that gave the room any sort of personality. It looked sanitary … lonely.

"This is how he lived?"

"Yeah, dude. He was more into his computers than real life."

"His last name was Potrey?" I asked, remembering the Hotmail address.

"Yeah, dude."

My mind raced, trying to connect the dots. It settled on a detail I'd almost forgotten. "You said there was a burn mark on the floor of your parent's cabin. Can you describe it?"

He scratched his ample belly. "I can do one better, dude. Wait here." Footsteps thudded heavily down the stairs and came back shortly. "Here you go, dude," he uttered breathlessly. "My folks took a pic and sent it to me." A Dell laptop *thunked* into my palms, screen up showing a pic that froze my blood.

A twisty line burned into blond wood snaked round and round in a pattern that confused the eyes, causing them to blur and strain. What the hell had Alex been up to? Magic, obviously, but what kind? And how had he avoided detection?

"Jamie, your parent's cabin, can you get cell reception there?" I couldn't take my eyes off that head-splitting pattern.

"Nope. Can't get diddly squat. Only a land line."

Well, that explained how magic went undetected. It cost an arm and a leg to make the sensors, and it was much more efficient to piggyback a cell phone satellite than to send up several of our own. The down side was that there were some places we could not monitor.

Mind spinning, I sat down heavily on the bed before my knees could weaken. I saw something there that put the whole thing together ... The picture became complete.

The door had opened inward toward the bed, so I hadn't seen the poster that decorated that side. Not until I sat on the bed. I imagine that Casey must have sat just as I had, staring at it ... wondering ... dreaming. Then he'd found someone who could make his dreams come true.

It was an old poster, tattered and worn, edges curling, old enough that the white border had started to turn a light sepia color. A poster of a man in a blue one-piece with an equally blue woman at his side against a black background. He had his arms raised, and a cobalt ray of light shot up unto the dark sky. A disk, also blue, floated in that ray just above his hands. I recognized it from one of my all-time favorite movies. In fact, I had that movie on my smart phone. The word emblazoned like a banner at the bottom said it all.

TRON.

Oh crap.

"Sorry, boss. I investigated the trail you set me on, but it was a dead end. Couldn't find out a damn thing." The pleasant burn of Blue Ice warmed me.

BB took a sip from his snifter and licked his lips, eyeing me steadily. "That's too bad."

"Yeah, too bad. What are you going to do now?"

He shook his head. "Nothing to do, Kal. We can't get rid of it and it's spread throughout cyberspace. We can only pray it doesn't cripple the World Wide Web."

I studied his carefully neutral face then raised my tumbler, looking at the light refracting through the clear liquid and ice. "You're not worried at all, are you? You just wanted answers. I think that somehow you have a countermeasure to this ghost if it chooses to be malicious."

"Yes." His affirmation hung in the air between us.

I pointed a finger. "You, sir, want to use this thing to the Bureau's advantage. An asset that no other agency possesses."

BB snorted and took another sip. "A fine killer you are, Kal. So fine I forget sometimes that you are far more intelligent than you look."

"A compliment?"

"An observation."

"So now what, boss?"

"So now you and your team take your vacations. Go get drunk, get laid, or see your family. Have some fun."

I let the rest of the vodka slither down my throat. "Thanks, boss."

"You got a wifi signal, kid?"

"Yes, sir."

"Yes, *Kal*. 'Sir' is my Dad." I stretched on the steps, enjoying the view of the Washington Monument, America's answer to an Egyptian obelisk. Made me wonder if all the stories of the Masons and the Illuminati were true. The afternoon sun felt warm and silky on my face and warmed the pale stone of the Lincoln Memorial. Honest Abe stared out of the shadows, his wise gaze piercing me through with stony wisdom. I tipped our fifth President a wink and turned to the young magician sitting next to me. "Kid, how did the Bureau find you?"

Alex looked up from where he sat next to me, his body bent protectively over the laptop resting on his thighs. "Kal?"

"You had to have done something to attract the Bureau's attention. What was it?"

He nodded. "It was Elmo, my dachshund. A car hit him and I

tried to heal him. That set off the sensors near my house."

I pursed my lips. "Did it work?"

"No. I didn't have enough knowledge of canine anatomy. He died anyway." The kid sounded very sad.

"Good. That answers that."

Silence stretched between us for a couple of minutes before he asked, "Why did you want to talk here, Kal?"

"What I want to say, kid, is something I don't want the Bureau overhearing." My level stare made him shift uncomfortably.

"What?" he asked.

The sun felt so good, the day so fine I almost let it pass for the moment, but plans had begun to spin round in my head and I needed to see clearly the terrain on which I found myself deployed.

Time to dive on in. "Alex, I know about Casey."

The young magician's face turned to stone.

"I know you and he tried to interface with a computer and that you wound up translating him directly into the machine. Am I right?"

Not a twitch. Alex stared at the laptop with his hands gripping it tight.

"You and he were friends, maybe for a long time. After discovering your affinity for magic, which you surmised was the manipulation of Dark Energy, you shared your knowledge with him. He grew excited. His favorite movie was *Tron*, so he had fantasies of the computer world twirling in his fevered brain. He bugged you so much, pleaded with you, that you decided to indulge him, because you were burning with curiosity yourself.

"After all this time you had opened yourself up to someone about your ability, which you had dabbled in and toyed with, and it felt so good to share that burden of knowledge. Hell, you had no idea what would happen. You and he figured that he would just attune himself to a computer, to accelerate his mind and truly *understand* the electronic world. How am I doing so far?"

He nodded, tears beginning at the corners of his eyes.

"You found an affinity between magic and silver, heck, maybe even gold."

"Silver," he croaked.

"Right. So you used silver wire to amplify your spell, but you got it wrong." I sighed. "How did you even figure out how to Shape the spell?"

"From my research," he whispered. "It was supposed to be a protection spell, to keep out evil influences while working magic."

"And what did it turn out to be?"

"A minor Amplification spell."

"So you amplified the Communion spell you cast on Casey and wound up translating him directly into the computer you used." I shook my head in wonder. "It's a miracle that you didn't drain yourself dry right into the grave."

"Almost," he cried softly, scourged by memories. "I passed out and woke up two days later. By that time it was too late. Casey had used the DSL to get out of there and into cyberspace."

"Oh, you idiots … what a pair of knuckleheads!" I shook my head. "So, to keep his parents quiet, Casey's sending them emails and altering the records at MIT to show that he's been attending classes. He's even been helping Jaime with school in return for the illusion that he still lives in that house off-campus. Problem is, Jaime folds too easy, but he's all you and Casey have."

"You found Jaime?"

"Kid, I was born during the day, but it wasn't yesterday. Of course I found him. And got quite the story." I leaned in close. "How long did you think you could keep this up?"

"I dunno. Long time, I guess."

Butterflies fluttered about my stomach as I contemplated my next move, the words that would have me skittering on the edge of betrayal. Of the Bureau, of my contract, of my conscience. Was it in me? To do this thing? Thinking back to Leena's screams as she faced something beyond her understanding, a monster that defied reason, I came to one inescapable conclusion.

You bet your ass.

"Casey, I know you're listening," I stated firmly.

The laptop speakers gave out a buzzing, hissing sound that hung in the air for a few seconds before resolving into words. "I am here, Mr. Hakala."

I grinned, feeling a little sick. That voice was well beyond creepy. "My father's Mr. Hakala. Call me Kal."

"Yes, Kal."

"I haven't given the Director your real name. You're safe for now, unless you try something foolish or … unwise. I don't think you were a bad guy, Casey, just naive and a little foolish."

"I would have to agree with you there."

"One thing … you're a *Tron* fan. How is life inside the machine?"

Bzzzzz …"More terrifying, more fascinating that I could have imagined. This is a world of pure math and impeccable logic." He paused. "I think I will be very happy here."

"Good. A fulfilled spirit. I like that." A deep breath. "If you do try something foolish or unwise, the Director has countermeasures in place to purge you from the system. If they don't, your true name will be known and used against you in an exorcism. You got me?"

"Got you. But why tell me this?"

"I'm not that altruistic, trust me. I need your help and this is my way of buying some goodwill." Alex's head came up—hope lighting his eyes—and the speakers buzzed.

"Help?"

"Yeah. There's a monster I need to kill."

Chapter Twenty

Best Laid Plans and Other Myths

Still no sleep and my legs felt like so much rubber. Good thing the Royal Suite at the Four Seasons in Georgetown offered an impressive reason to stay awake. The 1,000 foot furnished terrace kept me marveling at the city lights below. The vodka I was swilling helped, too. Kauffman Luxury Vintage. At $225 a bottle, it was the most expensive I'd ever had. Worth it, too.

Warehouse … gone. Counting Special Branch and Agents, over twenty-five dead, the worst defeat in Bureau history. The President, normally so calm, grew apoplectic at the news and spent several hours talking to the British PM. I would've loved to have been a fly on the wall listening to that conversation. BB and the Joint Chiefs were scrambling to recruit agents, but it would take years to replace the Special Branch R&D magicians torn apart by Margaret's ghouls.

The brutal losses suffered killed any thought of celebrating; instead we found ourselves ensconced in the swankiest hotel in DC licking our wounds. As the hero of the hour, I had the catbird seat, the largest and finest room in the place. I was served the finest foods and the finest booze. It didn't matter; everything tasted like ashes.

As a guest of the Bureau, Dad had the Potomac Suite, probably the ritziest room he had ever slept in. Not that he gave a damn … his idea of fancy included linen napkins and beer served in a frosted glass. However, I wanted him to live it up a little. He deserved it. I reckoned he was running up a decent sized long distance bill talking to Mom.

Earlier that day, still dragging and shambling, BB had debriefed me in the Capitol Suite, the place already hooked up with secure lines to the Oval Office and the various Alphabet Agencies. He'd taken my statement with the usual aplomb and then dropped the bombshell on me.

"I'm sorry, Kal, but I can't let you go right now."

"What do you mean 'right now'?" I protested from my spot on the sofa. "You have me for five more months." BB had ensconced himself in a huge leather recliner brought special by nauseatingly subservient hotel staff. The damn thing looked like it was eating him. As we talked, a laptop resting on his thighs chimed every now and then. It may have looked like a Dell, but I was sure that BB would've been able to hack NATO with it.

"I appreciate that, Kal, I really do, but our losses necessitate drastic measures, and I'm invoking the Emergency Acts Clause in your contract."

The Emergency Acts Clause. Terrific. Basically, a provision that states that the Director can do anything he wants, within reason, if he feels that an emergency warrants its use, said clause needing to be confirmed by the President. I had the sneaking suspicion that it had been.

"For how long?" I growled.

BB heard something then, something in my voice usually reserved for the monsters I'd had to kill over the years. He shifted slightly in his seat and I knew he was prepared to draw the Ruger LCP from its holster in the small of his back.

Really? After all these years? I suppressed a scowl of annoyance. "You should know me better than that, boss."

He had the grace to look chagrined. "Yes, I should. I'm sorry, Kal, for just a second you looked … savage."

"Please answer the question."

"A year-and-a-half, maybe two."

Crap. That just wouldn't do. Keeping my face impassive, I tossed off a brief nod and stood.

"Where are you going, Kal?"

It wasn't hard to sound tired and resigned. "I haven't seen my parents in years. Going to visit my father."

I made my way to the hotel's west wing, to the Presidential Suite. After a sharp knock, Ilena answered the door, dressed in a fluffy white hotel bathrobe, brown hair a tangled wet halo around her head.

"Kal!" The petite magician cried before flinging herself into my arms. Not much to her, but she hit hard enough to rock me back on my heels. "Good to see you're all right!" she cried into my shoulder.

For a moment I savored the fresh, clean scent of her hair and the taut body under the robe. A tasty morsel of a woman, pretty in a girl-next-door sort of way. It was the first time I'd ever been within arm's length. Nice.

"Easy, Tex," I drawled with a smile, disentangling myself. "Where's Alex?"

Hooking her arm through mine, she led me into the suite. Done up in thick white shag, the place looked like you'd expect to see the President holding office there. Understated elegance combined with functionality. The spacious one-bedroom suite had been enlarged to three with the addition of connecting rooms, turning it into a head-of-state's wet dream.

The slightly disheveled figure of Carl, one of other surviving magicians, bounded up from the couch where he had been watching the 42-inch flat-screen TV.

"Hey, Kal, good to see you're okay," he enthused, shaking my hand. Lean and hard, his narrow face, dark hair, and thin blade of a nose gave him the appearance of a more dangerous Errol Flynn. From the detritus around the couch, I guessed he'd finished off the mini bar.

"Good to see you, too, Carl," I replied. "Here to see Alex."

"In his bedroom." With a final grin he went back to SportsCenter and Cheetos.

Alex had the largest bedroom, with carpeting so soft you could sleep on it and never miss a bed, dark wood furniture and velvety soft leather chairs that felt like you were nestling back into the womb. The young magician sat in one of those chairs surrounded by a bevy of white-uniformed ladies who administered a mani-pedi.

"Jesus, kid. How metrosexual of you," I laughed as I pulled a wad of twenties from the pocket of my jeans. I peeled a few off, setting them out for eager hands to grab. "Here, ladies, lunch is on me. Take care … buh-bye now."

Ilena laughed and kissed my cheek, sensing that I wanted to be alone with the young man, and left.

"What's wrong, Kal?" Alex asked, removing cotton balls from between his toes.

My smile slowly faded. "I've come to collect on the rest of the debt."

His face sobered instantly.

"Kid, you got any gems on you?"

He nodded.

"How many?"

"Maybe three or four. A couple of low-level stones and one high-level Shaped with a defensive spell."

"That steroid spell Win—Margaret used … you know its Shape?"

He nodded. "Her earrings had been discharged, but she had a ruby ring that hadn't been activated yet. The gang and I examined it after we checked in. Seems simple enough, but if abused, it will tear your muscles apart."

"And the gems from the smashed coil? Did they have spells Shaped into them?"

"Yes, but it'll take weeks to figure out the dynamics and complexities of those spells. They're Shaped so differently from anything else I've seen."

"But you can figure it out, can't you?"

He looked almost offended. "Of course."

"Good. I'll need two things from you; First …"

Next came Dom's room, the Grand Premier. Before the Bureau it would have had me drooling and barking at the moon, astounded by my good fortune, but when Dom opened the door, it seemed plain, pedestrian. Damn, I'd become jaded.

"Boss!" he exclaimed from the depths of his fluffy white robe. What was with the robes? I made a mental note to put mine on when I got back to the suite.

"Nice robe, Dom."

He stroked the soft material. "Yeah, it is. But it's a little gay."

We both shared a small laugh. He gestured me to come in, but I waved him off. "Nah, Dom. I need some help."

"What?" His hairy face transformed into a mask of concern. "Anything, boss. You know that."

From the front pocket of my jeans I produced a list. "I need all of these before tonight."

Reading the list, his face cleared. "Hell, we have most of these here. The rest I have to go back to Warehouse to get."

I lowered my voice. "Dom, this has to done on the QT. No one is to know," I whispered conspiratorially.

A pugnacious look overcame him. "What? Even from BB?"

Mentally crossing my fingers, I nodded.

"Would I get into trouble if he finds out?"

"You might."

"Cool."

So I sat under stars I couldn't see and pondered life in the Bureau and everything I'd given up to be right where I sat, on the largest, most luxuriant balcony ever designed for a hotel.

A ruby and an emerald glinted from two rings on my right hand and I ran a thumb over both, feeling the cool stones on my skin. Another gulp of hideously expensive vodka later and I felt it, like a rotten tooth needing to be pulled. Or a monster that needed to be killed.

I checked my cell's readout. "You're late." More vodka burned down my throat.

No answer, just a silence pregnant with menace.

By the pricking of my thumbs …

"You're a little predictable, you know that?"

The soft scuff of a boot on tile.

Something wicked this way comes…

Turning, I met the vampire's soulless pink gaze. "Been a long time," I breathed, clamping down hard on rising anger. "Ten years."

Its grin dripped spiky malevolence.

"How did she convince you not to start another nest? What did she do for you? To you?" My voice rumbled from deep within. "What did she promise you? Why would a predator care so much for prey?" I had no hope for an answer, didn't even know if it understood what was said. It looked like there would be some answers I'd never get before it died.

I could live with that.

It had the same lean pale face, the same long spidery fingers. Hell, even the same Indiana Jones/cowboy wannabe outfit. It was as if no time had passed since it had kidnapped Winnie. But there was one detail, one I knew it would possess. I looked at its fingers and smiled grimly. The vamp now wore rings.

I showed him mine. "Equal playing field, fang-face."

Bloodless flatworm lips split to whisper in that broken glass voice, "Twice you have offended me. No more."

"*Fasthair,*" I whispered and the emerald gleamed. Power such as I'd never known flooded through me like the rush of molten metal and time decided to take a vacation.

So still, everything had become set in amber, frozen in the lake of time while I skimmed above, impervious to its clutches. My fists hit the vamp in the chest before it could react, before it could phase, sending it flying through the glass wall into the suite. It crashed into the sofa and flipped-flopped onto the floor next to an interior wall. Diamond points of glass settled around its body in slow motion.

Despite the screaming pain in my fists and arms, I rocketed

through the broken wall and launched myself through the air at the vamp. It hissed and a ring glowed white. I passed through the space it had occupied less than a second before.

To my heightened perceptions, the wall it had crouched in front of came at me slowly, but I knew my skull would hit hard enough to shatter like Humpty Dumpty. Twisting violently, feeling the wrenching tear of back muscles, I managed to hammer into it with my spine instead of head, spreading the impact evenly. It still hurt like the blazes.

Before my battered body could fall to the floor it snatched me, holding me a good two feet in the air. It gurgled, numbing spittle flying from its lips.

It was laughing.

Rage welled up inside, a virtually endless supply ready for my use. But not this time. I clamped down on the fury and continued to fight cold, kicking and thrashing. It continued to laugh as its mouth came closer to my throat.

Closer still. The toe of one boot impacted on its shin with no effect and I could see the joy, the delight at my imminent death in its pale pink eyes. Its mouth opened wide, revealing the spikes of its teeth.

They clamped on my throat. No pain, only a numb pressure.

"Poisonnow," I gurgled.

The ruby glowed for an instant.

Paralysis gripped my body and I went slack in its arms. It continued to laugh as it gulped the hot coppery blood spurting into its mouth. Reflexively, its arms encircled my shoulders, pulling me closer in an obscene embrace to feed its hunger.

Blood gouted from my mouth. I smiled redly as my hand reached under my jacket to the small of my back. Thank god the anti-venom spell in the ruby had worked or I would've felt rather silly. A rosewood stake came free from my waistband.

"Go to hell," I uttered thickly through the blood in my throat. Its eyes widened in surprise.

The inch thick stake blurred forward, through the opening of its leather duster, propelled by my hyped-up muscles through its dun-colored button-down, cleaving through flesh and into its black heart.

It screamed its agony at the uncaring universe, the steam-kettle shriek tearing at my ears and splitting my skull. The most beautiful sound I'd ever heard.

Thump thump.

I watched my arterial blood hit the wall in crimson slow motion.

Thump thump.

Dom and Alex burst through the door, moving as if wading through treacle. If I hadn't been dying, I would've laughed. My hyper senses painted the scene in a humorous light; I had beaten the Dead Pool by eleven hours.

Thump thump

Cold. Hands and feet so icy.

Thump thump.

I smiled, everything felt so far away and peace finally beckoned to me like a long lost lover.

Thump thump.

The last thing I saw before I died was the flare of white light from my wristwatch.

Thump thump.

Chapter Twenty-One

A Time of all Things Ending

"Damn. Damn and bloody hell." BB stared at the corpse of his best man, blood slowly turning black around the body as it coagulated. The vampire had already been disposed of, agents and surviving Special Branch magicians working together to rid the hotel of the damning evidence.

"Oh my god!" came a guttural voice from behind. Pekka Hakala rushed passed the smaller man and dropped to his knees next to his son, broad, peasant face twisted in grief. Strong arms lifted the dead man as if he were a child. "Oh, my son … my son." His graying head bent over Kal's face, tears starting from pale blue eyes. A few moments later he began to mutter in Finnish, the same words over and over again. *Minun hyvä poika, minun hyvä poika.*

My good boy, BB mentally translated. During the ten years he'd known Kal, he'd picked up some Finnish. He brutally quashed his own welling sadness and turned to Alex, who'd just entered.

"How did he get in here?" BB asked roughly, waving at the elder Hakala.

"I don't know, boss." The young magician's eyes were full of tears. "He barreled right past me. Don't think a spell would have stopped him, either."

BB sighed. "Alex, bring up his will."

The young magician nodded and produced a RediPad. His fingers flew over the virtual keyboard until he found what he was looking for. "Kal wished to be returned to his parents in Minnesota and cremated immediately."

"Help Mr. Hakala make the arrangements." The Director shook his head. "Full Naval honors. Bill it to the Bureau."

The magician nodded.

Three days later a small copper urn entered the ground at the Wildwood Cemetery outside Grand Rapids, Minnesota. There was no gravestone yet—it was still on order—but the turnout of people marked the dead better than any monument of granite. The surviving members of Team Epsilon attended, as well as many of the agents who could tear themselves away from the rebuilding of the Bureau. Almost a hundred townsfolk circled the ceremony, there to pay homage to the semi-famous football hero they had rooted for on many a Saturday.

The American flag, folded carefully, was presented by Dom to a ravaged Terhi Hakala, still young-looking despite the gray that trailed through her black, black hair. Pekka Hakala stood in his Marine uniform, his many medals shining, a rock that weathered the storm of grief all around. Seven men in Navy Blues lifted rifles and fired. Once. Twice. Three times. A twenty-one gun salute for a fallen SEAL.

Dom turned away, a lump in his throat and tears flowing from his eyes, mourning the only agent he had ever looked up to. He wondered if he should transfer to Special Branch. The desire for the adventuresome life of an agent had paled.

A flat-faced Native American with waist-length hair, clad in jeans, snakeskin boots, and a black button down approached the grave. From a pocket he produced a black Recon 1 and set it in the hole next to the copper urn. "Damn, white boy," he muttered, shaking his head. "Damn."

After the Native American paid his respects, a woman with skin the color of coffee with a slight dollop of cream walked forward and knelt at the grave.

"Thank you for your honesty," was all she said as tears fell into the hole. With a whisper of a black cotton skirt, she rejoined the crowd.

The one thing the funeral didn't have was the BSI Director,

who had found himself with the unenviable task of rebuilding the most secret, most funded agency in the world, along with creating new protocols for its security.

On the very outskirts of the crowd, face shaded by a wide-brimmed black hat and veil, clad in a white blouse with black jacket and skirt, a woman stood apart with her son, a ginger-aired skinny little boy with pale blue eyes, also clad in black formal wear. They were still and resolute, waiting for the crowd to depart. Eventually only they remained, standing in the afternoon sun. The two walked to the freshly turned earth and stopped, staring at the grave.

"Mom, who was he?" asked the boy.

The woman looked at the dark soil for a long while before answering. "A friend. From long, long ago."

"Was he one of the good guys?"

"I thought so. Once."

"What do you mean 'once'?"

She gave a small sigh, a bitter and sad sound. "I think he was a haunted man."

"Haunted? Like by a ghost?"

No joy touched the smile behind the black veil. "I think … I think that's exactly right. By a ghost."

Denver's changeable weather irritated Wilkes more than he liked to admit. One day hot, the next cold, you never knew what the wind from the north or from the Rockies would bring.

As he made his way down the sidewalk, the late day's shadows cooling the air, he marveled at the temerity of his phone call. He didn't know what made him pick up the card that weeks ago he'd shoved into the back of his desk drawer, but when he had looked for some extra paper clips and saw the thick laminated edge poking out from under a box of staples, he felt almost compelled to grab it.

'Kal Hakala' it read, along with a phone number. On a whim he dialed and the man on the other end knew who he was and invited him to Papadeaux for dinner. The thought of sinking his teeth into a bone-in prime ribeye was too much to resist.

When he entered the restaurant, he asked the pretty brunette hostess if someone waited for him. Smiling, she led him to a secluded table in the back. The tall man there stood and shook his hand gravely; his homely face a neutral mask, as neutral as the color of his Armani suit.

"Detective Wilkes, it's good to meet you. My name is Ayre."

The big man sat and studied the other. "What's this about, sir?"

Not fazed in the least by the Detective's blunt approach, Ayre stared unblinking into his eyes. "I've come to offer you a job."

Epilogue

"Kalevi?"

Mumble mumble.

"Kalevi? Wake up."

Mom, I'm tired.

"I know, son. But you have to wake up."

Please. Five more minutes.

"I know you can hear me, Kalevi. Come back."

But it's peaceful here and the covers are so warm.

"Come on, son. Come on."

My eyes slitted open, the light far too bright. "Gah … whatsa matter?"

"Oh, thank god!" Mom cried. Why was she crying?

A rough voice said, "You had us worried, boy." Dad sounded awful, like he'd been crying, too. What the hell?

"Throat … water," I managed.

Blurry shadows moved and a straw touched my lips. Greedily I sipped at the cool water it offered. Images flashed in my mind's eye. Was I dead?

"Easy now … drink too much too quickly and you'll sick up," Mom murmured in my ear.

"Better." A lot better. I remembered … I *had* died. Glad to see it didn't take.

Alex's face swam into view. "I thought we might have lost you for good. You've been in a coma for a week, Kal. "

"Good thing my death was only temporary," I said in a painful rasp. "I see the soul gem worked."

The young magician held up my watch. The crystal on the back looked burned and blackened. "Yeah, I wasn't sure it would. Trapped your life energy pretty well, all things considered. I was afraid there would be some bleed out and not enough would remain to reanimate your body."

I groped toward my throat, feeling small lines of scars crisscrossing my flesh. "Healing worked, too." Canting my head side to side, I saw that I lay in the guest bedroom, the warm yellow walls glowing in the morning sun. It had once been my sister's room. Appropriate.

He nodded. "Putting flesh back together proved to be the easy part, even the muscle and bone damage from the magical steroids. The difficult bit was replenishing your blood supply. Good thing you had a couple of donors."

My parent's nodded and displayed the gauze pads on the inside of their elbows.

Alex held up something for me to see—a toy Winnebago. "Managed to smuggle these little guys in." Faint music wafted from the toy. *Cancion Del Mariachi,* I think.

My smile stretched parched lips. "Good to see they weathered the rough handling."

Dad laughed. "They've been quite a help around the house. I don't know how we lived without them before." He shook his head. "The old place has never looked so good or been so clean."

I changed the subject. "The funeral?"

"BB wasn't there. Couldn't make it because he's overseeing rebuilding the Bureau. But it was a beautiful affair. Everyone cried."

Relief washed over me. BB had proven over the years to be one of the sharpest knives in the drawer. Pulling the wool over his eyes was rarer than a total eclipse of the sun. Or an honest politician. "Thank god."

Mom smiled through the trails of tears on her cheeks. "I'm glad you're finally free of the Bureau, son."

My answering grin felt stiff. I wasn't free yet. "Mom ... how are you doing on your training?"

Dad's broad face smiled even wider. For a moment I thought his lips would meet in the back of his head. "It's a good thing your mother is a quick study. Your friend Alex taught her a few spells that could come handy around the house."

Mom thrust the straw between my lips again and smiled. "I'm not that talented, but it *is* fun to do."

A thought burst into the forefront of my tired brain. "Ghost? Is he here?"

Alex held up a laptop hooked to an Ethernet cable. *Bzzzz* ..."Right here, Kal."

"Thank god ... you had no problems with sending the video?"

"The only problem was fooling the Bureau's sniffer programs, and that was simplicity itself."

"So, Dad, you can recreate it?"

He scratched his head. "I've built Tesla coils in school, easy as pie. This thing, with that pattern of gems, gives me the willies. But I think I can pull it off. With a magician's help, that is."

"As long as the cell phone companies don't install any towers, your folks will be fine." Alex looked at Mom speculatively. "She catches on quick. A correspondence course in magic and she's at the top of the class."

Mom smiled. "I'm the only one in class."

"Thanks Alex, Ghost. I appreciate everything." The idea had come to me after I had found out Ghost's identity; if he could send emails to his friend Jaime undetected, he could do the same with Mom, set up a line of communication untouched by Bureau sniffer programs. Little 'packages' of data that could help Mom become a magician. And I had been right ... Her 'feelings' were a lot more than mere psychic awareness. The fact that my parent's place was so far out of sensor range that she could turn all her neighbors into tree frogs and it wouldn't create a blip on the Bureau's radar, keeping her relatively safe.

Bzzzzz ..."You're welcome, Kal. I must admit, I had some fun tweaking the Bureau's nose."

"A question, Kal." Alex leaned over me, voice becoming soft. "Why now? Couldn't you wait until BB released you from the

Emergency Clause?"

I sighed. "He was never going to release me, Alex, because he didn't believe that I destroyed the coil by accident. Our beloved Director is far too cunning to be fooled for long." My own voice lowered to a growl. "Besides, I checked with Dom ... I'm the only one he invoked the Clause for. He knew which way the wind blew. I had to get out, now—before he put two and two together and we all faced the crap storm."

He nodded and said, "Two issues, though, Kal. One: your mom is still kind of a novice. It takes a lot of practice to hold the Shape of the spells in your mind. No offence, ma'am." Mom waved his worry away. "Two: you need some large, high-quality gems at max charge to fully utilize the coil."

Mom and Dad just smiled. Alex threw me a confused look. "You forget how much I got paid," I laughed. "Mom and Dad have been accessing our joint account for years, buying all manner of high-quality gems."

"I should have known," he said ruefully. "I should have known."

"Yes, you should have."

"So, white boy, what now?" Canton entered the room, teeth at full wattage.

"Glad you made it, redskin." My heart did a little happy dance. No one else I'd rather have on my six than him.

"You kidding? I wouldn't have missed this for all the tea in China." His full-power smile dimmed slightly. "But couldn't your mother have told me *before* the funeral? Lost my best knife."

Laughing hurt my throat, but I didn't care. "Buddy, you ain't seen nothing yet. Dad?"

From the bedroom closet Dad pulled down a polished pine box about twenty inches long. The letters CA were etched into the lid.

"Had Dad order you one," I told him

Canton's eyes flew wide as opened the box. "I don't freaking believe this," he breathed reverently, pulling out a long knife. A twin to my own Bowie, except the hilt was carved from walnut instead of rosewood. "Knew you were okay, white boy, the second I met you." His eyes shone. "Now what?"

Mom answered for the both of us. "Now we kill a monster." Her normally elfin face had become savage. It's a commonly held belief that the female of the species is the most dangerous. Looking at Mom, I knew it to be true.

"Yeah, buddy, it's time to kill a monster."

I have a promise to keep.

And miles to go before I sleep.

Follow the continuing
adventures of Kal Hakala in
What Happens in Vegas Dies in Vegas
Coming Soon from Camel Press

Born in Helsinki, Finland (The Land of the Uncommonly Stubborn), **Mark Everett Stone** arrived in the U.S. at a young age and promptly dove into the world of the fantastic. Starting at age seven with the *Iliad* and the *Odyssey*, he went on to consume every scrap of Norse Mythology he could get his grubby little paws on. At age thirteen he graduated to Tolkien and Heinlein, building up a book collection that soon rivaled the local public library's.

In college Mark majored in Journalism and minored in English. The newspaper business wasn't for him, so he did what every good writer does: find work in a wide variety of fields that included catering, bartending, and restaurant management. After getting married, he sold Hyundais (before they became popular) and, because he lives in Colorado, Subarus. Eventually he matured enough to be able to sit down and just *write*.

Mark is feverishly working on his next book, *The Judas Line*, while his amazingly patient wife, Brandie, keeps him and their two sons, Aeden and Gabriel, in check. You can find Mark on the Web at www.markeverettstone.camelpress.com.

www.ingramcontent.com/pod-product-compliance
Lightning Source LLC
Chambersburg PA
CBHW010440100726

47904CB00008B/2418